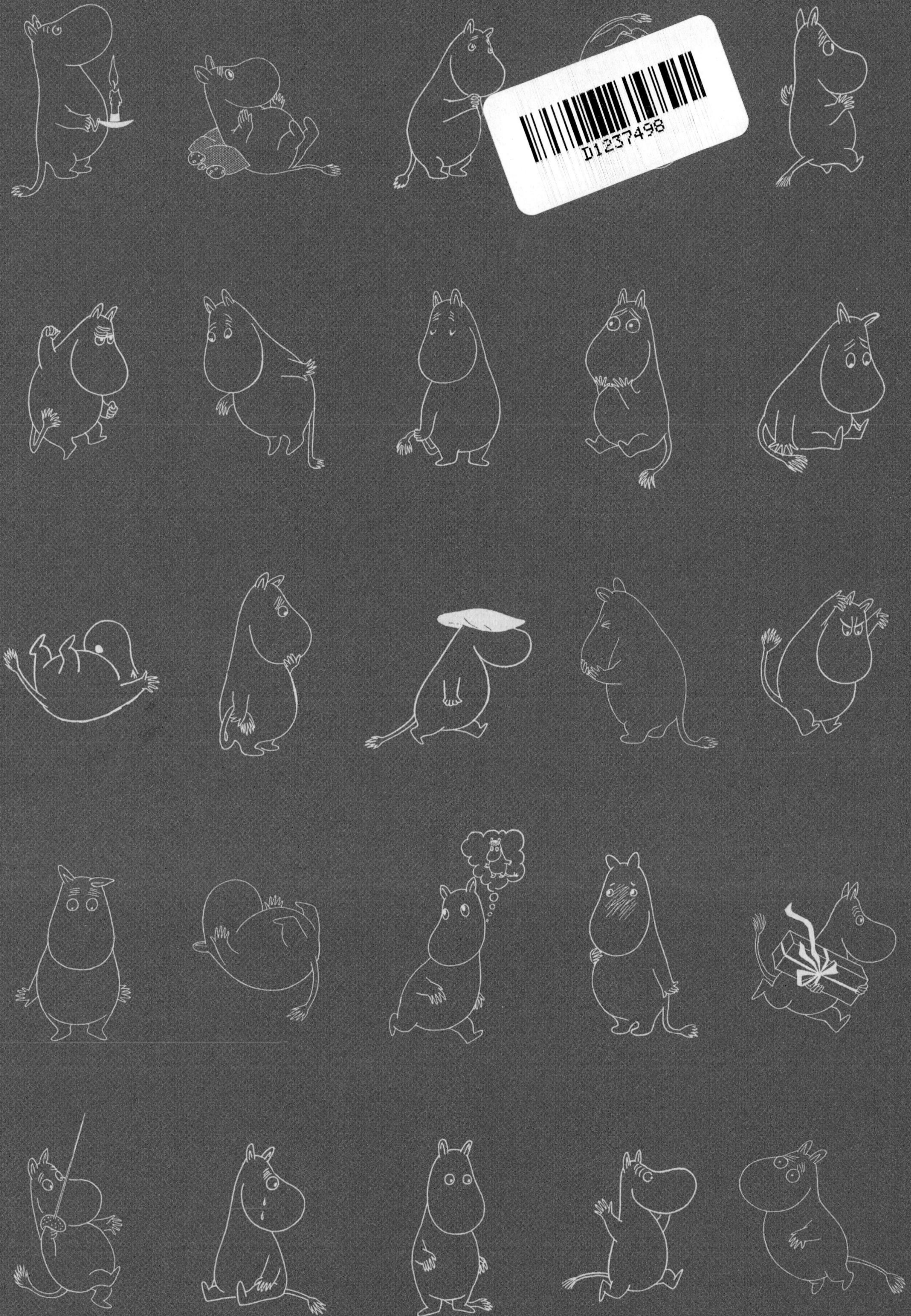

THE COMPLETE TOVE JANSSON

MOOMIN

COMIC STRIP

Drawn & Quarterly

MONTRÉAL

Moomin Book Three: The Complete Tove Jansson Comic Strip by Tove Jansson
ISBN 978-1-897299-55-5

First Printing: September 2008
10 9 8 7 6 5 4 3 2 1

Printed in Singapore

Library and Archives Canada Cataloguing in Publication
Jansson, Tove
    Moomin : the complete Tove Jansson comic strip / Tove Jansson.
Originally published in the Evening news, London, 1953-1959.
ISBN 1-894937-80-5 (bk. 1).--ISBN 978-1-897299-19-7 (bk. 2).--ISBN 978-1-897299-55-5 (bk. 3)
    I. Title.
PN6738.M66]35 2006   741.5'94897   C2006-902218-6

Drawn & Quarterly
Post Office Box 48056
Montreal, Quebec
Canada H2V 4S8
www.drawnandquarterly.com

Distributed in the USA and abroad by:
Farrar, Straus and Giroux
19 Union Square West
New York, NY 10003
Orders: 888 330 8477

Distributed in Canada by:
Raincoast Books
9050 Shaughnessy Street
Vancouver, BC V6P 6E5
Orders: 800 663 5714

Distributed in the United Kingdom by:
Publishers Group U.K.
8 The Arena
Mollison Avenue
Enfield Middlesex EN3 7NL
Orders: 0208 804 0400

MOOMIN

VOLUME THREE

9. Moomin Falls in Love

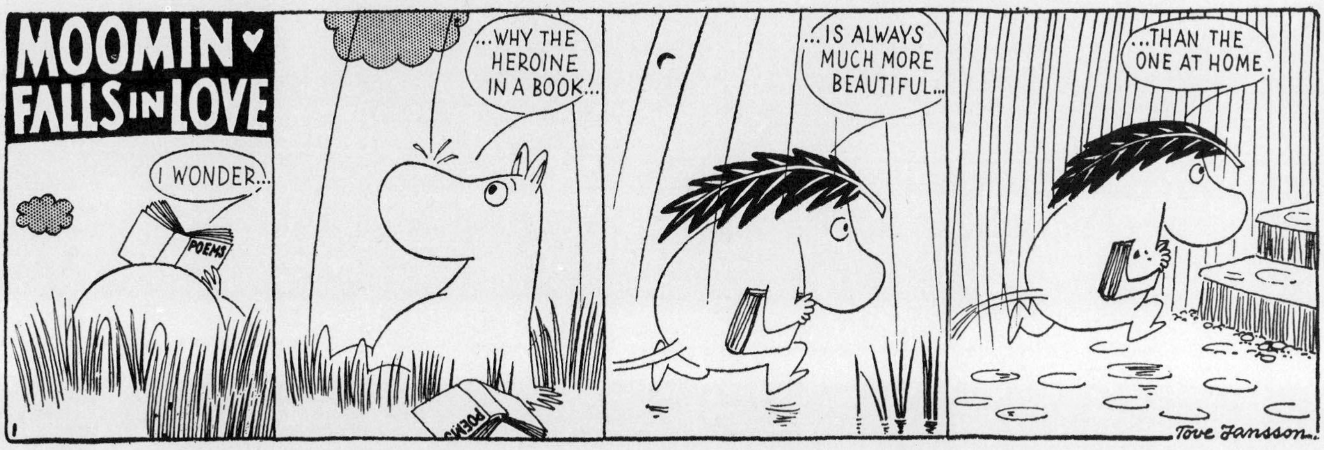

MOOMIN FALLS IN LOVE
I WONDER...
POEMS
...WHY THE HEROINE IN A BOOK...
...IS ALWAYS MUCH MORE BEAUTIFUL...
...THAN THE ONE AT HOME.
Tove Jansson

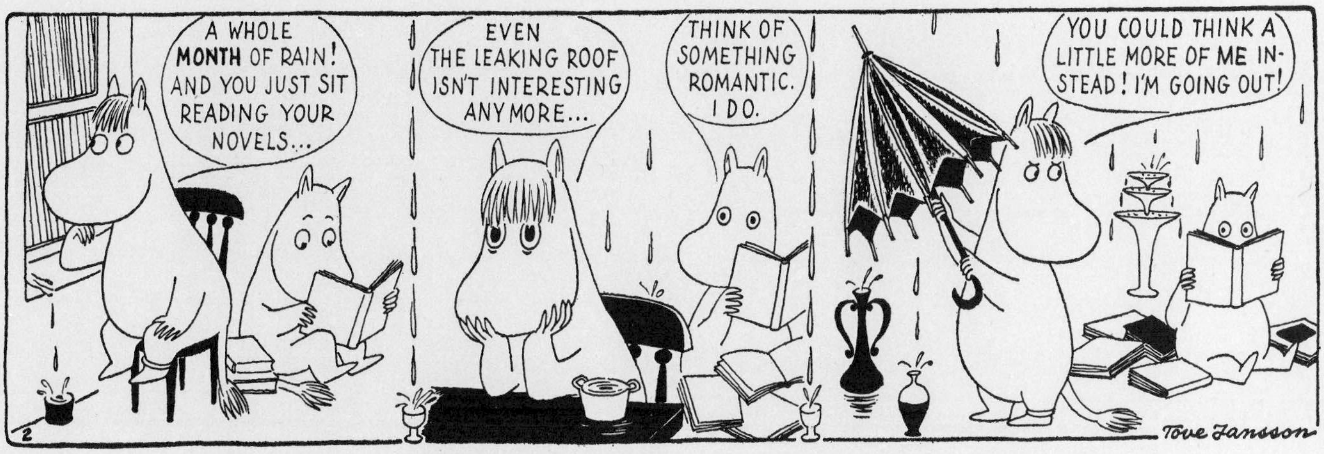

A WHOLE MONTH OF RAIN! AND YOU JUST SIT READING YOUR NOVELS...
EVEN THE LEAKING ROOF ISN'T INTERESTING ANYMORE...
THINK OF SOMETHING ROMANTIC. I DO.
YOU COULD THINK A LITTLE MORE OF ME INSTEAD! I'M GOING OUT!
Tove Jansson

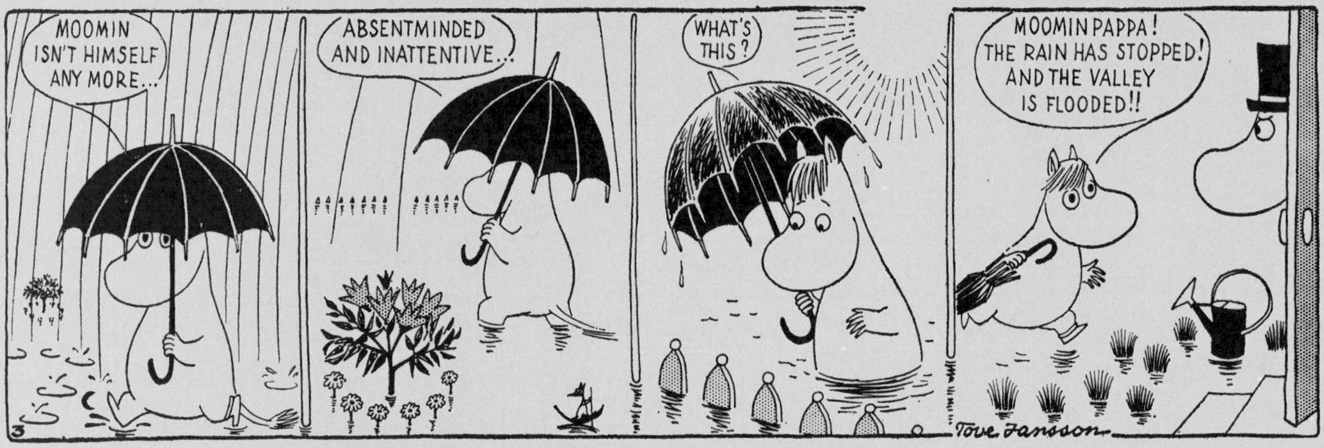
MOOMIN ISN'T HIMSELF ANY MORE...
ABSENTMINDED AND INATTENTIVE...
WHAT'S THIS?
MOOMINPAPPA! THE RAIN HAS STOPPED! AND THE VALLEY IS FLOODED!!
Tove Jansson

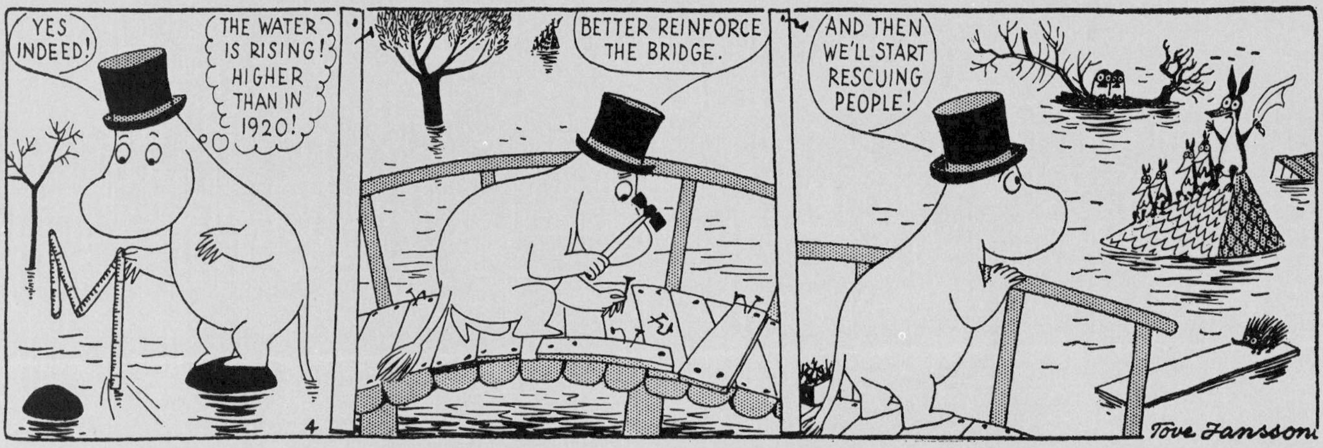
YES INDEED!
THE WATER IS RISING! HIGHER THAN IN 1920!
BETTER REINFORCE THE BRIDGE.
AND THEN WE'LL START RESCUING PEOPLE!
Tove Jansson

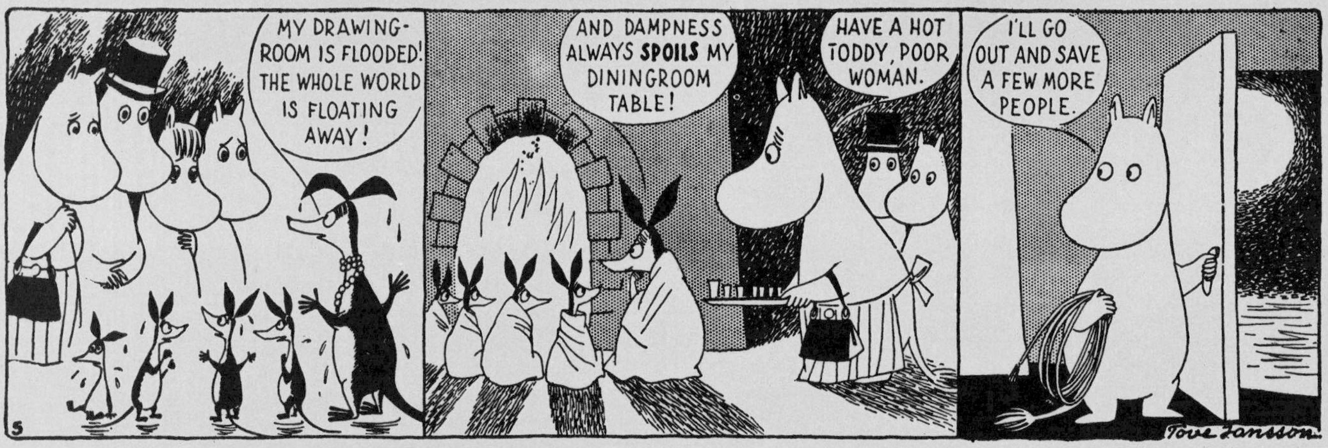
MY DRAWING-ROOM IS FLOODED! THE WHOLE WORLD IS FLOATING AWAY!
AND DAMPNESS ALWAYS SPOILS MY DININGROOM TABLE!
HAVE A HOT TODDY, POOR WOMAN.
I'LL GO OUT AND SAVE A FEW MORE PEOPLE.
Tove Jansson

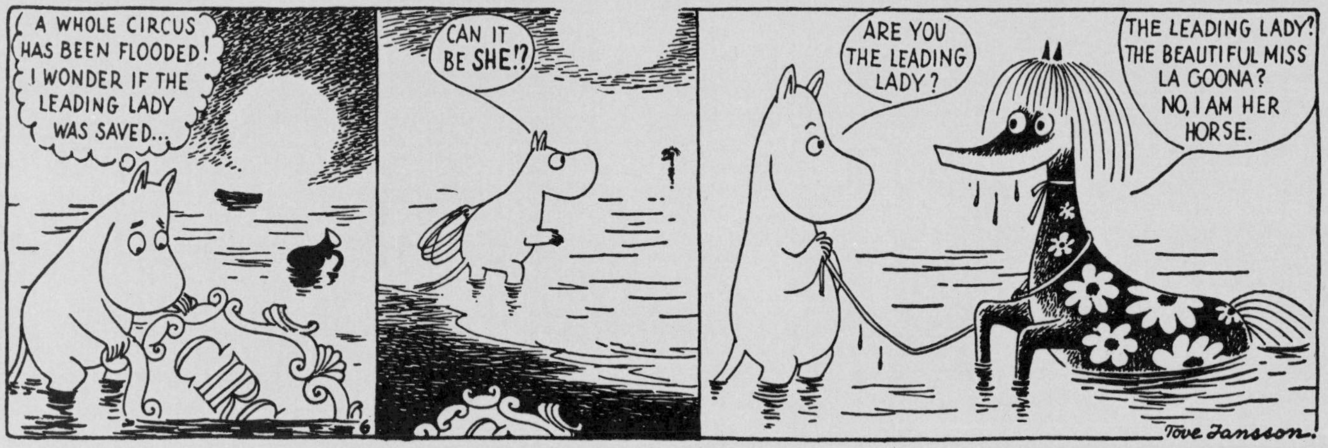
A WHOLE CIRCUS HAS BEEN FLOODED! I WONDER IF THE LEADING LADY WAS SAVED...
CAN IT BE SHE!?
ARE YOU THE LEADING LADY?
THE LEADING LADY? THE BEAUTIFUL MISS LA GOONA? NO, I AM HER HORSE.
Tove Jansson

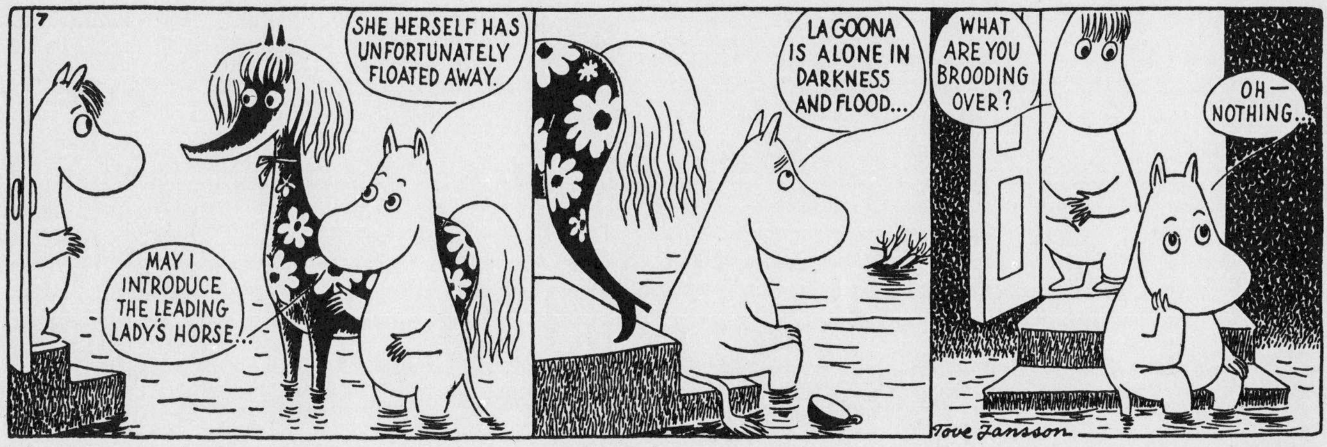
7
SHE HERSELF HAS UNFORTUNATELY FLOATED AWAY.
MAY I INTRODUCE THE LEADING LADY'S HORSE...
LA GOONA IS ALONE IN DARKNESS AND FLOOD...
WHAT ARE YOU BROODING OVER?
OH— NOTHING...
Tove Jansson

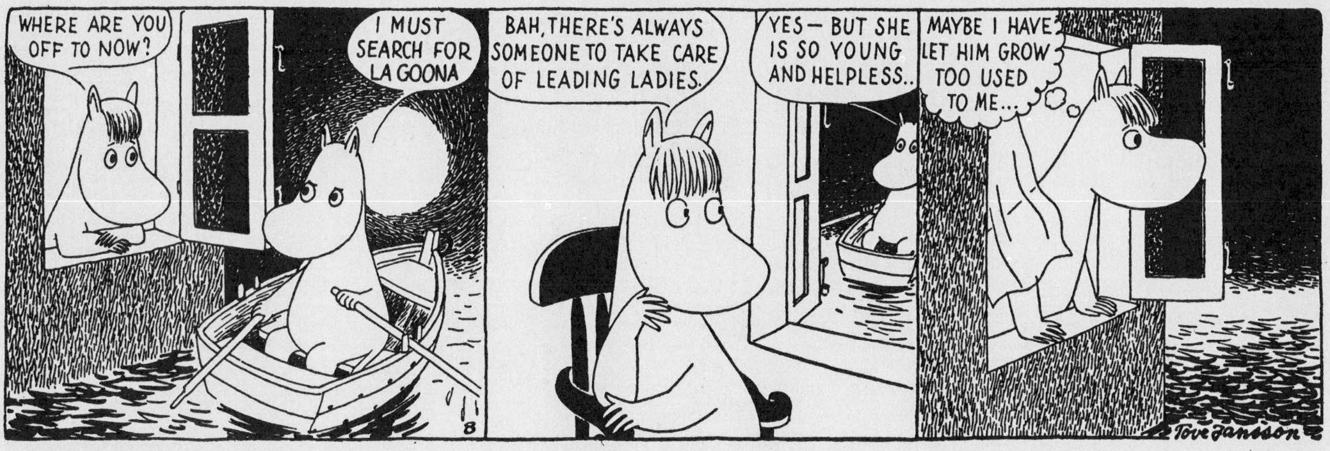
WHERE ARE YOU OFF TO NOW?
I MUST SEARCH FOR LA GOONA
8
BAH, THERE'S ALWAYS SOMEONE TO TAKE CARE OF LEADING LADIES.
YES— BUT SHE IS SO YOUNG AND HELPLESS..
MAYBE I HAVE LET HIM GROW TOO USED TO ME...
Tove Jansson

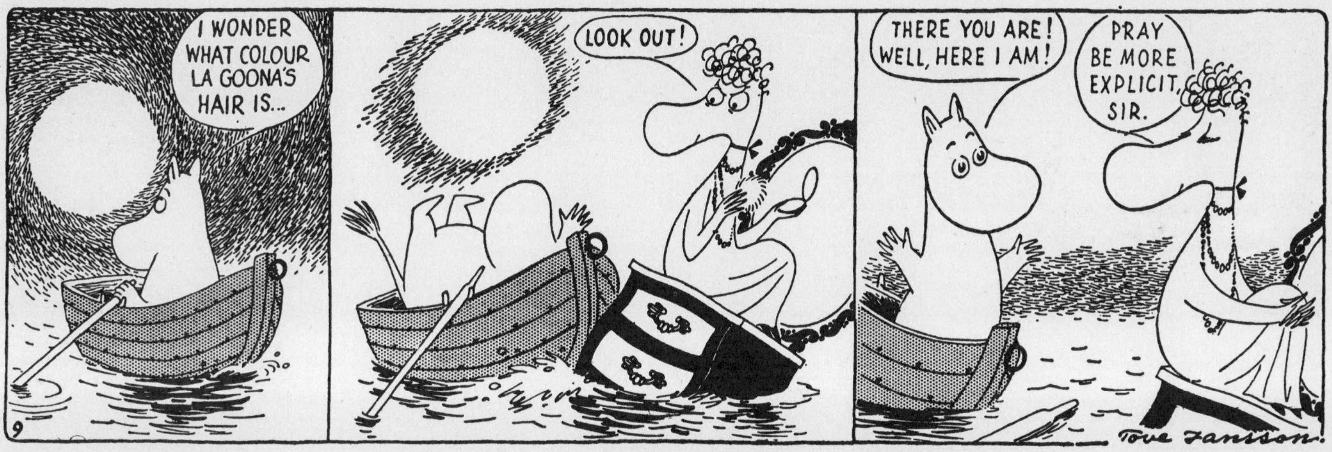
I WONDER WHAT COLOUR LA GOONA'S HAIR IS...
9
LOOK OUT!
THERE YOU ARE! WELL, HERE I AM!
PRAY BE MORE EXPLICIT, SIR.
Tove Jansson

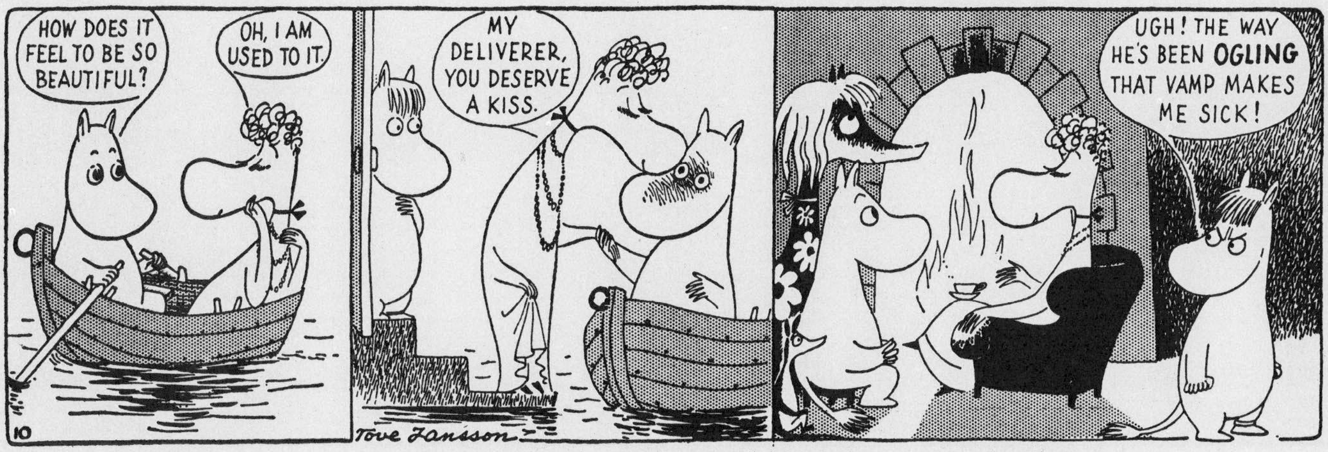
HOW DOES IT FEEL TO BE SO BEAUTIFUL?
OH, I AM USED TO IT.
10
MY DELIVERER, YOU DESERVE A KISS.
Tove Jansson
UGH! THE WAY HE'S BEEN OGLING THAT VAMP MAKES ME SICK!

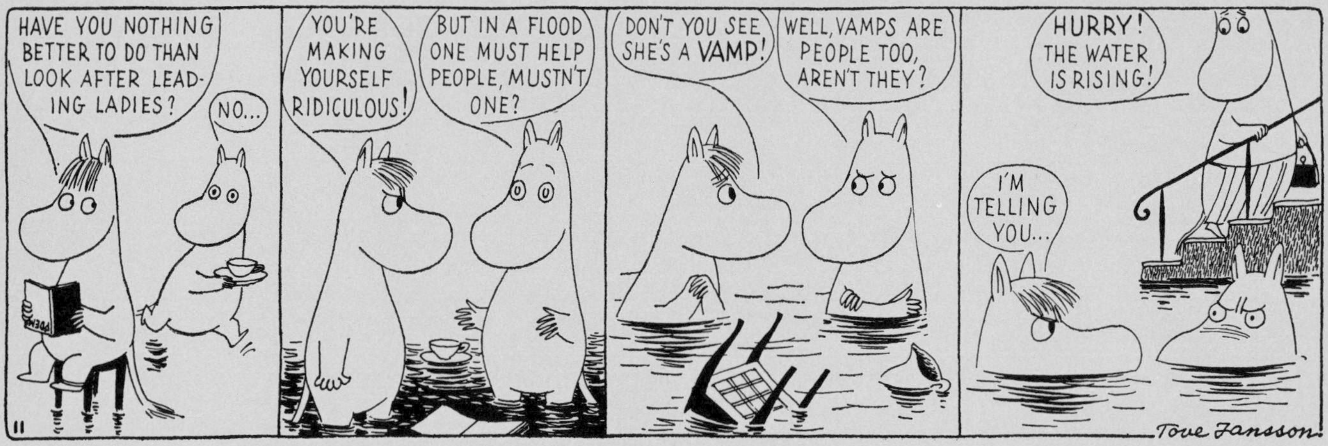
HAVE YOU NOTHING BETTER TO DO THAN LOOK AFTER LEADING LADIES?
NO...
YOU'RE MAKING YOURSELF RIDICULOUS!
BUT IN A FLOOD ONE MUST HELP PEOPLE, MUSTN'T ONE?
DON'T YOU SEE SHE'S A VAMP!
WELL, VAMPS ARE PEOPLE TOO, AREN'T THEY?
HURRY! THE WATER IS RISING!
I'M TELLING YOU...
11
Tove Jansson

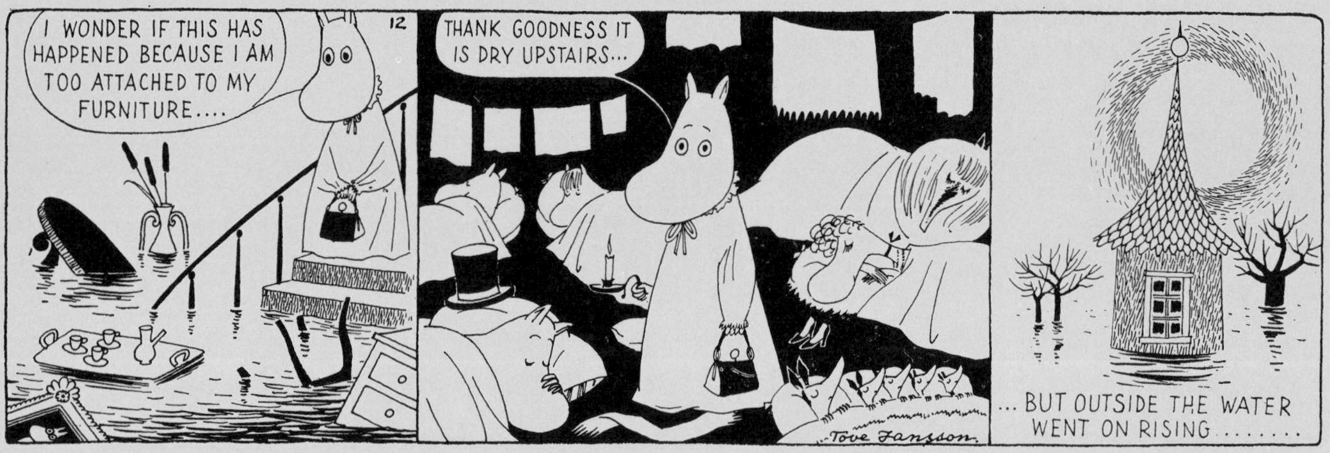
12
I WONDER IF THIS HAS HAPPENED BECAUSE I AM TOO ATTACHED TO MY FURNITURE....
THANK GOODNESS IT IS DRY UPSTAIRS...
Tove Jansson
... BUT OUTSIDE THE WATER WENT ON RISING ....

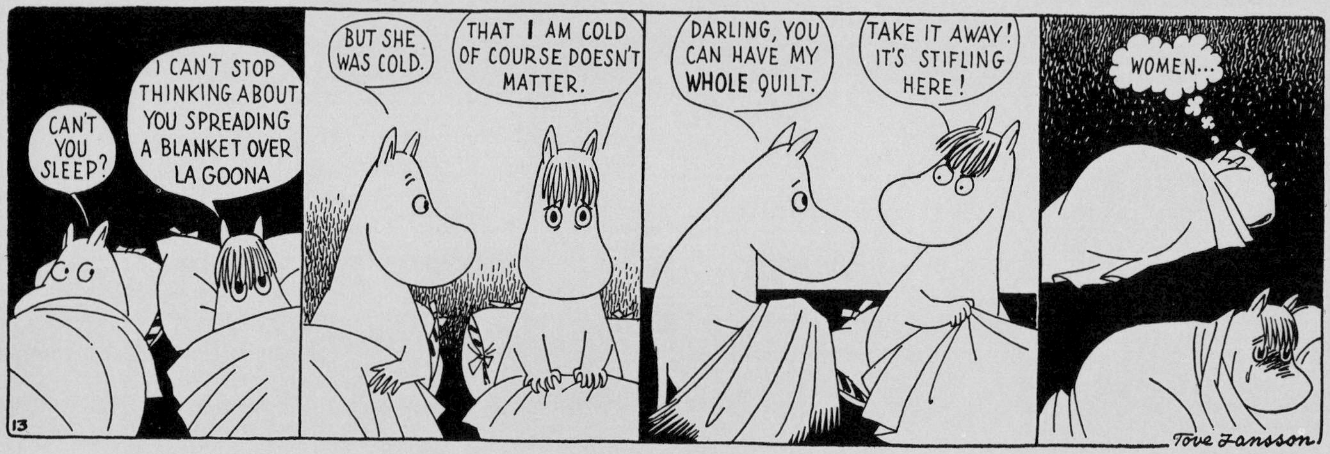
CAN'T YOU SLEEP?
I CAN'T STOP THINKING ABOUT YOU SPREADING A BLANKET OVER LA GOONA
BUT SHE WAS COLD.
THAT I AM COLD OF COURSE DOESN'T MATTER.
DARLING, YOU CAN HAVE MY WHOLE QUILT.
TAKE IT AWAY! IT'S STIFLING HERE!
WOMEN...
13
Tove Jansson

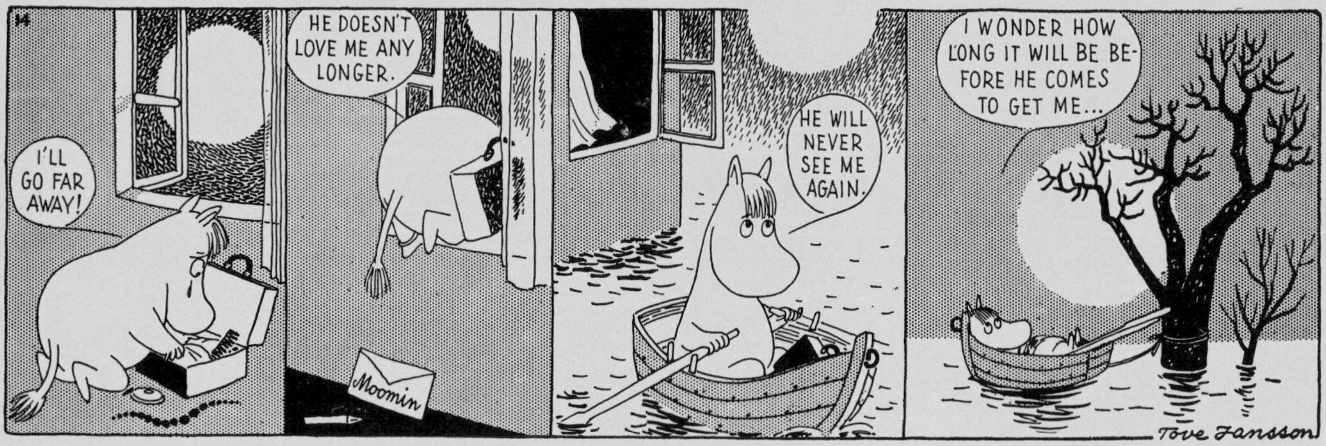
14
I'LL GO FAR AWAY!
HE DOESN'T LOVE ME ANY LONGER.
Moomin
HE WILL NEVER SEE ME AGAIN.
I WONDER HOW LONG IT WILL BE BEFORE HE COMES TO GET ME...
Tove Jansson

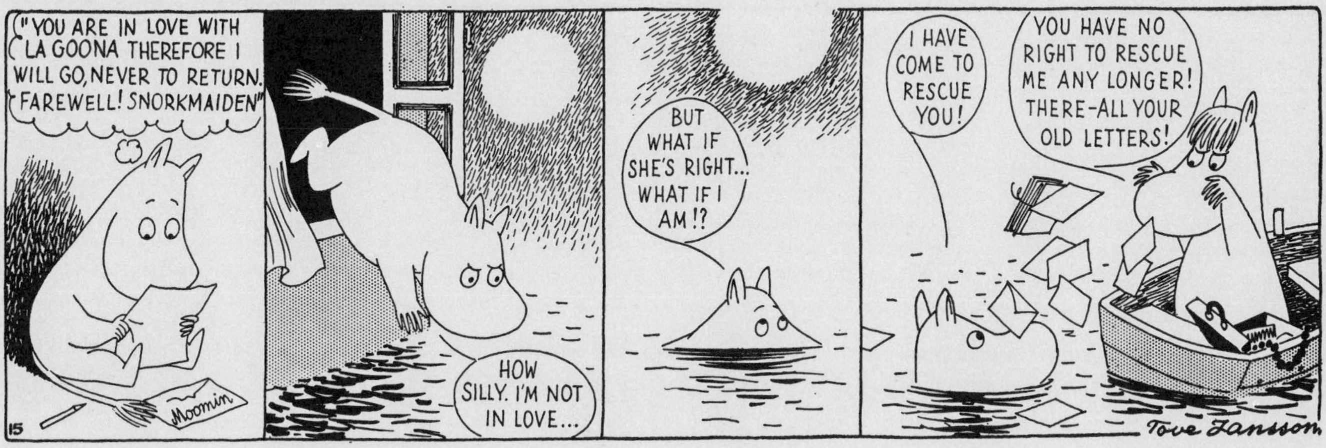
15
"YOU ARE IN LOVE WITH LA GOONA THEREFORE I WILL GO, NEVER TO RETURN. FAREWELL! SNORKMAIDEN"
Moomin
BUT WHAT IF SHE'S RIGHT... WHAT IF I AM!?
HOW SILLY. I'M NOT IN LOVE...
I HAVE COME TO RESCUE YOU!
YOU HAVE NO RIGHT TO RESCUE ME ANY LONGER! THERE–ALL YOUR OLD LETTERS!
Tove Jansson

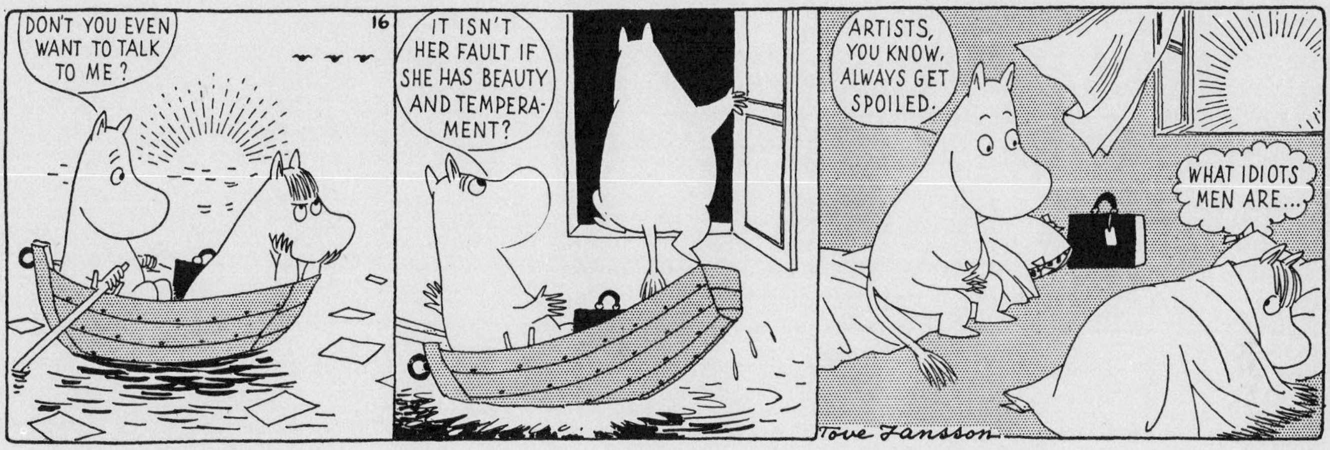
16
DON'T YOU EVEN WANT TO TALK TO ME?
IT ISN'T HER FAULT IF SHE HAS BEAUTY AND TEMPERAMENT?
ARTISTS, YOU KNOW, ALWAYS GET SPOILED.
WHAT IDIOTS MEN ARE...
Tove Jansson

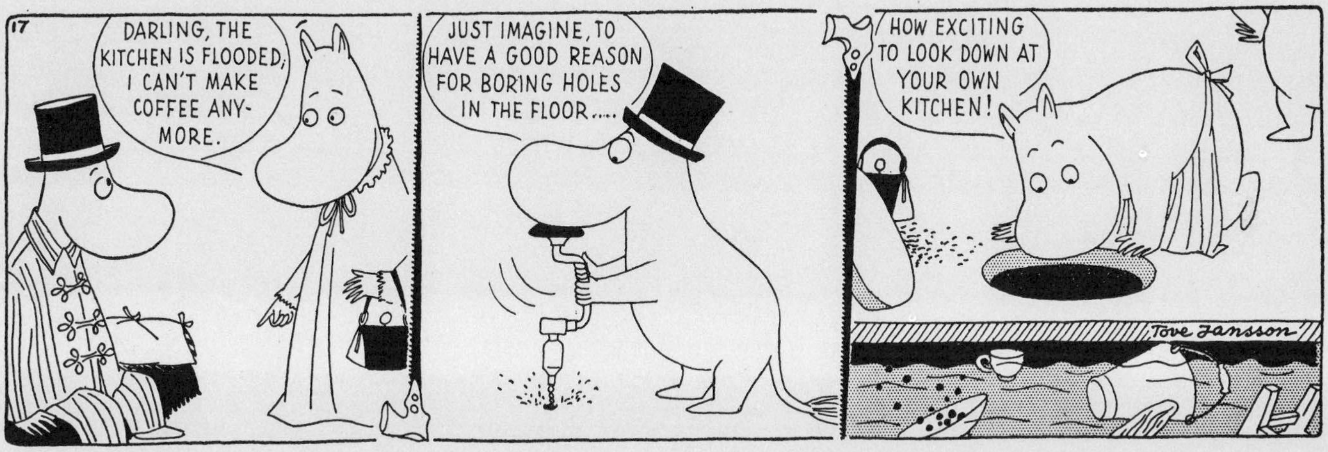
17
DARLING, THE KITCHEN IS FLOODED; I CAN'T MAKE COFFEE ANYMORE.
JUST IMAGINE, TO HAVE A GOOD REASON FOR BORING HOLES IN THE FLOOR.....
HOW EXCITING TO LOOK DOWN AT YOUR OWN KITCHEN!
Tove Jansson

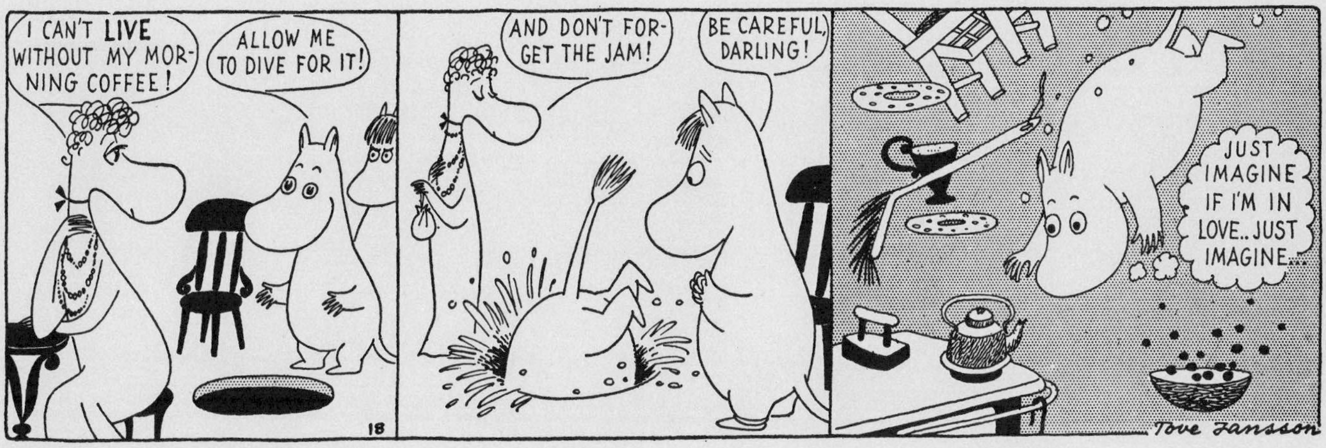
I CAN'T LIVE WITHOUT MY MORNING COFFEE!
ALLOW ME TO DIVE FOR IT!
18
AND DON'T FORGET THE JAM!
BE CAREFUL, DARLING!
JUST IMAGINE IF I'M IN LOVE.. JUST IMAGINE...
Tove Jansson

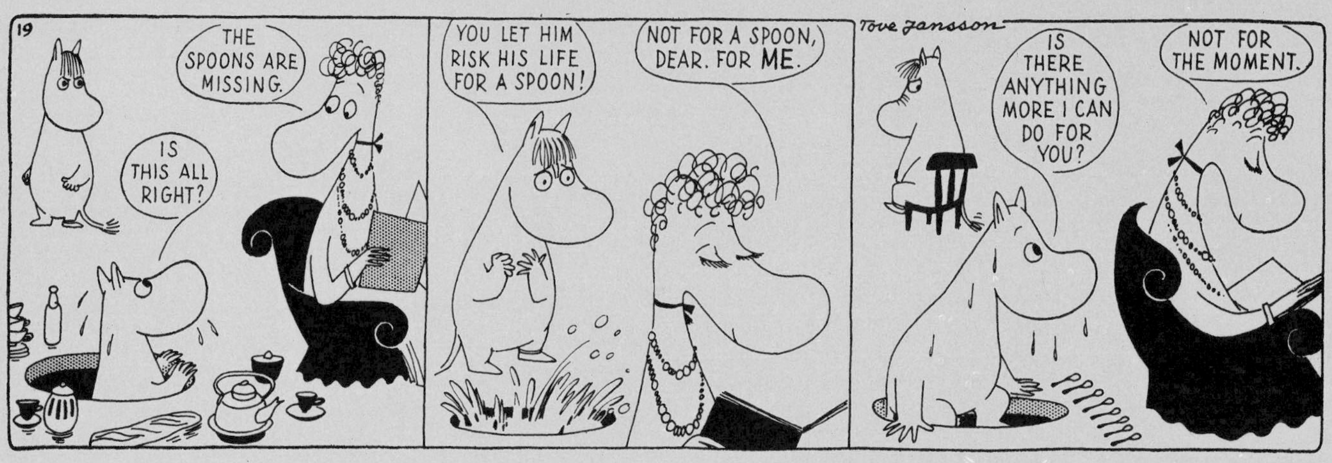
19
THE SPOONS ARE MISSING.
IS THIS ALL RIGHT?
YOU LET HIM RISK HIS LIFE FOR A SPOON!
NOT FOR A SPOON, DEAR. FOR **ME**.
Tove Jansson
IS THERE ANYTHING MORE I CAN DO FOR YOU?
NOT FOR THE MOMENT.

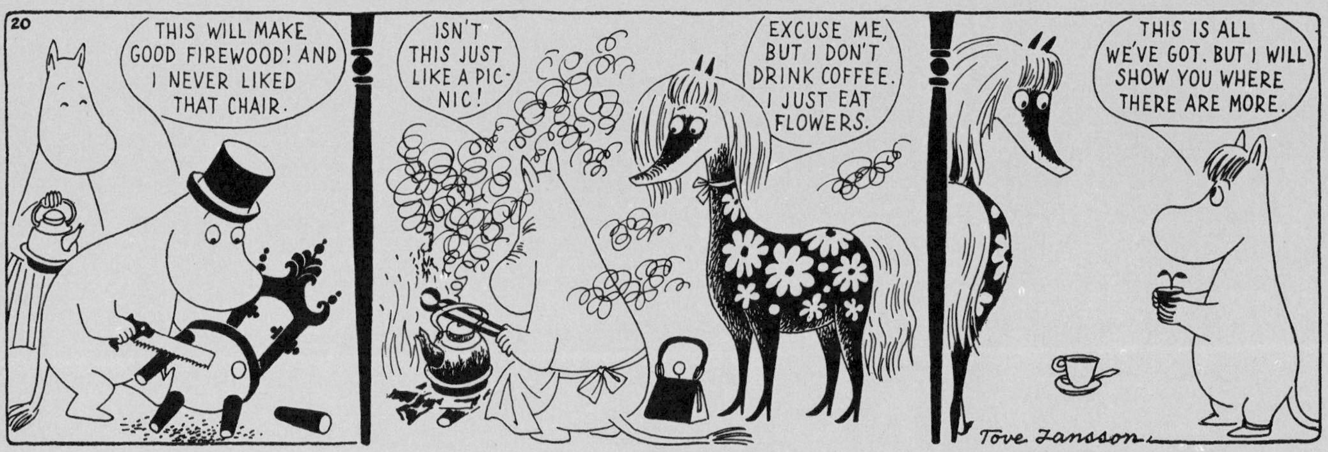
20
THIS WILL MAKE GOOD FIREWOOD! AND I NEVER LIKED THAT CHAIR.
ISN'T THIS JUST LIKE A PIC-NIC!
EXCUSE ME, BUT I DON'T DRINK COFFEE. I JUST EAT FLOWERS.
THIS IS ALL WE'VE GOT. BUT I WILL SHOW YOU WHERE THERE ARE MORE.
Tove Jansson

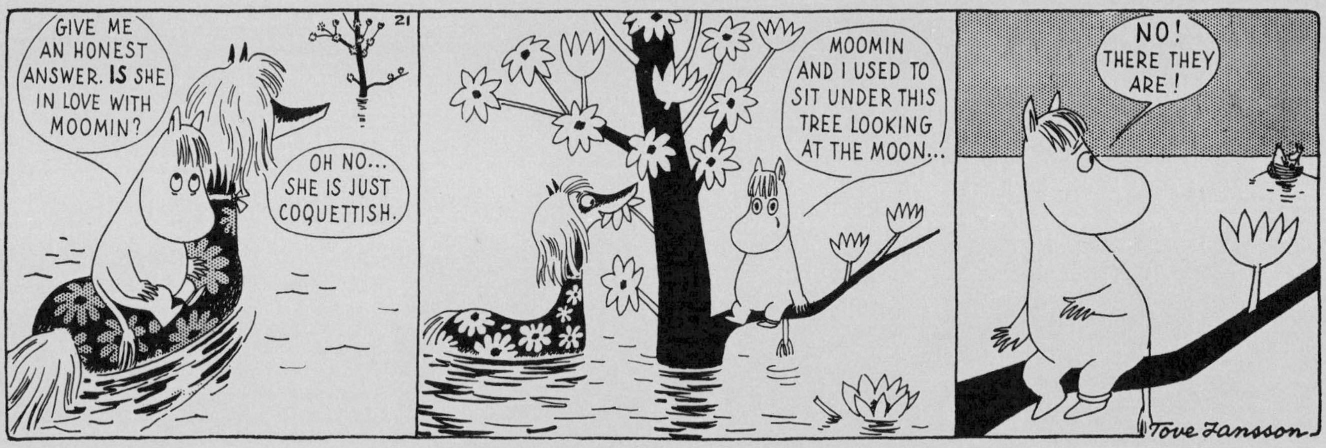
21
GIVE ME AN HONEST ANSWER. **IS** SHE IN LOVE WITH MOOMIN?
OH NO... SHE IS JUST COQUETTISH.
MOOMIN AND I USED TO SIT UNDER THIS TREE LOOKING AT THE MOON...
NO! THERE THEY ARE!
Tove Jansson

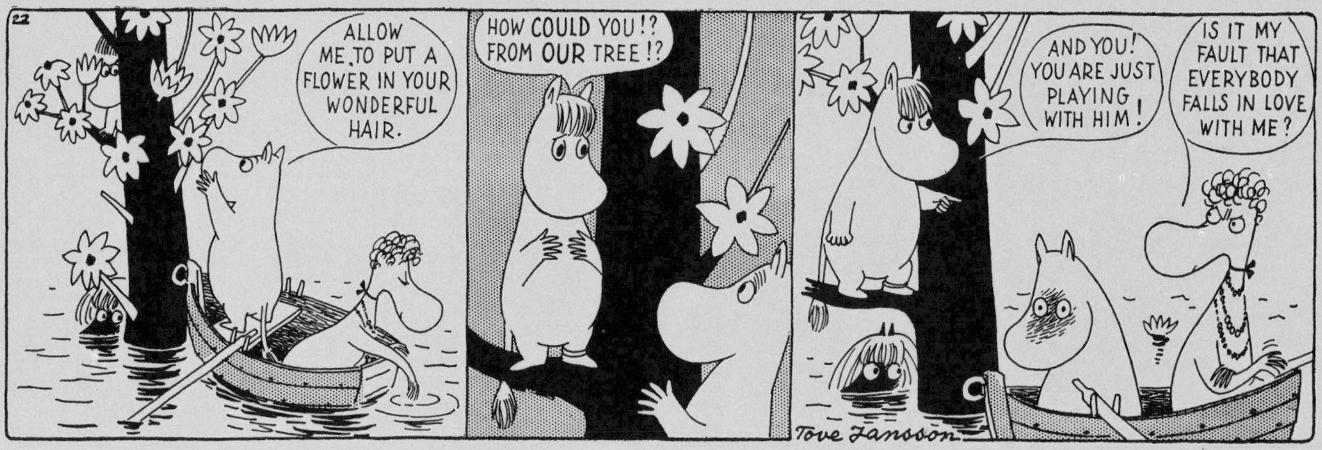
22
ALLOW ME TO PUT A FLOWER IN YOUR WONDERFUL HAIR.
HOW **COULD** YOU!? FROM **OUR** TREE!?
AND YOU! YOU ARE JUST PLAYING WITH HIM!
IS IT MY FAULT THAT EVERYBODY FALLS IN LOVE WITH ME?
Tove Jansson

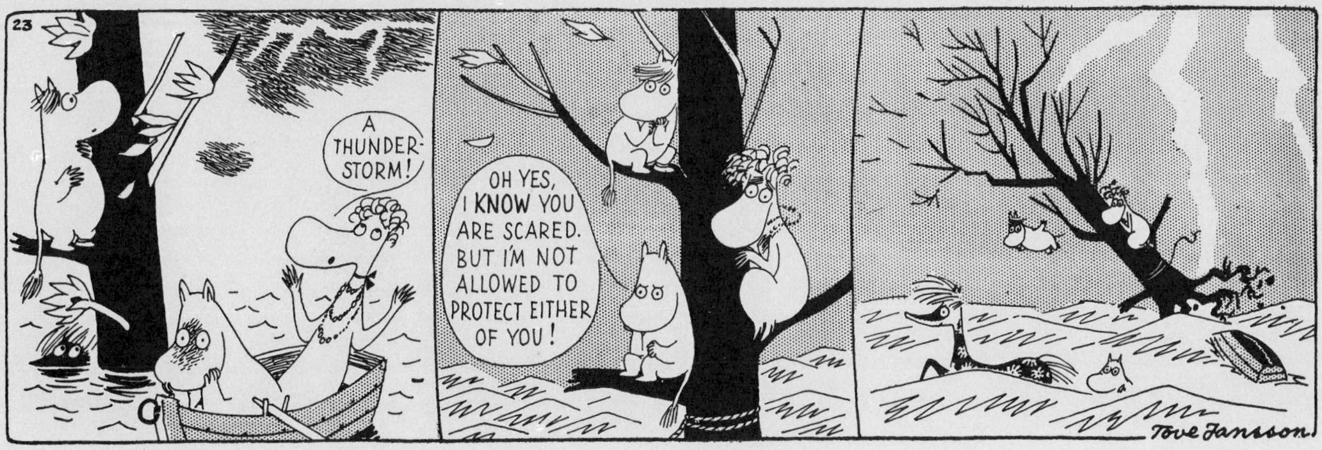
23
A THUNDER-STORM!
OH YES, I KNOW YOU ARE SCARED. BUT I'M NOT ALLOWED TO PROTECT EITHER OF YOU!
Tove Jansson

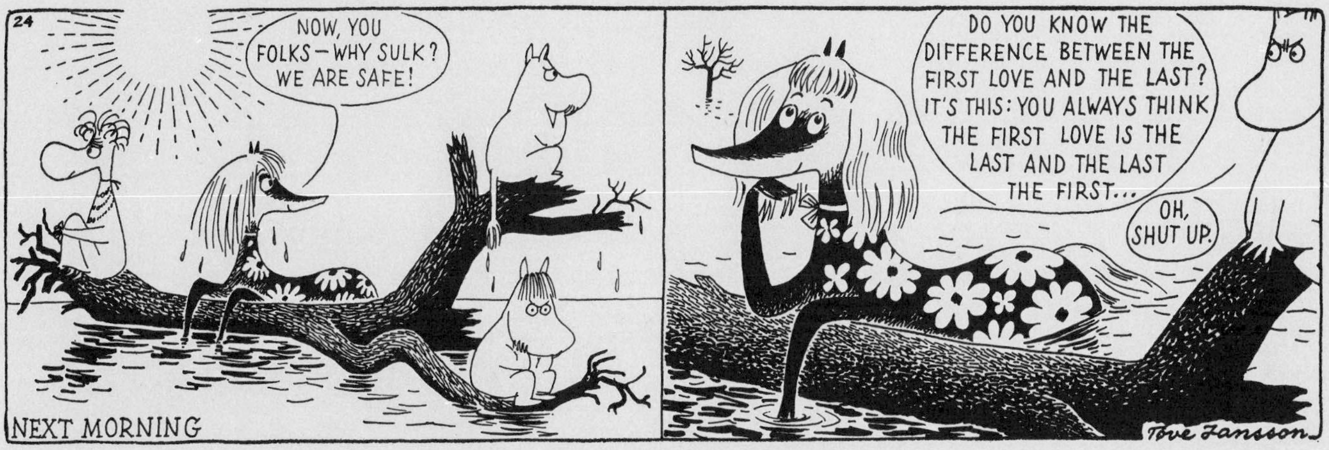
24
NOW, YOU FOLKS – WHY SULK? WE ARE SAFE!
NEXT MORNING
DO YOU KNOW THE DIFFERENCE BETWEEN THE FIRST LOVE AND THE LAST? IT'S THIS: YOU ALWAYS THINK THE FIRST LOVE IS THE LAST AND THE LAST THE FIRST...
OH, SHUT UP.
Tove Jansson

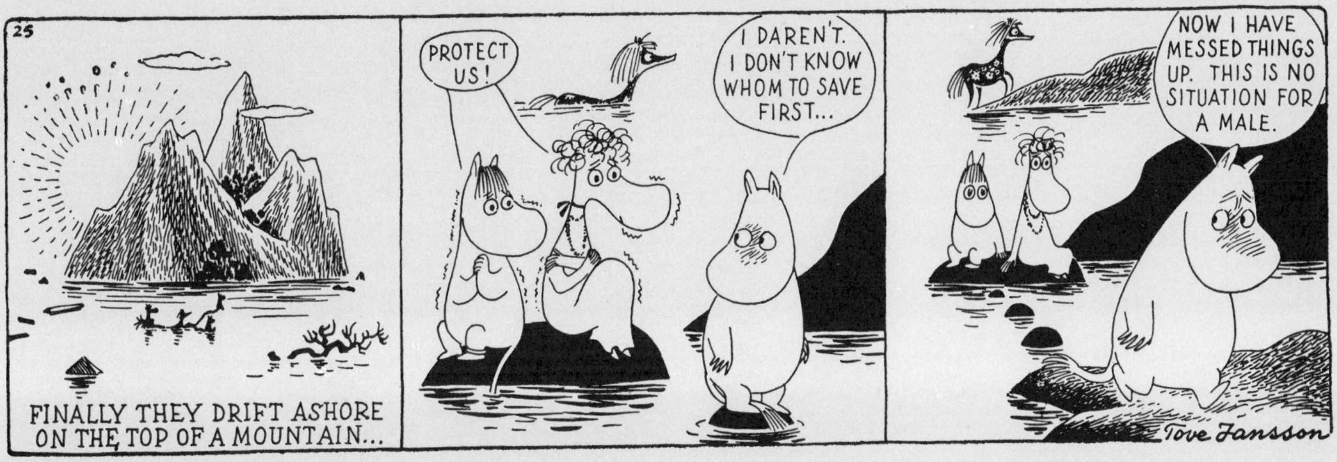
25
FINALLY THEY DRIFT ASHORE ON THE TOP OF A MOUNTAIN...
PROTECT US!
I DAREN'T. I DON'T KNOW WHOM TO SAVE FIRST...
NOW I HAVE MESSED THINGS UP. THIS IS NO SITUATION FOR A MALE.
Tove Jansson

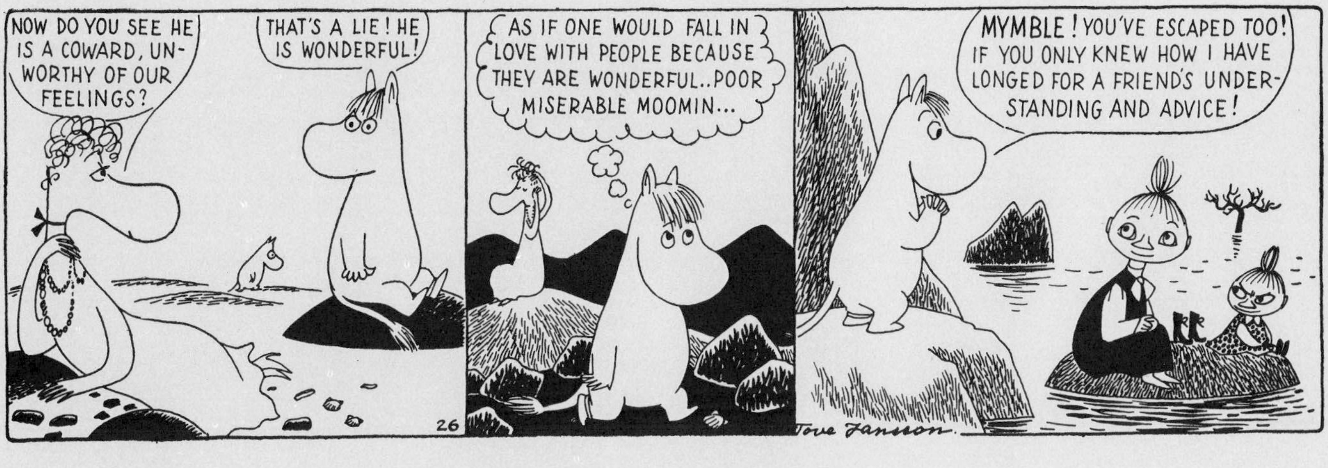
NOW DO YOU SEE HE IS A COWARD, UNWORTHY OF OUR FEELINGS?
THAT'S A LIE! HE IS WONDERFUL!
26
AS IF ONE WOULD FALL IN LOVE WITH PEOPLE BECAUSE THEY ARE WONDERFUL.. POOR MISERABLE MOOMIN...
MYMBLE! YOU'VE ESCAPED TOO! IF YOU ONLY KNEW HOW I HAVE LONGED FOR A FRIEND'S UNDERSTANDING AND ADVICE!
Tove Jansson

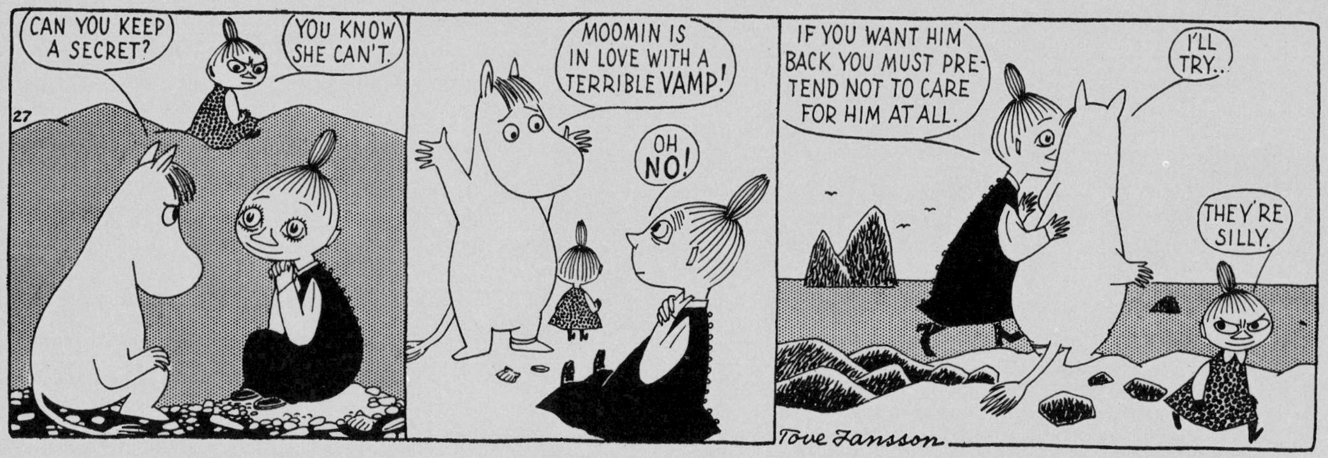
27
CAN YOU KEEP A SECRET?
YOU KNOW SHE CAN'T.
MOOMIN IS IN LOVE WITH A TERRIBLE VAMP!
OH NO!
IF YOU WANT HIM BACK YOU MUST PRETEND NOT TO CARE FOR HIM AT ALL.
I'LL TRY..
THEY'RE SILLY.
Tove Jansson

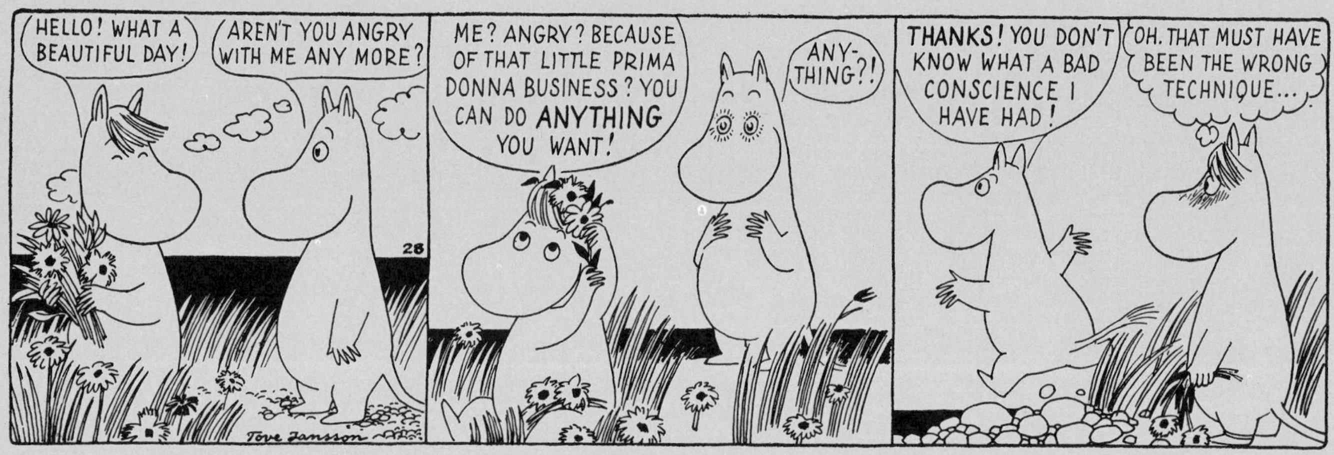
HELLO! WHAT A BEAUTIFUL DAY!
AREN'T YOU ANGRY WITH ME ANY MORE?
28
ME? ANGRY? BECAUSE OF THAT LITTLE PRIMA DONNA BUSINESS? YOU CAN DO ANYTHING YOU WANT!
ANY-THING?!
THANKS! YOU DON'T KNOW WHAT A BAD CONSCIENCE I HAVE HAD!
OH. THAT MUST HAVE BEEN THE WRONG TECHNIQUE...
Tove Jansson

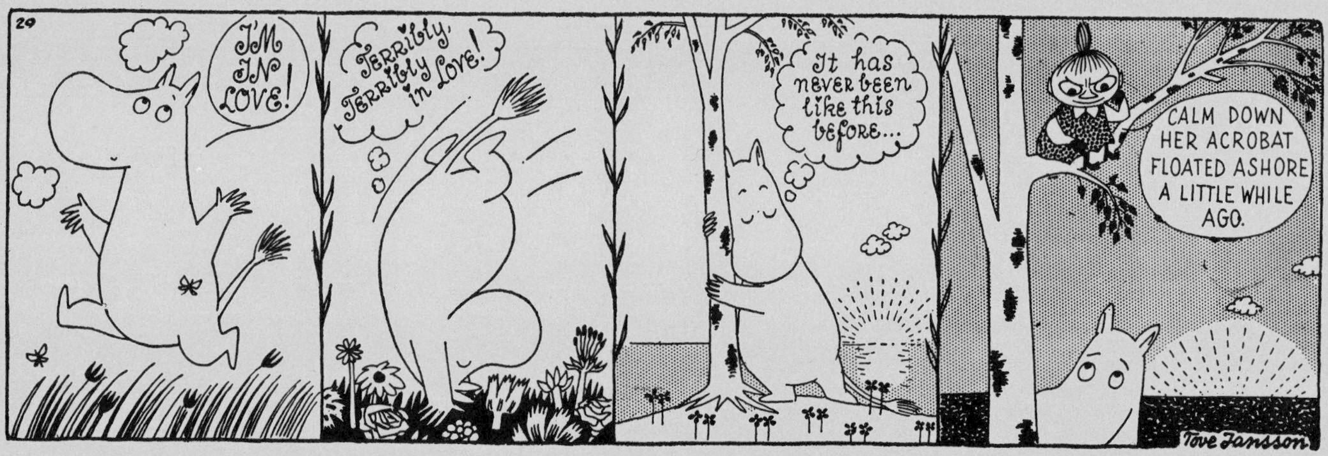
29
I'M IN LOVE!
Terribly, Terribly in Love!
It has never been like this before...
CALM DOWN HER ACROBAT FLOATED ASHORE A LITTLE WHILE AGO.
Tove Jansson

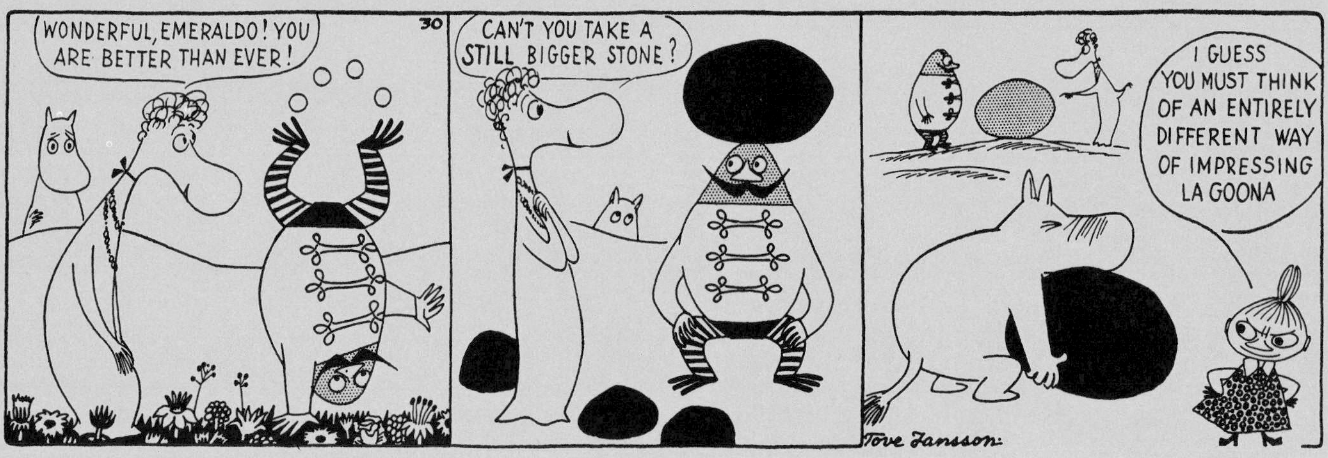
WONDERFUL, EMERALDO! YOU ARE BETTER THAN EVER!
30
CAN'T YOU TAKE A STILL BIGGER STONE?
I GUESS YOU MUST THINK OF AN ENTIRELY DIFFERENT WAY OF IMPRESSING LA GOONA
Tove Jansson

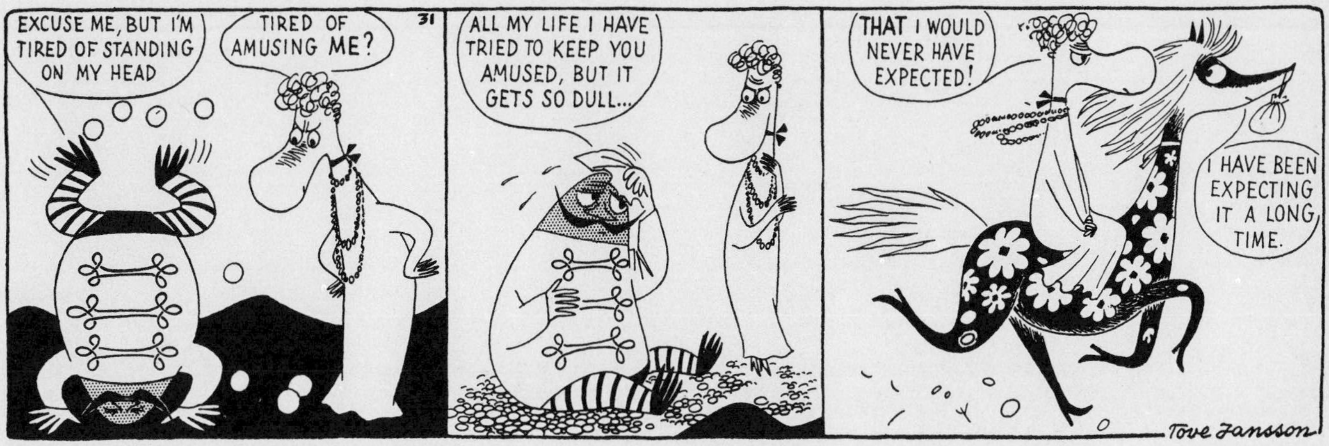
31
EXCUSE ME, BUT I'M TIRED OF STANDING ON MY HEAD
TIRED OF AMUSING ME?
ALL MY LIFE I HAVE TRIED TO KEEP YOU AMUSED, BUT IT GETS SO DULL...
THAT I WOULD NEVER HAVE EXPECTED!
I HAVE BEEN EXPECTING IT A LONG TIME.
Tove Jansson

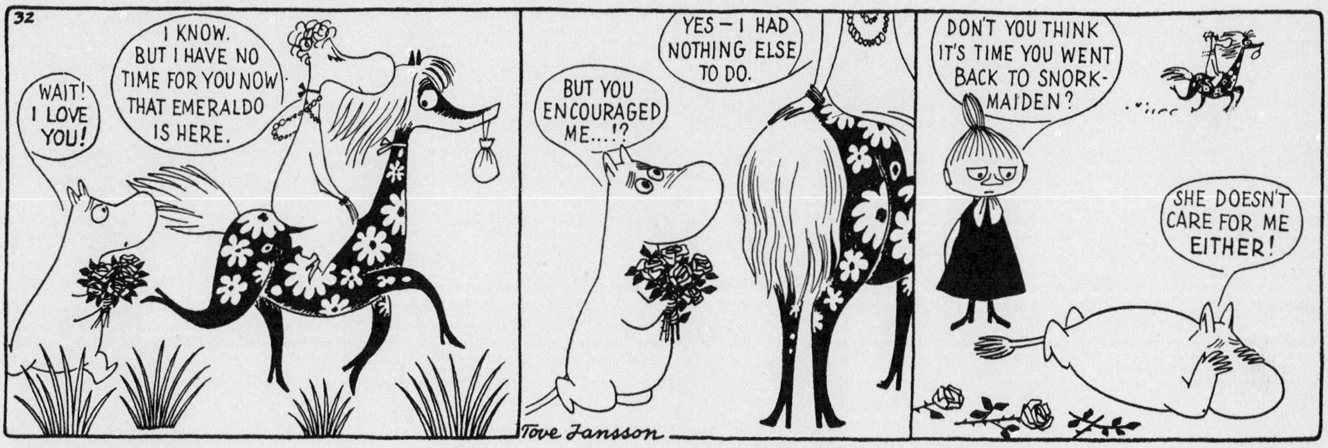
32
WAIT! I LOVE YOU!
I KNOW. BUT I HAVE NO TIME FOR YOU NOW THAT EMERALDO IS HERE.
BUT YOU ENCOURAGED ME...!?
YES – I HAD NOTHING ELSE TO DO.
Tove Jansson
DON'T YOU THINK IT'S TIME YOU WENT BACK TO SNORK-MAIDEN?
SHE DOESN'T CARE FOR ME EITHER!

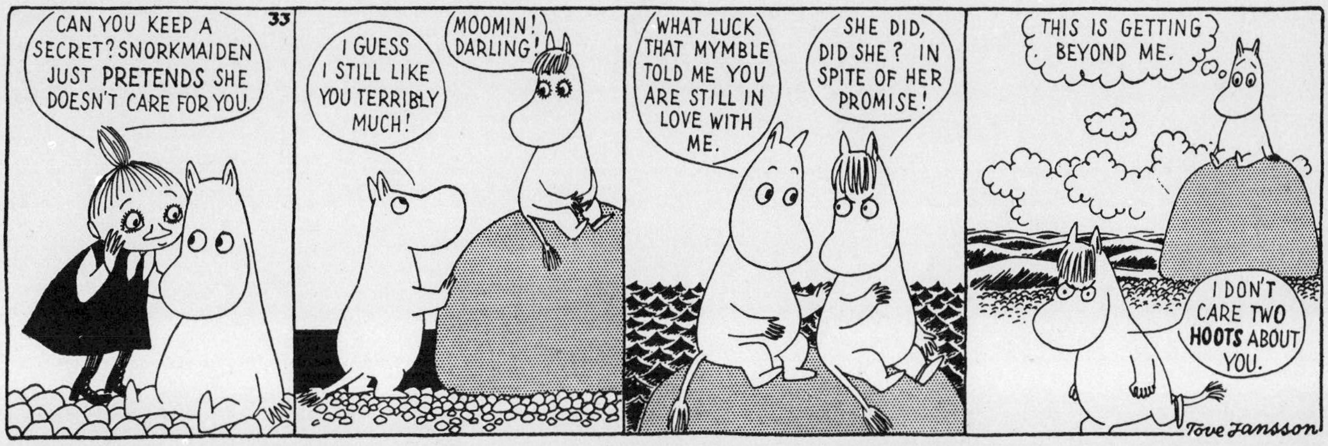
33
CAN YOU KEEP A SECRET? SNORKMAIDEN JUST PRETENDS SHE DOESN'T CARE FOR YOU.
I GUESS I STILL LIKE YOU TERRIBLY MUCH!
MOOMIN! DARLING!
WHAT LUCK THAT MYMBLE TOLD ME YOU ARE STILL IN LOVE WITH ME.
SHE DID, DID SHE? IN SPITE OF HER PROMISE!
THIS IS GETTING BEYOND ME.
I DON'T CARE TWO HOOTS ABOUT YOU.
Tove Jansson

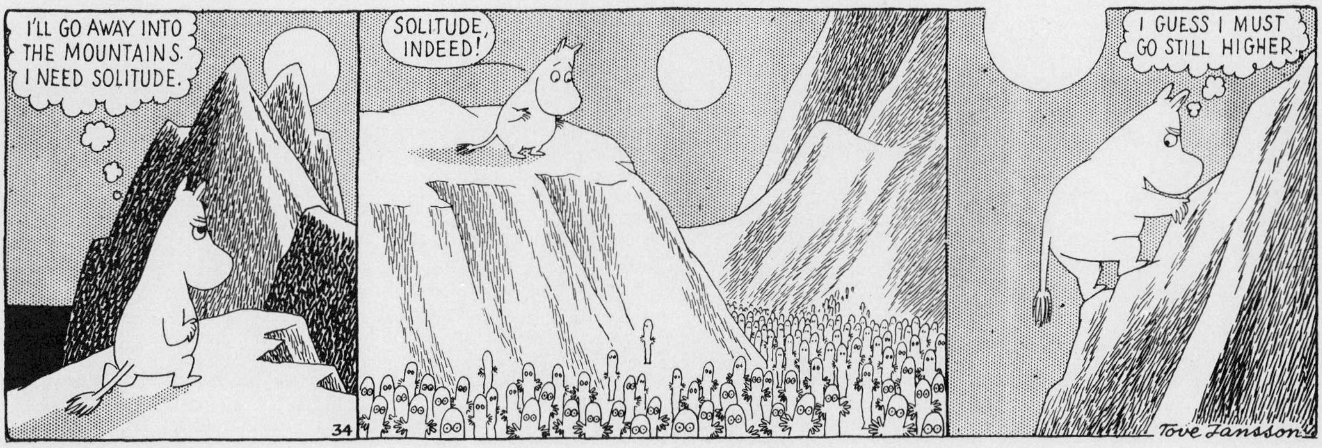
I'LL GO AWAY INTO THE MOUNTAINS. I NEED SOLITUDE.
34
SOLITUDE, INDEED!
I GUESS I MUST GO STILL HIGHER.
Tove Jansson

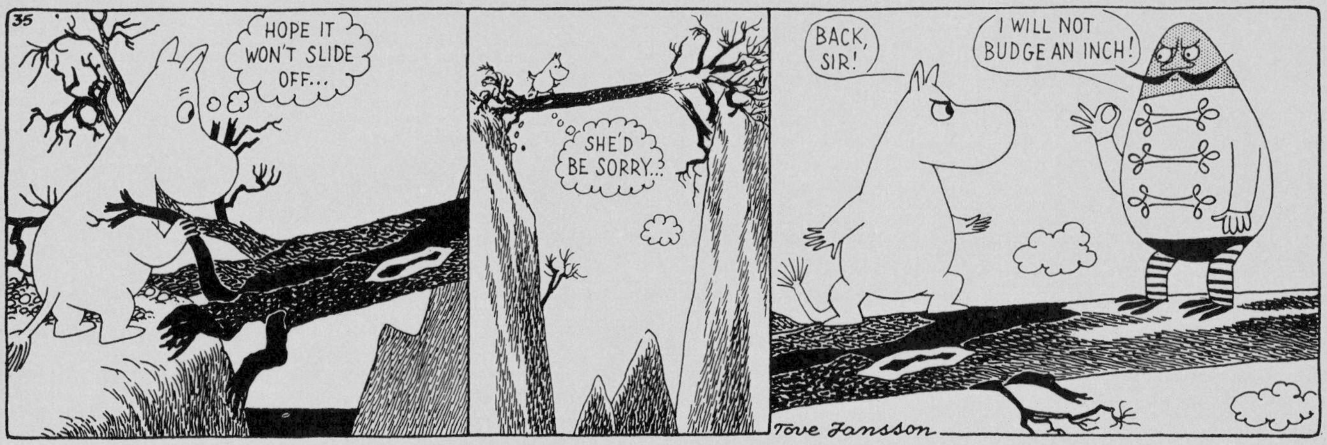
35
HOPE IT WON'T SLIDE OFF...
SHE'D BE SORRY..?
BACK, SIR!
I WILL NOT BUDGE AN INCH!
Tove Jansson

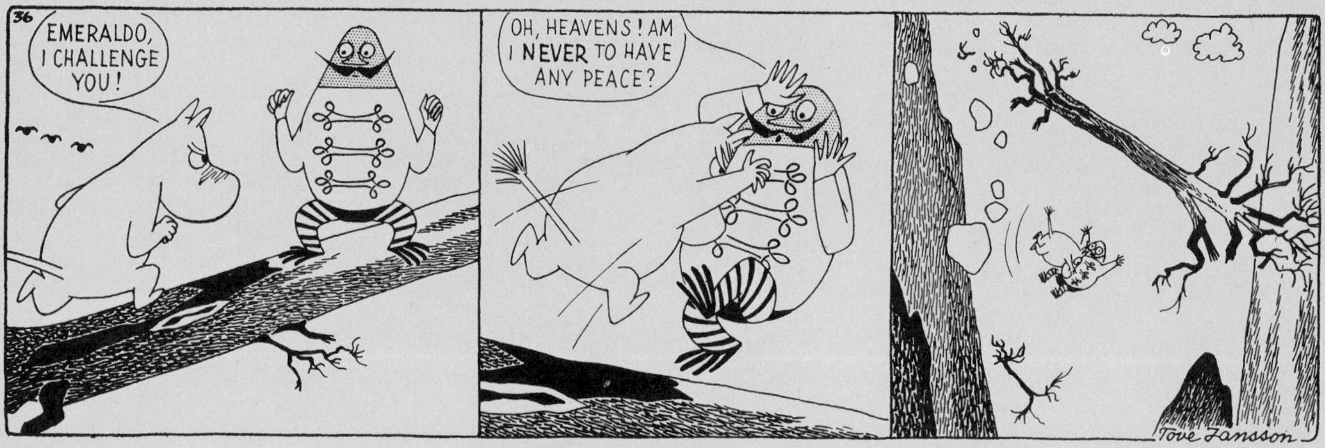
36
EMERALDO, I CHALLENGE YOU!
OH, HEAVENS! AM I NEVER TO HAVE ANY PEACE?
Tove Jansson

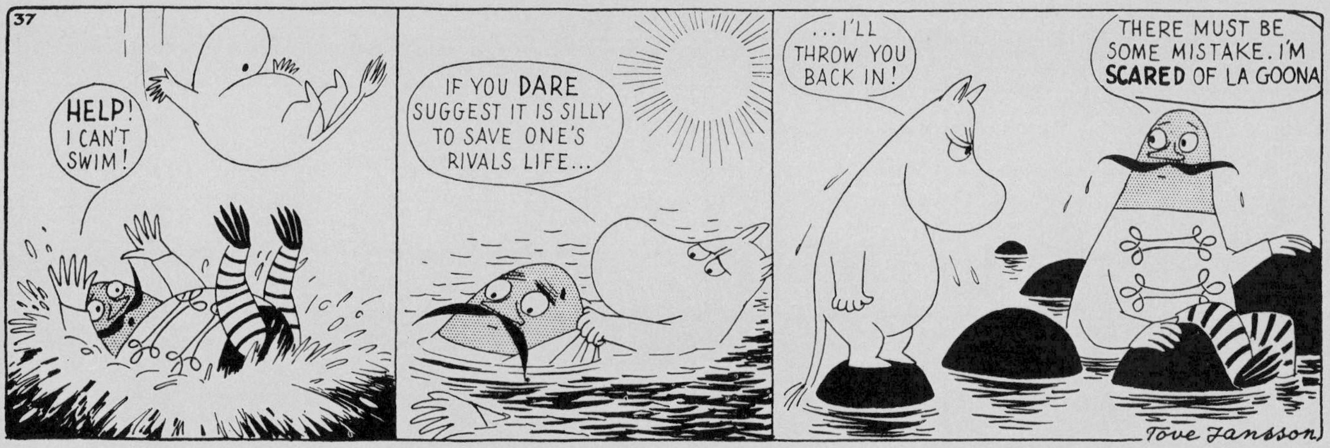
37
HELP! I CAN'T SWIM!
IF YOU DARE SUGGEST IT IS SILLY TO SAVE ONE'S RIVALS LIFE...
...I'LL THROW YOU BACK IN!
THERE MUST BE SOME MISTAKE. I'M SCARED OF LA GOONA
Tove Jansson

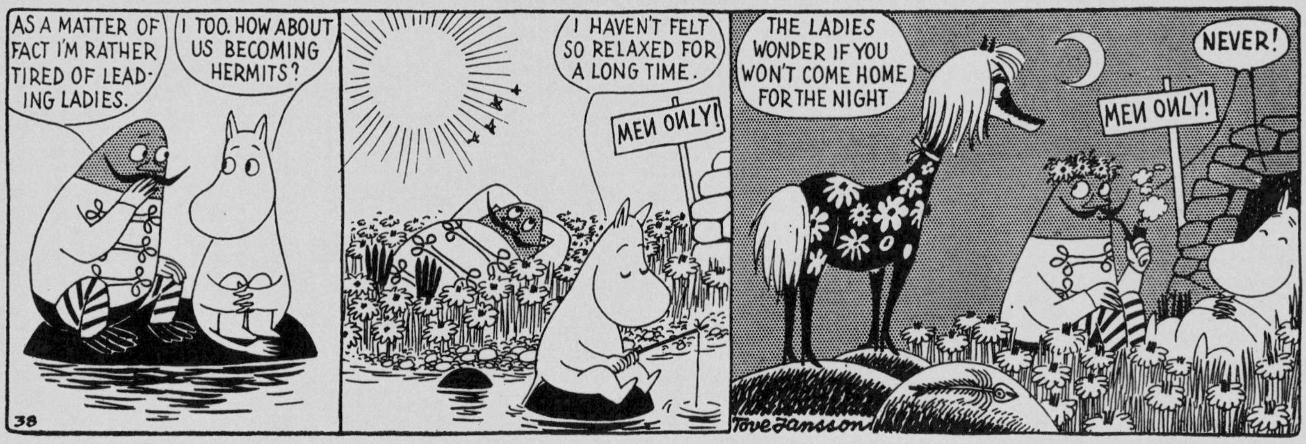
AS A MATTER OF FACT I'M RATHER TIRED OF LEADING LADIES.
I TOO. HOW ABOUT US BECOMING HERMITS?
38
I HAVEN'T FELT SO RELAXED FOR A LONG TIME.
MEN ONLY!
THE LADIES WONDER IF YOU WON'T COME HOME FOR THE NIGHT
NEVER!
MEN ONLY!
Tove Jansson

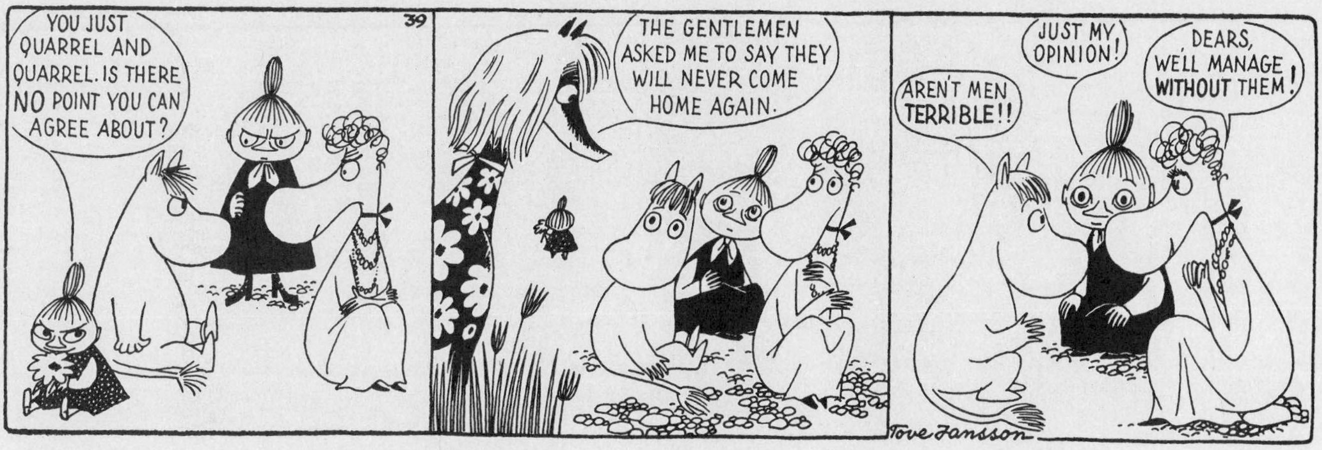
39
YOU JUST QUARREL AND QUARREL. IS THERE NO POINT YOU CAN AGREE ABOUT?
THE GENTLEMEN ASKED ME TO SAY THEY WILL NEVER COME HOME AGAIN.
AREN'T MEN TERRIBLE!!
JUST MY OPINION!
DEARS, WE'LL MANAGE WITHOUT THEM!
Tove Jansson

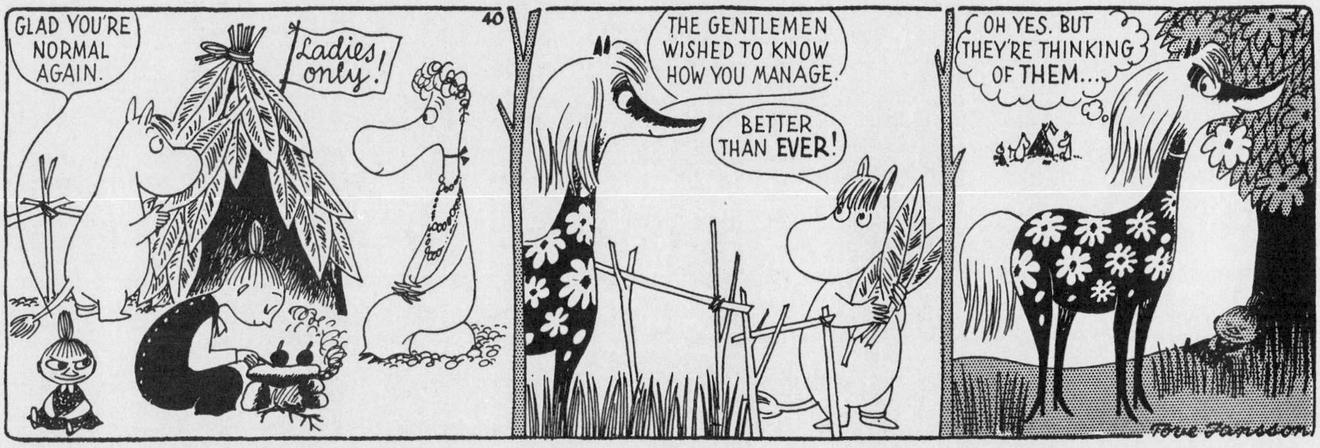
40
GLAD YOU'RE NORMAL AGAIN.
Ladies only!
THE GENTLEMEN WISHED TO KNOW HOW YOU MANAGE.
BETTER THAN EVER!
OH YES. BUT THEY'RE THINKING OF THEM....
Tove Jansson

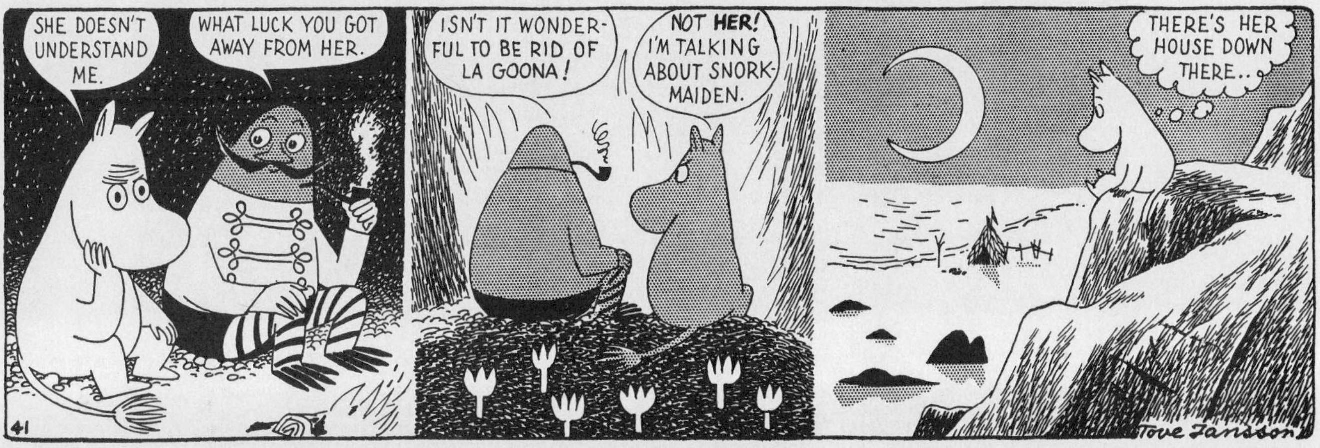
SHE DOESN'T UNDERSTAND ME.
WHAT LUCK YOU GOT AWAY FROM HER.
41
ISN'T IT WONDERFUL TO BE RID OF LA GOONA!
NOT HER! I'M TALKING ABOUT SNORK-MAIDEN.
THERE'S HER HOUSE DOWN THERE..
Tove Jansson

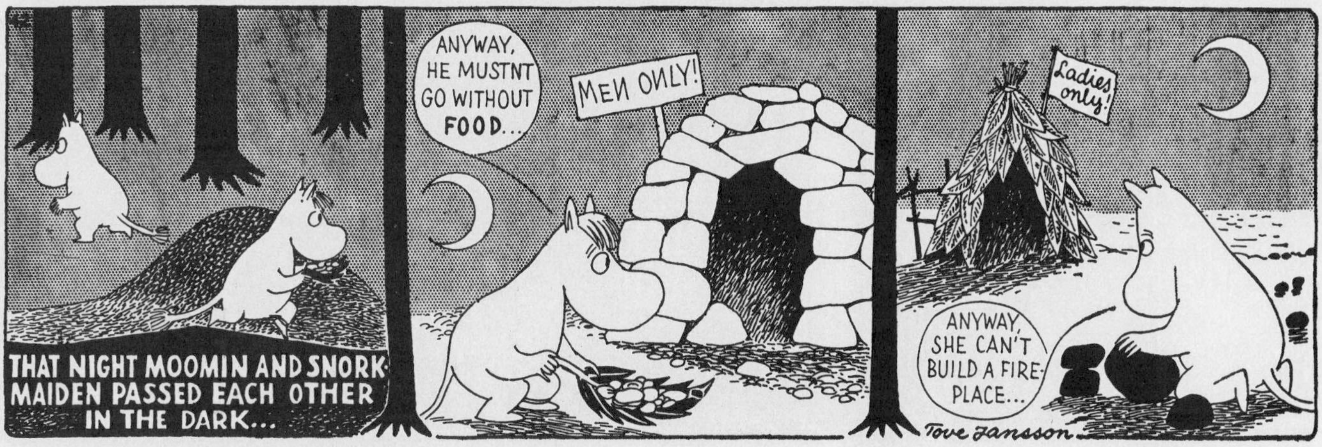
THAT NIGHT MOOMIN AND SNORK-MAIDEN PASSED EACH OTHER IN THE DARK...
ANYWAY, HE MUSTNT GO WITHOUT FOOD...
MEN ONLY!
Ladies only!
ANYWAY, SHE CAN'T BUILD A FIRE-PLACE...
Tove Jansson

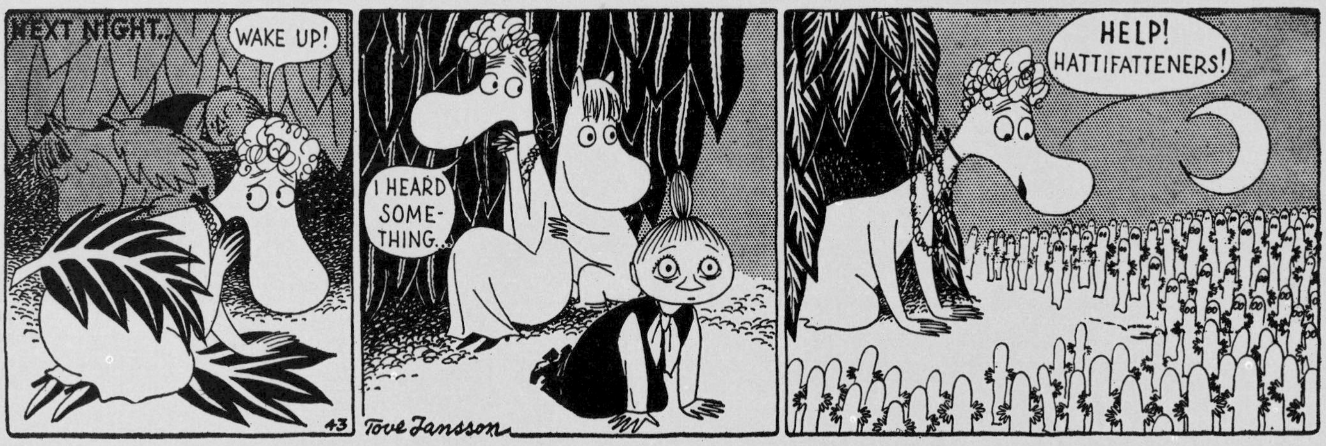
NEXT NIGHT...
WAKE UP!
I HEARD SOME-THING...
HELP! HATTIFATTENERS!
Tove Jansson

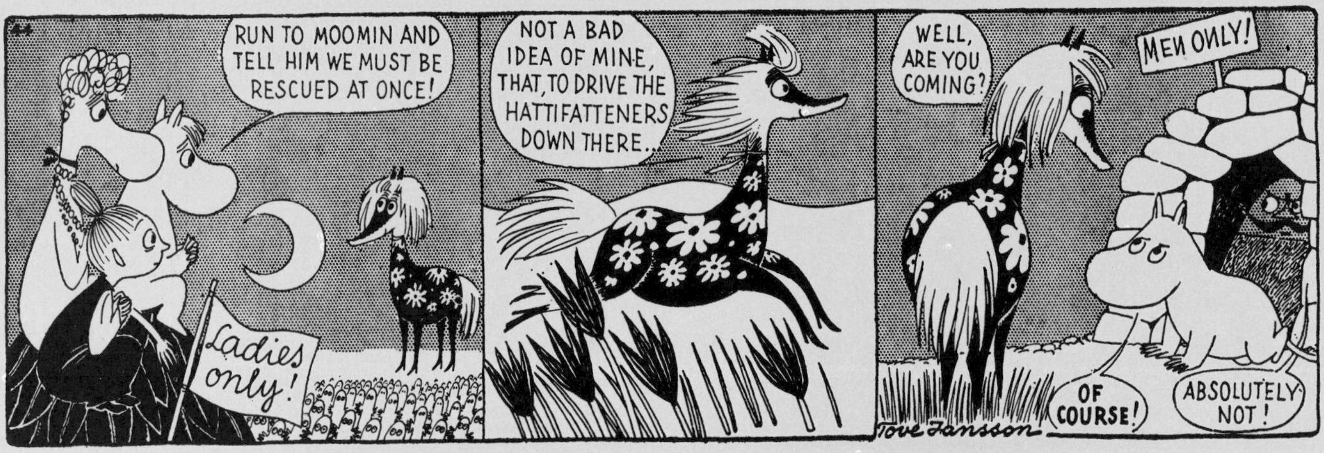
RUN TO MOOMIN AND TELL HIM WE MUST BE RESCUED AT ONCE!
Ladies only!
NOT A BAD IDEA OF MINE, THAT, TO DRIVE THE HATTIFATTENERS DOWN THERE...
WELL, ARE YOU COMING?
MEN ONLY!
OF COURSE!
ABSOLUTELY NOT!
Tove Jansson

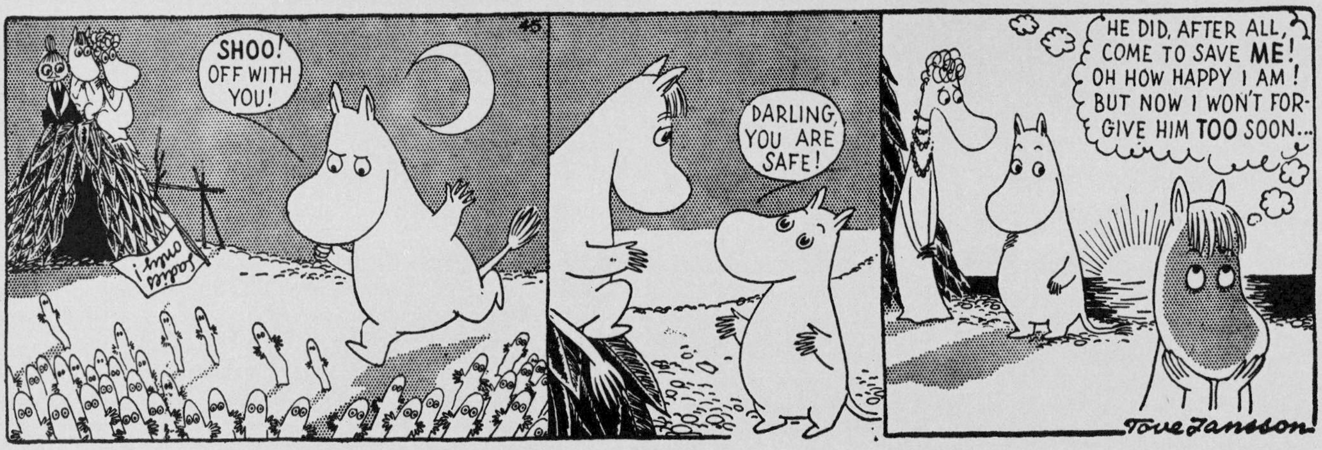
SHOO! OFF WITH YOU!
DARLING, YOU ARE SAFE!
HE DID, AFTER ALL, COME TO SAVE ME! OH HOW HAPPY I AM! BUT NOW I WON'T FOR-GIVE HIM TOO SOON...
Tove Jansson

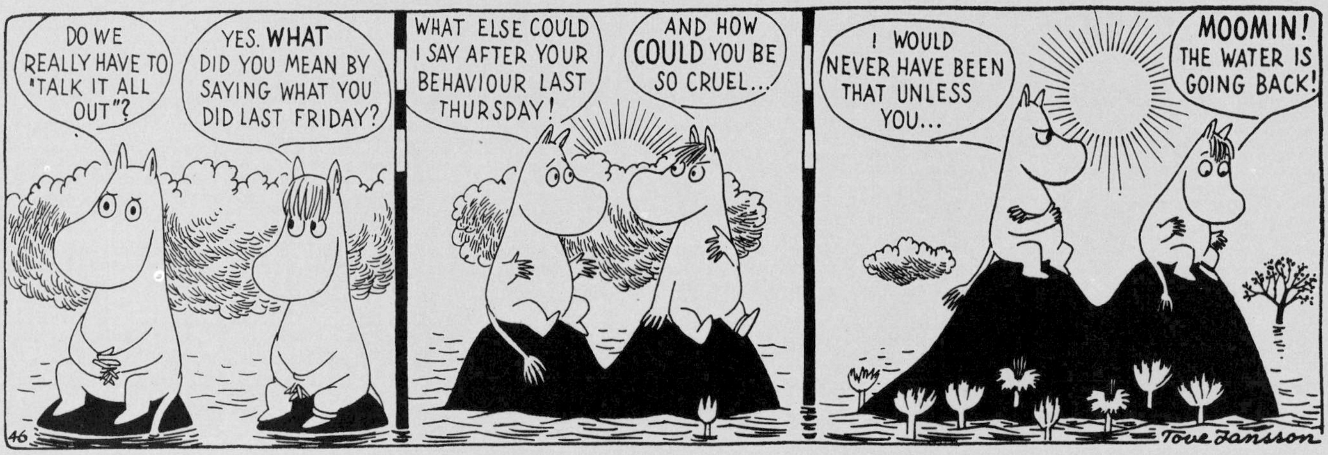
DO WE REALLY HAVE TO "TALK IT ALL OUT"?
YES. WHAT DID YOU MEAN BY SAYING WHAT YOU DID LAST FRIDAY?
WHAT ELSE COULD I SAY AFTER YOUR BEHAVIOUR LAST THURSDAY!
AND HOW COULD YOU BE SO CRUEL...
I WOULD NEVER HAVE BEEN THAT UNLESS YOU...
MOOMIN! THE WATER IS GOING BACK!
Tove Jansson

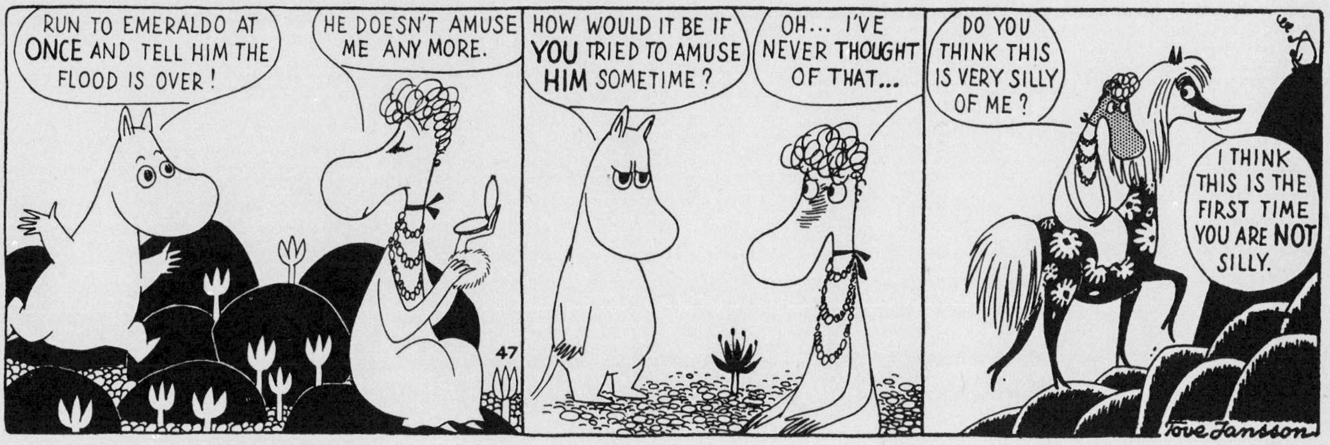
RUN TO EMERALDO AT ONCE AND TELL HIM THE FLOOD IS OVER!
HE DOESN'T AMUSE ME ANY MORE.
47
HOW WOULD IT BE IF YOU TRIED TO AMUSE HIM SOMETIME?
OH... I'VE NEVER THOUGHT OF THAT...
DO YOU THINK THIS IS VERY SILLY OF ME?
I THINK THIS IS THE FIRST TIME YOU ARE NOT SILLY.
Tove Jansson

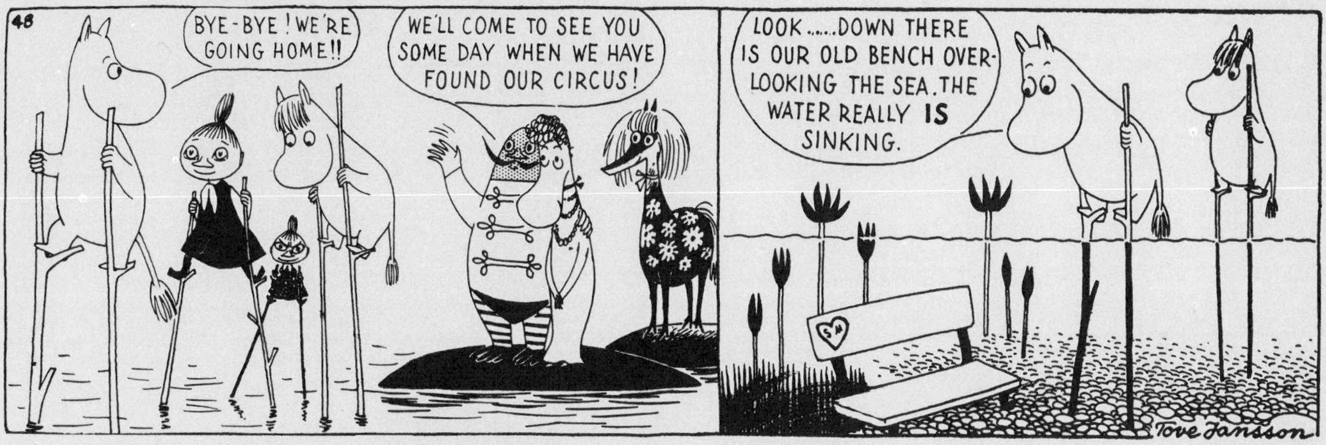
48
BYE-BYE! WE'RE GOING HOME!!
WE'LL COME TO SEE YOU SOME DAY WHEN WE HAVE FOUND OUR CIRCUS!
LOOK......DOWN THERE IS OUR OLD BENCH OVER-LOOKING THE SEA. THE WATER REALLY IS SINKING.
Tove Jansson

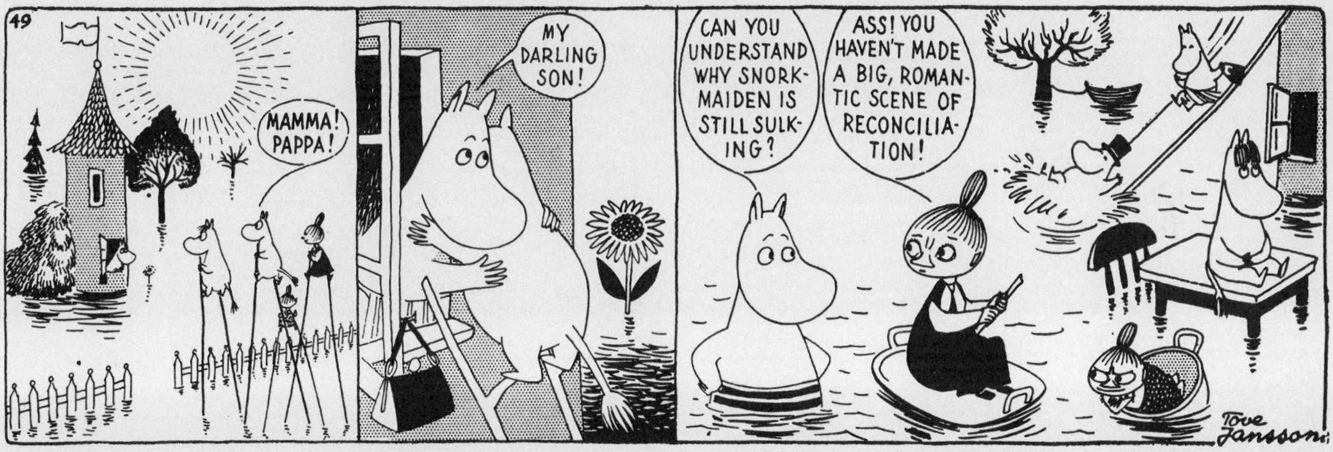
49
MAMMA! PAPPA!
MY DARLING SON!
CAN YOU UNDERSTAND WHY SNORK-MAIDEN IS STILL SULK-ING?
ASS! YOU HAVEN'T MADE A BIG, ROMAN-TIC SCENE OF RECONCILIA-TION!
Tove Jansson

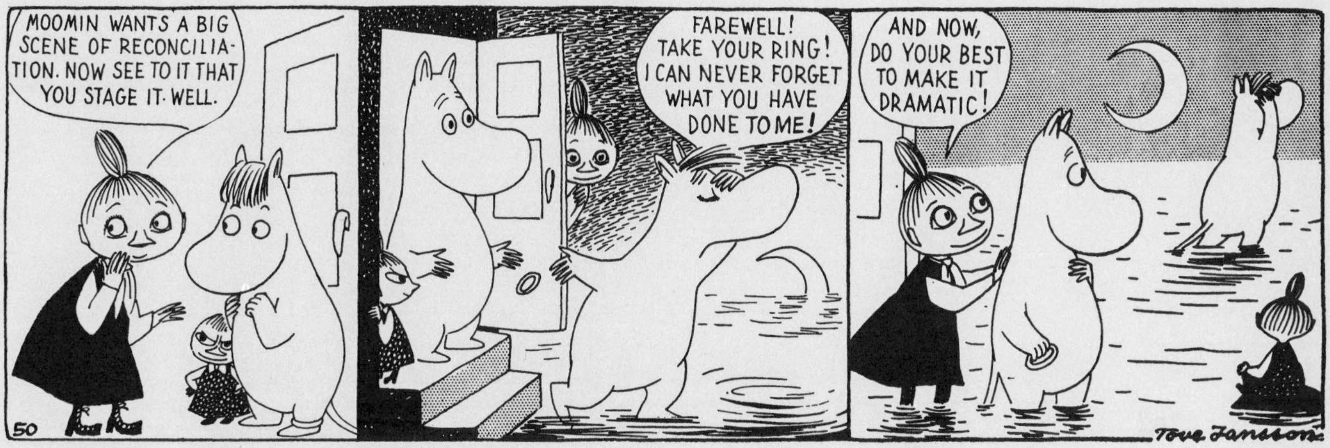
MOOMIN WANTS A BIG SCENE OF RECONCILIA-TION. NOW SEE TO IT THAT YOU STAGE IT WELL.
50
FAREWELL! TAKE YOUR RING! I CAN NEVER FORGET WHAT YOU HAVE DONE TO ME!
AND NOW, DO YOUR BEST TO MAKE IT DRAMATIC!
Tove Jansson

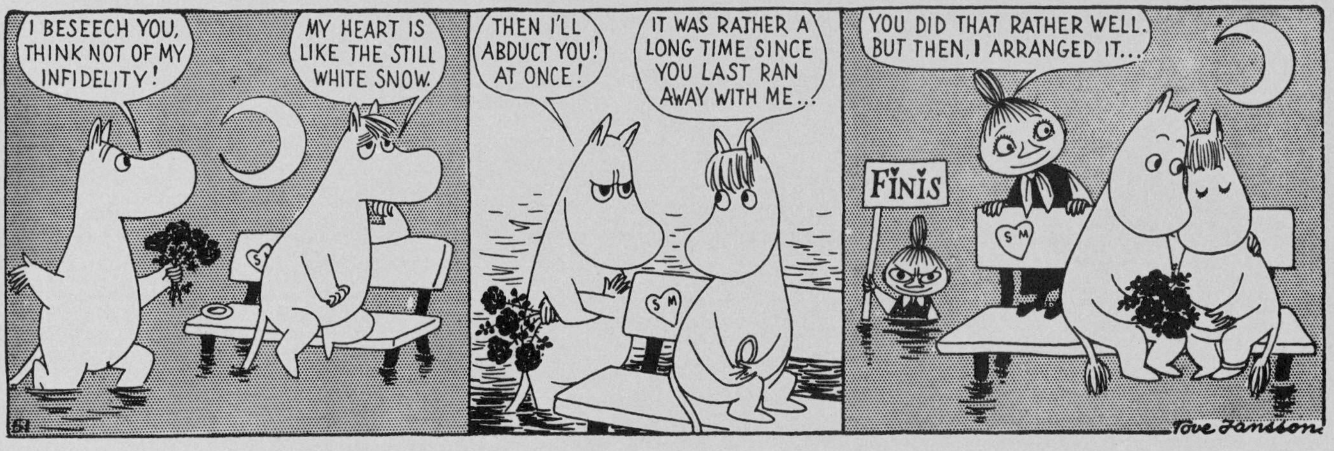
I BESEECH YOU, THINK NOT OF MY INFIDELITY!
MY HEART IS LIKE THE STILL WHITE SNOW.
THEN I'LL ABDUCT YOU! AT ONCE!
IT WAS RATHER A LONG TIME SINCE YOU LAST RAN AWAY WITH ME...
YOU DID THAT RATHER WELL. BUT THEN, I ARRANGED IT...
FINIS
Tove Jansson

10. Moominvalley Turns Jungle

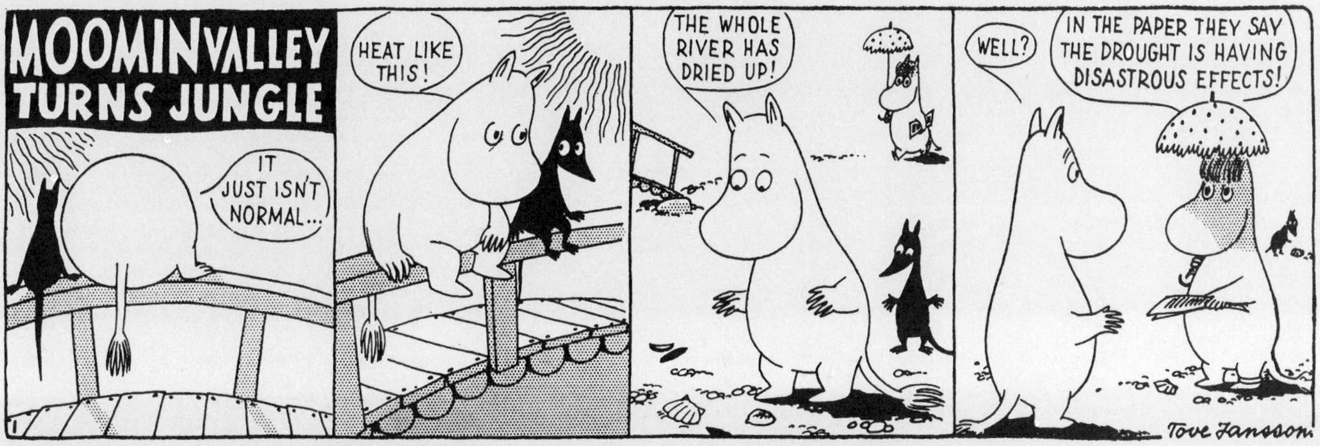
MOOMINVALLEY TURNS JUNGLE
IT JUST ISN'T NORMAL...
HEAT LIKE THIS!
THE WHOLE RIVER HAS DRIED UP!
WELL?
IN THE PAPER THEY SAY THE DROUGHT IS HAVING DISASTROUS EFFECTS!
Tove Jansson

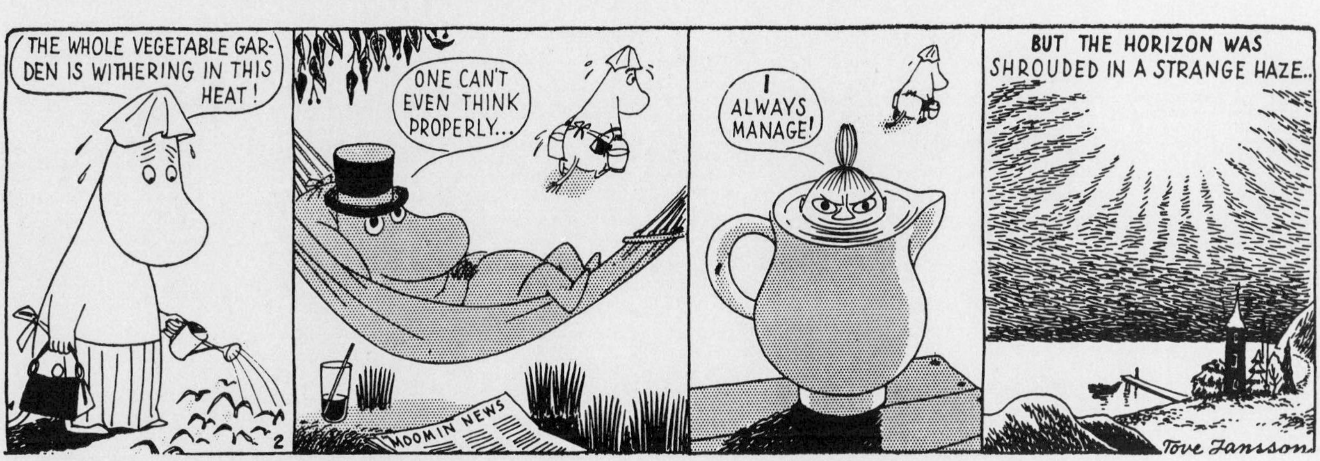
THE WHOLE VEGETABLE GARDEN IS WITHERING IN THIS HEAT!
ONE CAN'T EVEN THINK PROPERLY...
MOOMIN NEWS
I ALWAYS MANAGE!
BUT THE HORIZON WAS SHROUDED IN A STRANGE HAZE..
Tove Jansson

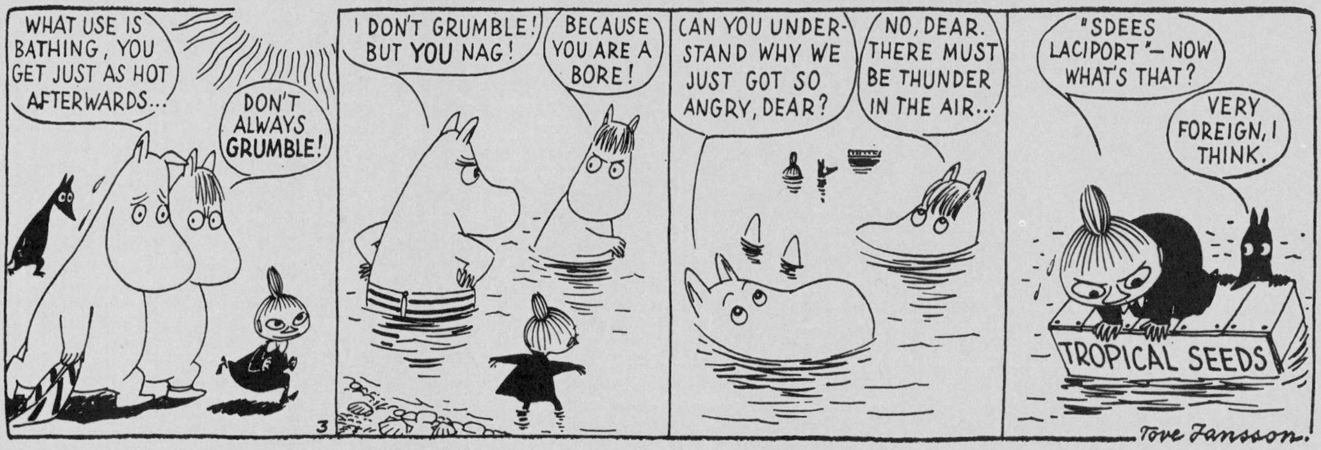
WHAT USE IS BATHING, YOU GET JUST AS HOT AFTERWARDS...
DON'T ALWAYS GRUMBLE!
3
I DON'T GRUMBLE! BUT YOU NAG!
BECAUSE YOU ARE A BORE!
CAN YOU UNDER-STAND WHY WE JUST GOT SO ANGRY, DEAR?
NO, DEAR. THERE MUST BE THUNDER IN THE AIR...
"SDEES LACIPORT"– NOW WHAT'S THAT?
VERY FOREIGN, I THINK.
TROPICAL SEEDS
Tove Jansson

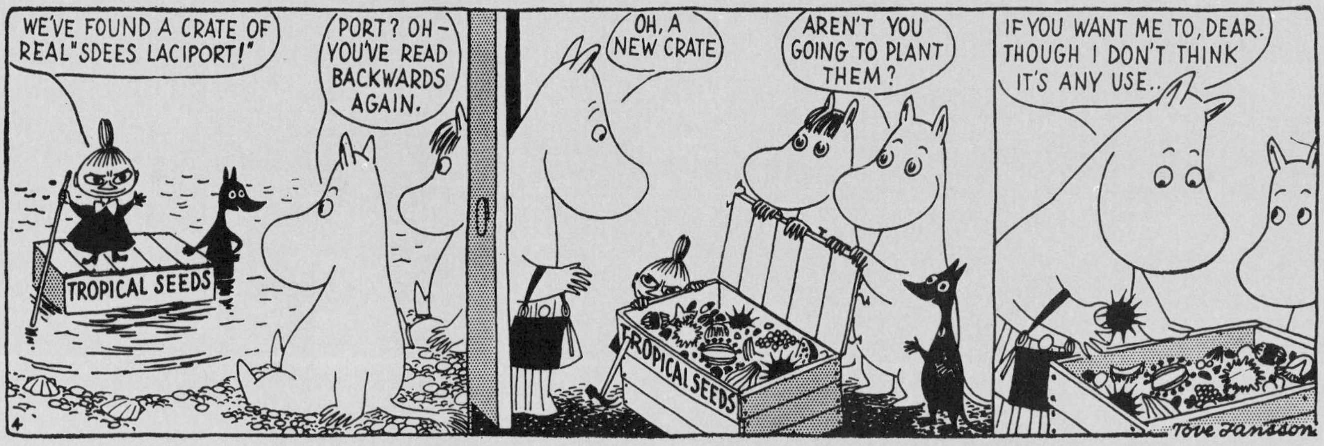
WE'VE FOUND A CRATE OF REAL "SDEES LACIPORT!"
TROPICAL SEEDS
PORT? OH– YOU'VE READ BACKWARDS AGAIN.
4
OH, A NEW CRATE
AREN'T YOU GOING TO PLANT THEM?
TROPICAL SEEDS
IF YOU WANT ME TO, DEAR. THOUGH I DON'T THINK IT'S ANY USE..
Tove Jansson

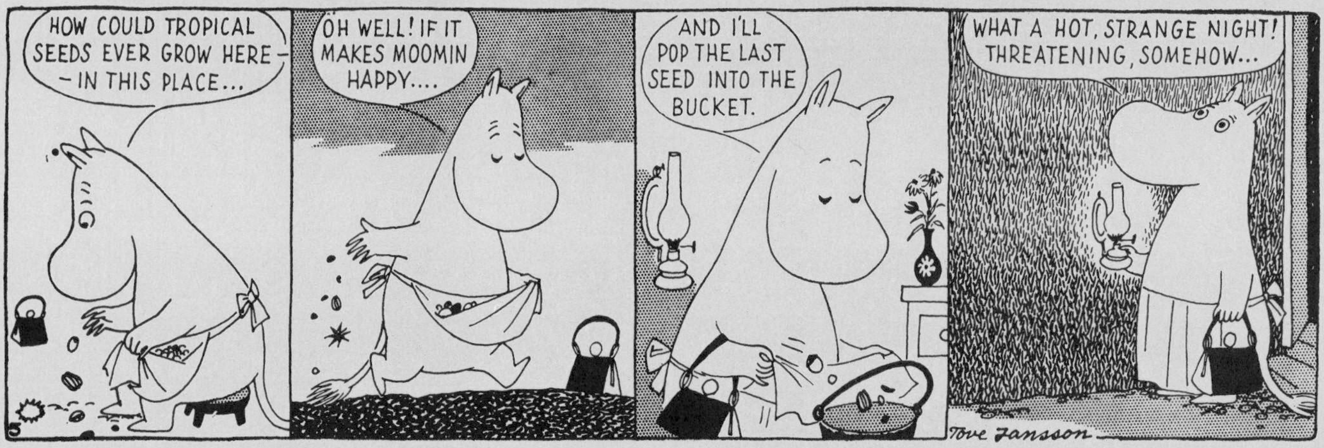
HOW COULD TROPICAL SEEDS EVER GROW HERE – IN THIS PLACE...
5
OH WELL! IF IT MAKES MOOMIN HAPPY....
AND I'LL POP THE LAST SEED INTO THE BUCKET.
WHAT A HOT, STRANGE NIGHT! THREATENING, SOMEHOW...
Tove Jansson

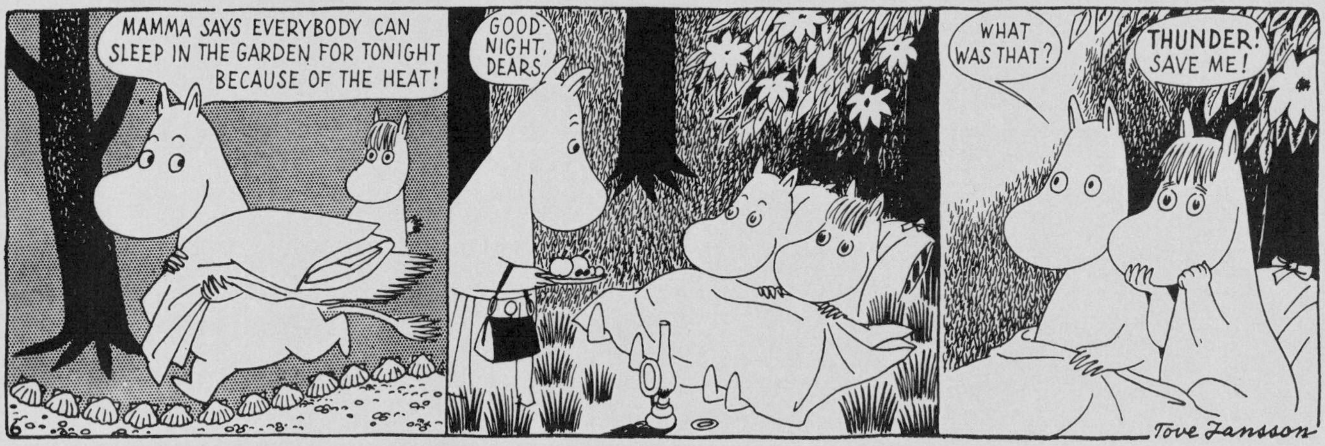
MAMMA SAYS EVERYBODY CAN SLEEP IN THE GARDEN FOR TONIGHT BECAUSE OF THE HEAT!
6
GOOD-NIGHT, DEARS.
WHAT WAS THAT?
THUNDER! SAVE ME!
Tove Jansson

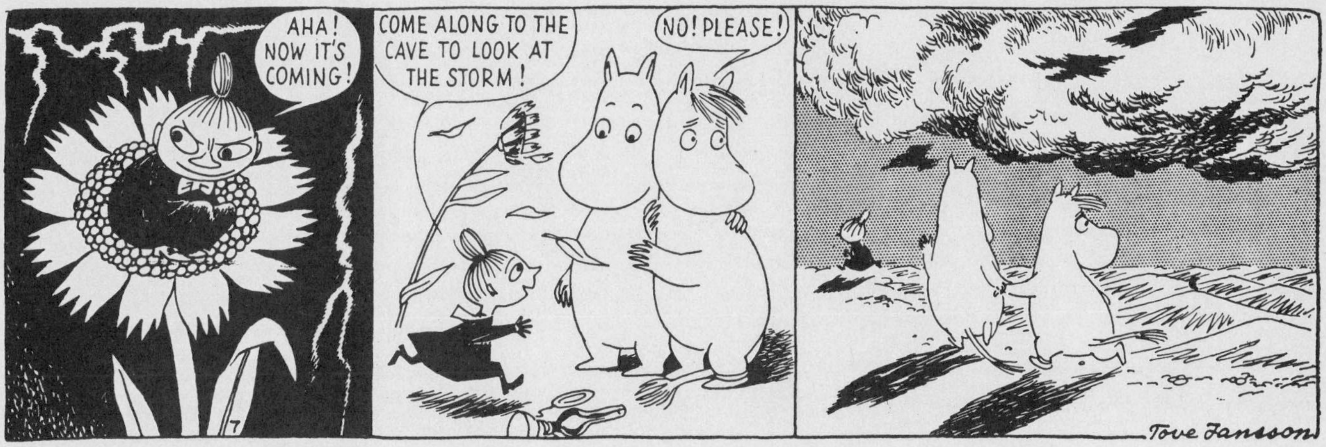
AHA! NOW IT'S COMING!
COME ALONG TO THE CAVE TO LOOK AT THE STORM!
NO! PLEASE!
Tove Jansson

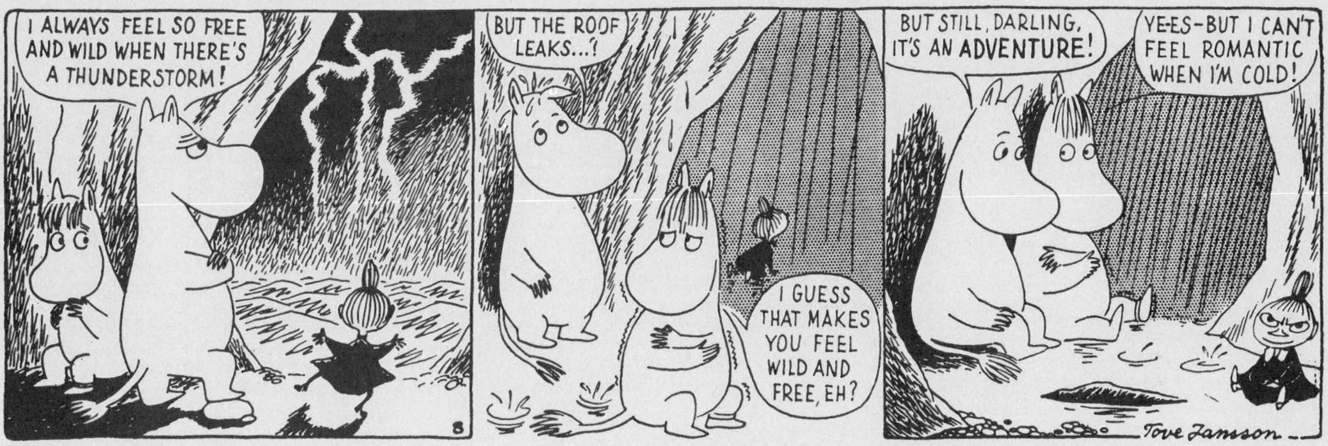
I ALWAYS FEEL SO FREE AND WILD WHEN THERE'S A THUNDERSTORM!
BUT THE ROOF LEAKS...!
I GUESS THAT MAKES YOU FEEL WILD AND FREE, EH?
BUT STILL, DARLING, IT'S AN ADVENTURE!
YE-ES–BUT I CAN'T FEEL ROMANTIC WHEN I'M COLD!
Tove Jansson

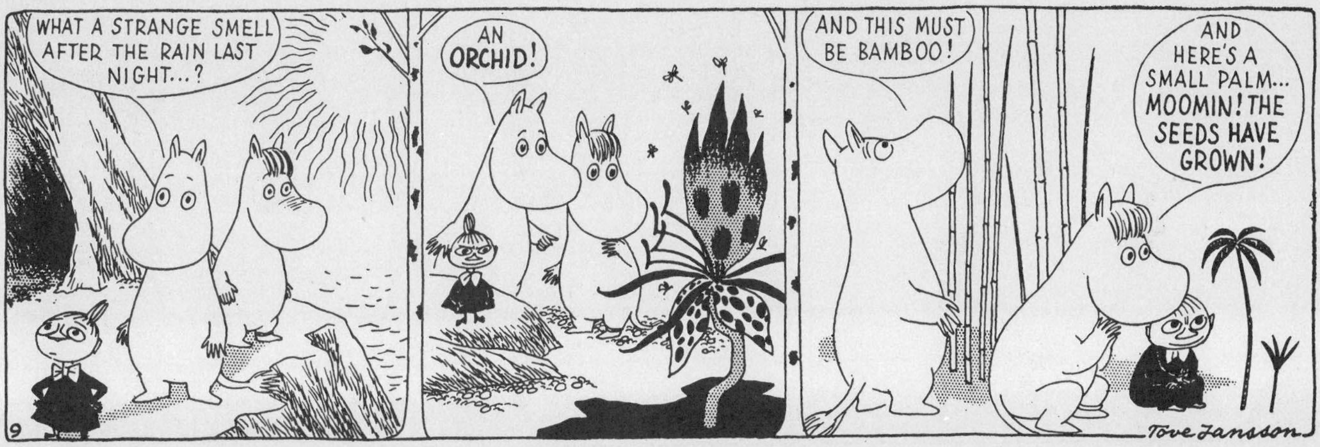
WHAT A STRANGE SMELL AFTER THE RAIN LAST NIGHT...?
AN ORCHID!
AND THIS MUST BE BAMBOO!
AND HERE'S A SMALL PALM... MOOMIN! THE SEEDS HAVE GROWN!
Tove Jansson

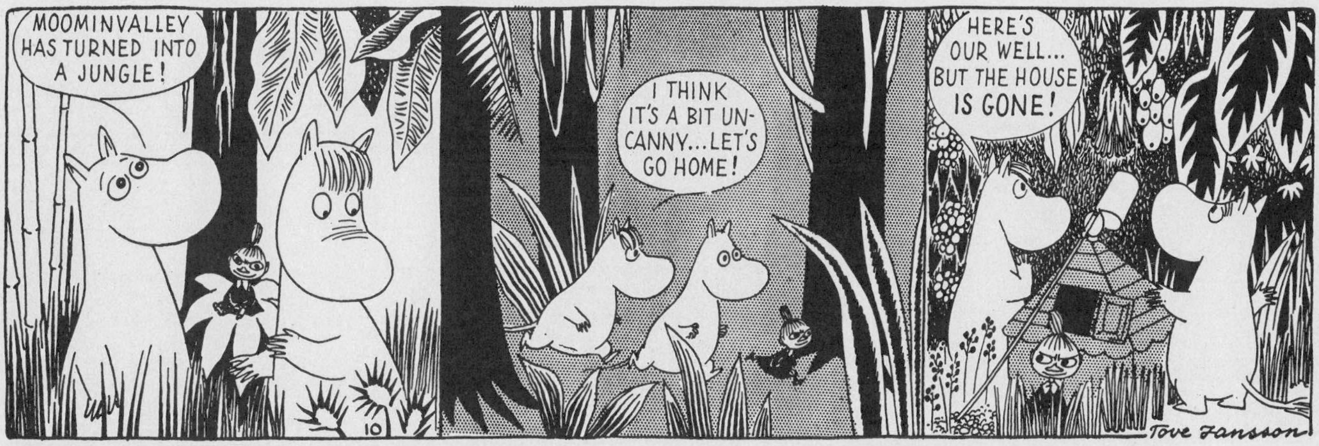
MOOMINVALLEY HAS TURNED INTO A JUNGLE!
I THINK IT'S A BIT UNCANNY...LET'S GO HOME!
HERE'S OUR WELL... BUT THE HOUSE IS GONE!
Tove Jansson

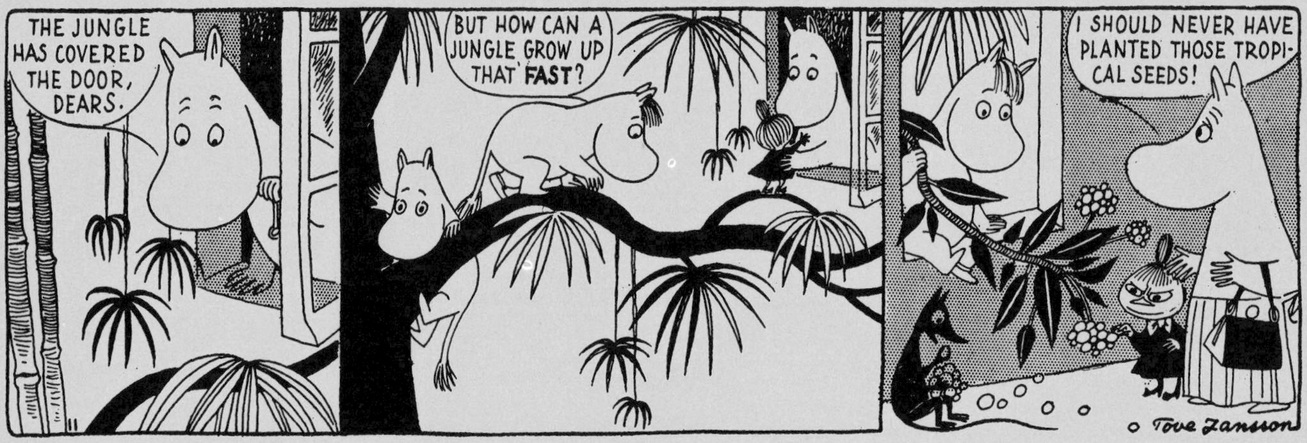
THE JUNGLE HAS COVERED THE DOOR, DEARS.
BUT HOW CAN A JUNGLE GROW UP THAT FAST?
I SHOULD NEVER HAVE PLANTED THOSE TROPICAL SEEDS!
Tove Jansson

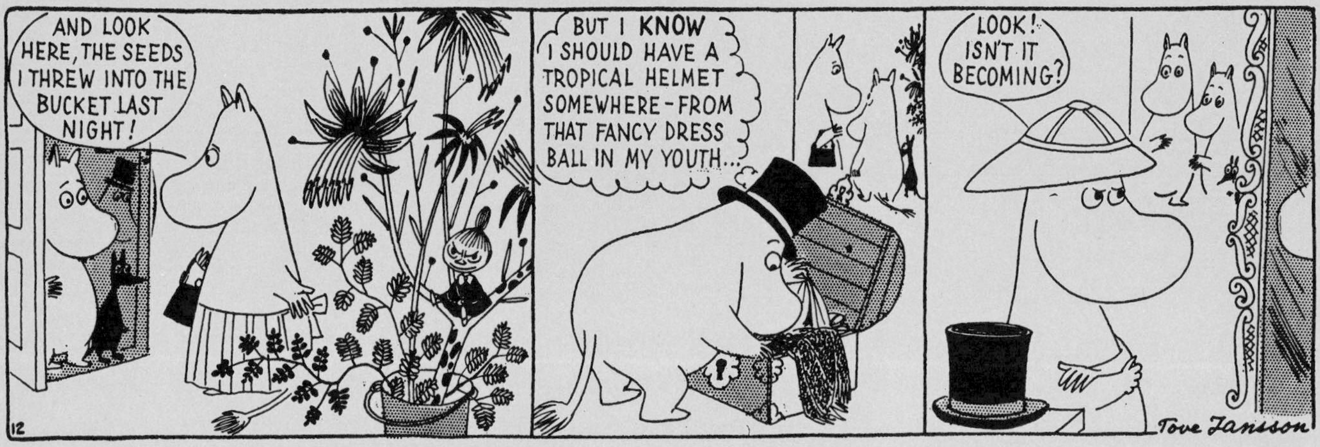
AND LOOK HERE, THE SEEDS I THREW INTO THE BUCKET LAST NIGHT!
BUT I KNOW I SHOULD HAVE A TROPICAL HELMET SOMEWHERE - FROM THAT FANCY DRESS BALL IN MY YOUTH...
LOOK! ISN'T IT BECOMING?
Tove Jansson

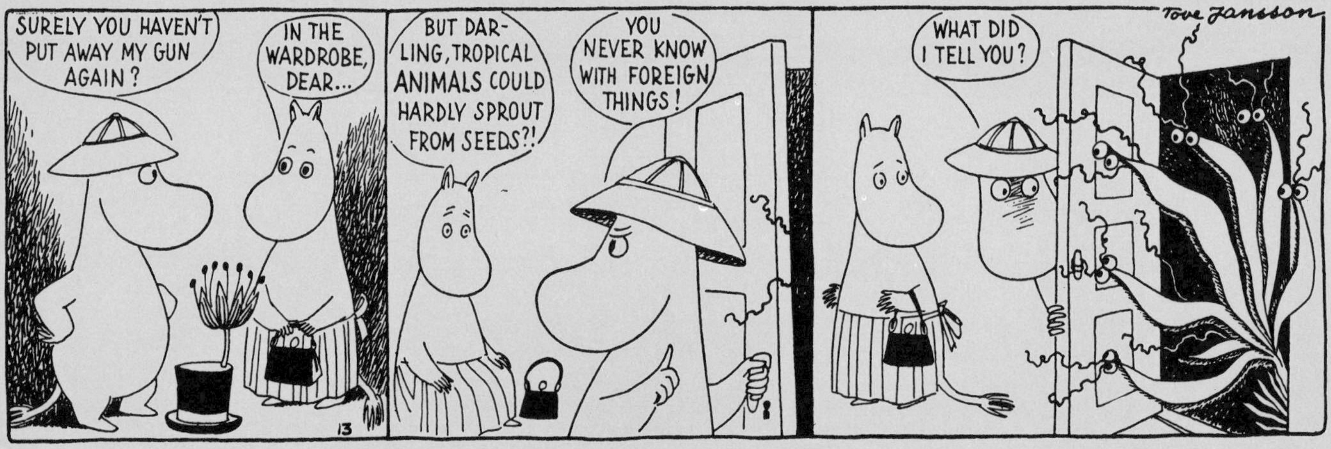
SURELY YOU HAVEN'T PUT AWAY MY GUN AGAIN?
IN THE WARDROBE, DEAR...
BUT DARLING, TROPICAL ANIMALS COULD HARDLY SPROUT FROM SEEDS?!
YOU NEVER KNOW WITH FOREIGN THINGS!
WHAT DID I TELL YOU?
Tove Jansson

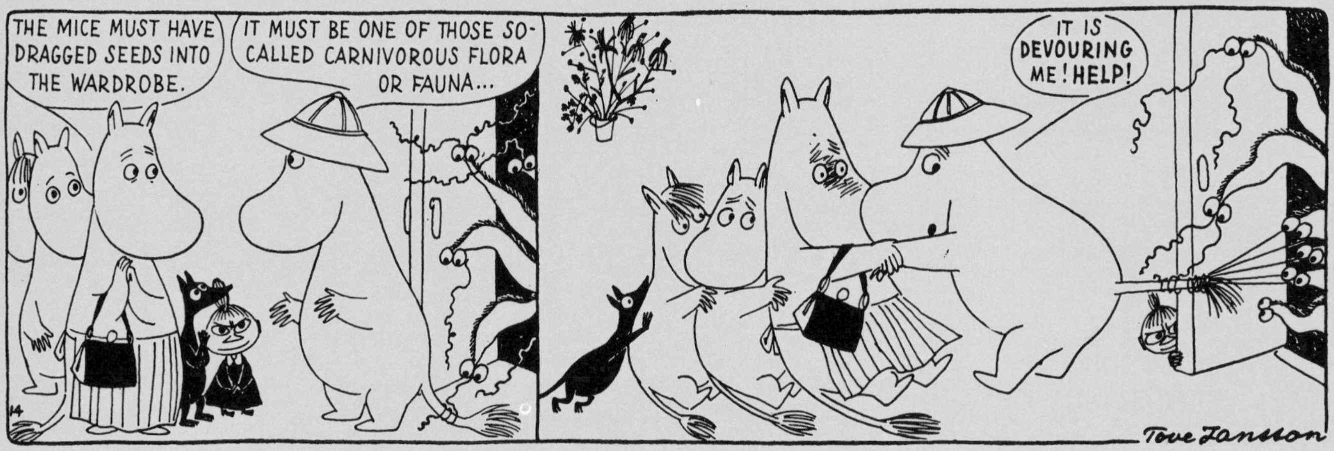
THE MICE MUST HAVE DRAGGED SEEDS INTO THE WARDROBE.
IT MUST BE ONE OF THOSE SO-CALLED CARNIVOROUS FLORA OR FAUNA...
IT IS DEVOURING ME! HELP!
Tove Jansson

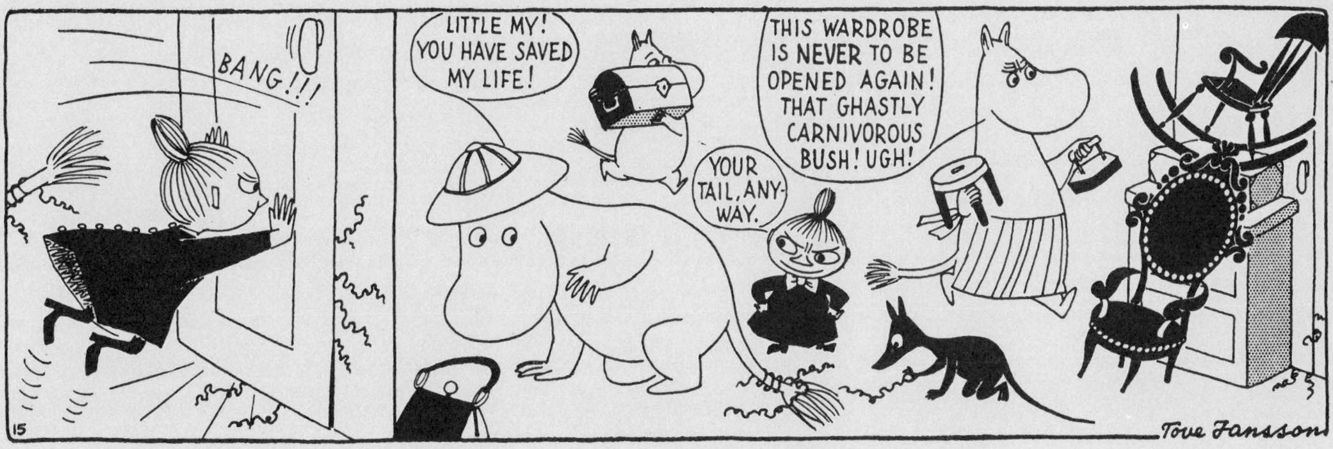
BANG!!!
15
LITTLE MY! YOU HAVE SAVED MY LIFE!
YOUR TAIL, ANY-WAY.
THIS WARDROBE IS NEVER TO BE OPENED AGAIN! THAT GHASTLY CARNIVOROUS BUSH! UGH!
Tove Jansson

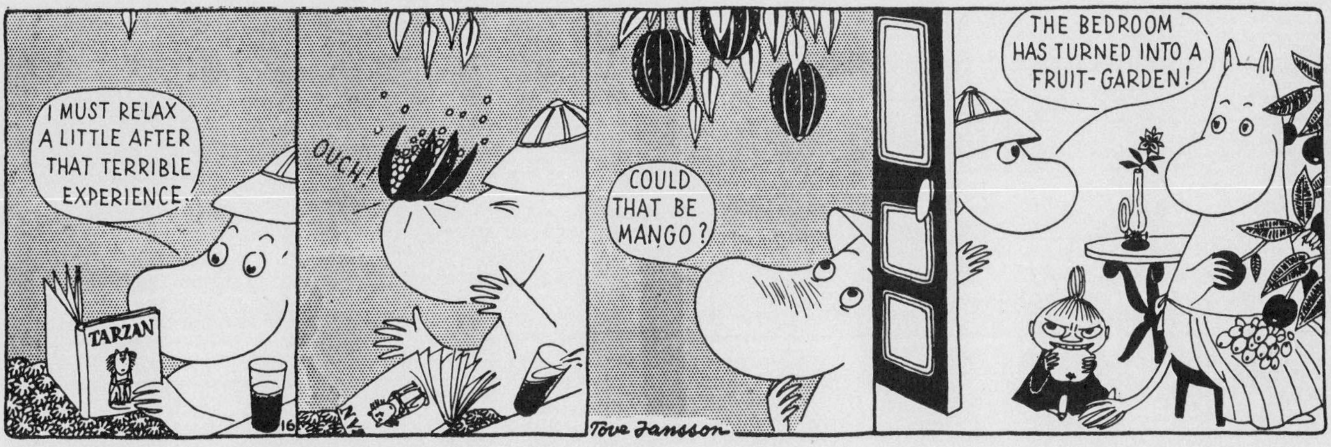
I MUST RELAX A LITTLE AFTER THAT TERRIBLE EXPERIENCE.
TARZAN
16
OUCH!
COULD THAT BE MANGO?
Tove Jansson
THE BEDROOM HAS TURNED INTO A FRUIT-GARDEN!

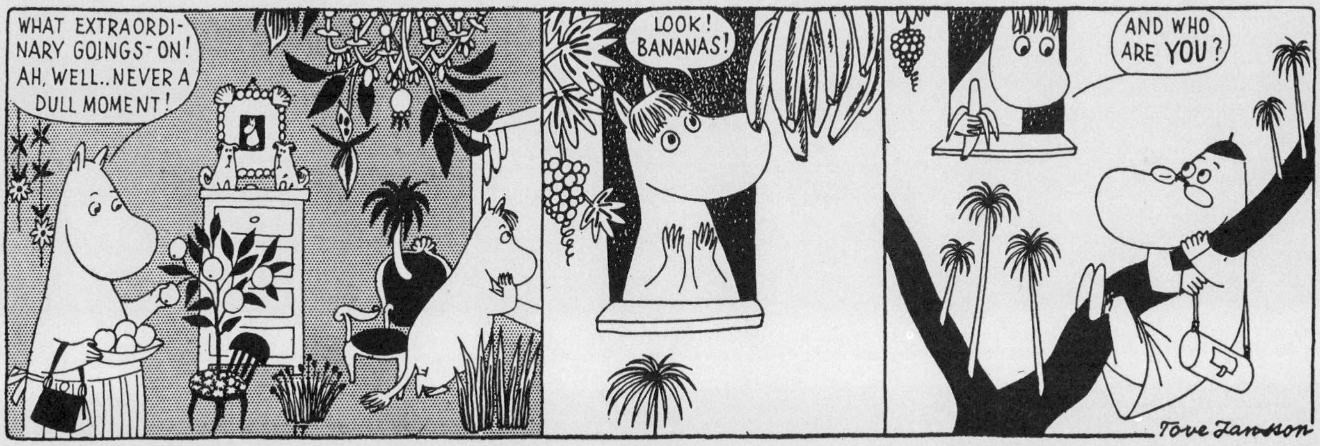
WHAT EXTRAORDI-NARY GOINGS-ON! AH, WELL.. NEVER A DULL MOMENT!
LOOK! BANANAS!
AND WHO ARE YOU?
Tove Jansson

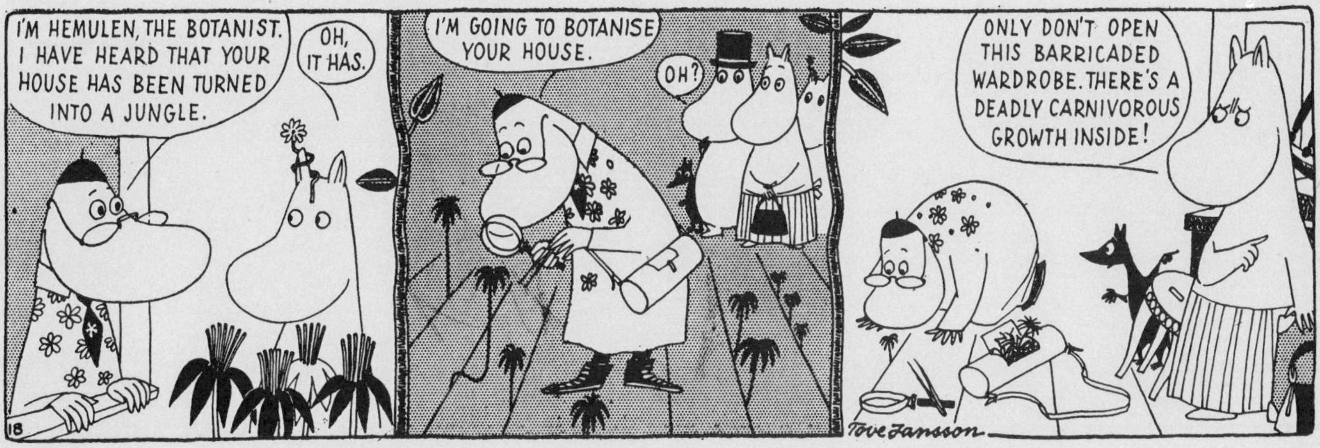
I'M HEMULEN, THE BOTANIST. I HAVE HEARD THAT YOUR HOUSE HAS BEEN TURNED INTO A JUNGLE.
OH, IT HAS.
18
I'M GOING TO BOTANISE YOUR HOUSE.
OH?
ONLY DON'T OPEN THIS BARRICADED WARDROBE. THERE'S A DEADLY CARNIVOROUS GROWTH INSIDE!
Tove Jansson

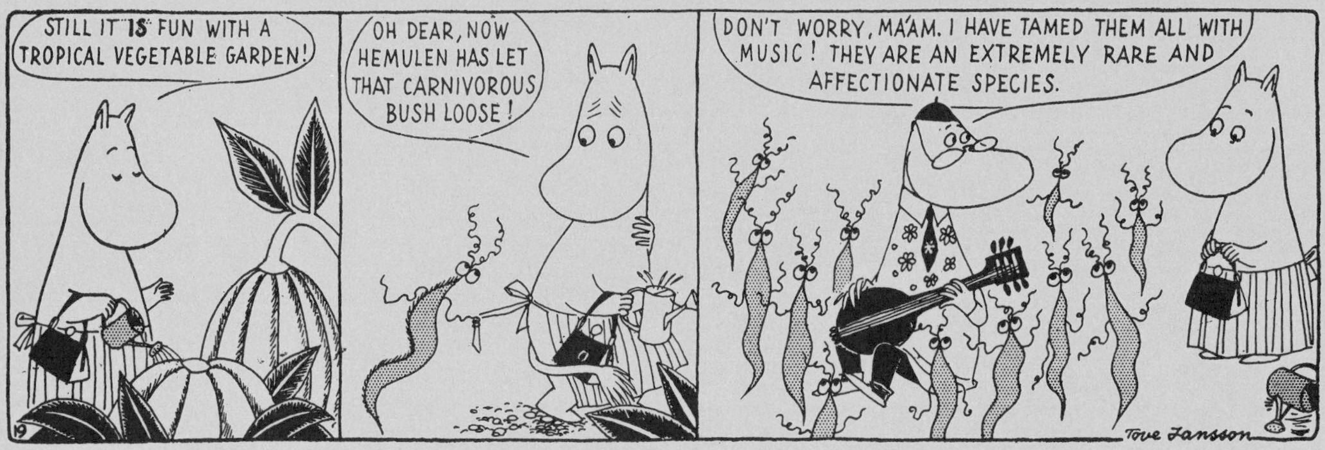
STILL IT IS FUN WITH A TROPICAL VEGETABLE GARDEN!
OH DEAR, NOW HEMULEN HAS LET THAT CARNIVOROUS BUSH LOOSE!
DON'T WORRY, MA'AM. I HAVE TAMED THEM ALL WITH MUSIC! THEY ARE AN EXTREMELY RARE AND AFFECTIONATE SPECIES.
Tove Jansson

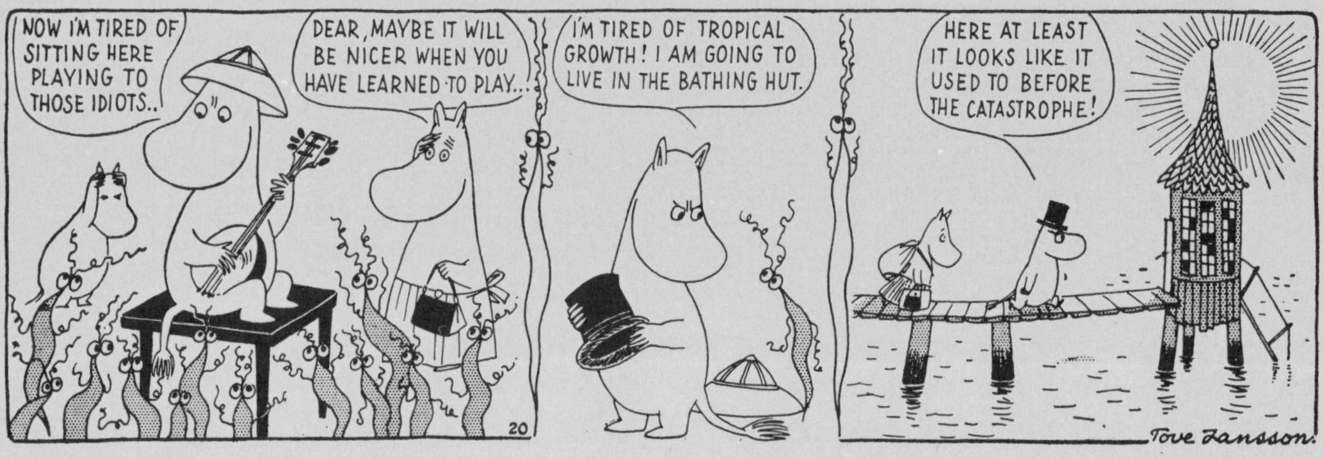
NOW I'M TIRED OF SITTING HERE PLAYING TO THOSE IDIOTS..
DEAR, MAYBE IT WILL BE NICER WHEN YOU HAVE LEARNED TO PLAY...
I'M TIRED OF TROPICAL GROWTH! I AM GOING TO LIVE IN THE BATHING HUT.
HERE AT LEAST IT LOOKS LIKE IT USED TO BEFORE THE CATASTROPHE!
Tove Jansson

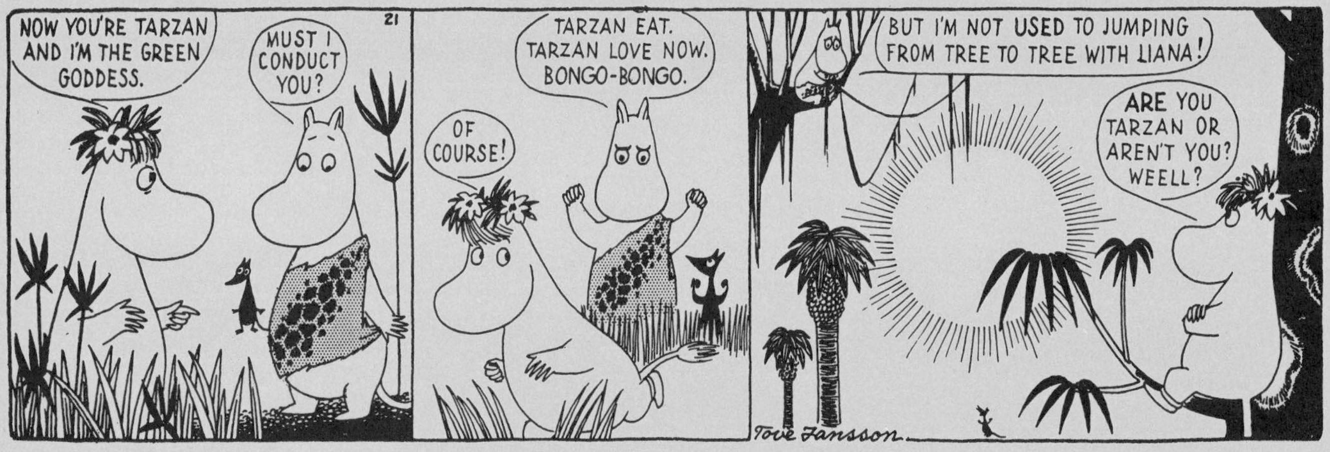
NOW YOU'RE TARZAN AND I'M THE GREEN GODDESS.
MUST I CONDUCT YOU?
TARZAN EAT. TARZAN LOVE NOW. BONGO-BONGO.
OF COURSE!
BUT I'M NOT USED TO JUMPING FROM TREE TO TREE WITH LIANA!
ARE YOU TARZAN OR AREN'T YOU? WEELL?
Tove Jansson

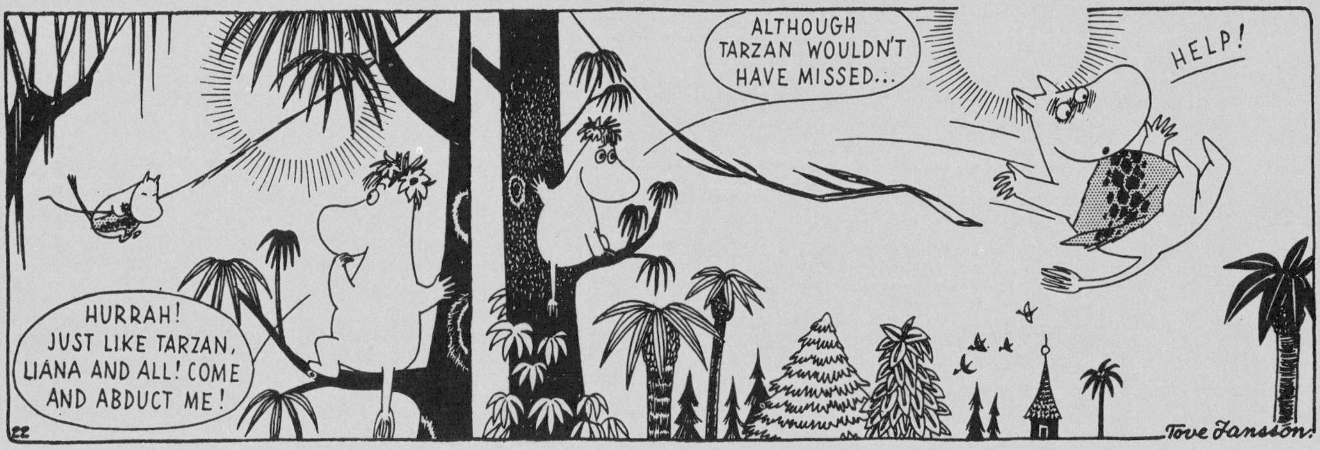
HURRAH! JUST LIKE TARZAN, LIANA AND ALL! COME AND ABDUCT ME!
ALTHOUGH TARZAN WOULDN'T HAVE MISSED...
HELP!
Tove Jansson

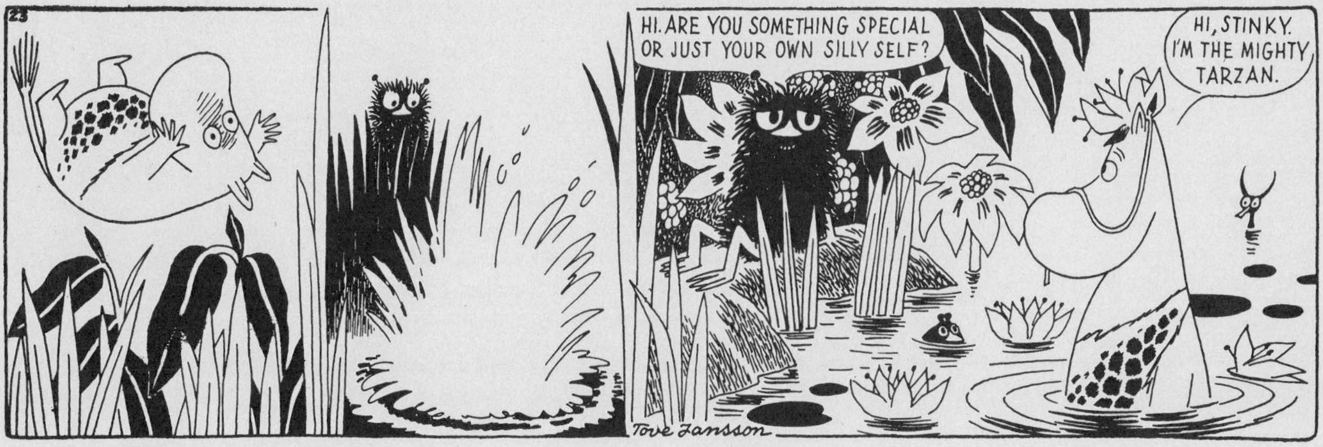
HI. ARE YOU SOMETHING SPECIAL OR JUST YOUR OWN SILLY SELF?
HI, STINKY. I'M THE MIGHTY TARZAN.
Tove Jansson

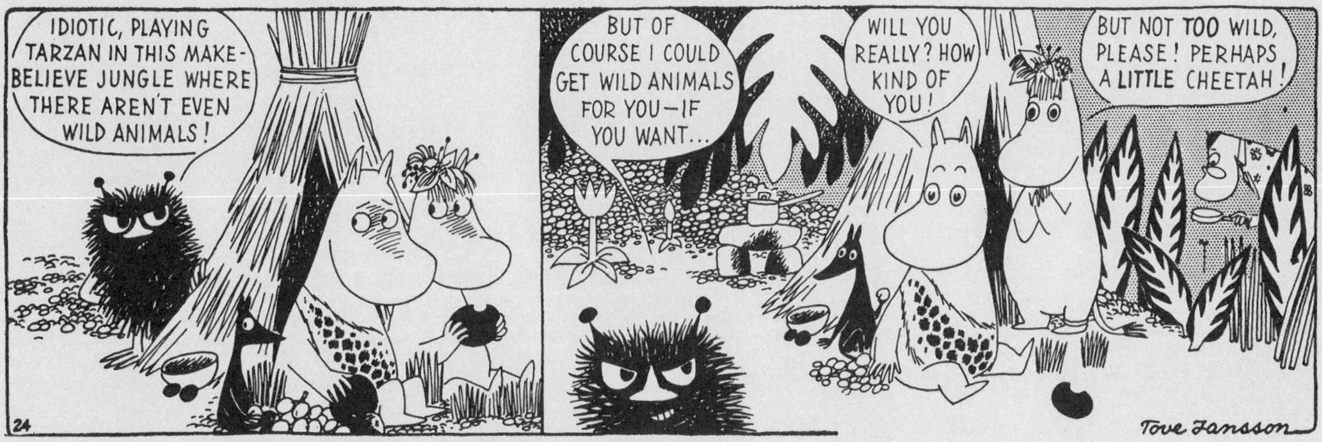
IDIOTIC, PLAYING TARZAN IN THIS MAKE-BELIEVE JUNGLE WHERE THERE AREN'T EVEN WILD ANIMALS!
BUT OF COURSE I COULD GET WILD ANIMALS FOR YOU—IF YOU WANT...
WILL YOU REALLY? HOW KIND OF YOU!
BUT NOT TOO WILD, PLEASE! PERHAPS A LITTLE CHEETAH!
Tove Jansson

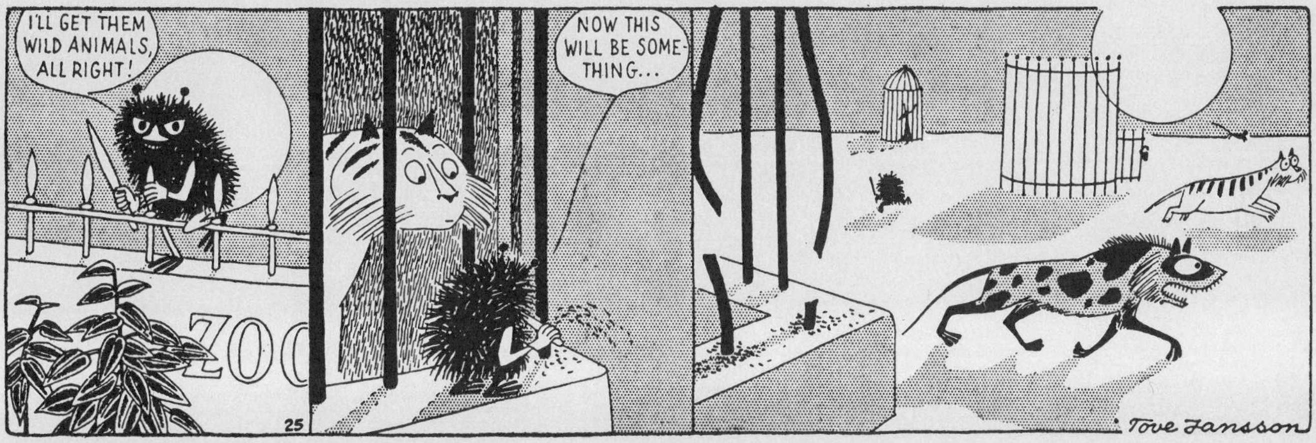
I'LL GET THEM WILD ANIMALS, ALL RIGHT!
ZOO
NOW THIS WILL BE SOMETHING...
Tove Jansson

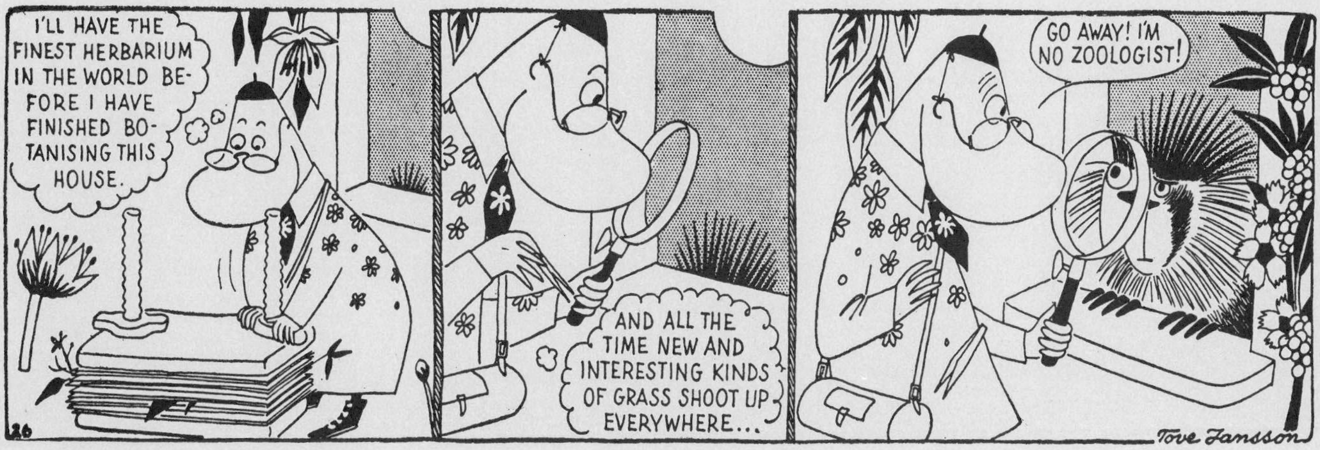
I'LL HAVE THE FINEST HERBARIUM IN THE WORLD BEFORE I HAVE FINISHED BOTANISING THIS HOUSE.
AND ALL THE TIME NEW AND INTERESTING KINDS OF GRASS SHOOT UP EVERYWHERE...
GO AWAY! I'M NO ZOOLOGIST!
Tove Jansson

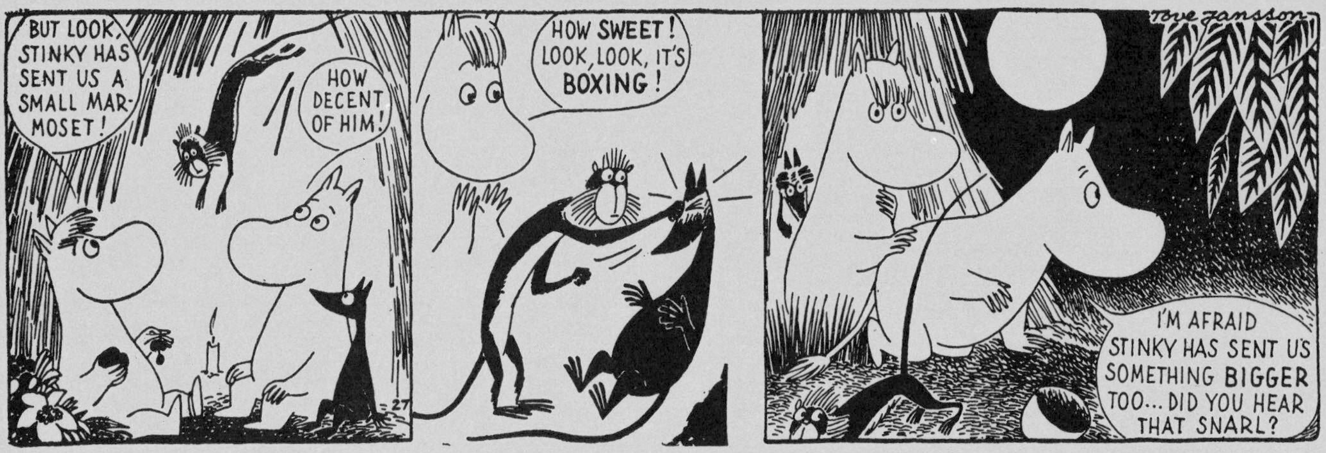
BUT LOOK, STINKY HAS SENT US A SMALL MARMOSET!
HOW DECENT OF HIM!
27
HOW SWEET! LOOK, LOOK, IT'S BOXING!
Tove Jansson
I'M AFRAID STINKY HAS SENT US SOMETHING BIGGER TOO... DID YOU HEAR THAT SNARL?

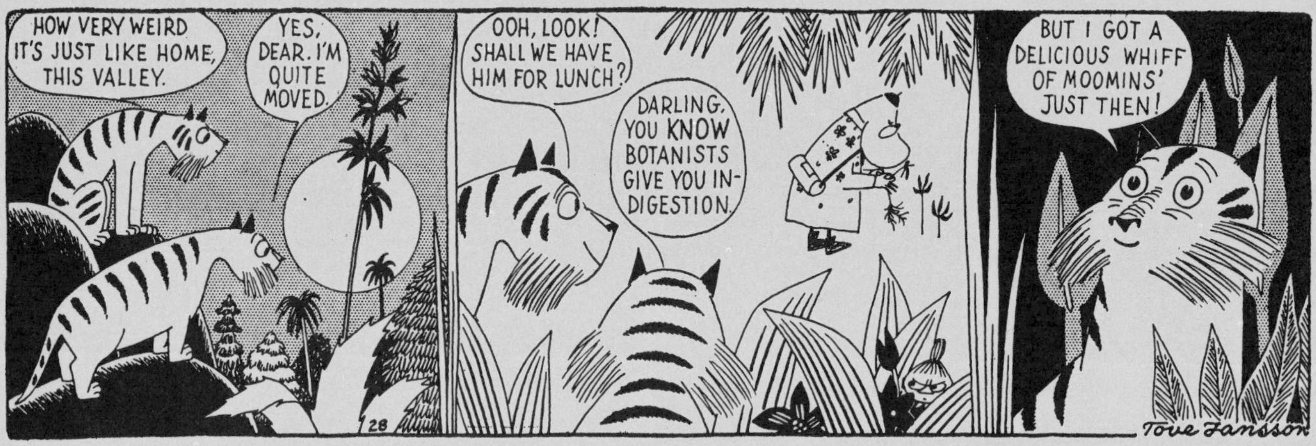
HOW VERY WEIRD IT'S JUST LIKE HOME, THIS VALLEY.
YES, DEAR. I'M QUITE MOVED.
28
OOH, LOOK! SHALL WE HAVE HIM FOR LUNCH?
DARLING, YOU KNOW BOTANISTS GIVE YOU INDIGESTION.
BUT I GOT A DELICIOUS WHIFF OF MOOMINS' JUST THEN!
Tove Jansson

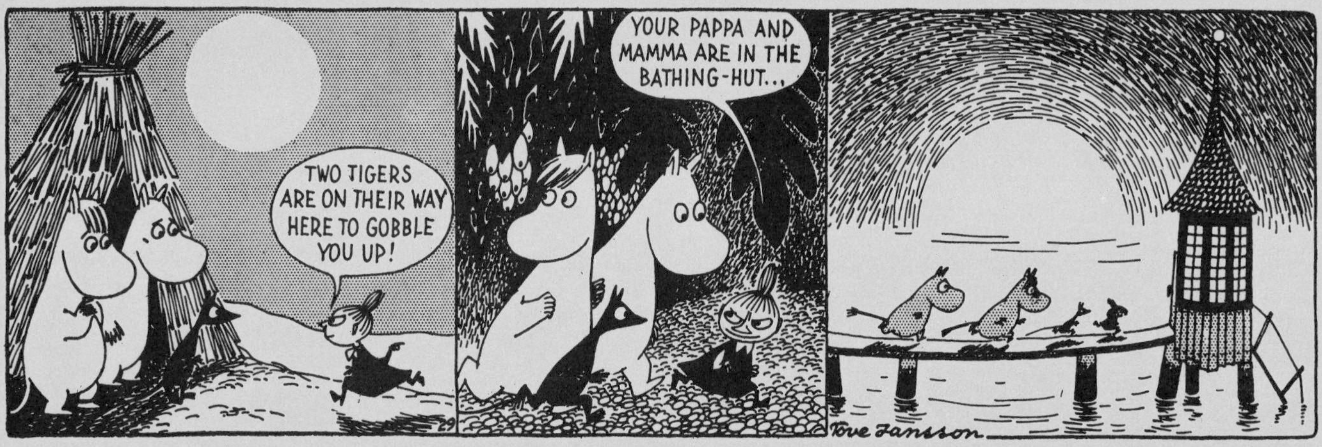
TWO TIGERS ARE ON THEIR WAY HERE TO GOBBLE YOU UP!
29
YOUR PAPPA AND MAMMA ARE IN THE BATHING-HUT...
Tove Jansson

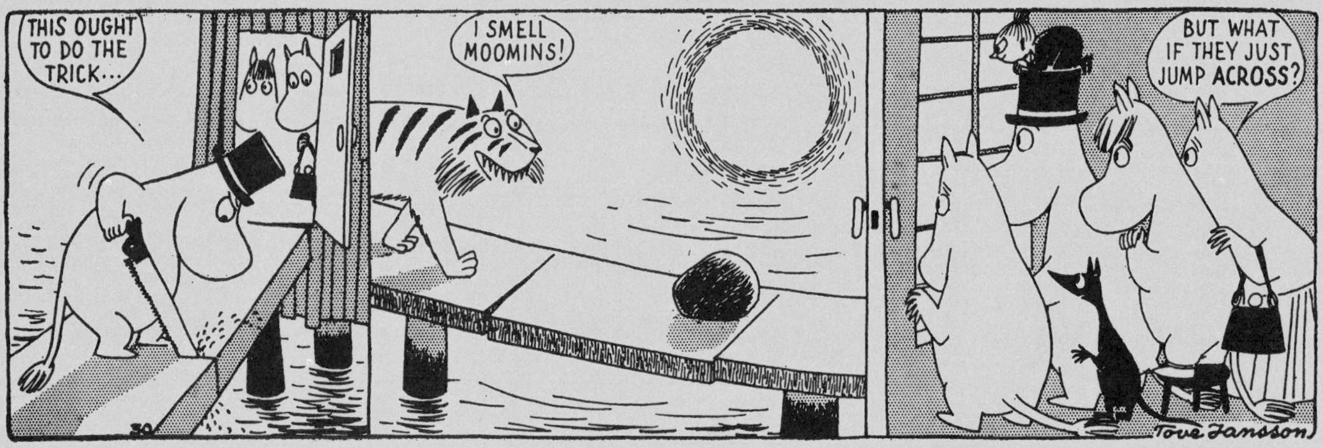
THIS OUGHT TO DO THE TRICK...
30
I SMELL MOOMINS!
BUT WHAT IF THEY JUST JUMP ACROSS?
Tove Jansson

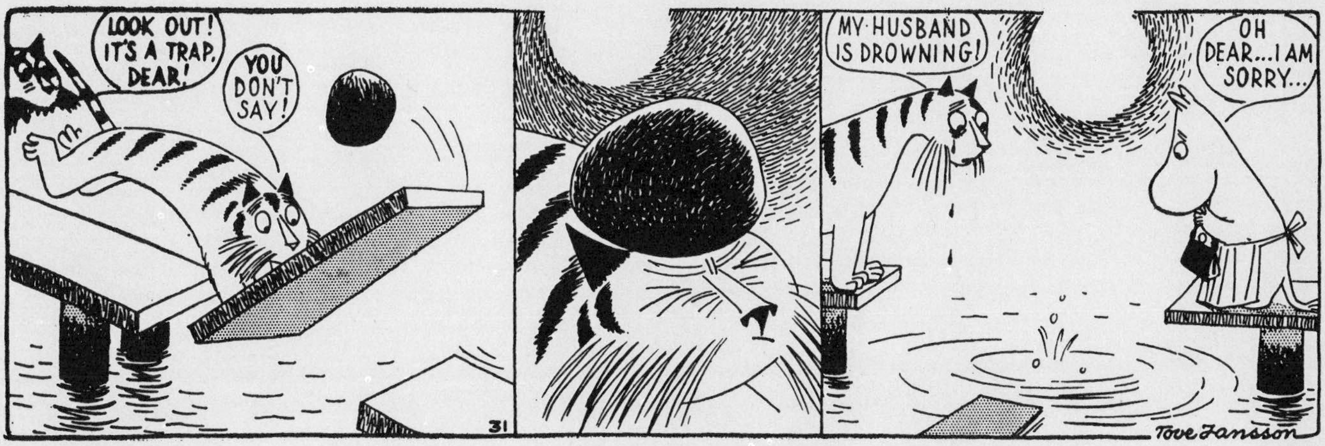
LOOK OUT! IT'S A TRAP, DEAR!
YOU DON'T SAY!
31
MY HUSBAND IS DROWNING!
OH DEAR... I AM SORRY...
Tove Jansson

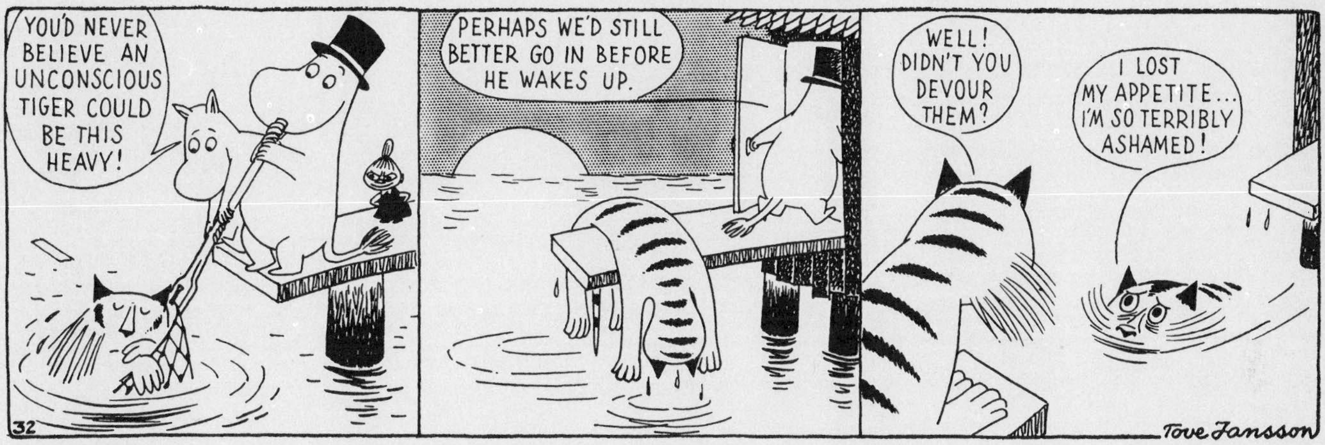
YOU'D NEVER BELIEVE AN UNCONSCIOUS TIGER COULD BE THIS HEAVY!
32
PERHAPS WE'D STILL BETTER GO IN BEFORE HE WAKES UP.
WELL! DIDN'T YOU DEVOUR THEM?
I LOST MY APPETITE... I'M SO TERRIBLY ASHAMED!
Tove Jansson

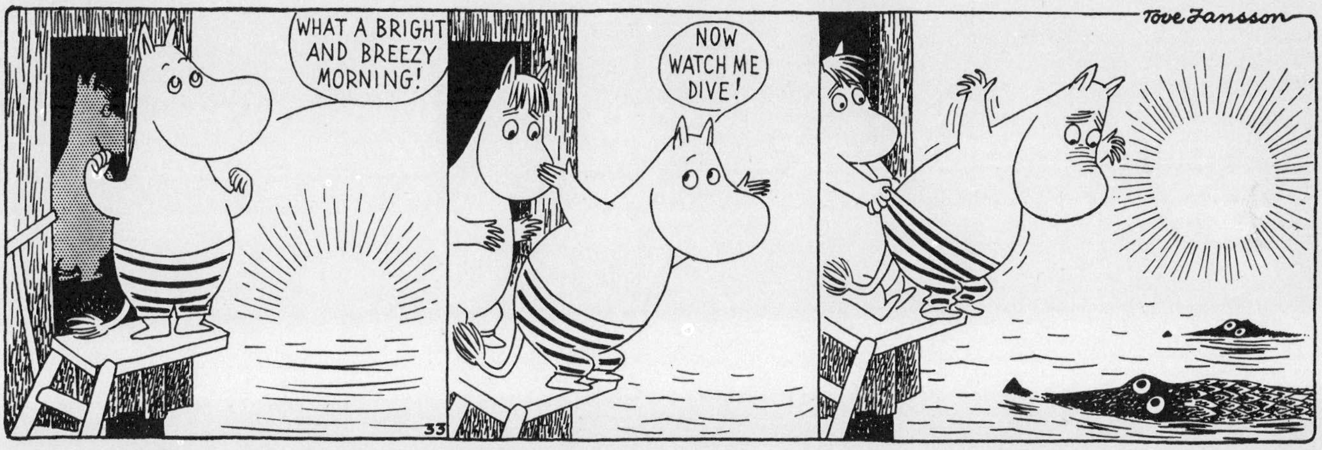
WHAT A BRIGHT AND BREEZY MORNING!
NOW WATCH ME DIVE!
33
Tove Jansson

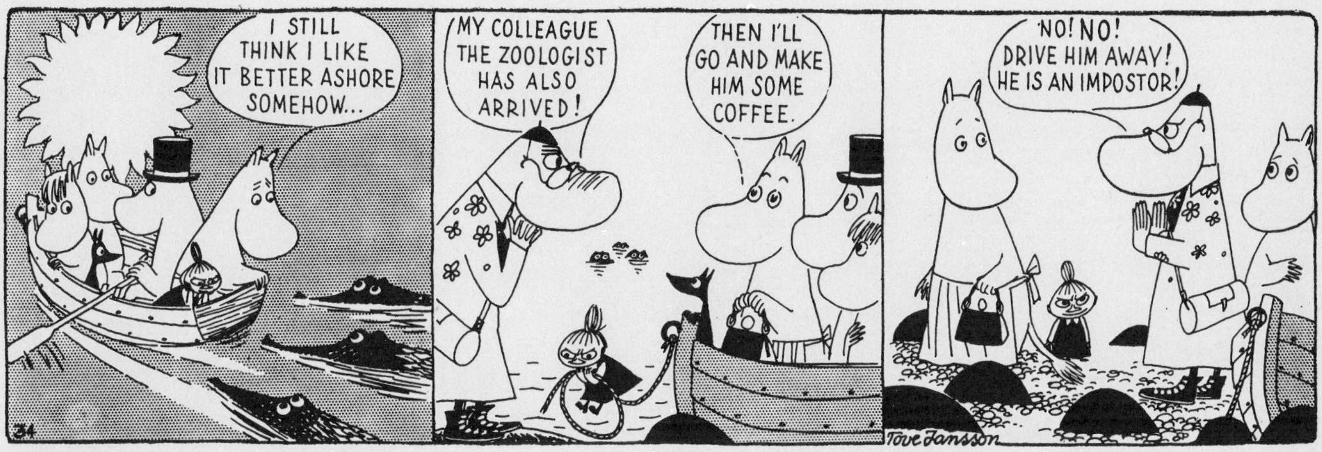
I STILL THINK I LIKE IT BETTER ASHORE SOMEHOW...
34
MY COLLEAGUE THE ZOOLOGIST HAS ALSO ARRIVED!
THEN I'LL GO AND MAKE HIM SOME COFFEE.
NO! NO! DRIVE HIM AWAY! HE IS AN IMPOSTOR!
Tove Jansson

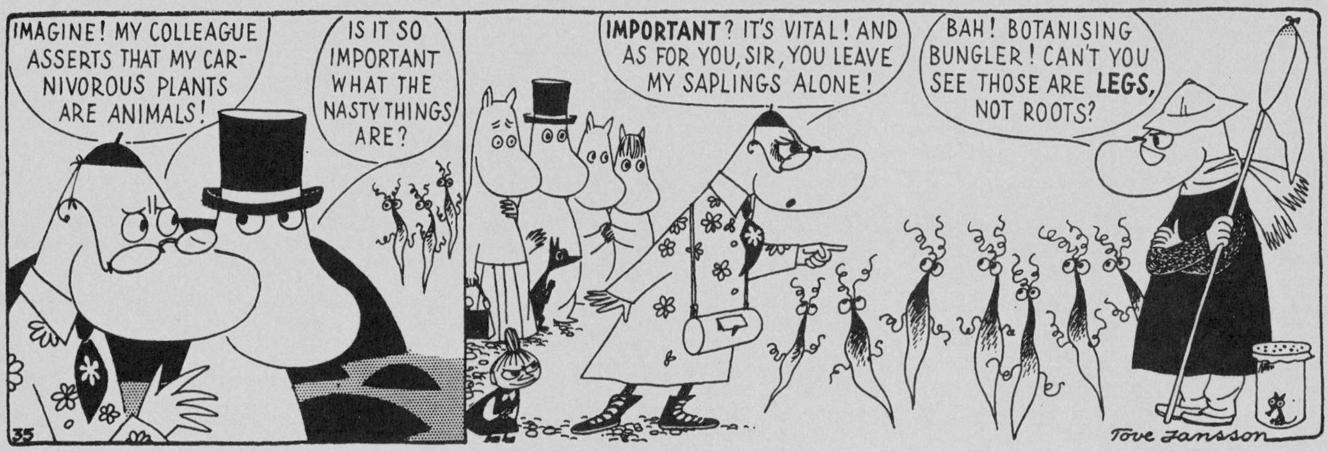
IMAGINE! MY COLLEAGUE ASSERTS THAT MY CARNIVOROUS PLANTS ARE ANIMALS!
IS IT SO IMPORTANT WHAT THE NASTY THINGS ARE?
IMPORTANT? IT'S VITAL! AND AS FOR YOU, SIR, YOU LEAVE MY SAPLINGS ALONE!
BAH! BOTANISING BUNGLER! CAN'T YOU SEE THOSE ARE LEGS, NOT ROOTS?
35
Tove Jansson

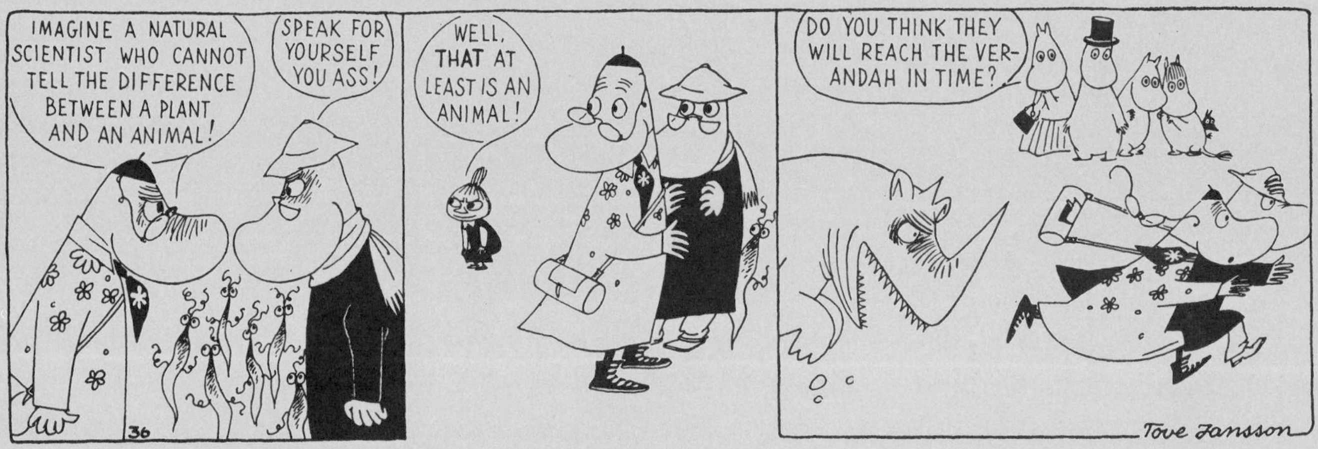
IMAGINE A NATURAL SCIENTIST WHO CANNOT TELL THE DIFFERENCE BETWEEN A PLANT AND AN ANIMAL!
SPEAK FOR YOURSELF YOU ASS!
WELL, THAT AT LEAST IS AN ANIMAL!
DO YOU THINK THEY WILL REACH THE VERANDAH IN TIME?
36
Tove Jansson

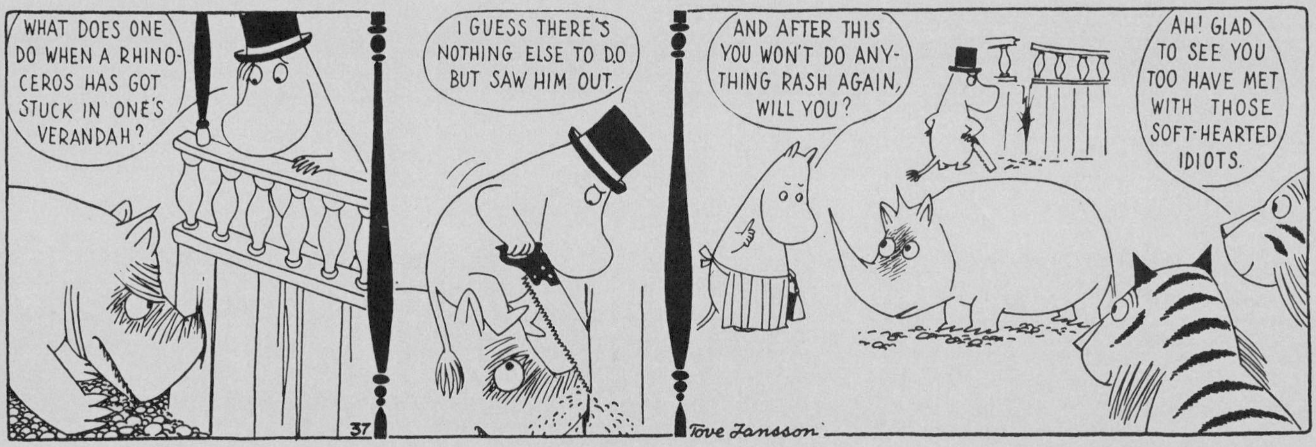
WHAT DOES ONE DO WHEN A RHINOCEROS HAS GOT STUCK IN ONE'S VERANDAH?
I GUESS THERE'S NOTHING ELSE TO DO BUT SAW HIM OUT.
AND AFTER THIS YOU WON'T DO ANYTHING RASH AGAIN, WILL YOU?
AH! GLAD TO SEE YOU TOO HAVE MET WITH THOSE SOFT-HEARTED IDIOTS.
37
Tove Jansson

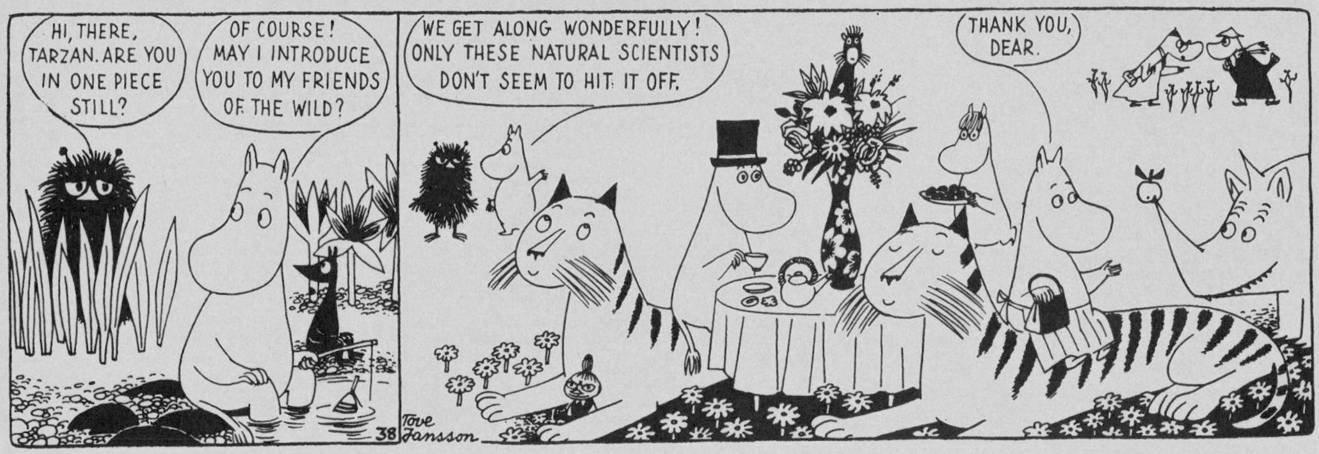
HI, THERE, TARZAN. ARE YOU IN ONE PIECE STILL?
OF COURSE! MAY I INTRODUCE YOU TO MY FRIENDS OF THE WILD?
WE GET ALONG WONDERFULLY! ONLY THESE NATURAL SCIENTISTS DON'T SEEM TO HIT IT OFF.
THANK YOU, DEAR.
38
Tove Jansson

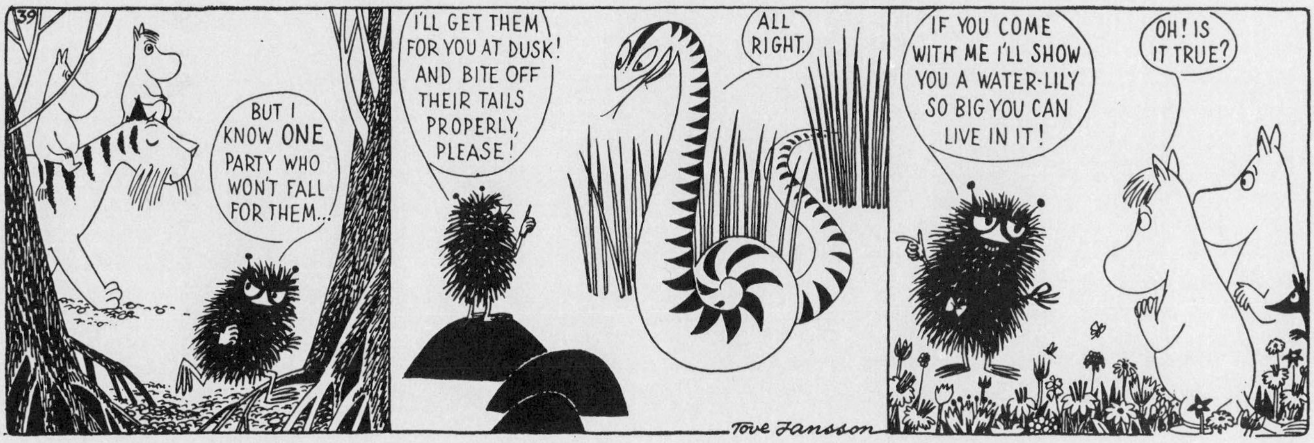
39
BUT I KNOW ONE PARTY WHO WON'T FALL FOR THEM...
I'LL GET THEM FOR YOU AT DUSK! AND BITE OFF THEIR TAILS PROPERLY, PLEASE!
ALL RIGHT.
IF YOU COME WITH ME I'LL SHOW YOU A WATER-LILY SO BIG YOU CAN LIVE IN IT!
OH! IS IT TRUE?
Tove Jansson

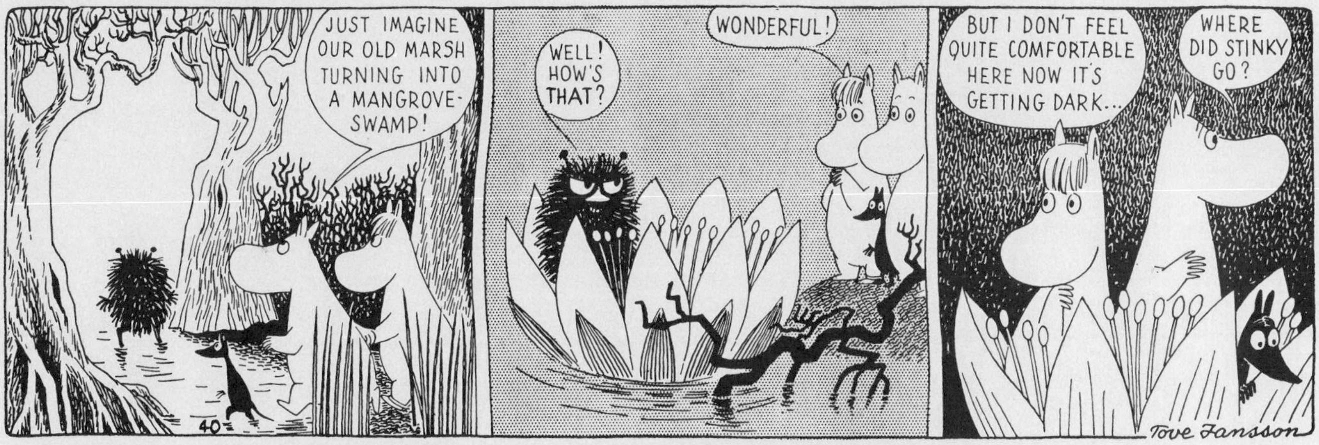
40
JUST IMAGINE OUR OLD MARSH TURNING INTO A MANGROVE-SWAMP!
WELL! HOW'S THAT?
WONDERFUL!
BUT I DON'T FEEL QUITE COMFORTABLE HERE NOW IT'S GETTING DARK...
WHERE DID STINKY GO?
Tove Jansson

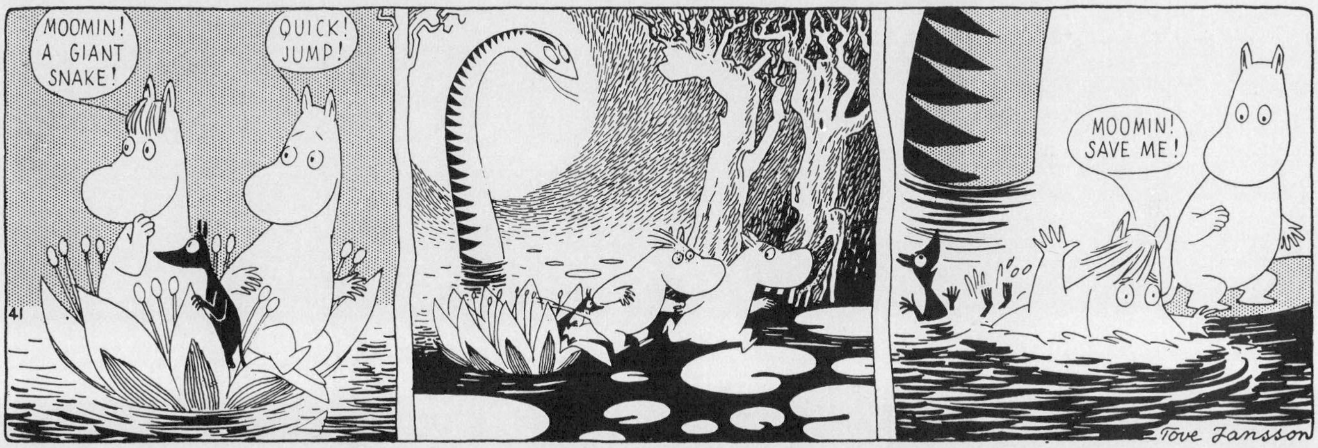
41
MOOMIN! A GIANT SNAKE!
QUICK! JUMP!
MOOMIN! SAVE ME!
Tove Jansson

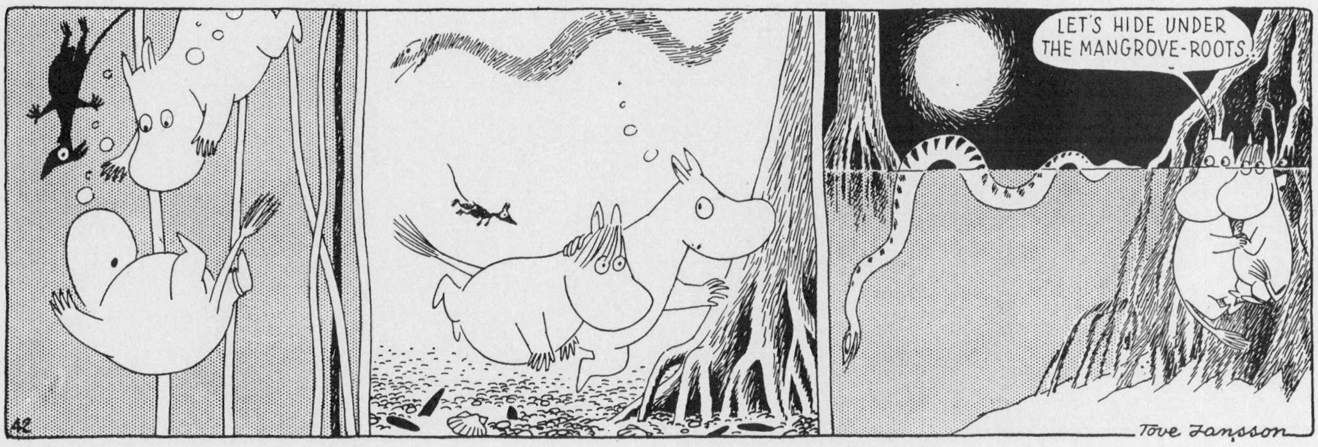
42
LET'S HIDE UNDER THE MANGROVE-ROOTS.
Tove Jansson

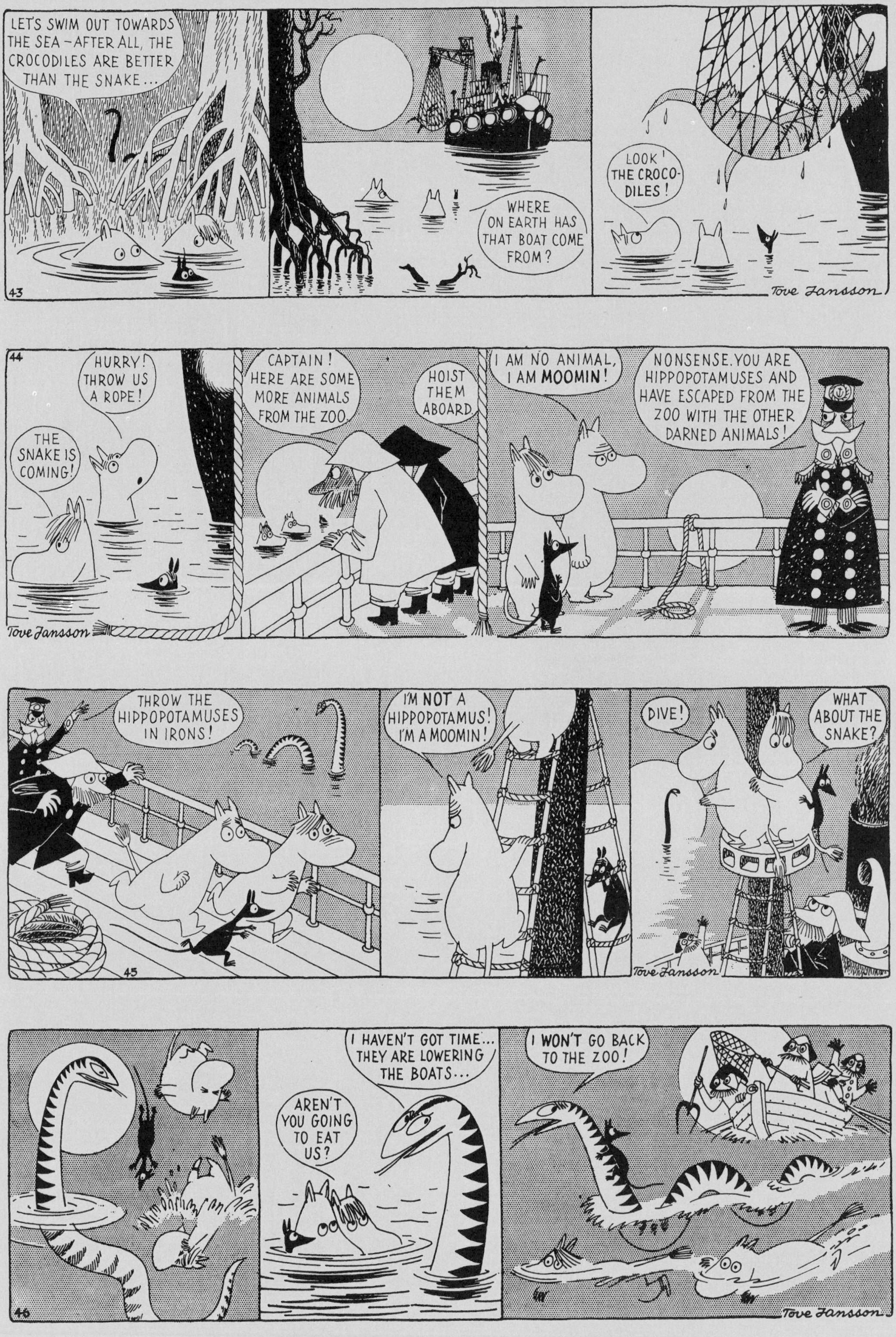
LET'S SWIM OUT TOWARDS THE SEA – AFTER ALL, THE CROCODILES ARE BETTER THAN THE SNAKE...
43
WHERE ON EARTH HAS THAT BOAT COME FROM?
LOOK! THE CROCODILES!
Tove Jansson
44
HURRY! THROW US A ROPE!
THE SNAKE IS COMING!
Tove Jansson
CAPTAIN! HERE ARE SOME MORE ANIMALS FROM THE ZOO.
HOIST THEM ABOARD.
I AM NO ANIMAL, I AM MOOMIN!
NONSENSE. YOU ARE HIPPOPOTAMUSES AND HAVE ESCAPED FROM THE ZOO WITH THE OTHER DARNED ANIMALS!
THROW THE HIPPOPOTAMUSES IN IRONS!
45
I'M NOT A HIPPOPOTAMUS! I'M A MOOMIN!
DIVE!
WHAT ABOUT THE SNAKE?
Tove Jansson
46
AREN'T YOU GOING TO EAT US?
I HAVEN'T GOT TIME... THEY ARE LOWERING THE BOATS...
I WON'T GO BACK TO THE ZOO!
Tove Jansson

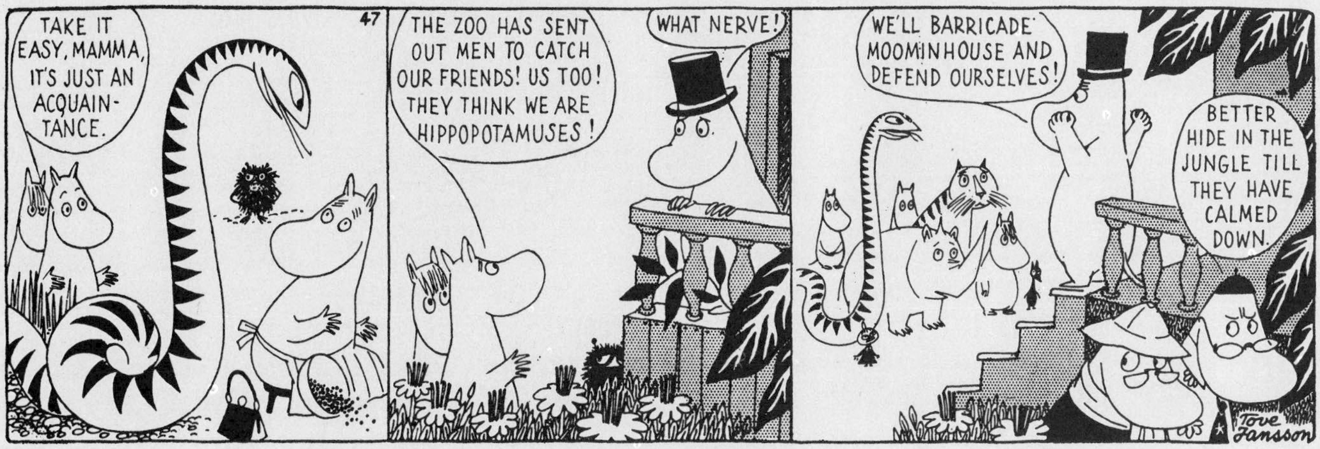
47
TAKE IT EASY, MAMMA, IT'S JUST AN ACQUAIN-TANCE.
THE ZOO HAS SENT OUT MEN TO CATCH OUR FRIENDS! US TOO! THEY THINK WE ARE HIPPOPOTAMUSES!
WHAT NERVE!
WE'LL BARRICADE MOOMINHOUSE AND DEFEND OURSELVES!
BETTER HIDE IN THE JUNGLE TILL THEY HAVE CALMED DOWN.
Tove Jansson

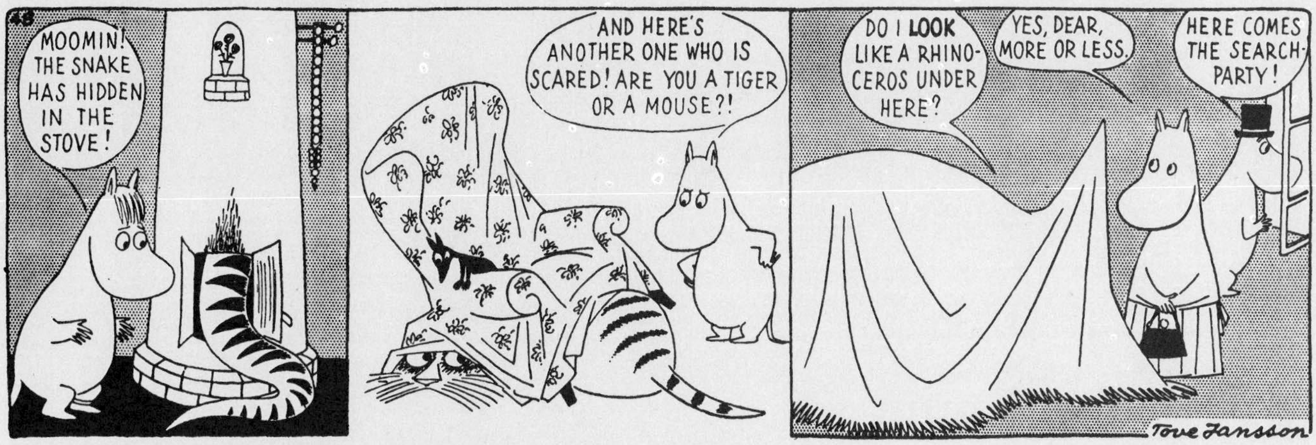
48
MOOMIN! THE SNAKE HAS HIDDEN IN THE STOVE!
AND HERE'S ANOTHER ONE WHO IS SCARED! ARE YOU A TIGER OR A MOUSE?!
DO I LOOK LIKE A RHINO-CEROS UNDER HERE?
YES, DEAR, MORE OR LESS.
HERE COMES THE SEARCH-PARTY!
Tove Jansson

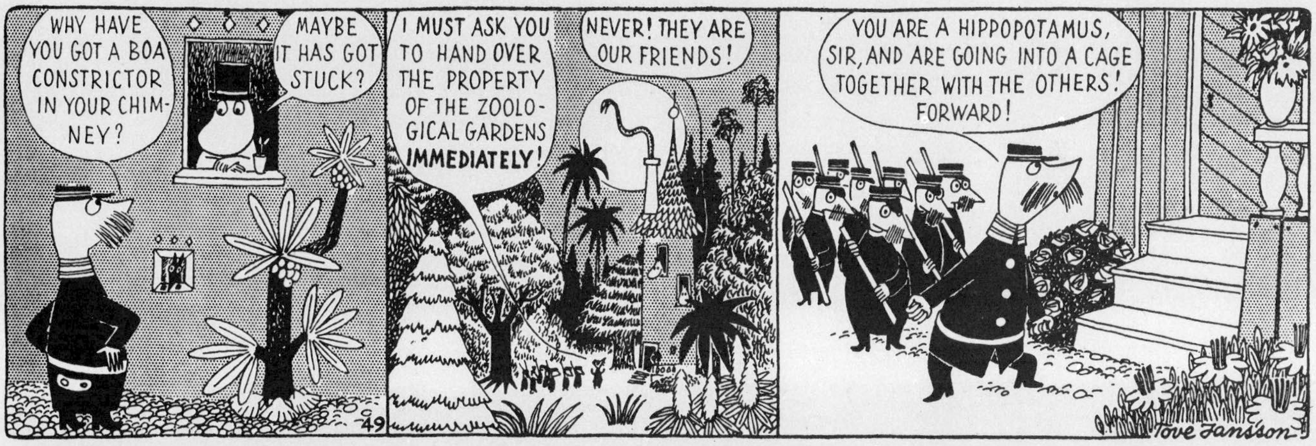
WHY HAVE YOU GOT A BOA CONSTRICTOR IN YOUR CHIM-NEY?
MAYBE IT HAS GOT STUCK?
I MUST ASK YOU TO HAND OVER THE PROPERTY OF THE ZOOLO-GICAL GARDENS IMMEDIATELY!
NEVER! THEY ARE OUR FRIENDS!
49
YOU ARE A HIPPOPOTAMUS, SIR, AND ARE GOING INTO A CAGE TOGETHER WITH THE OTHERS! FORWARD!
Tove Jansson

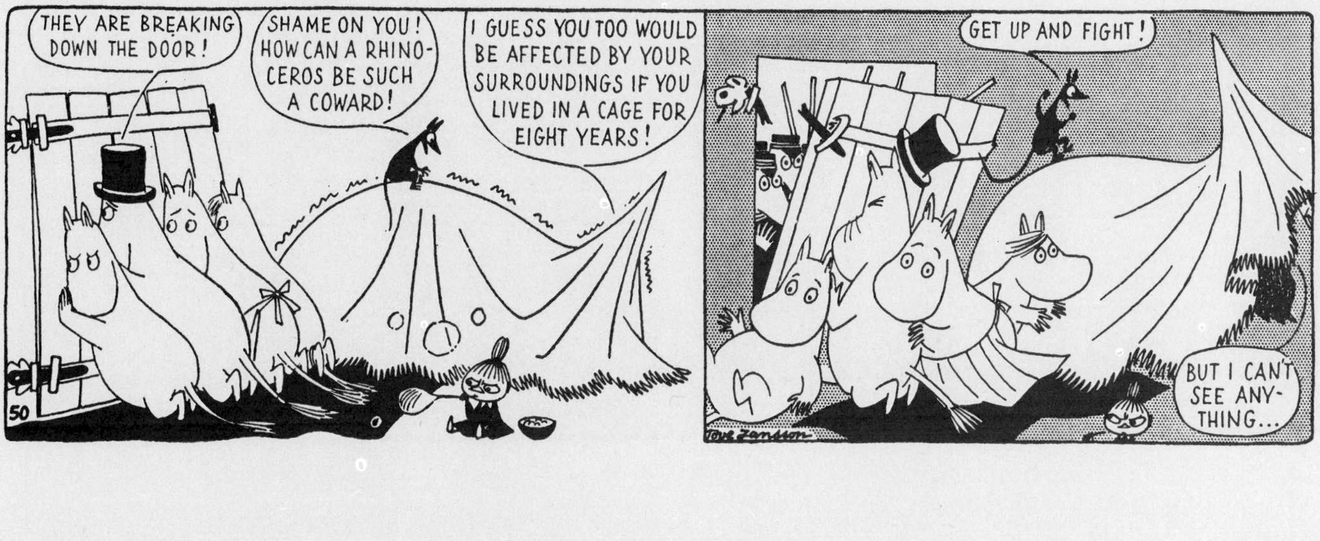
THEY ARE BREAKING DOWN THE DOOR!
SHAME ON YOU! HOW CAN A RHINO-CEROS BE SUCH A COWARD!
I GUESS YOU TOO WOULD BE AFFECTED BY YOUR SURROUNDINGS IF YOU LIVED IN A CAGE FOR EIGHT YEARS!
50
GET UP AND FIGHT!
BUT I CAN'T SEE ANY-THING...
Tove Jansson

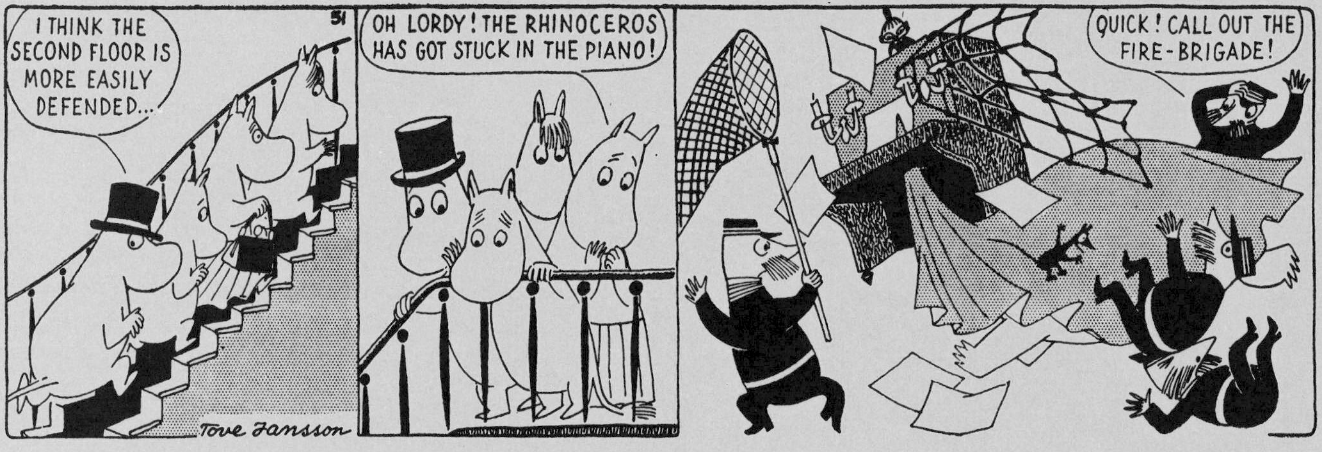
51
I THINK THE SECOND FLOOR IS MORE EASILY DEFENDED...
Tove Jansson
OH LORDY! THE RHINOCEROS HAS GOT STUCK IN THE PIANO!
QUICK! CALL OUT THE FIRE-BRIGADE!

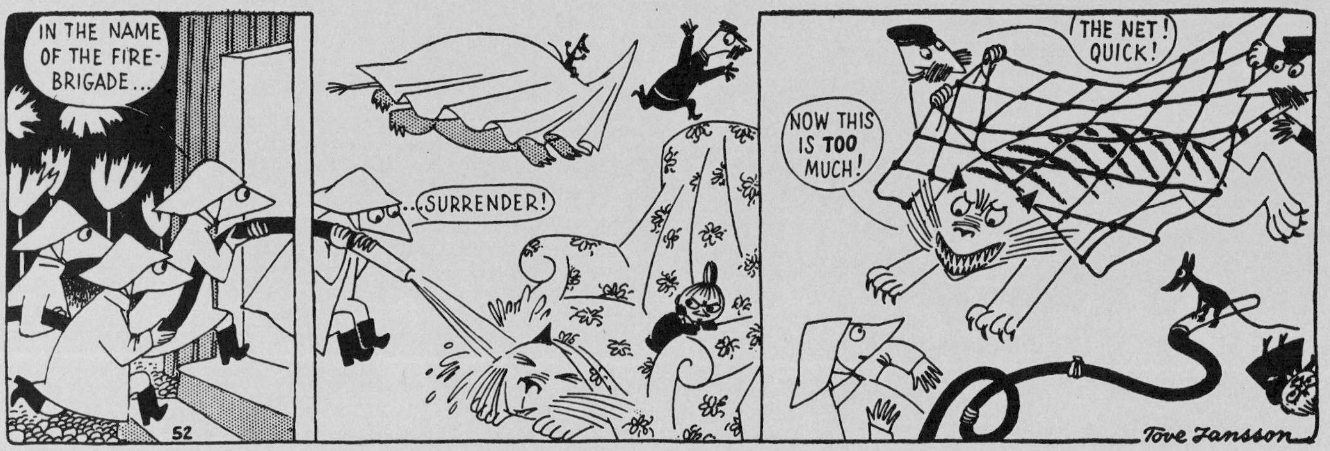
IN THE NAME OF THE FIRE-BRIGADE...
52
...SURRENDER!
THE NET! QUICK!
NOW THIS IS **TOO** MUCH!
Tove Jansson

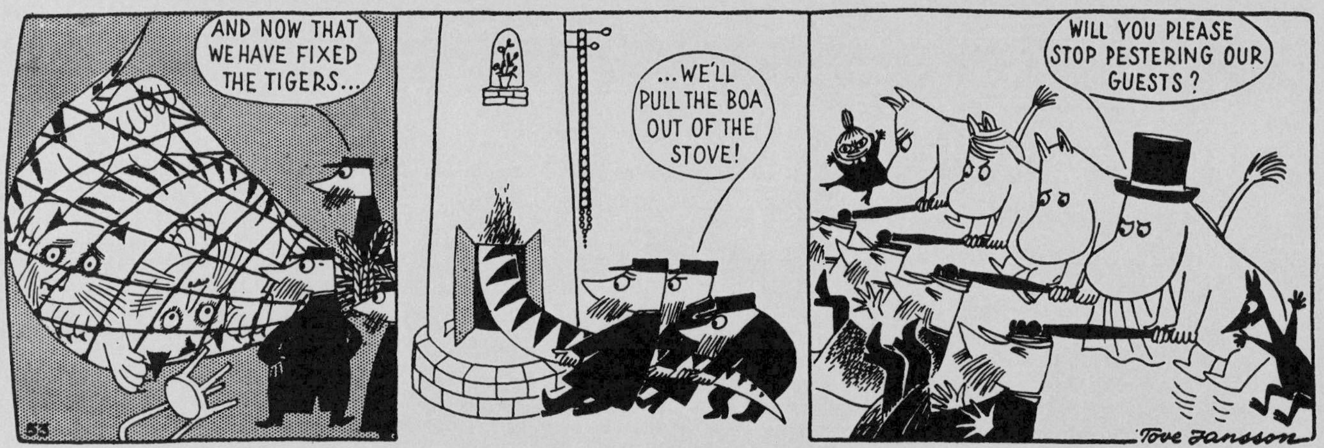
AND NOW THAT WE HAVE FIXED THE TIGERS...
53
...WE'LL PULL THE BOA OUT OF THE STOVE!
WILL YOU PLEASE STOP PESTERING OUR GUESTS?
Tove Jansson

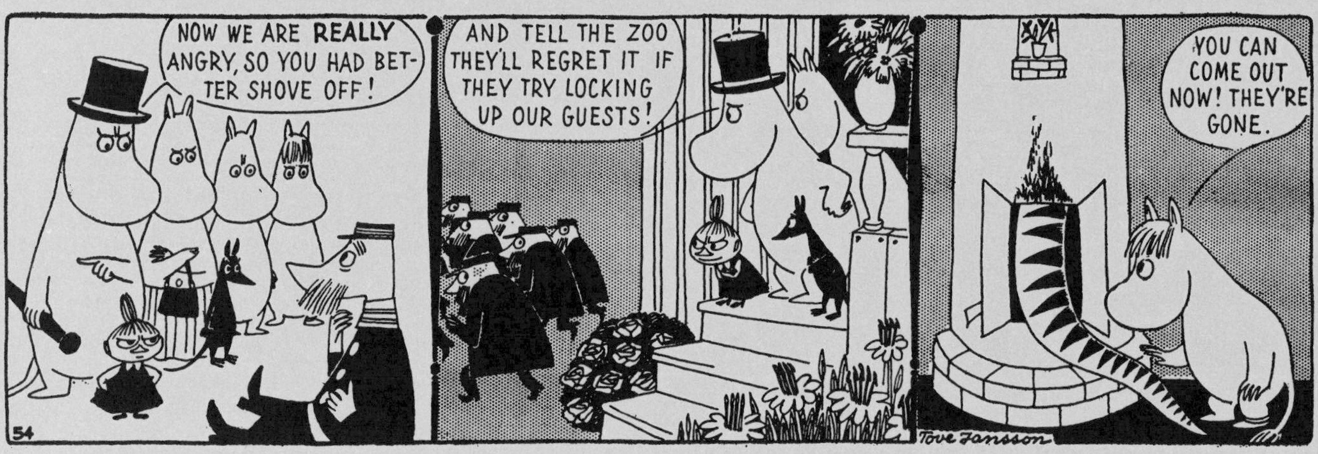
NOW WE ARE **REALLY** ANGRY, SO YOU HAD BETTER SHOVE OFF!
54
AND TELL THE ZOO THEY'LL REGRET IT IF THEY TRY LOCKING UP OUR GUESTS!
YOU CAN COME OUT NOW! THEY'RE GONE.
Tove Jansson

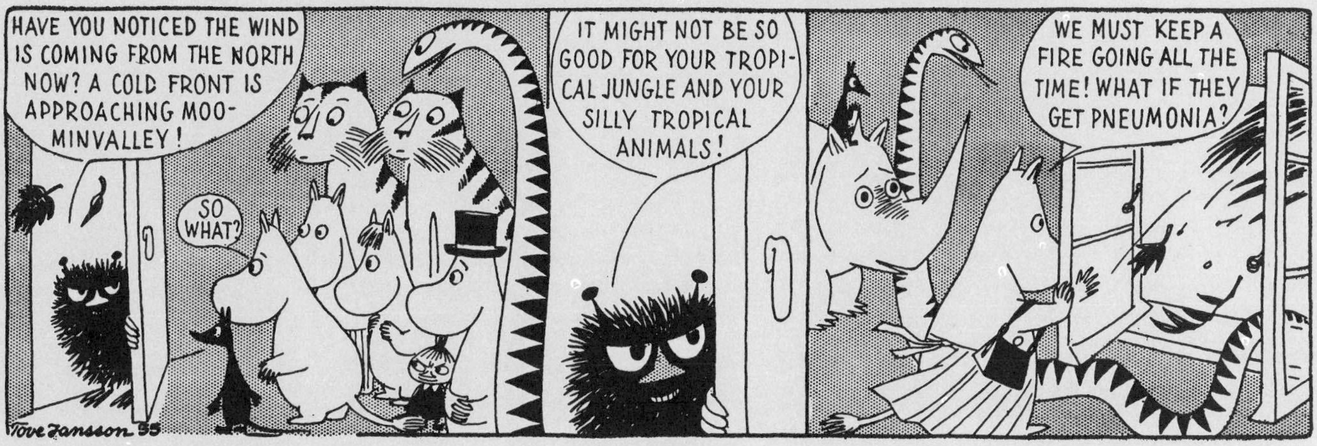
HAVE YOU NOTICED THE WIND IS COMING FROM THE NORTH NOW? A COLD FRONT IS APPROACHING MOO-MINVALLEY!
SO WHAT?
IT MIGHT NOT BE SO GOOD FOR YOUR TROPI-CAL JUNGLE AND YOUR SILLY TROPICAL ANIMALS!
WE MUST KEEP A FIRE GOING ALL THE TIME! WHAT IF THEY GET PNEUMONIA?
Tove Jansson 55

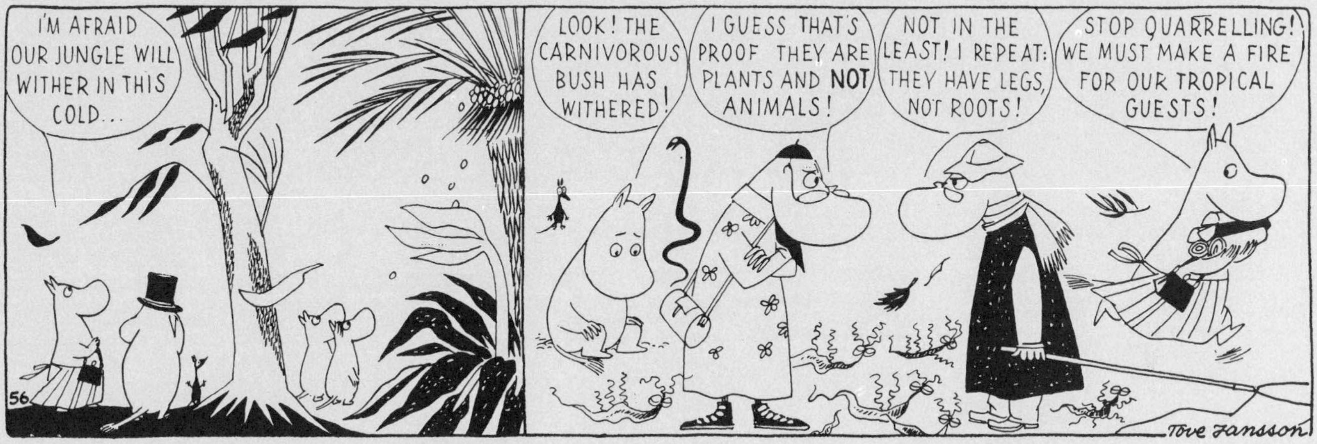
56
I'M AFRAID OUR JUNGLE WILL WITHER IN THIS COLD...
LOOK! THE CARNIVOROUS BUSH HAS WITHERED!
I GUESS THAT'S PROOF THEY ARE PLANTS AND NOT ANIMALS!
NOT IN THE LEAST! I REPEAT: THEY HAVE LEGS, NOT ROOTS!
STOP QUARRELLING! WE MUST MAKE A FIRE FOR OUR TROPICAL GUESTS!
Tove Jansson

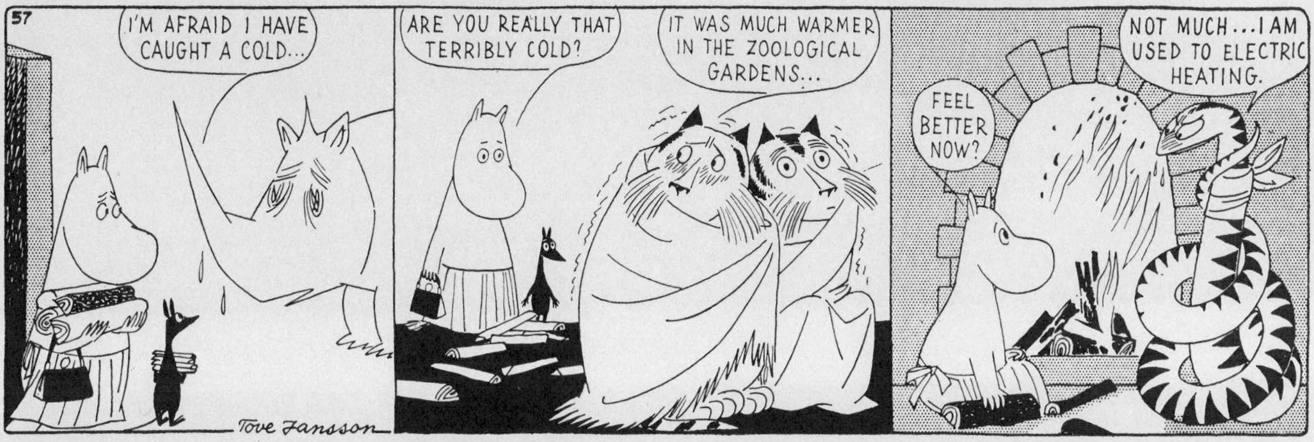
57
I'M AFRAID I HAVE CAUGHT A COLD...
Tove Jansson
ARE YOU REALLY THAT TERRIBLY COLD?
IT WAS MUCH WARMER IN THE ZOOLOGICAL GARDENS...
FEEL BETTER NOW?
NOT MUCH...I AM USED TO ELECTRIC HEATING.

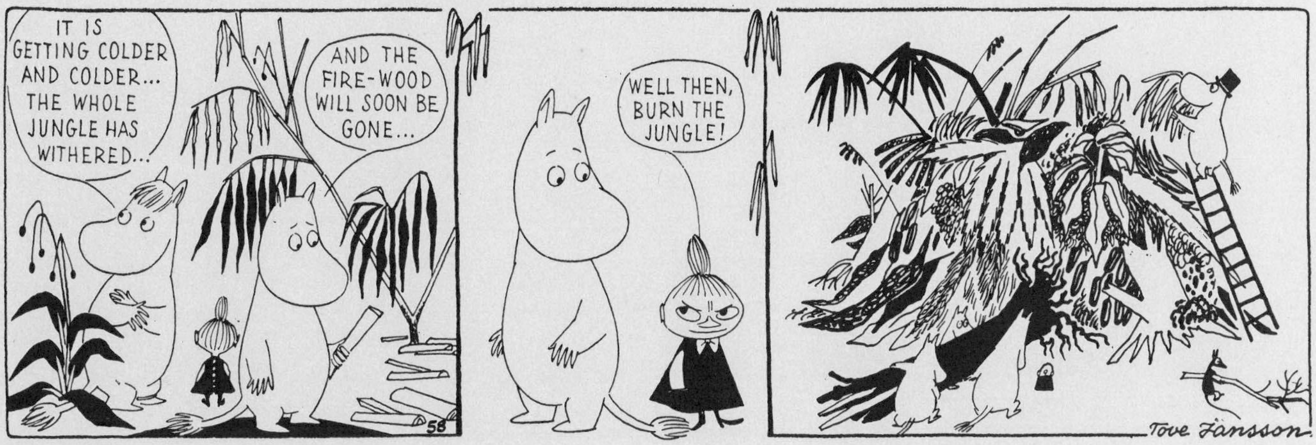
IT IS GETTING COLDER AND COLDER... THE WHOLE JUNGLE HAS WITHERED...
AND THE FIRE-WOOD WILL SOON BE GONE...
58
WELL THEN, BURN THE JUNGLE!
Tove Jansson

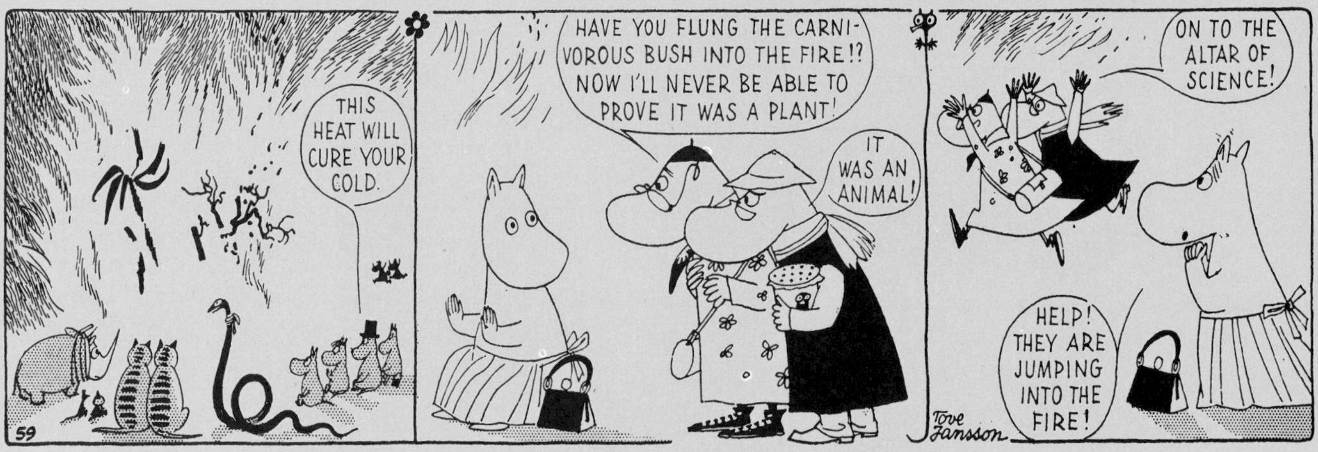
59
THIS HEAT WILL CURE YOUR COLD.
HAVE YOU FLUNG THE CARNIVOROUS BUSH INTO THE FIRE!? NOW I'LL NEVER BE ABLE TO PROVE IT WAS A PLANT!
IT WAS AN ANIMAL!
ON TO THE ALTAR OF SCIENCE!
HELP! THEY ARE JUMPING INTO THE FIRE!
Tove Jansson

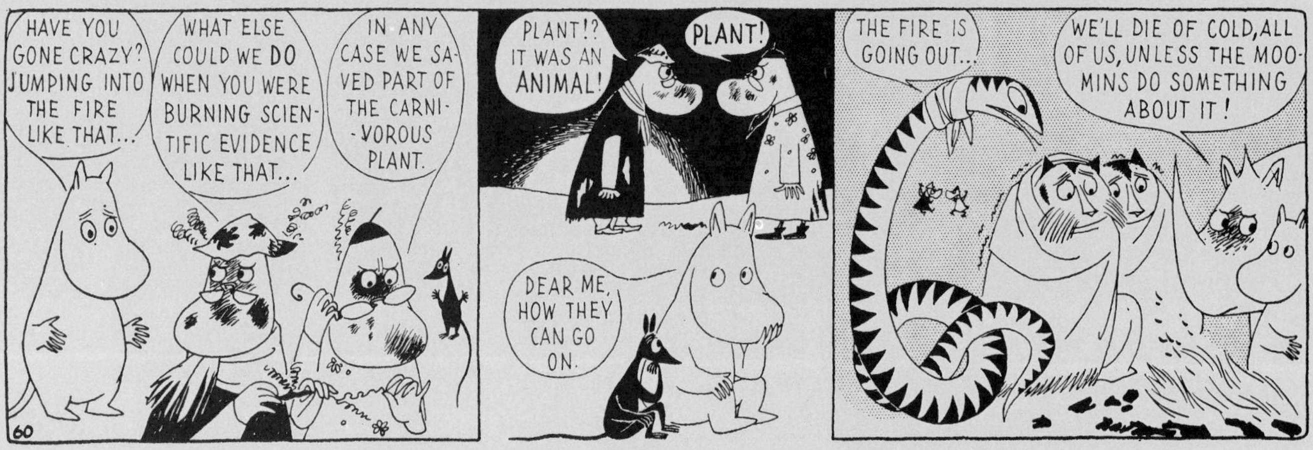
60
HAVE YOU GONE CRAZY? JUMPING INTO THE FIRE LIKE THAT...
WHAT ELSE COULD WE DO WHEN YOU WERE BURNING SCIENTIFIC EVIDENCE LIKE THAT...
IN ANY CASE WE SAVED PART OF THE CARNIVOROUS PLANT.
PLANT!? IT WAS AN ANIMAL!
PLANT!
DEAR ME, HOW THEY CAN GO ON.
THE FIRE IS GOING OUT...
WE'LL DIE OF COLD, ALL OF US, UNLESS THE MOOMINS DO SOMETHING ABOUT IT!

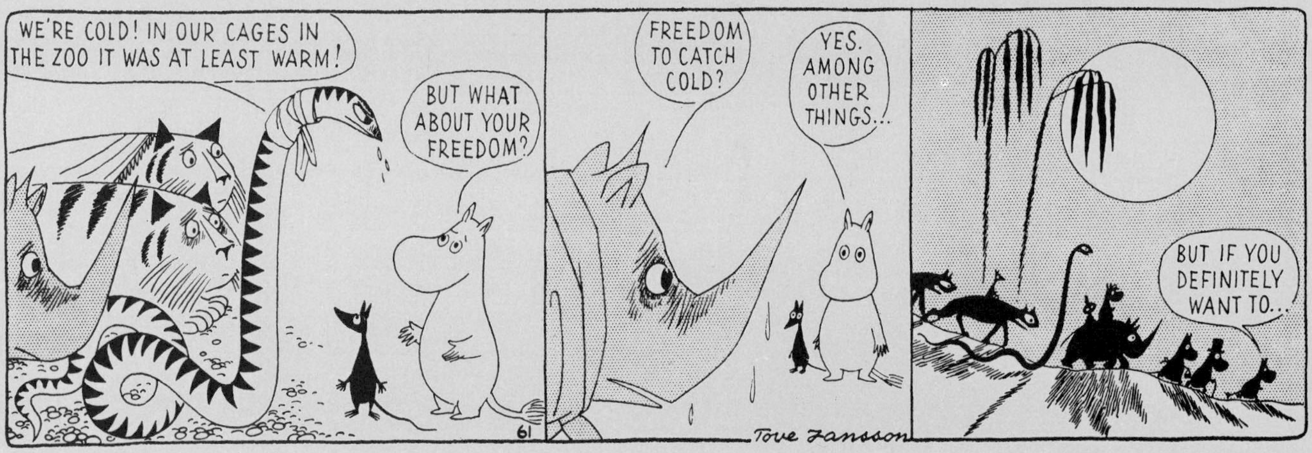
61
WE'RE COLD! IN OUR CAGES IN THE ZOO IT WAS AT LEAST WARM!
BUT WHAT ABOUT YOUR FREEDOM?
FREEDOM TO CATCH COLD?
YES. AMONG OTHER THINGS...
Tove Jansson
BUT IF YOU DEFINITELY WANT TO...

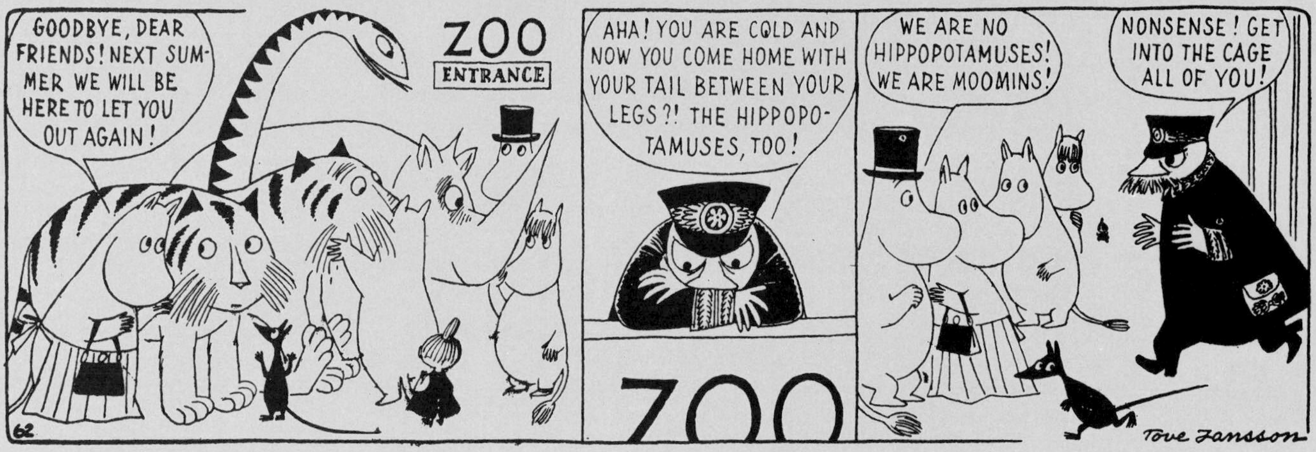
62
GOODBYE, DEAR FRIENDS! NEXT SUMMER WE WILL BE HERE TO LET YOU OUT AGAIN!
ZOO
ENTRANCE
AHA! YOU ARE COLD AND NOW YOU COME HOME WITH YOUR TAIL BETWEEN YOUR LEGS?! THE HIPPOPOTAMUSES, TOO!
ZOO
WE ARE NO HIPPOPOTAMUSES! WE ARE MOOMINS!
NONSENSE! GET INTO THE CAGE ALL OF YOU!
Tove Jansson

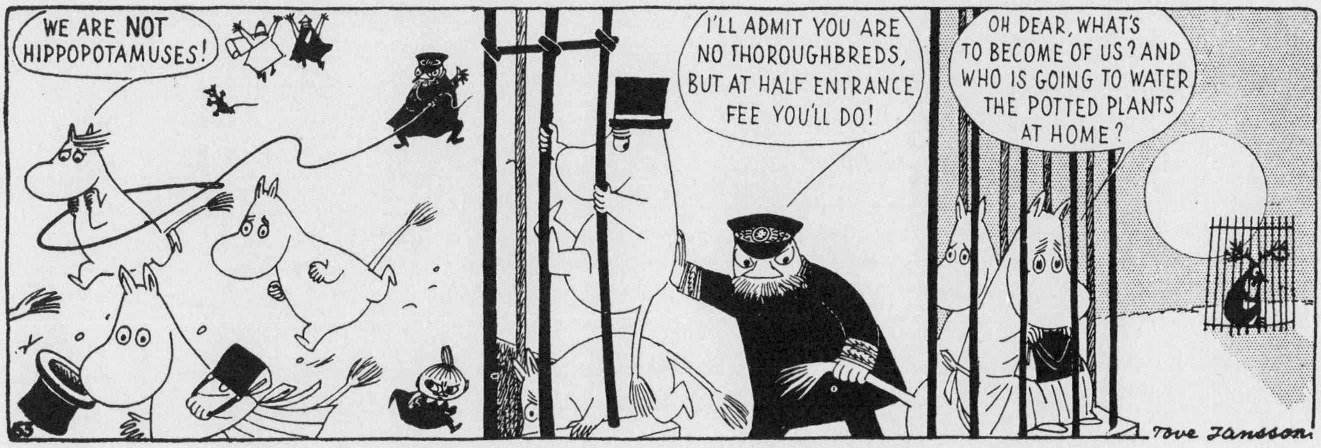
WE ARE NOT HIPPOPOTAMUSES!
I'LL ADMIT YOU ARE NO THOROUGHBREDS, BUT AT HALF ENTRANCE FEE YOU'LL DO!
OH DEAR, WHAT'S TO BECOME OF US? AND WHO IS GOING TO WATER THE POTTED PLANTS AT HOME?
Tove Jansson.

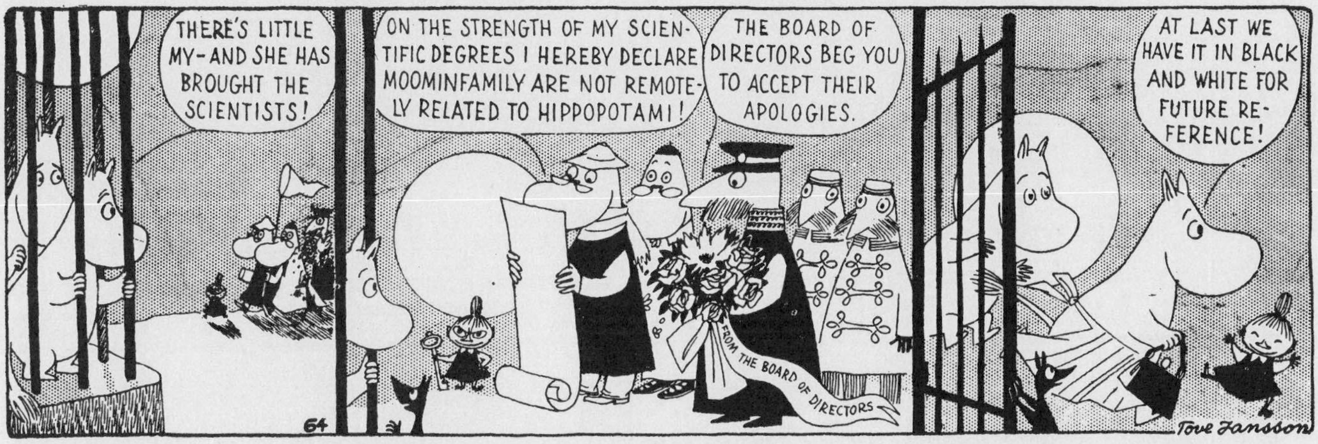
THERE'S LITTLE MY – AND SHE HAS BROUGHT THE SCIENTISTS!
64
ON THE STRENGTH OF MY SCIENTIFIC DEGREES I HEREBY DECLARE MOOMINFAMILY ARE NOT REMOTELY RELATED TO HIPPOPOTAMI!
THE BOARD OF DIRECTORS BEG YOU TO ACCEPT THEIR APOLOGIES.
FROM THE BOARD OF DIRECTORS
AT LAST WE HAVE IT IN BLACK AND WHITE FOR FUTURE REFERENCE!
Tove Jansson

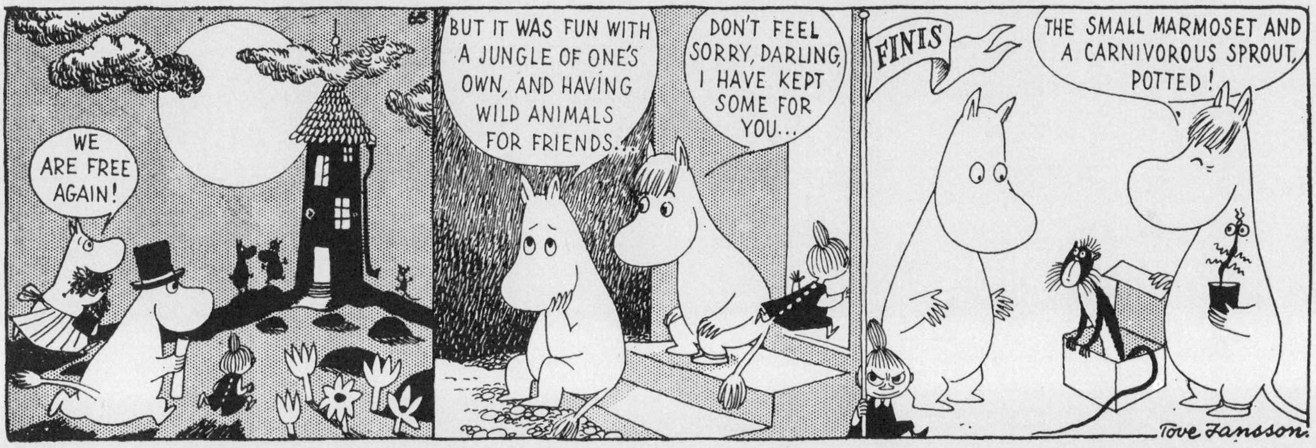
WE ARE FREE AGAIN!
BUT IT WAS FUN WITH A JUNGLE OF ONE'S OWN, AND HAVING WILD ANIMALS FOR FRIENDS...
DON'T FEEL SORRY, DARLING, I HAVE KEPT SOME FOR YOU...
FINIS
THE SMALL MARMOSET AND A CARNIVOROUS SPROUT, POTTED!
Tove Jansson.

11. Moomin and the Martians

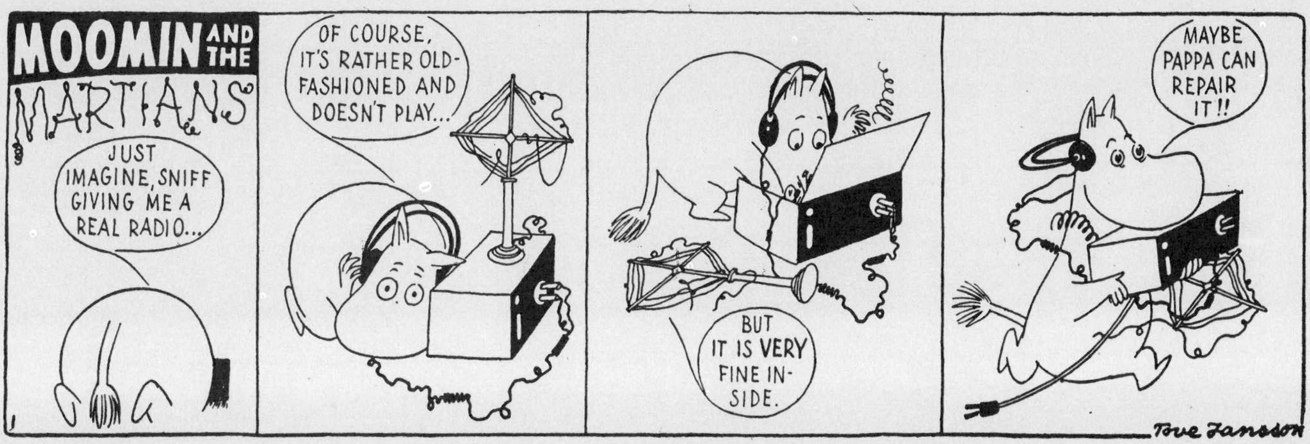

MOOMIN AND THE MARTIANS
1
JUST IMAGINE, SNIFF GIVING ME A REAL RADIO...
OF COURSE, IT'S RATHER OLD-FASHIONED AND DOESN'T PLAY...
BUT IT IS VERY FINE INSIDE.
MAYBE PAPPA CAN REPAIR IT!!
Tove Jansson

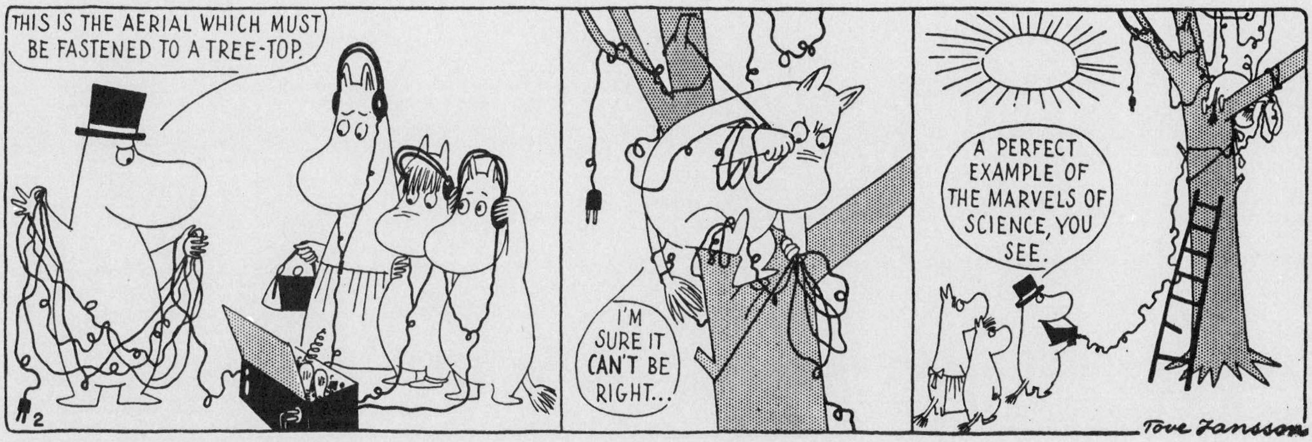

THIS IS THE AERIAL WHICH MUST BE FASTENED TO A TREE-TOP.
2
I'M SURE IT CAN'T BE RIGHT...
A PERFECT EXAMPLE OF THE MARVELS OF SCIENCE, YOU SEE.
Tove Jansson

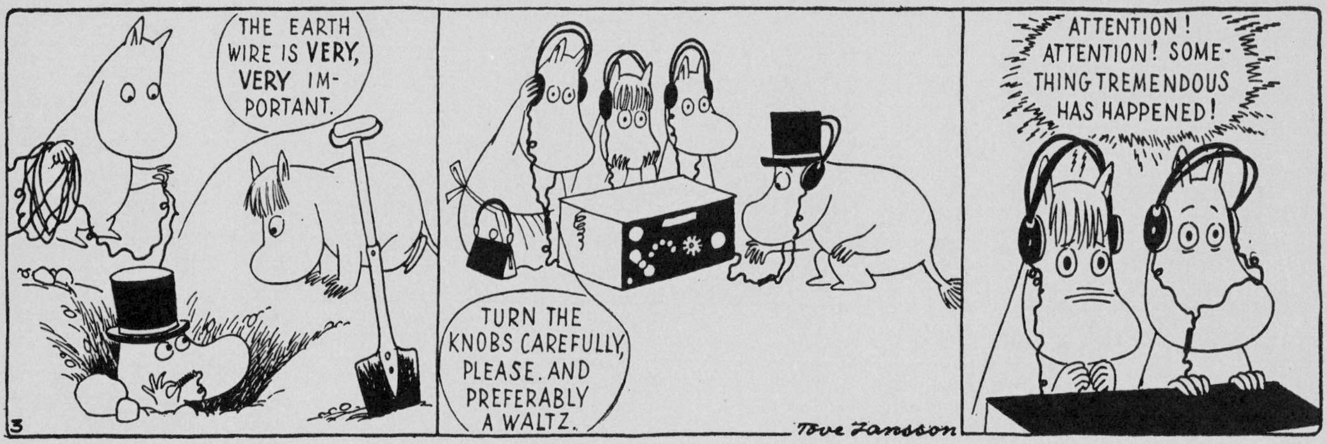
3
THE EARTH WIRE IS VERY, VERY IMPORTANT.
TURN THE KNOBS CAREFULLY, PLEASE. AND PREFERABLY A WALTZ.
ATTENTION! ATTENTION! SOMETHING TREMENDOUS HAS HAPPENED!
Tove Jansson

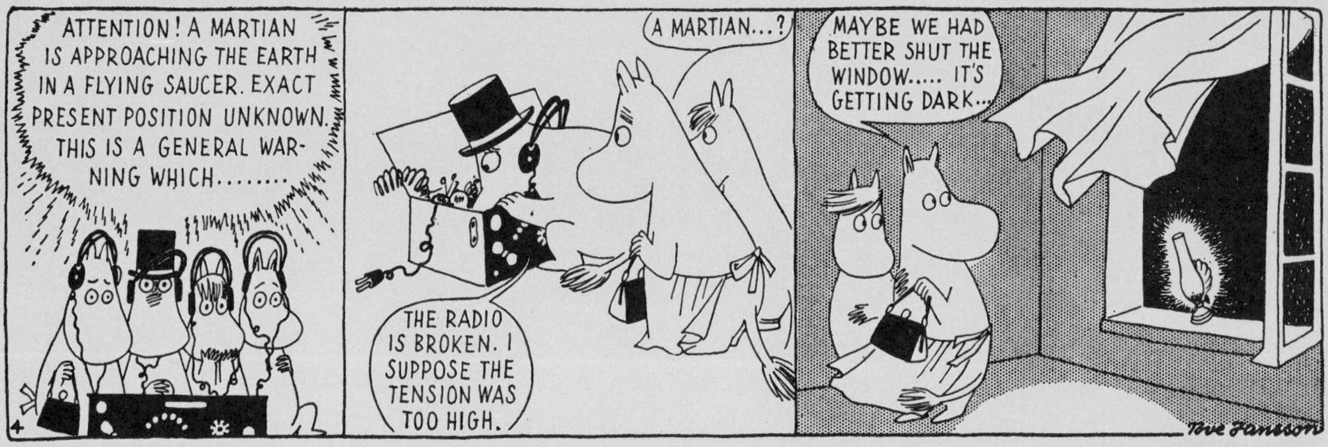
4
ATTENTION! A MARTIAN IS APPROACHING THE EARTH IN A FLYING SAUCER. EXACT PRESENT POSITION UNKNOWN. THIS IS A GENERAL WARNING WHICH........
A MARTIAN...?
THE RADIO IS BROKEN. I SUPPOSE THE TENSION WAS TOO HIGH.
MAYBE WE HAD BETTER SHUT THE WINDOW..... IT'S GETTING DARK...
Tove Jansson

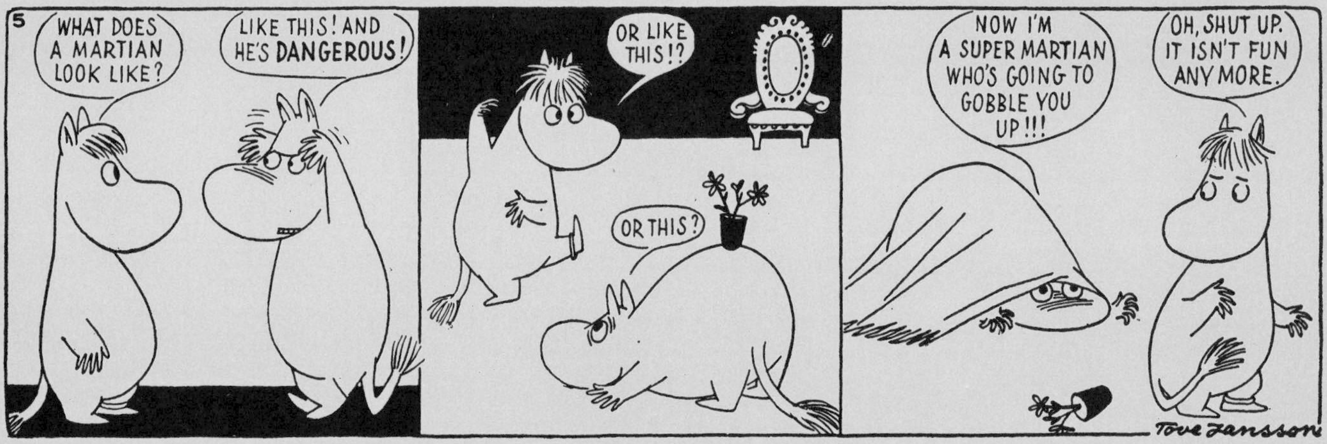
5
WHAT DOES A MARTIAN LOOK LIKE?
LIKE THIS! AND HE'S DANGEROUS!
OR LIKE THIS!?
OR THIS?
NOW I'M A SUPER MARTIAN WHO'S GOING TO GOBBLE YOU UP!!!
OH, SHUT UP. IT ISN'T FUN ANY MORE.
Tove Jansson

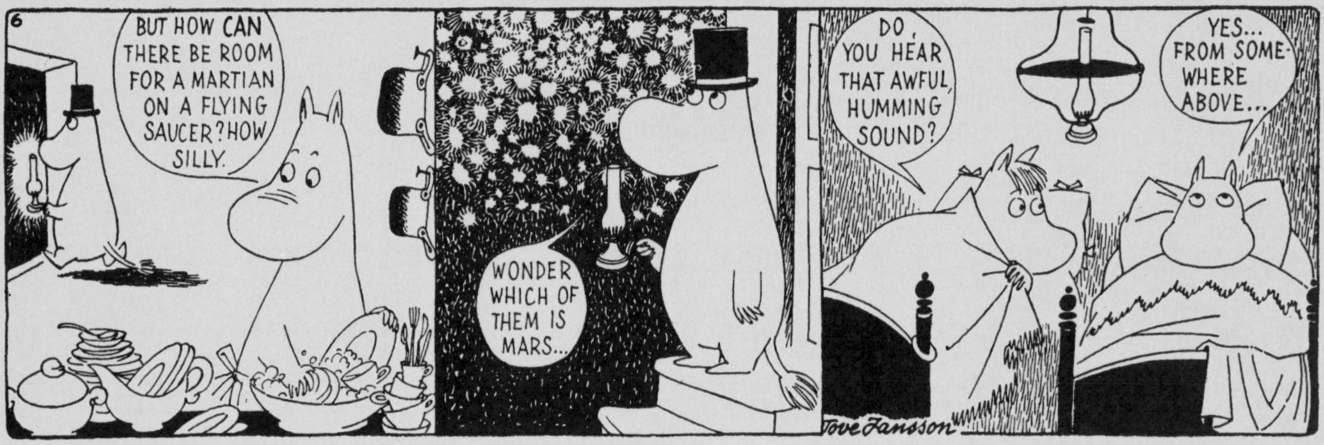
6
BUT HOW CAN THERE BE ROOM FOR A MARTIAN ON A FLYING SAUCER? HOW SILLY.
WONDER WHICH OF THEM IS MARS...
DO, YOU HEAR THAT AWFUL, HUMMING SOUND?
YES... FROM SOMEWHERE ABOVE...
Tove Jansson

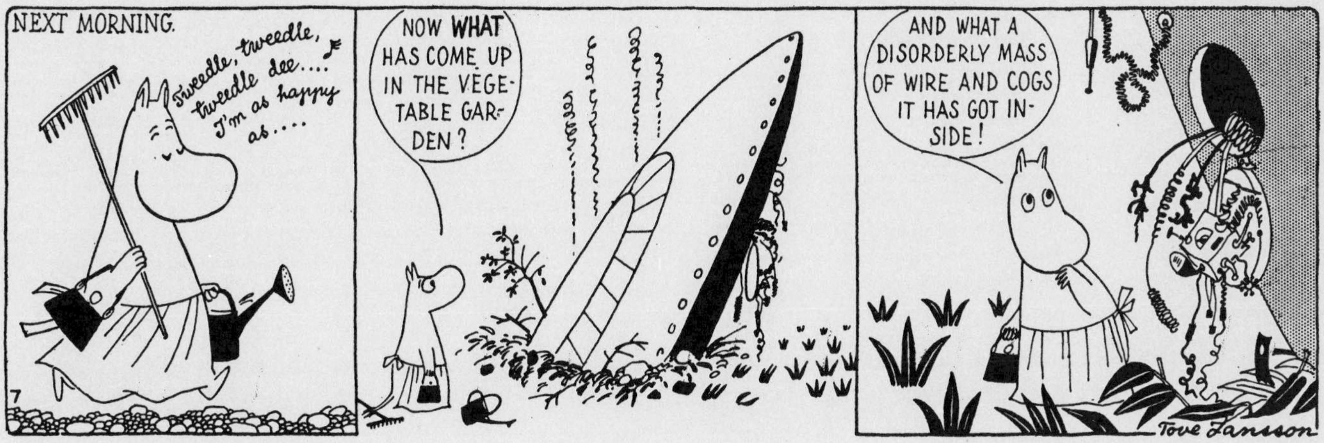
NEXT MORNING.
Tweedle, tweedle, tweedle dee.... I'm as happy as....
NOW WHAT HAS COME UP IN THE VEGETABLE GARDEN?
AND WHAT A DISORDERLY MASS OF WIRE AND COGS IT HAS GOT INSIDE!
Tove Jansson

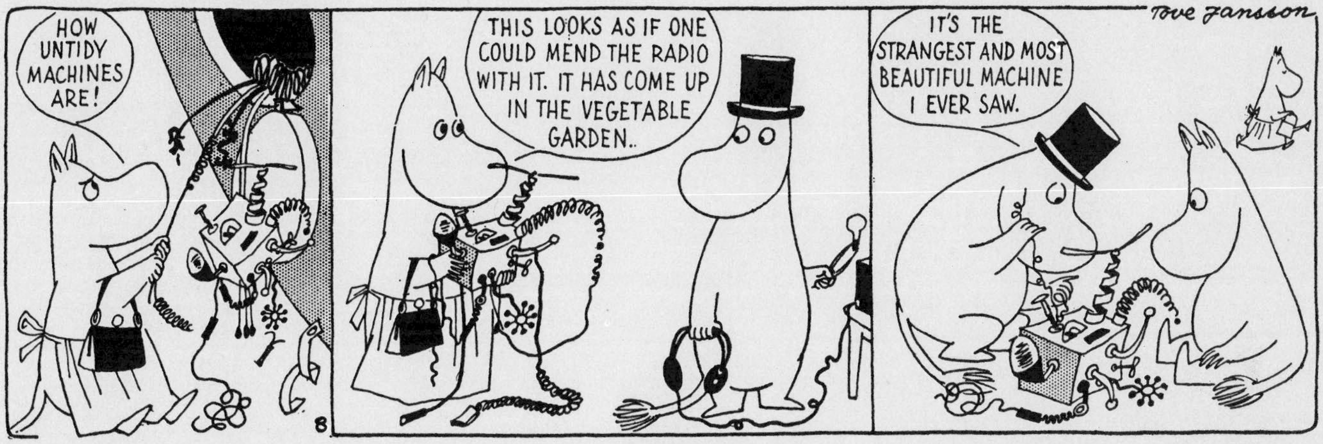
HOW UNTIDY MACHINES ARE!
THIS LOOKS AS IF ONE COULD MEND THE RADIO WITH IT. IT HAS COME UP IN THE VEGETABLE GARDEN..
IT'S THE STRANGEST AND MOST BEAUTIFUL MACHINE I EVER SAW.
Tove Jansson

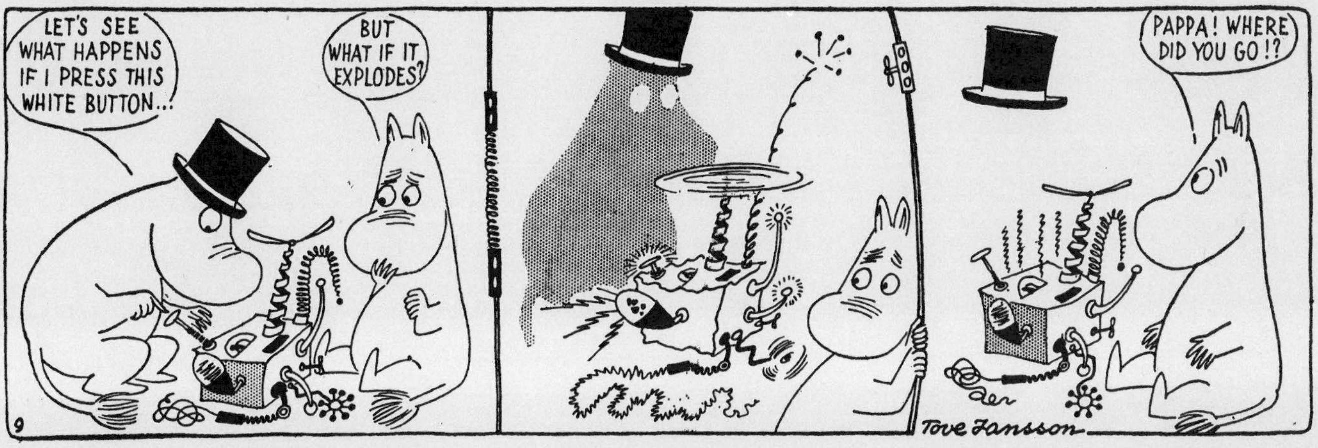
LET'S SEE WHAT HAPPENS IF I PRESS THIS WHITE BUTTON...
BUT WHAT IF IT EXPLODES?
PAPPA! WHERE DID YOU GO!?
Tove Jansson

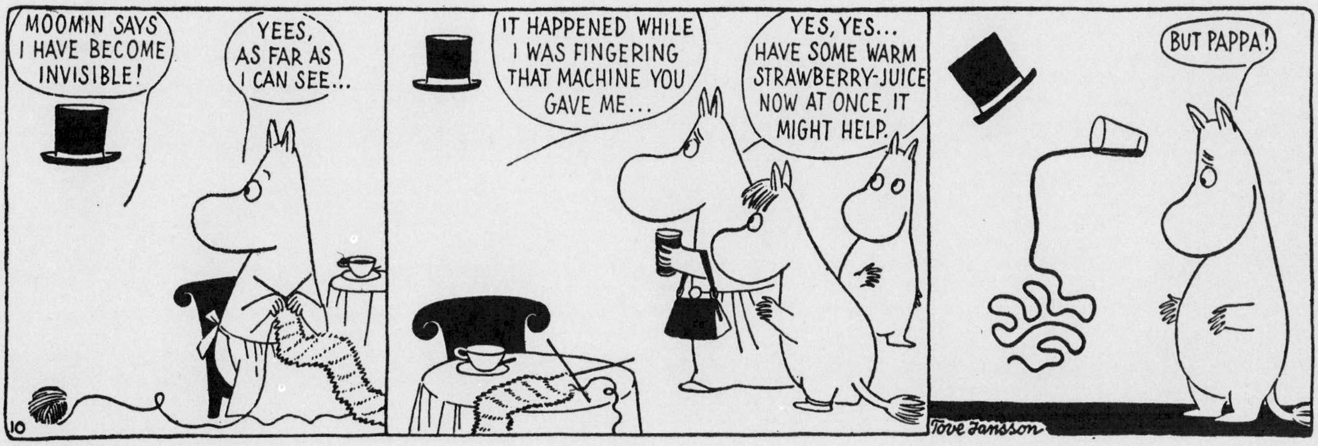
MOOMIN SAYS I HAVE BECOME INVISIBLE!
YEES, AS FAR AS I CAN SEE...
IT HAPPENED WHILE I WAS FINGERING THAT MACHINE YOU GAVE ME...
YES, YES... HAVE SOME WARM STRAWBERRY-JUICE NOW AT ONCE, IT MIGHT HELP.
BUT PAPPA!
Tove Jansson

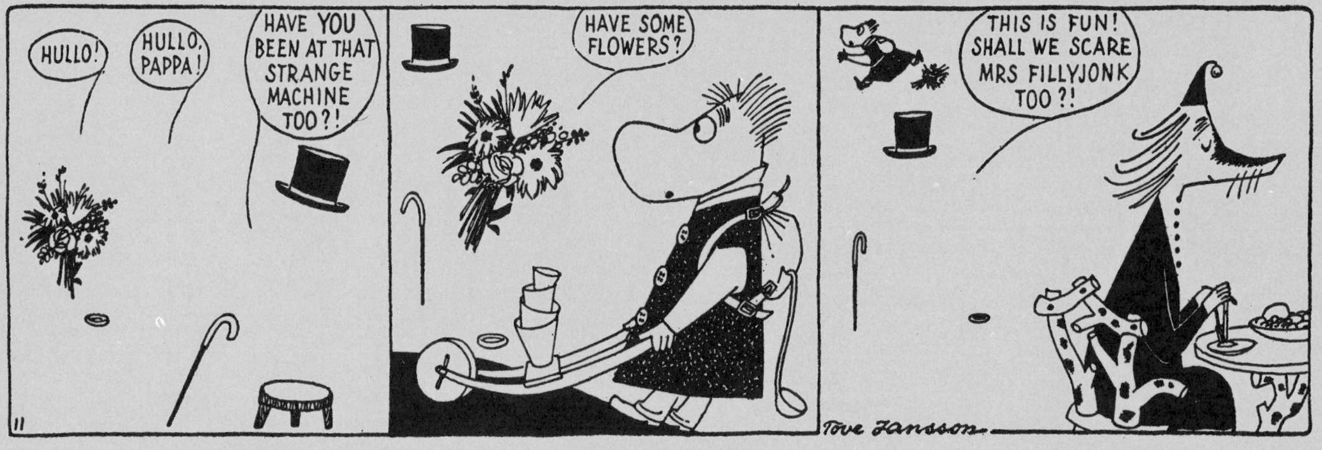
11
HULLO!
HULLO, PAPPA!
HAVE YOU BEEN AT THAT STRANGE MACHINE TOO?!
HAVE SOME FLOWERS?
THIS IS FUN! SHALL WE SCARE MRS FILLYJONK TOO?!
Tove Jansson

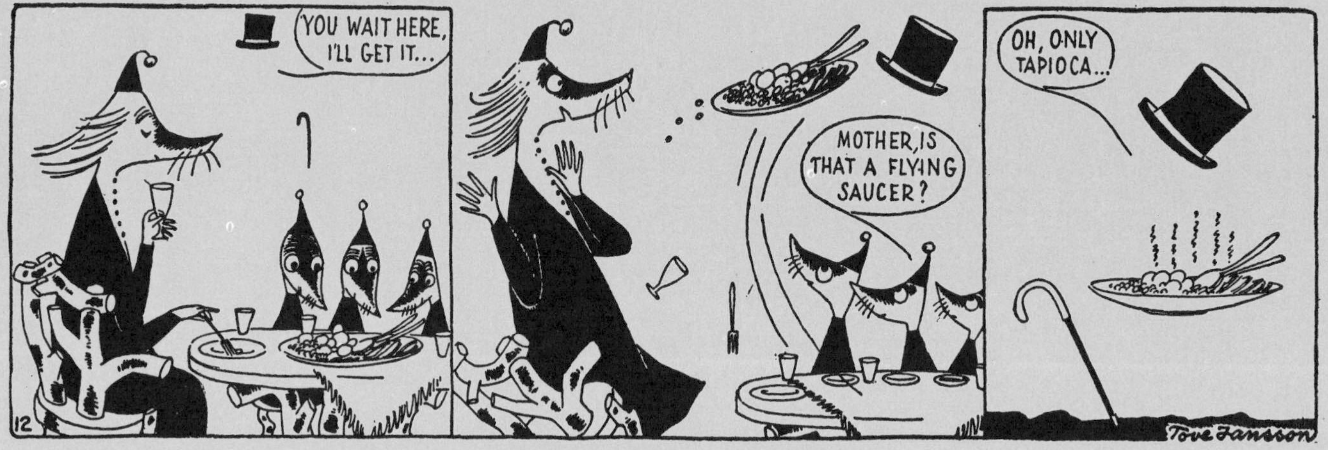
12
YOU WAIT HERE, I'LL GET IT...
MOTHER, IS THAT A FLYING SAUCER?
OH, ONLY TAPIOCA...
Tove Jansson

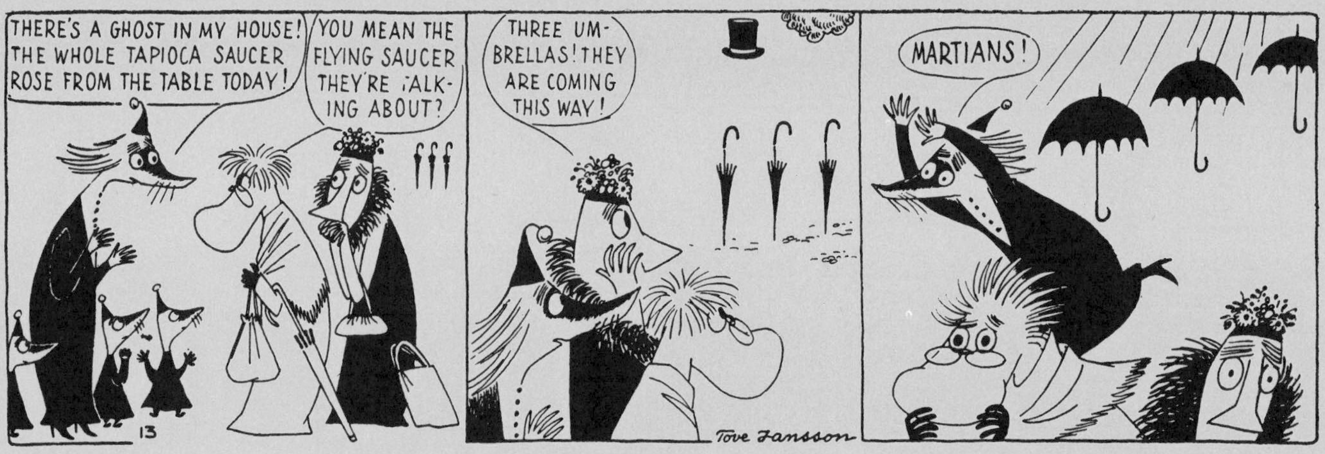
13
THERE'S A GHOST IN MY HOUSE! THE WHOLE TAPIOCA SAUCER ROSE FROM THE TABLE TODAY!
YOU MEAN THE FLYING SAUCER THEY'RE TALK-ING ABOUT?
THREE UM-BRELLAS! THEY ARE COMING THIS WAY!
MARTIANS!
Tove Jansson

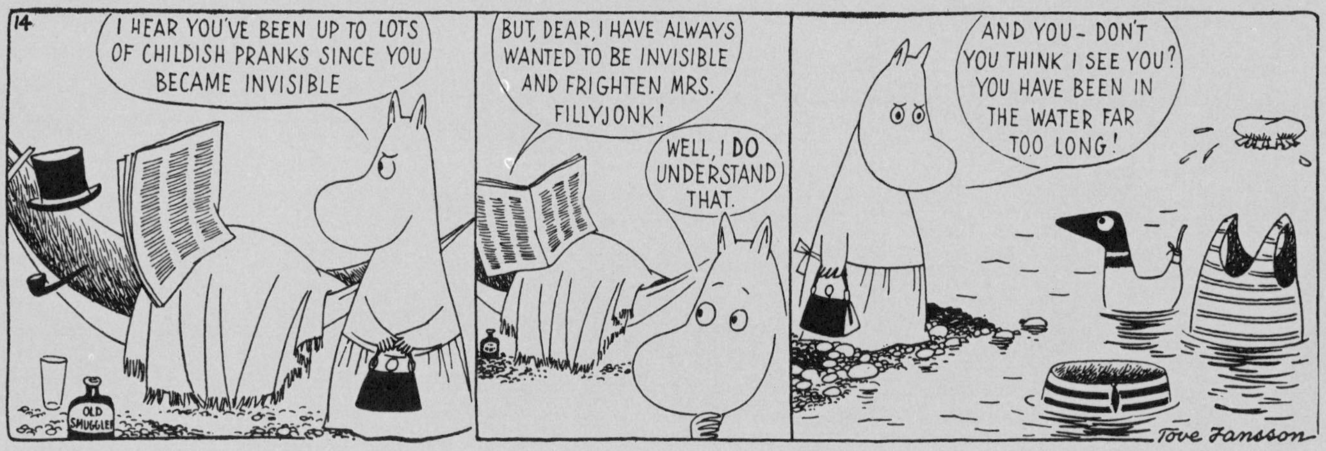
14
I HEAR YOU'VE BEEN UP TO LOTS OF CHILDISH PRANKS SINCE YOU BECAME INVISIBLE
OLD SMUGGLER
BUT, DEAR, I HAVE ALWAYS WANTED TO BE INVISIBLE AND FRIGHTEN MRS. FILLYJONK!
WELL, I DO UNDERSTAND THAT.
AND YOU - DON'T YOU THINK I SEE YOU? YOU HAVE BEEN IN THE WATER FAR TOO LONG!
Tove Jansson

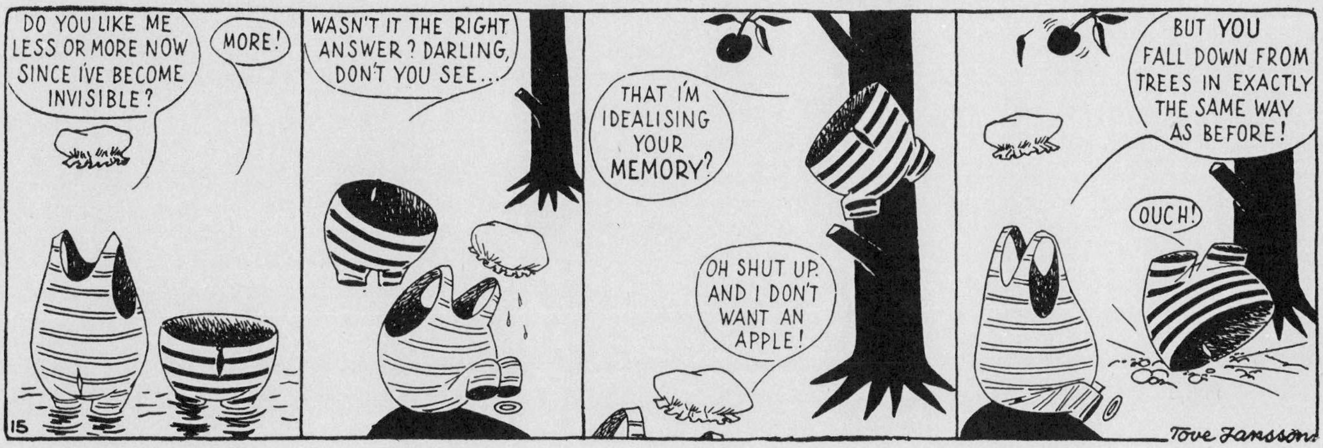
DO YOU LIKE ME LESS OR MORE NOW SINCE I'VE BECOME INVISIBLE?
MORE!
WASN'T IT THE RIGHT ANSWER? DARLING, DON'T YOU SEE...
THAT I'M IDEALISING YOUR MEMORY?
OH SHUT UP. AND I DON'T WANT AN APPLE!
BUT YOU FALL DOWN FROM TREES IN EXACTLY THE SAME WAY AS BEFORE!
OUCH!
15
Tove Jansson

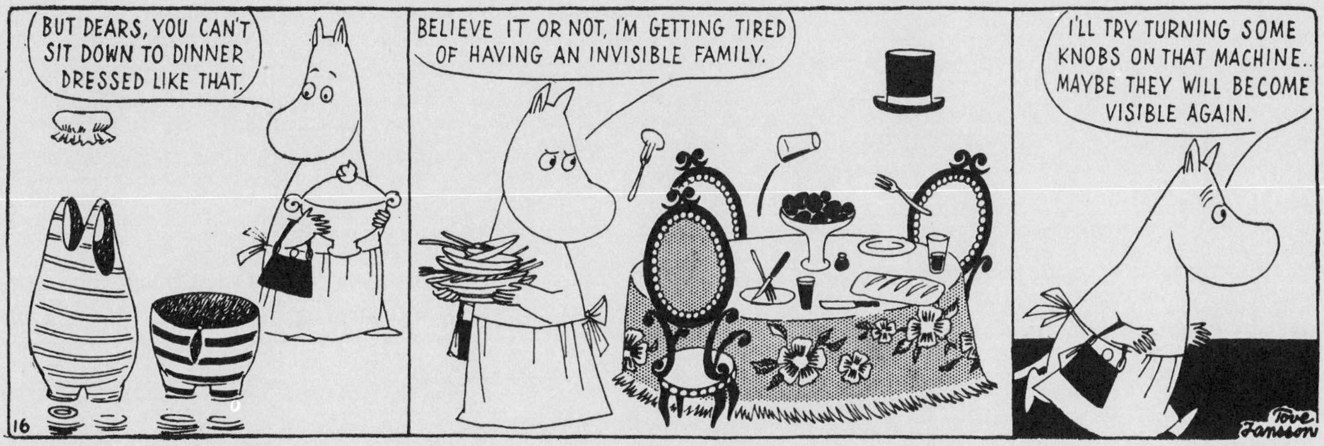
BUT DEARS, YOU CAN'T SIT DOWN TO DINNER DRESSED LIKE THAT.
BELIEVE IT OR NOT, I'M GETTING TIRED OF HAVING AN INVISIBLE FAMILY.
I'LL TRY TURNING SOME KNOBS ON THAT MACHINE.. MAYBE THEY WILL BECOME VISIBLE AGAIN.
16
Tove Jansson

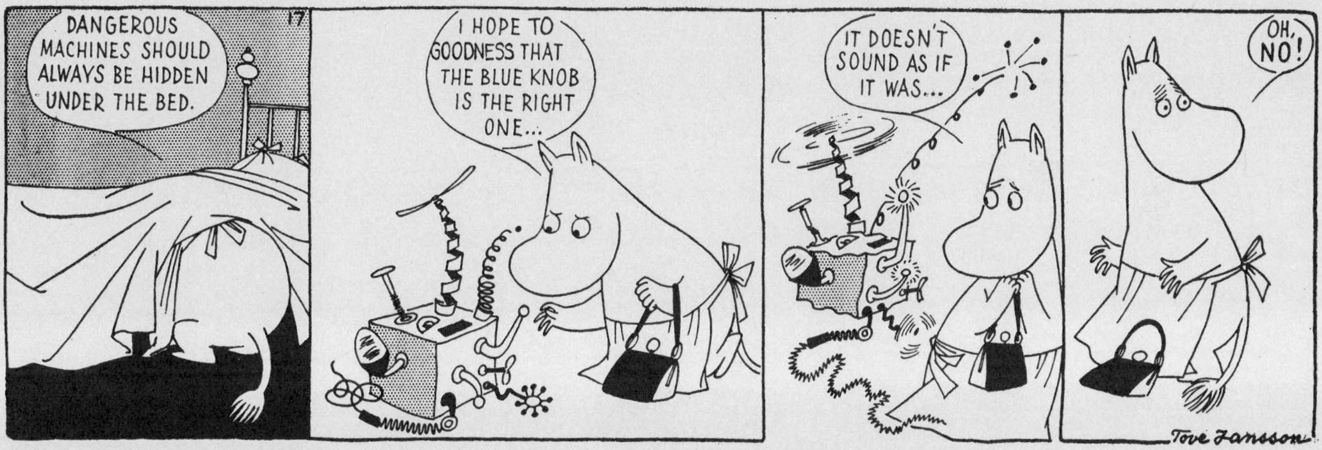
DANGEROUS MACHINES SHOULD ALWAYS BE HIDDEN UNDER THE BED.
17
I HOPE TO GOODNESS THAT THE BLUE KNOB IS THE RIGHT ONE...
IT DOESN'T SOUND AS IF IT WAS...
OH, NO!
Tove Jansson

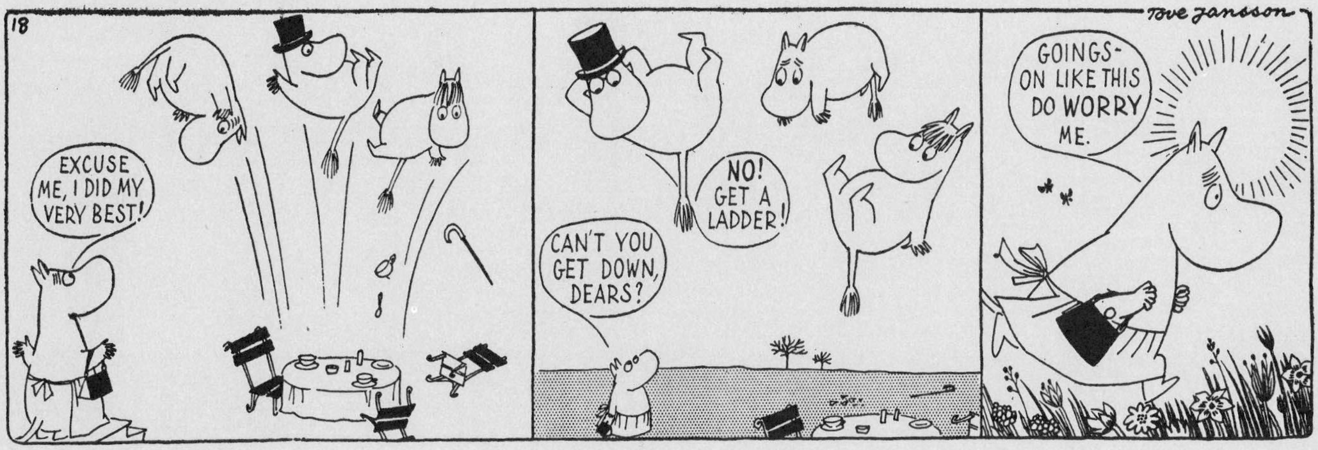
18
Tove Jansson
EXCUSE ME, I DID MY VERY BEST!
NO! GET A LADDER!
CAN'T YOU GET DOWN, DEARS?
GOINGS-ON LIKE THIS DO WORRY ME.

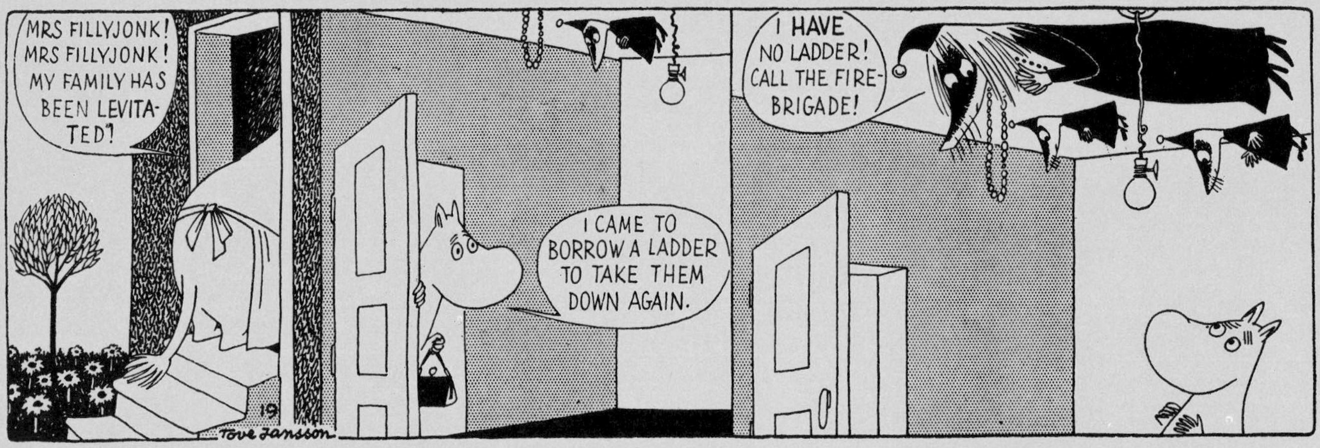
MRS FILLYJONK! MRS FILLYJONK! MY FAMILY HAS BEEN LEVITATED!
I CAME TO BORROW A LADDER TO TAKE THEM DOWN AGAIN.
I HAVE NO LADDER! CALL THE FIRE-BRIGADE!
19
Tove Jansson

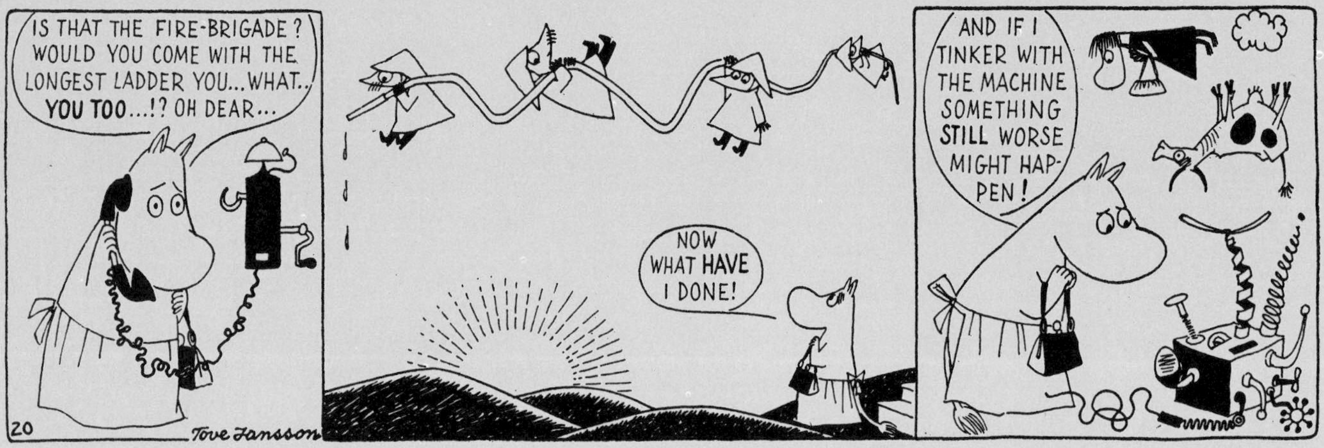
IS THAT THE FIRE-BRIGADE? WOULD YOU COME WITH THE LONGEST LADDER YOU...WHAT... YOU TOO...!? OH DEAR...
NOW WHAT HAVE I DONE!
AND IF I TINKER WITH THE MACHINE SOMETHING STILL WORSE MIGHT HAPPEN!
20
Tove Jansson

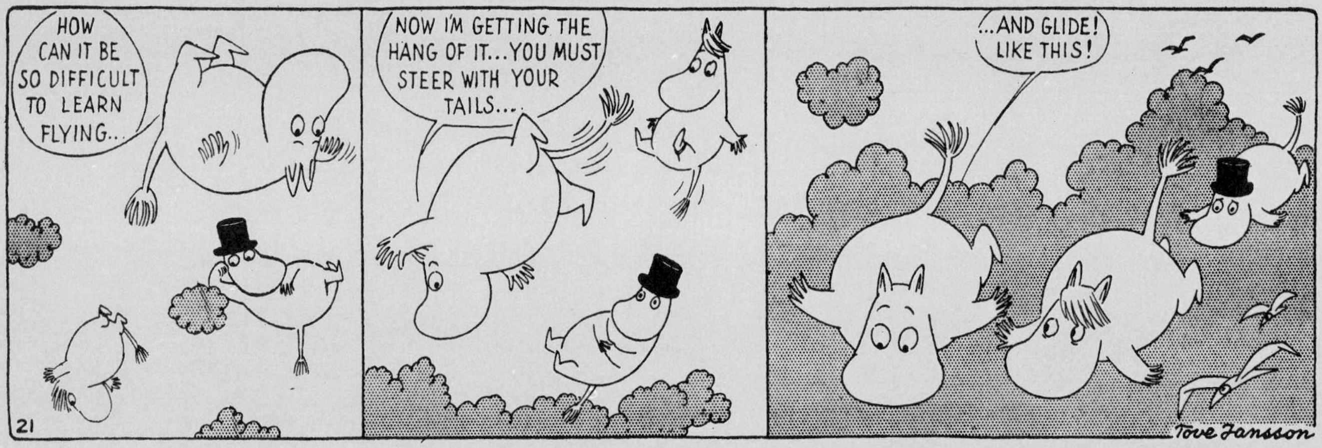
HOW CAN IT BE SO DIFFICULT TO LEARN FLYING...
NOW I'M GETTING THE HANG OF IT...YOU MUST STEER WITH YOUR TAILS....
...AND GLIDE! LIKE THIS!
21
Tove Jansson

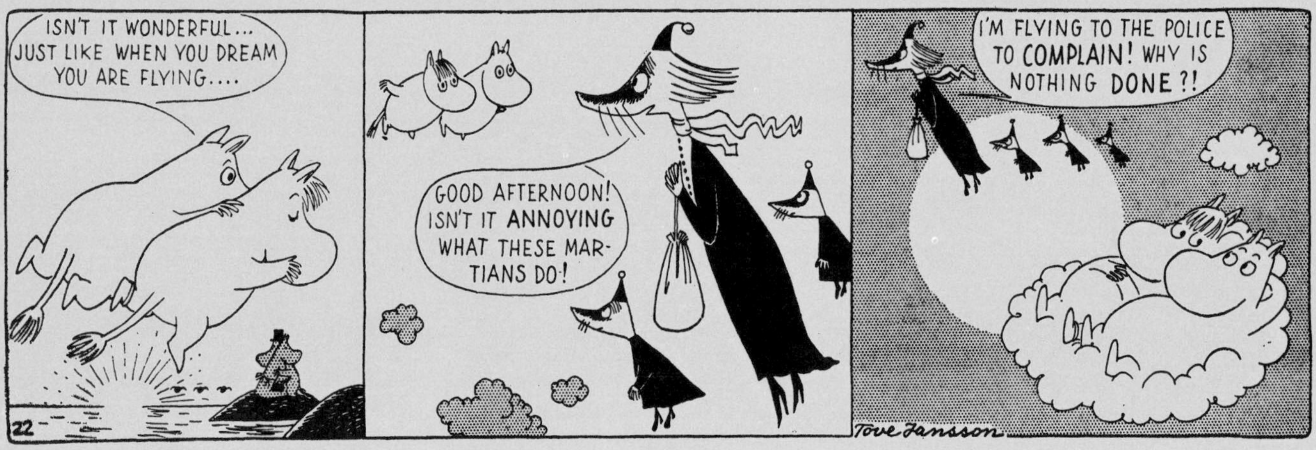
ISN'T IT WONDERFUL... JUST LIKE WHEN YOU DREAM YOU ARE FLYING....
GOOD AFTERNOON! ISN'T IT ANNOYING WHAT THESE MARTIANS DO!
I'M FLYING TO THE POLICE TO COMPLAIN! WHY IS NOTHING DONE?!
22
Tove Jansson

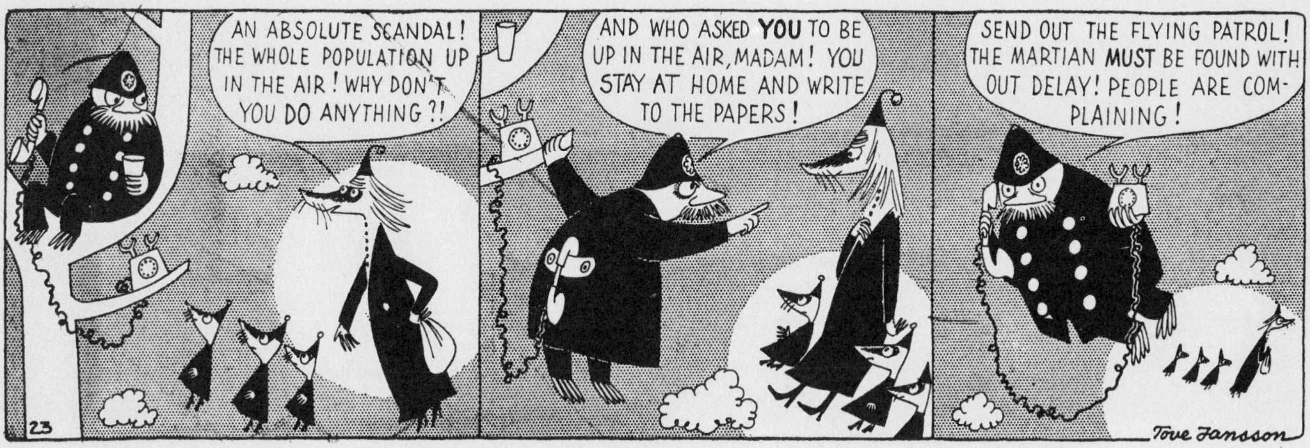
23
AN ABSOLUTE SCANDAL! THE WHOLE POPULATION UP IN THE AIR! WHY DON'T YOU DO ANYTHING?!
AND WHO ASKED **YOU** TO BE UP IN THE AIR, MADAM! YOU STAY AT HOME AND WRITE TO THE PAPERS!
SEND OUT THE FLYING PATROL! THE MARTIAN **MUST** BE FOUND WITHOUT DELAY! PEOPLE ARE COMPLAINING!
Tove Jansson

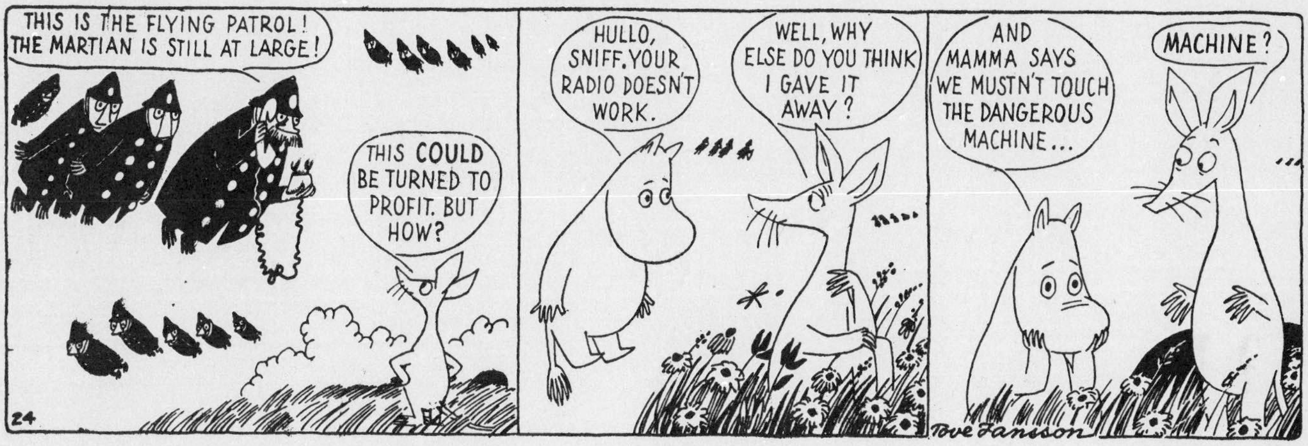
24
THIS IS THE FLYING PATROL! THE MARTIAN IS STILL AT LARGE!
THIS **COULD** BE TURNED TO PROFIT. BUT HOW?
HULLO, SNIFF. YOUR RADIO DOESN'T WORK.
WELL, WHY ELSE DO YOU THINK I GAVE IT AWAY?
AND MAMMA SAYS WE MUSTN'T TOUCH THE DANGEROUS MACHINE...
MACHINE?
Tove Jansson

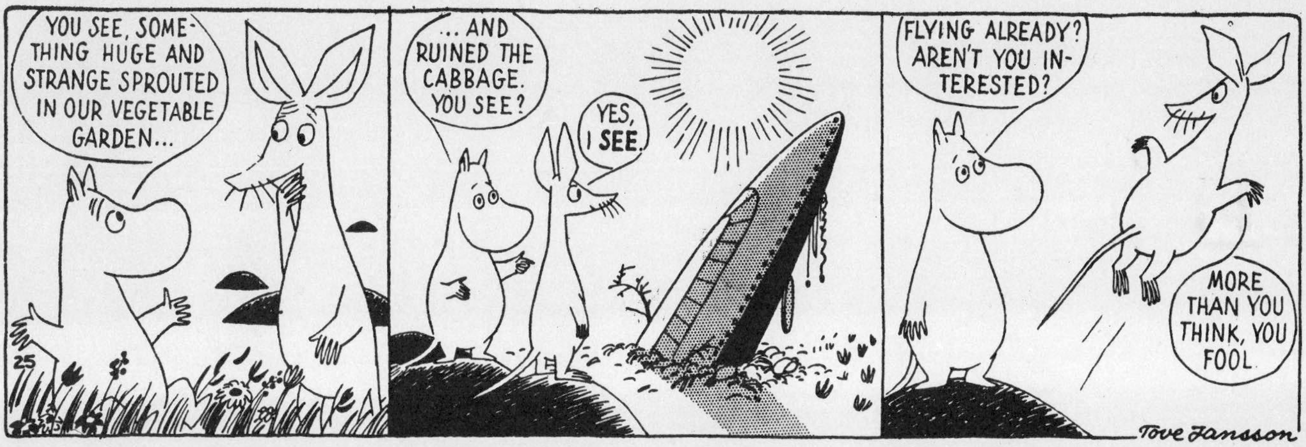
25
YOU SEE, SOMETHING HUGE AND STRANGE SPROUTED IN OUR VEGETABLE GARDEN...
...AND RUINED THE CABBAGE. YOU SEE?
YES, I **SEE**.
FLYING ALREADY? AREN'T YOU INTERESTED?
MORE THAN YOU THINK, YOU FOOL.
Tove Jansson

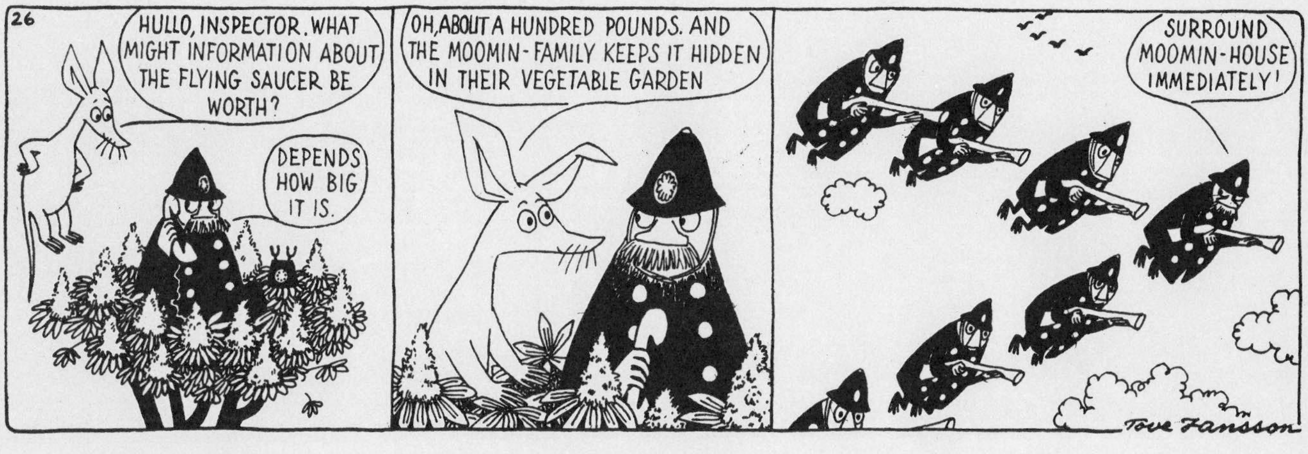
26
HULLO, INSPECTOR. WHAT MIGHT INFORMATION ABOUT THE FLYING SAUCER BE WORTH?
DEPENDS HOW BIG IT IS.
OH, ABOUT A HUNDRED POUNDS. AND THE MOOMIN-FAMILY KEEPS IT HIDDEN IN THEIR VEGETABLE GARDEN
SURROUND MOOMIN-HOUSE IMMEDIATELY!
Tove Jansson

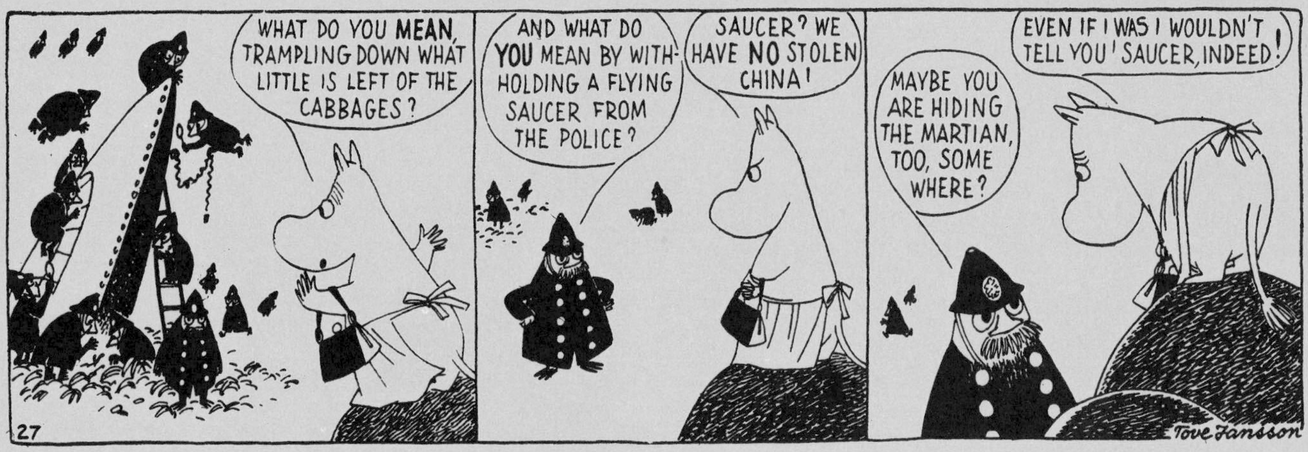
27
WHAT DO YOU MEAN, TRAMPLING DOWN WHAT LITTLE IS LEFT OF THE CABBAGES?
AND WHAT DO YOU MEAN BY WITH-HOLDING A FLYING SAUCER FROM THE POLICE?
SAUCER? WE HAVE NO STOLEN CHINA!
MAYBE YOU ARE HIDING THE MARTIAN, TOO, SOME WHERE?
EVEN IF I WAS I WOULDN'T TELL YOU! SAUCER, INDEED!
Tove Jansson

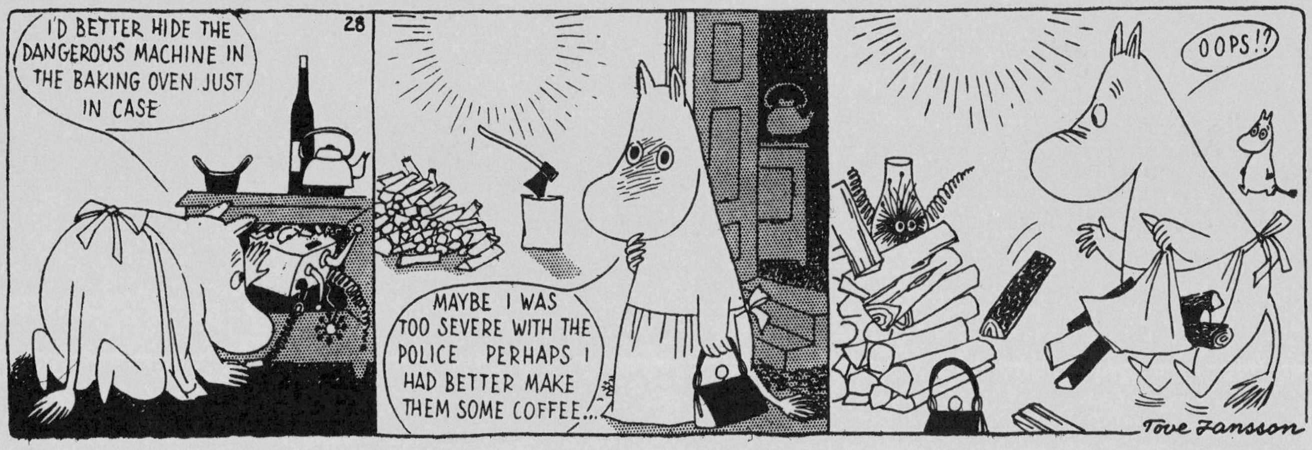
28
I'D BETTER HIDE THE DANGEROUS MACHINE IN THE BAKING OVEN JUST IN CASE
MAYBE I WAS TOO SEVERE WITH THE POLICE PERHAPS I HAD BETTER MAKE THEM SOME COFFEE...
OOPS!?
Tove Jansson

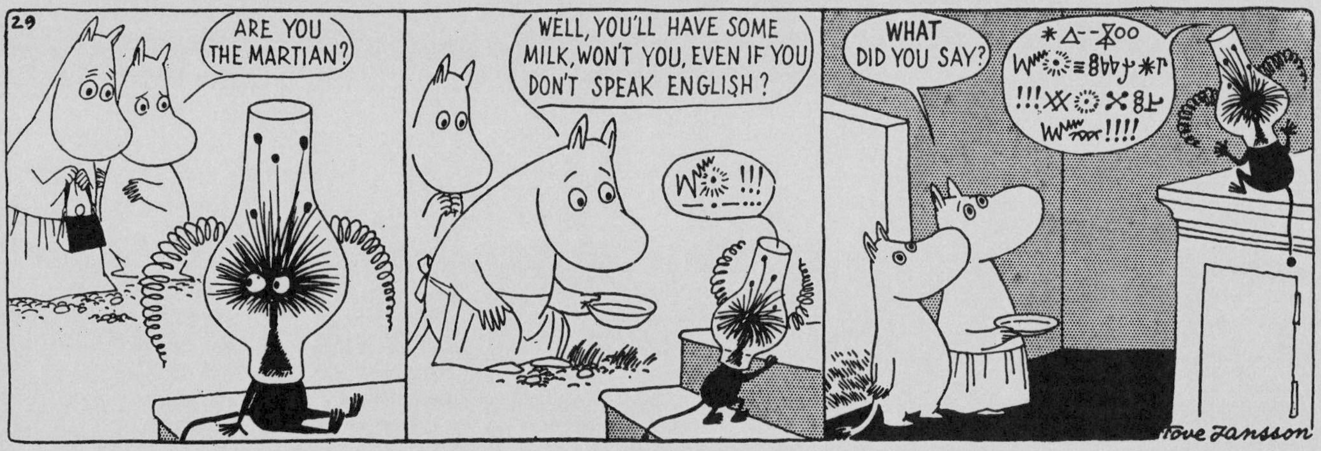
29
ARE YOU THE MARTIAN?
WELL, YOU'LL HAVE SOME MILK, WON'T YOU, EVEN IF YOU DON'T SPEAK ENGLISH?
WHAT DID YOU SAY?
Tove Jansson

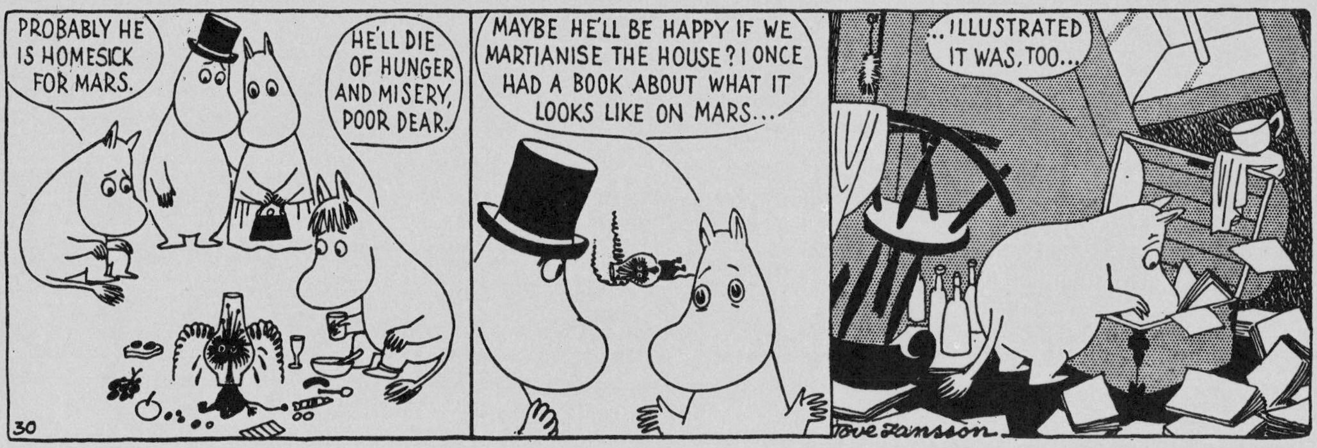
PROBABLY HE IS HOMESICK FOR MARS.
HE'LL DIE OF HUNGER AND MISERY, POOR DEAR.
30
MAYBE HE'LL BE HAPPY IF WE MARTIANISE THE HOUSE? I ONCE HAD A BOOK ABOUT WHAT IT LOOKS LIKE ON MARS...
...ILLUSTRATED IT WAS, TOO...
Tove Jansson

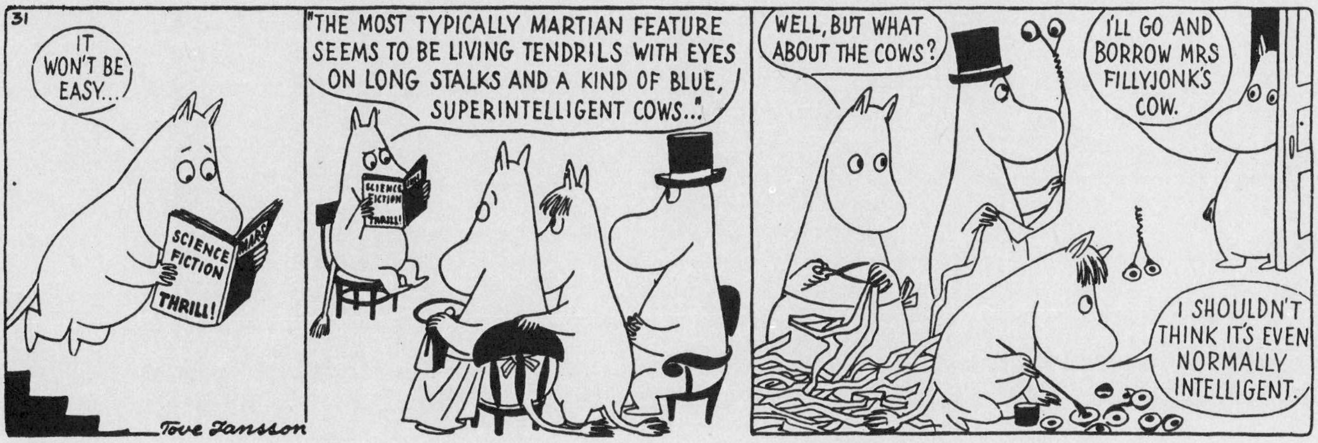
31
IT WON'T BE EASY...
SCIENCE FICTION THRILL!
MARS
Tove Jansson
"THE MOST TYPICALLY MARTIAN FEATURE SEEMS TO BE LIVING TENDRILS WITH EYES ON LONG STALKS AND A KIND OF BLUE, SUPERINTELLIGENT COWS..."
WELL, BUT WHAT ABOUT THE COWS?
I'LL GO AND BORROW MRS FILLYJONK'S COW.
I SHOULDN'T THINK IT'S EVEN NORMALLY INTELLIGENT.

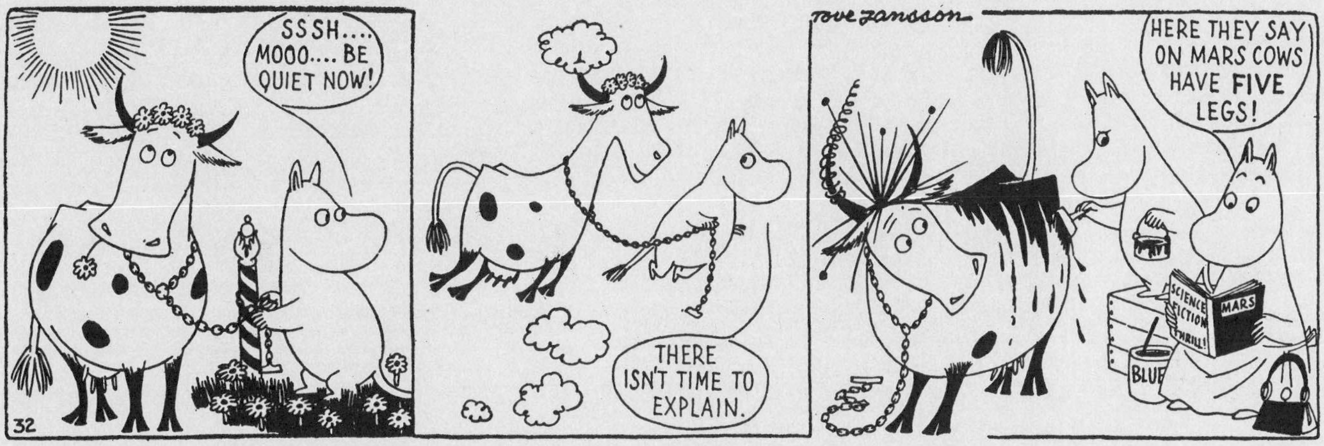
32
SSSH.... MOOO.... BE QUIET NOW!
THERE ISN'T TIME TO EXPLAIN.
Tove Jansson
HERE THEY SAY ON MARS COWS HAVE **FIVE** LEGS!
SCIENCE FICTION THRILL!
MARS
BLUE

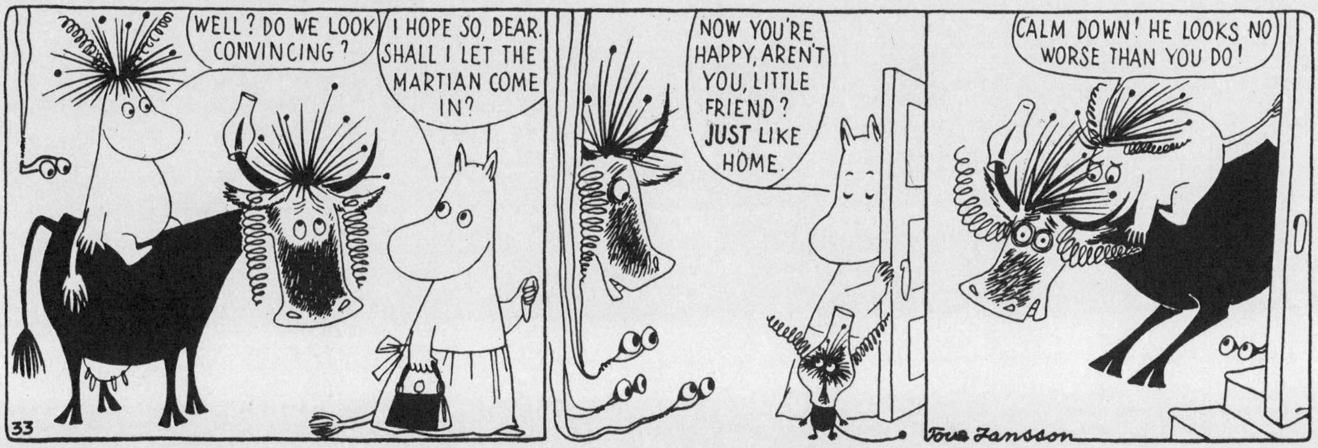
33
WELL? DO WE LOOK CONVINCING?
I HOPE SO, DEAR. SHALL I LET THE MARTIAN COME IN?
NOW YOU'RE HAPPY, AREN'T YOU, LITTLE FRIEND? **JUST** LIKE HOME.
CALM DOWN! HE LOOKS NO WORSE THAN YOU DO!
Tove Jansson

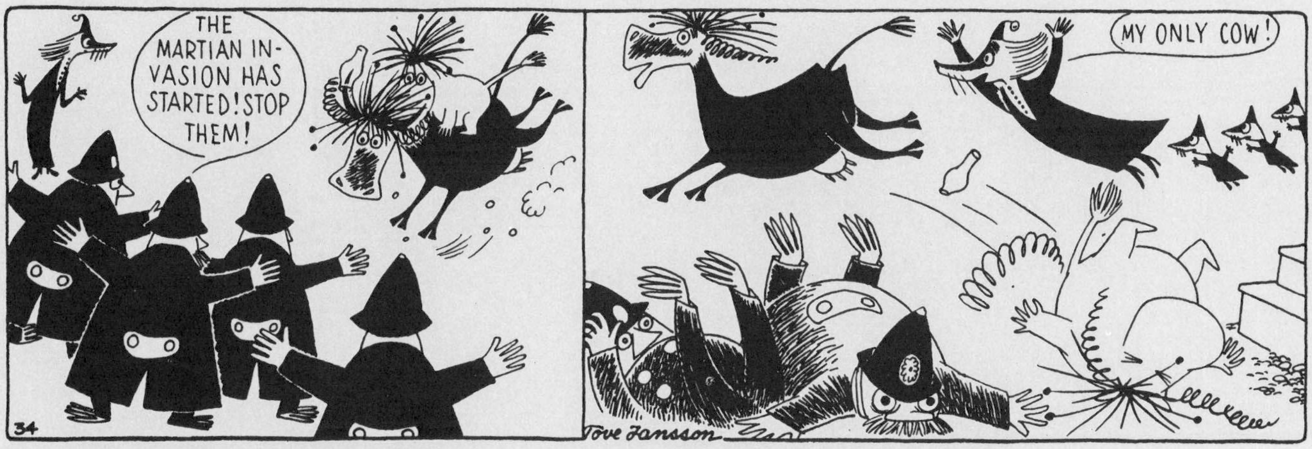
34
THE MARTIAN IN-VASION HAS STARTED! STOP THEM!
MY ONLY COW!
Tove Jansson

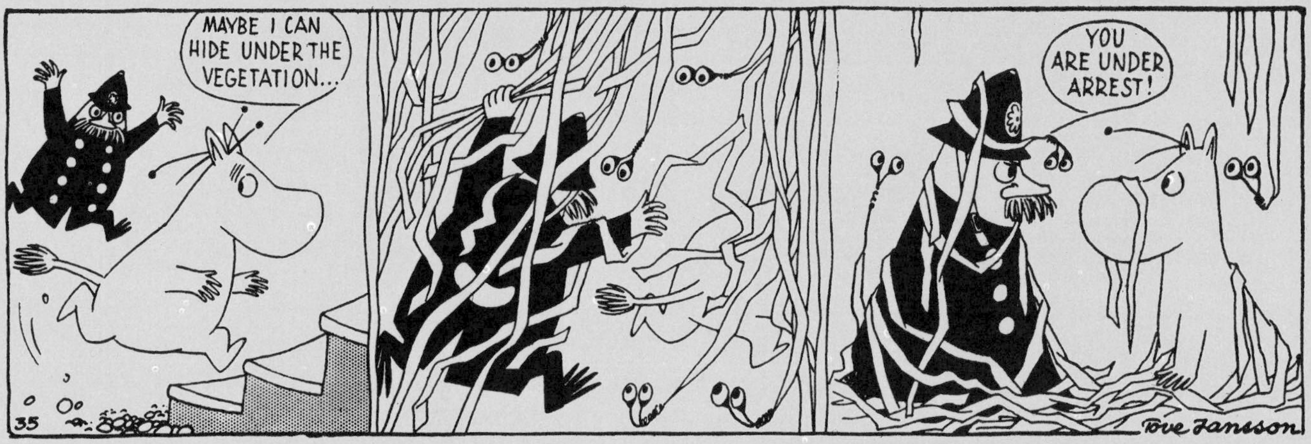
MAYBE I CAN HIDE UNDER THE VEGETATION...
YOU ARE UNDER ARREST!
35
Tove Jansson

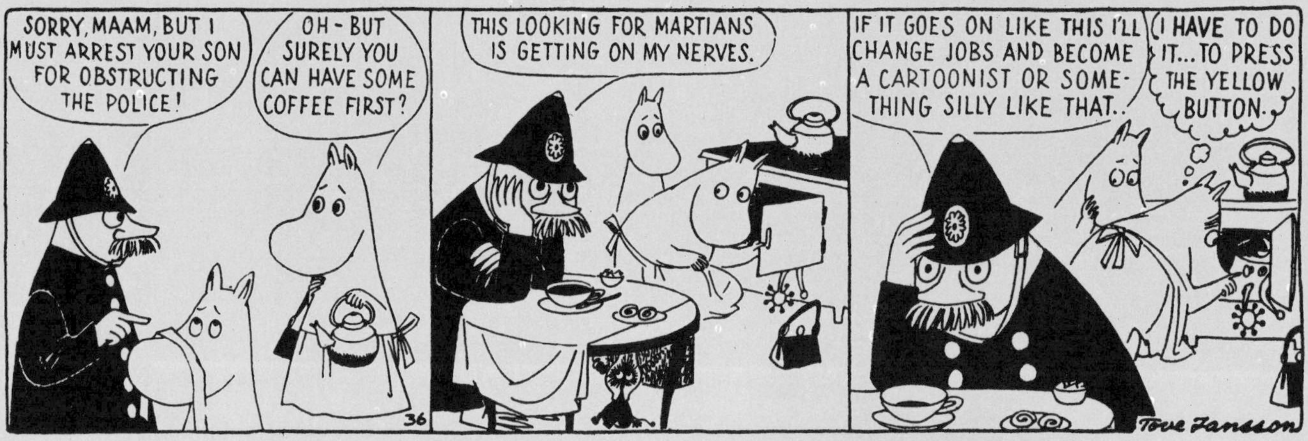
SORRY, MAAM, BUT I MUST ARREST YOUR SON FOR OBSTRUCTING THE POLICE!
OH - BUT SURELY YOU CAN HAVE SOME COFFEE FIRST?
36
THIS LOOKING FOR MARTIANS IS GETTING ON MY NERVES.
IF IT GOES ON LIKE THIS I'LL CHANGE JOBS AND BECOME A CARTOONIST OR SOMETHING SILLY LIKE THAT..
I HAVE TO DO IT... TO PRESS THE YELLOW BUTTON.
Tove Jansson

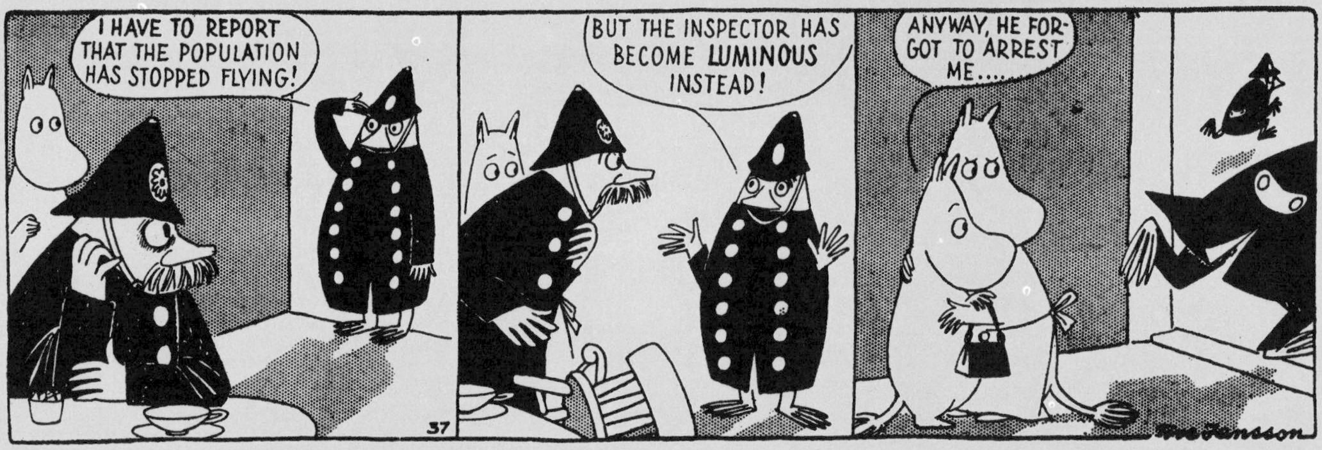
I HAVE TO REPORT THAT THE POPULATION HAS STOPPED FLYING!
37
BUT THE INSPECTOR HAS BECOME LUMINOUS INSTEAD!
ANYWAY, HE FORGOT TO ARREST ME.....

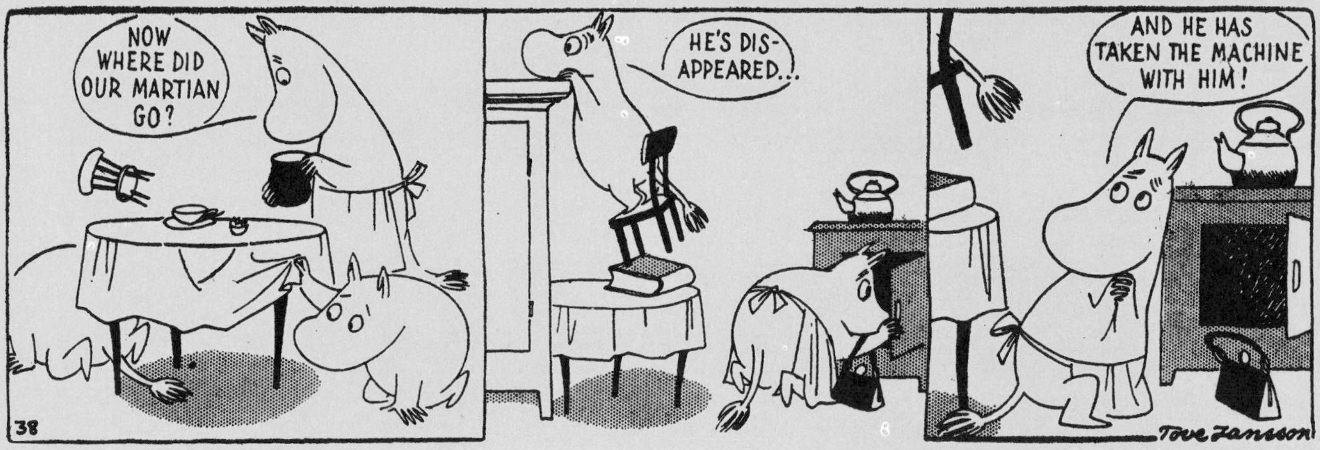
NOW WHERE DID OUR MARTIAN GO?
38
HE'S DISAPPEARED...
AND HE HAS TAKEN THE MACHINE WITH HIM!
Tove Jansson

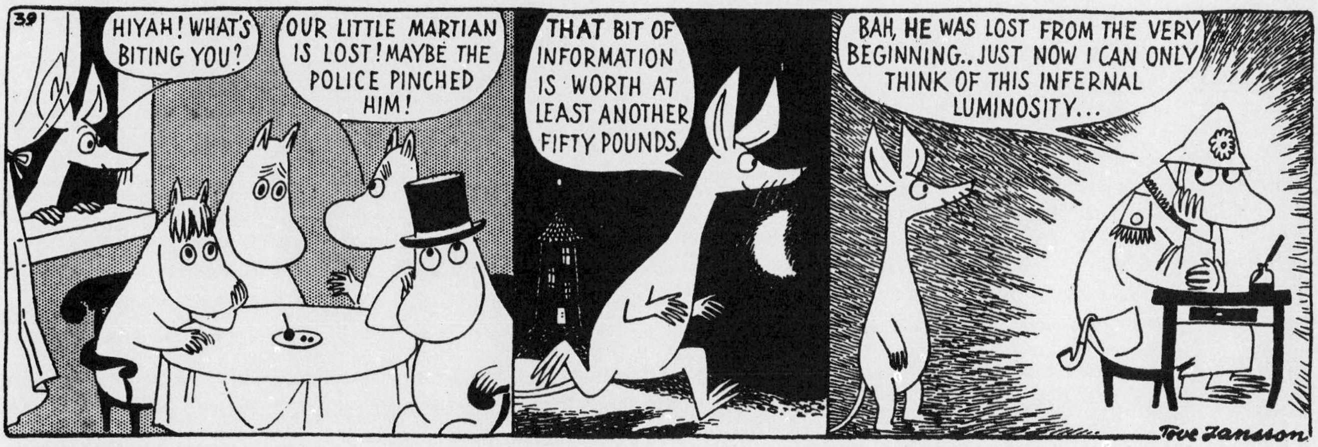
39
HIYAH! WHAT'S BITING YOU?
OUR LITTLE MARTIAN IS LOST! MAYBE THE POLICE PINCHED HIM!
THAT BIT OF INFORMATION IS WORTH AT LEAST ANOTHER FIFTY POUNDS.
BAH, HE WAS LOST FROM THE VERY BEGINNING.. JUST NOW I CAN ONLY THINK OF THIS INFERNAL LUMINOSITY...
Tove Jansson

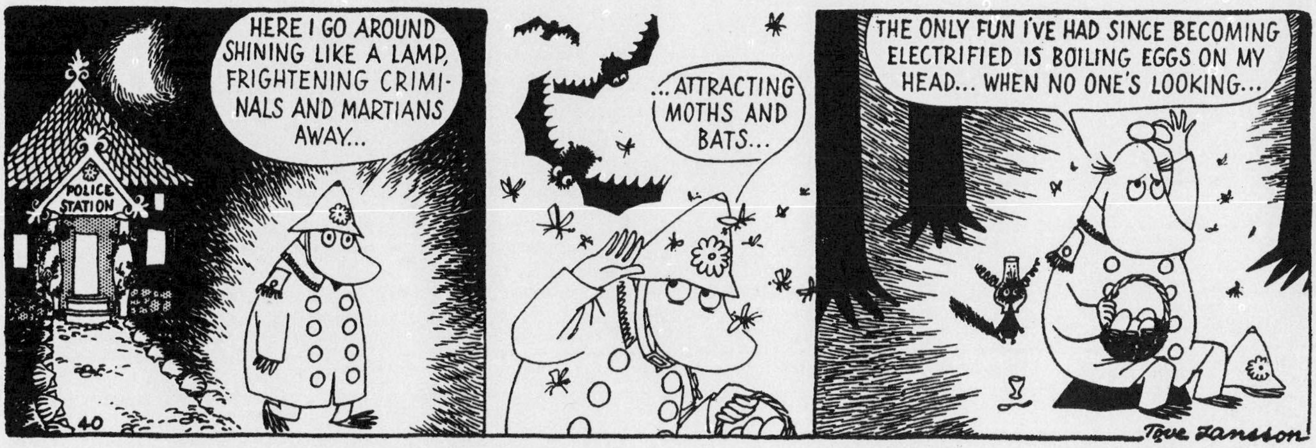
POLICE STATION
HERE I GO AROUND SHINING LIKE A LAMP, FRIGHTENING CRIMINALS AND MARTIANS AWAY...
40
...ATTRACTING MOTHS AND BATS...
THE ONLY FUN I'VE HAD SINCE BECOMING ELECTRIFIED IS BOILING EGGS ON MY HEAD... WHEN NO ONE'S LOOKING...
Tove Jansson

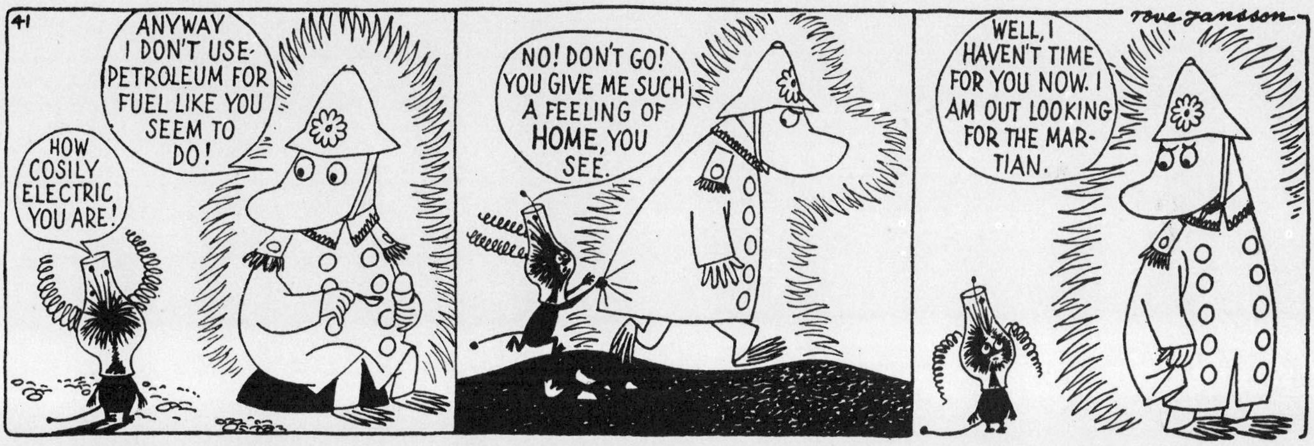
41
HOW COSILY ELECTRIC YOU ARE!
ANYWAY I DON'T USE PETROLEUM FOR FUEL LIKE YOU SEEM TO DO!
NO! DON'T GO! YOU GIVE ME SUCH A FEELING OF HOME, YOU SEE.
Tove Jansson
WELL, I HAVEN'T TIME FOR YOU NOW. I AM OUT LOOKING FOR THE MARTIAN.

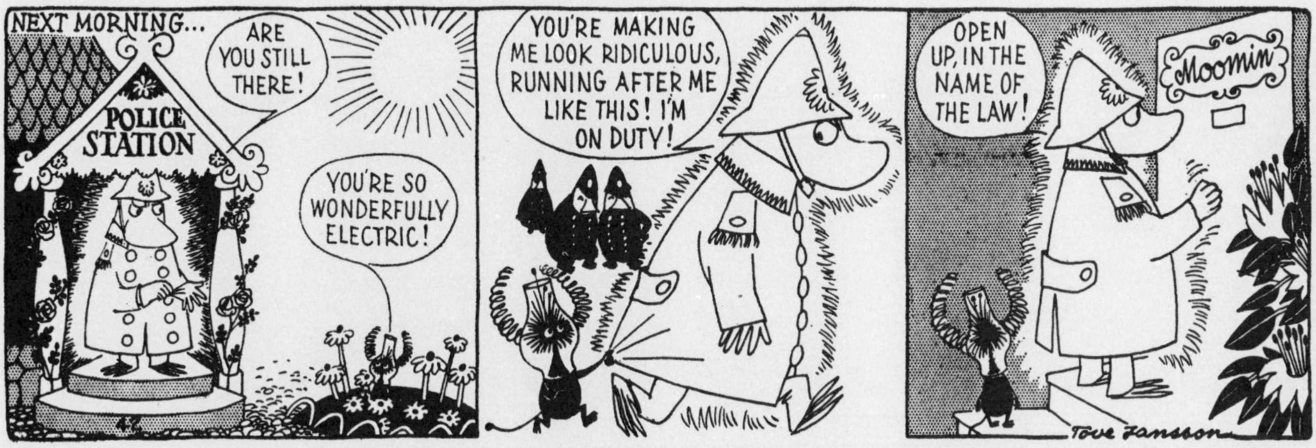
NEXT MORNING...
POLICE STATION
ARE YOU STILL THERE!
YOU'RE SO WONDERFULLY ELECTRIC!
YOU'RE MAKING ME LOOK RIDICULOUS, RUNNING AFTER ME LIKE THIS! I'M ON DUTY!
OPEN UP, IN THE NAME OF THE LAW!
Moomin
Tove Jansson

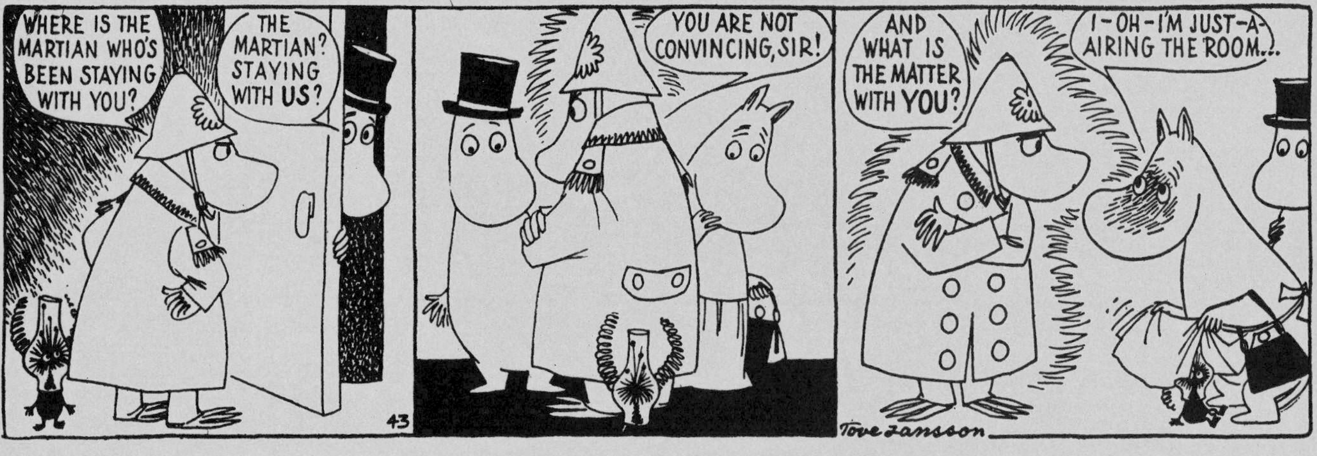
WHERE IS THE MARTIAN WHO'S BEEN STAYING WITH YOU?
THE MARTIAN? STAYING WITH US?
43
YOU ARE NOT CONVINCING, SIR!
AND WHAT IS THE MATTER WITH YOU?
I-OH-I'M JUST-A-AIRING THE ROOM...
Tove Jansson

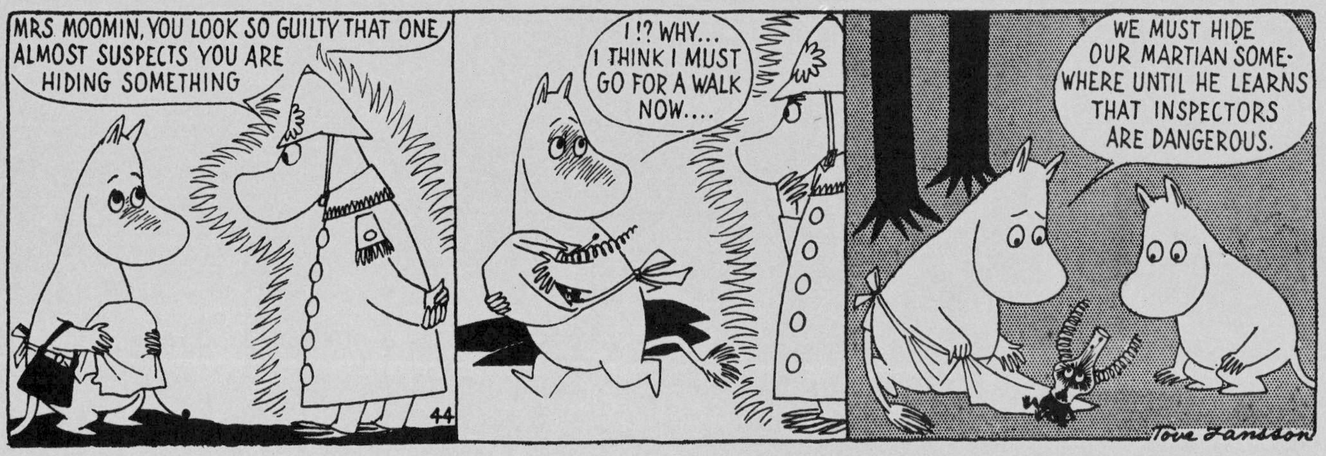
MRS. MOOMIN, YOU LOOK SO GUILTY THAT ONE ALMOST SUSPECTS YOU ARE HIDING SOMETHING
44
I!? WHY... I THINK I MUST GO FOR A WALK NOW....
WE MUST HIDE OUR MARTIAN SOMEWHERE UNTIL HE LEARNS THAT INSPECTORS ARE DANGEROUS.
Tove Jansson

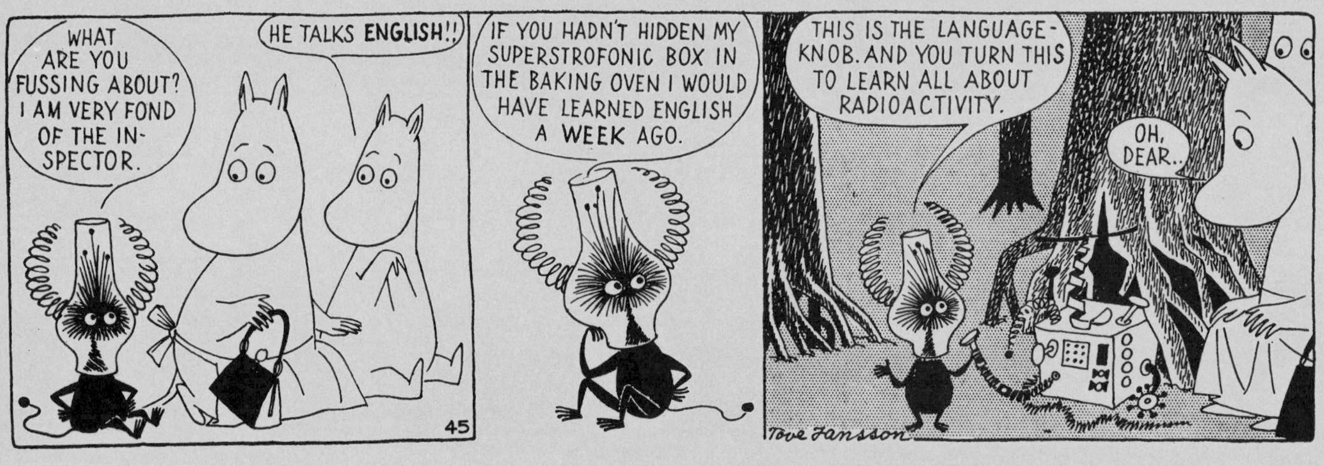
WHAT ARE YOU FUSSING ABOUT? I AM VERY FOND OF THE INSPECTOR.
HE TALKS ENGLISH!!
45
IF YOU HADN'T HIDDEN MY SUPERSTROFONIC BOX IN THE BAKING OVEN I WOULD HAVE LEARNED ENGLISH A WEEK AGO.
THIS IS THE LANGUAGE-KNOB. AND YOU TURN THIS TO LEARN ALL ABOUT RADIOACTIVITY.
OH, DEAR..
Tove Jansson

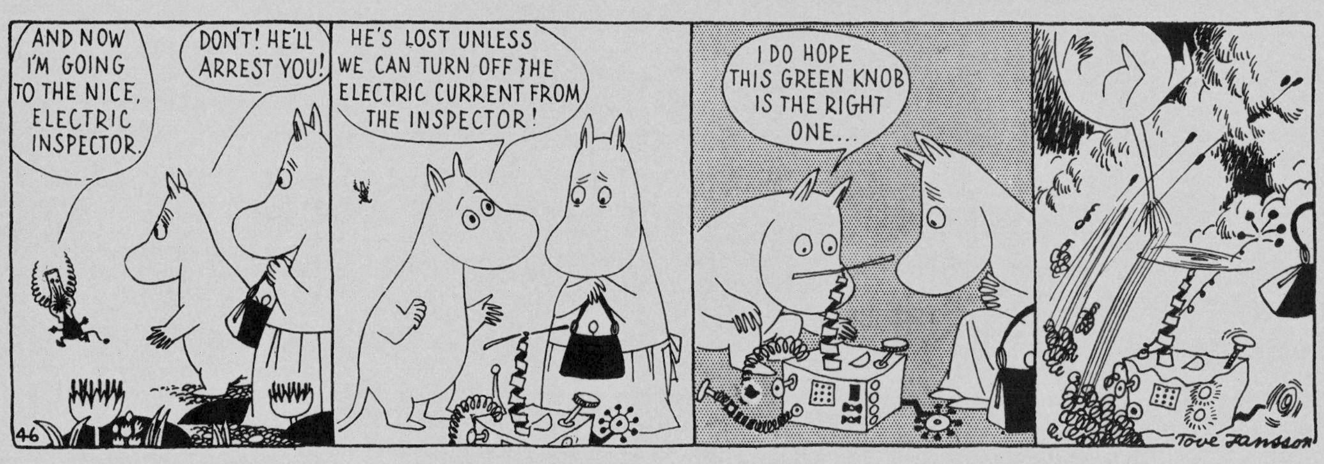
AND NOW I'M GOING TO THE NICE, ELECTRIC INSPECTOR.
DON'T! HE'LL ARREST YOU!
46
HE'S LOST UNLESS WE CAN TURN OFF THE ELECTRIC CURRENT FROM THE INSPECTOR!
I DO HOPE THIS GREEN KNOB IS THE RIGHT ONE...
Tove Jansson

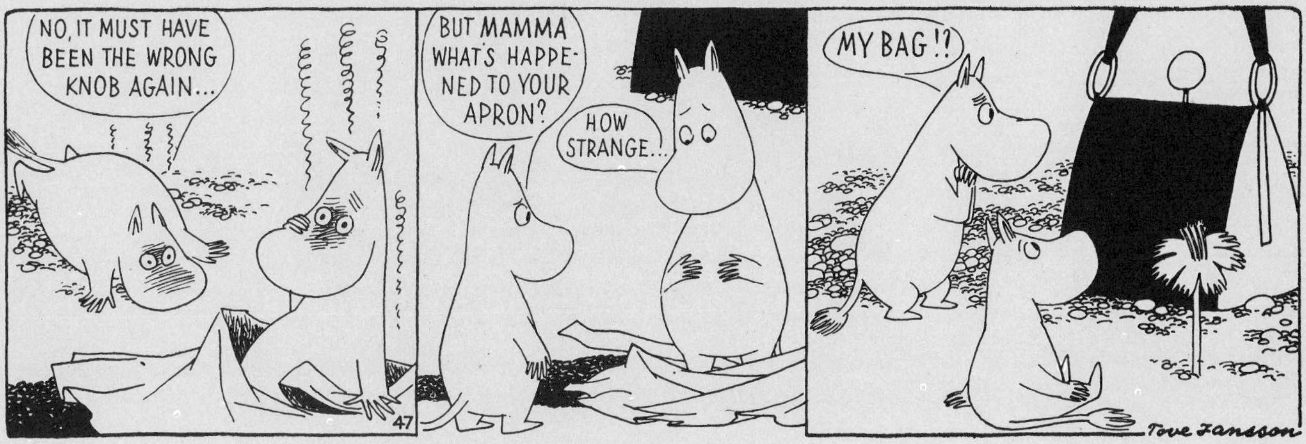
NO, IT MUST HAVE BEEN THE WRONG KNOB AGAIN...
47
BUT MAMMA WHAT'S HAPPENED TO YOUR APRON?
HOW STRANGE...
MY BAG!?
Tove Jansson

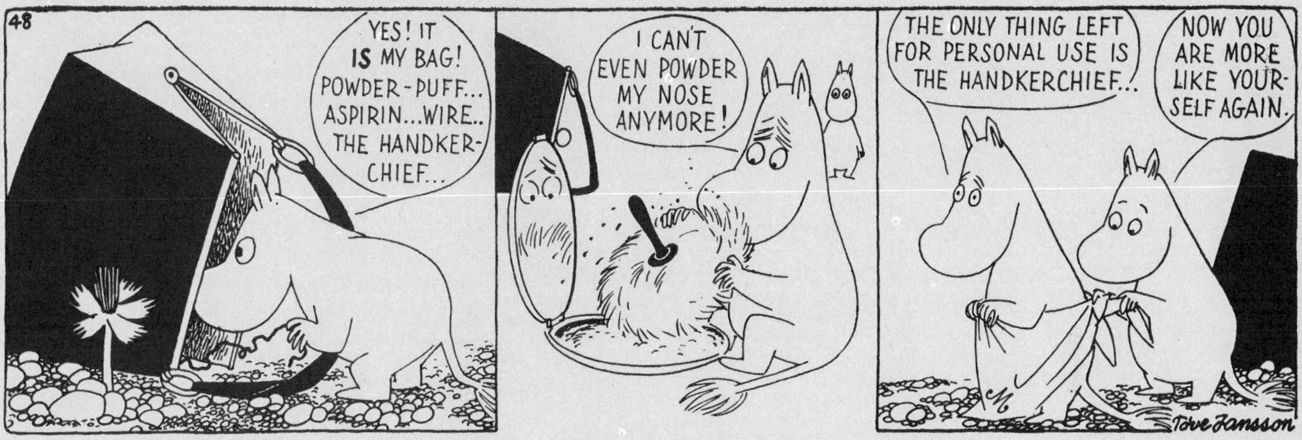
48
YES! IT IS MY BAG! POWDER-PUFF... ASPIRIN...WIRE.. THE HANDKERCHIEF...
I CAN'T EVEN POWDER MY NOSE ANYMORE!
THE ONLY THING LEFT FOR PERSONAL USE IS THE HANDKERCHIEF...
NOW YOU ARE MORE LIKE YOURSELF AGAIN.
Tove Jansson

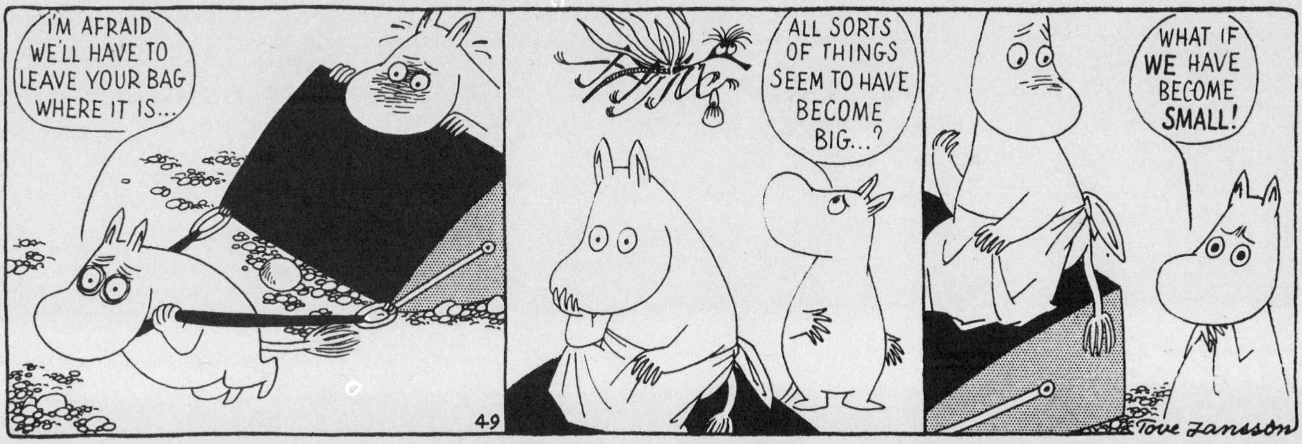
I'M AFRAID WE'LL HAVE TO LEAVE YOUR BAG WHERE IT IS...
49
ALL SORTS OF THINGS SEEM TO HAVE BECOME BIG...?
WHAT IF WE HAVE BECOME SMALL!
Tove Jansson

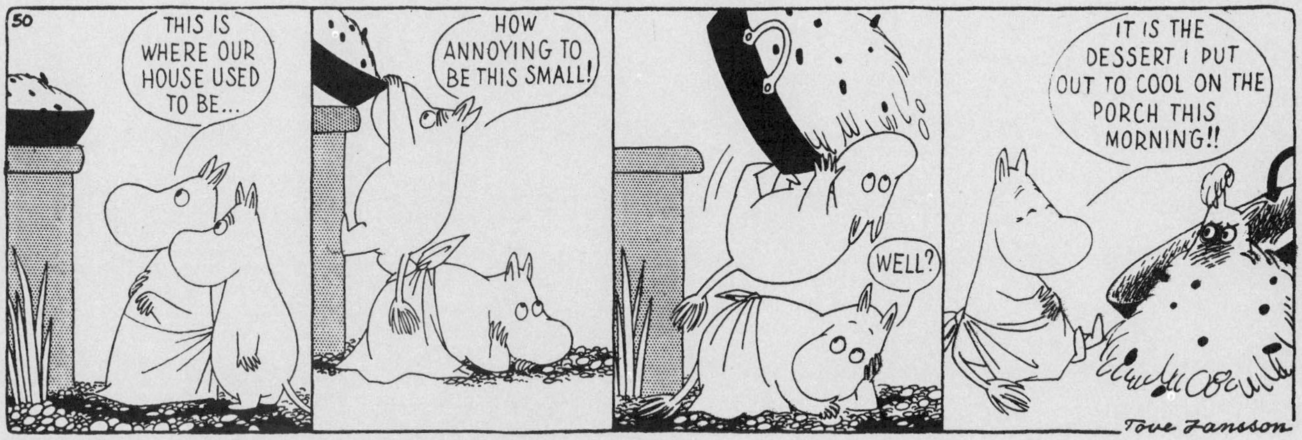
50
THIS IS WHERE OUR HOUSE USED TO BE...
HOW ANNOYING TO BE THIS SMALL!
WELL?
IT IS THE DESSERT I PUT OUT TO COOL ON THE PORCH THIS MORNING!!
Tove Jansson

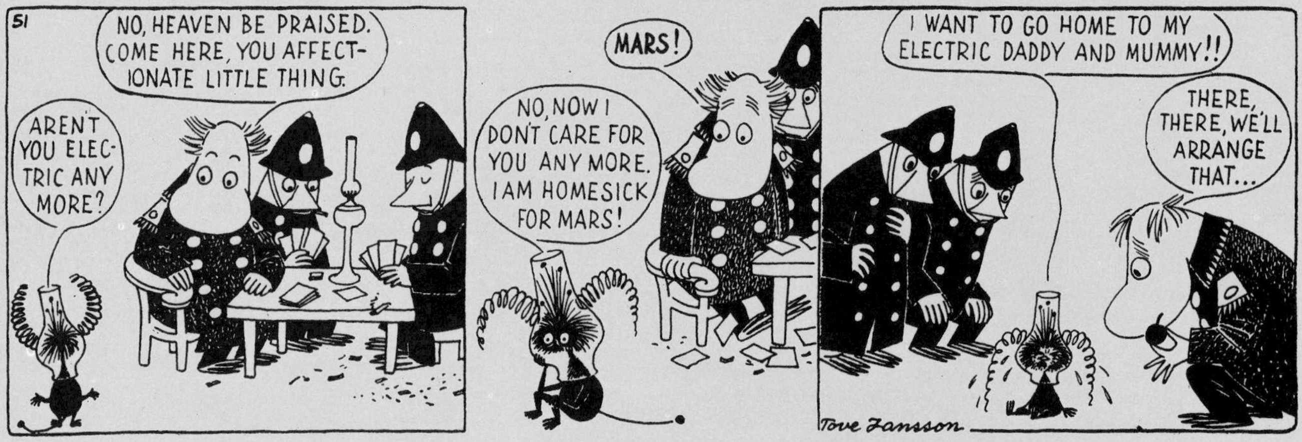
51
AREN'T YOU ELECTRIC ANY MORE?
NO, HEAVEN BE PRAISED. COME HERE, YOU AFFECTIONATE LITTLE THING.
NO, NOW I DON'T CARE FOR YOU ANY MORE. I AM HOMESICK FOR MARS!
MARS!
I WANT TO GO HOME TO MY ELECTRIC DADDY AND MUMMY!!
THERE, THERE, WE'LL ARRANGE THAT...
Tove Jansson

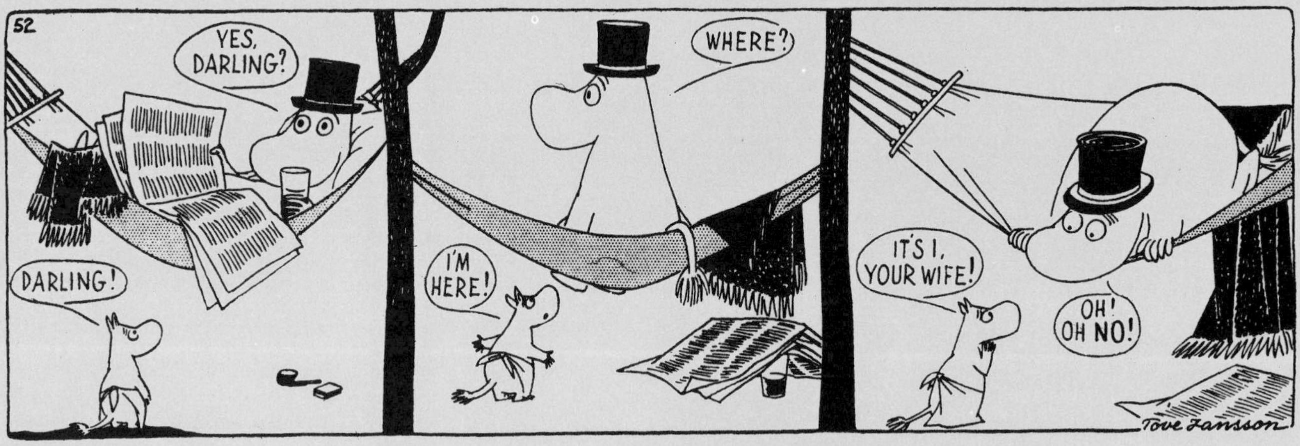
52
DARLING!
YES, DARLING?
I'M HERE!
WHERE?
IT'S I, YOUR WIFE!
OH! OH NO!
Tove Jansson

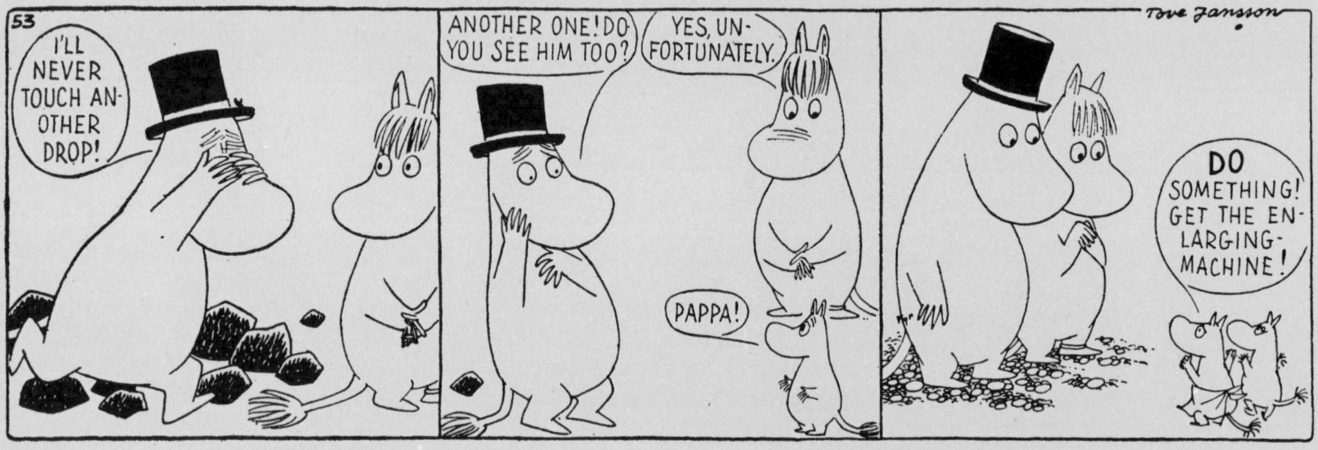
53
I'LL NEVER TOUCH ANOTHER DROP!
ANOTHER ONE! DO YOU SEE HIM TOO?
YES, UNFORTUNATELY.
PAPPA!
Tove Jansson
DO SOMETHING! GET THE ENLARGING-MACHINE!

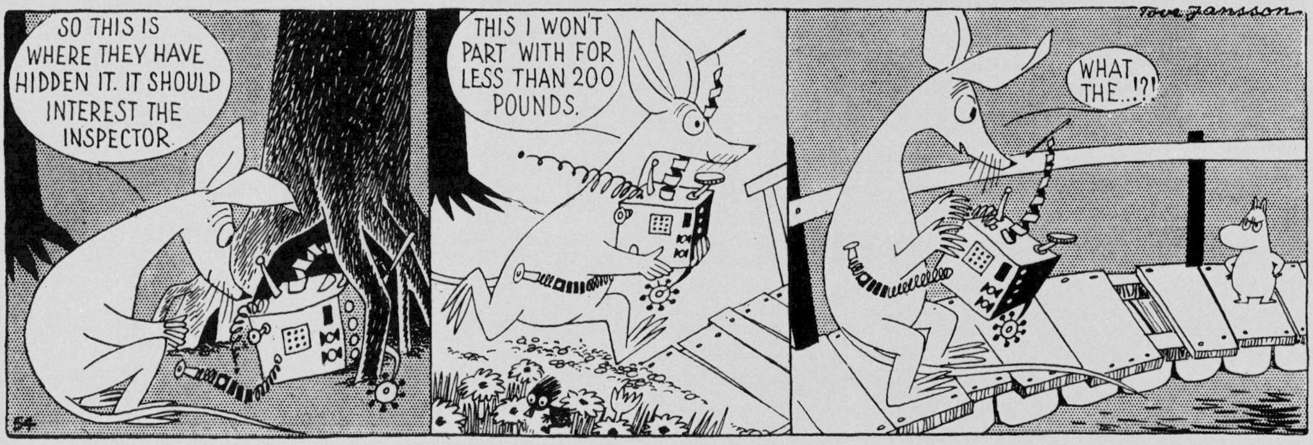
SO THIS IS WHERE THEY HAVE HIDDEN IT. IT SHOULD INTEREST THE INSPECTOR.
54
THIS I WON'T PART WITH FOR LESS THAN 200 POUNDS.
Tove Jansson
WHAT THE..!?!

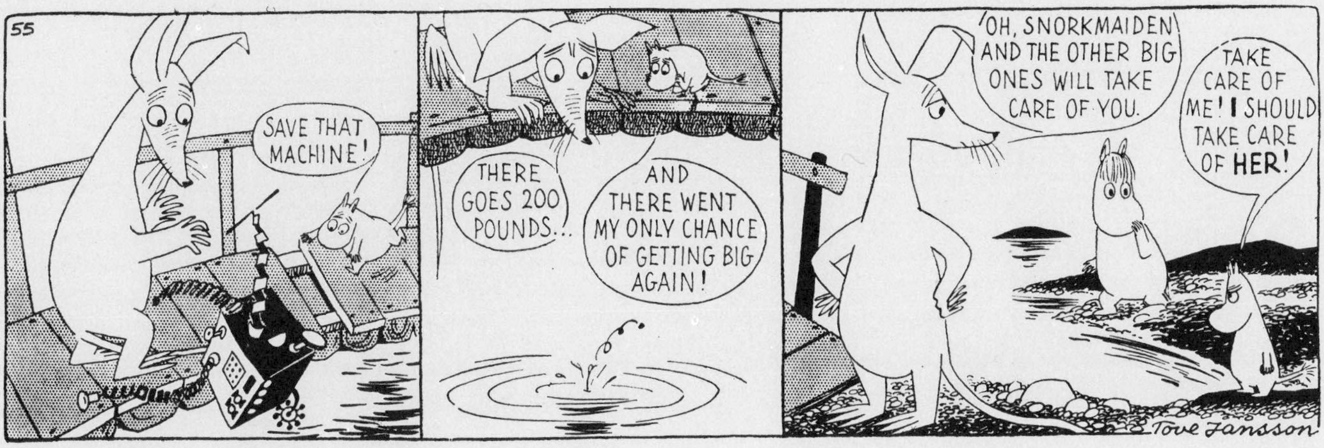
55
SAVE THAT MACHINE!
THERE GOES 200 POUNDS...
AND THERE WENT MY ONLY CHANCE OF GETTING BIG AGAIN!
OH, SNORKMAIDEN AND THE OTHER BIG ONES WILL TAKE CARE OF YOU.
TAKE CARE OF ME! I SHOULD TAKE CARE OF HER!
Tove Jansson

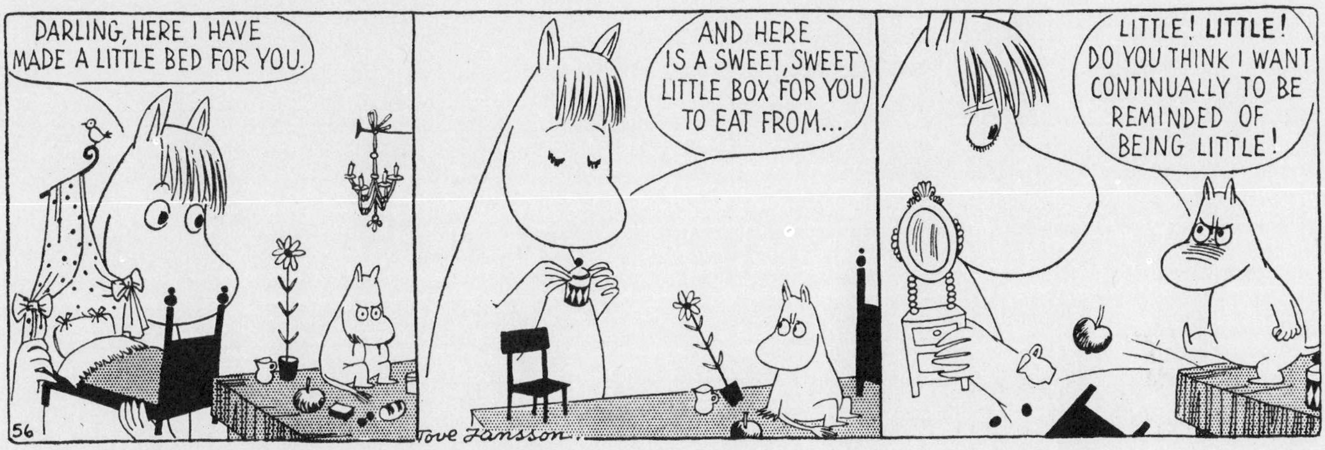
DARLING, HERE I HAVE MADE A LITTLE BED FOR YOU.
56
AND HERE IS A SWEET, SWEET LITTLE BOX FOR YOU TO EAT FROM...
Tove Jansson
LITTLE! LITTLE! DO YOU THINK I WANT CONTINUALLY TO BE REMINDED OF BEING LITTLE!

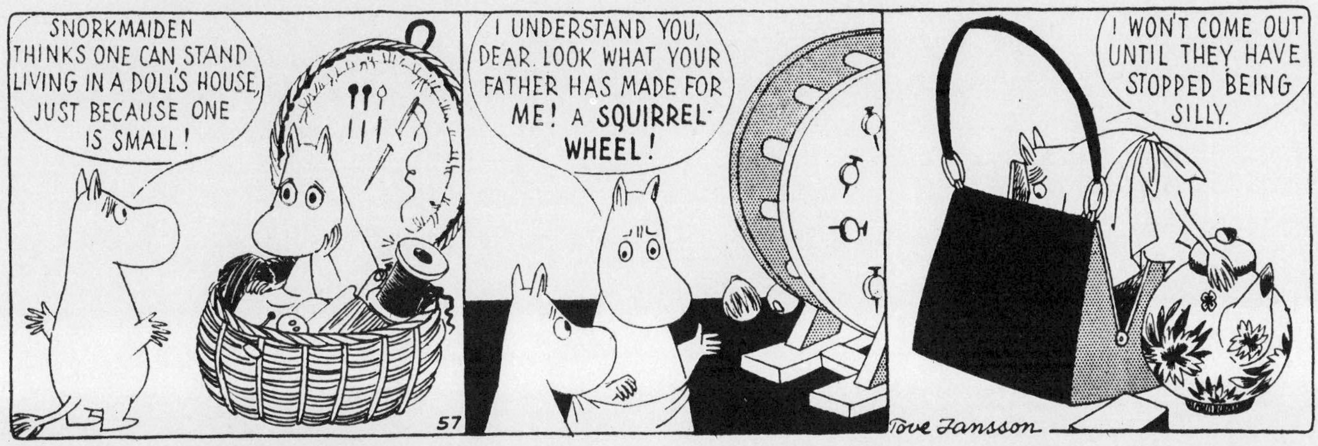
SNORKMAIDEN THINKS ONE CAN STAND LIVING IN A DOLL'S HOUSE, JUST BECAUSE ONE IS SMALL!
57
I UNDERSTAND YOU, DEAR. LOOK WHAT YOUR FATHER HAS MADE FOR ME! A SQUIRREL-WHEEL!
I WON'T COME OUT UNTIL THEY HAVE STOPPED BEING SILLY.
Tove Jansson

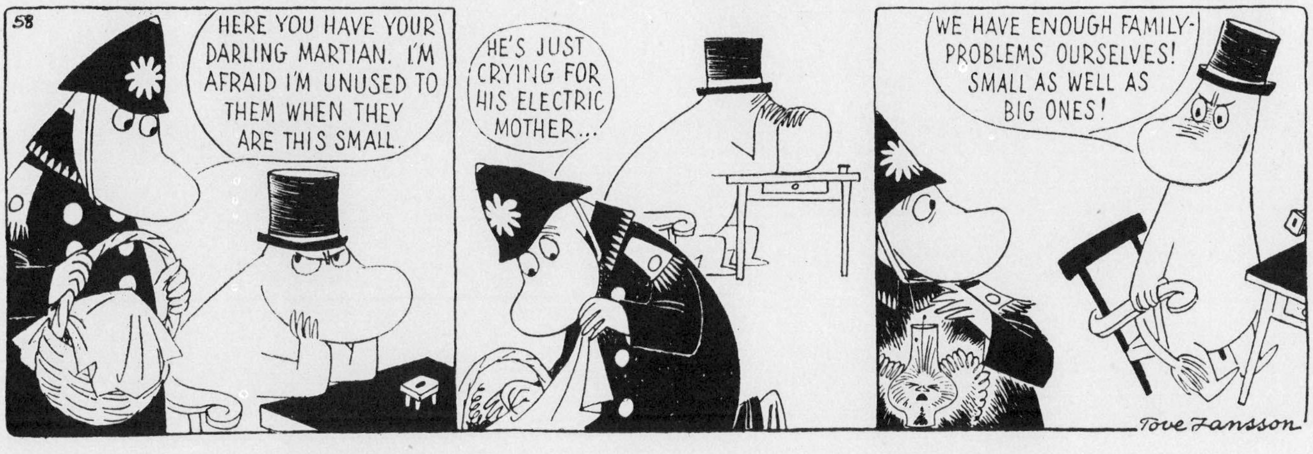
58
HERE YOU HAVE YOUR DARLING MARTIAN. I'M AFRAID I'M UNUSED TO THEM WHEN THEY ARE THIS SMALL.
HE'S JUST CRYING FOR HIS ELECTRIC MOTHER...
WE HAVE ENOUGH FAMILY-PROBLEMS OURSELVES! SMALL AS WELL AS BIG ONES!
Tove Jansson

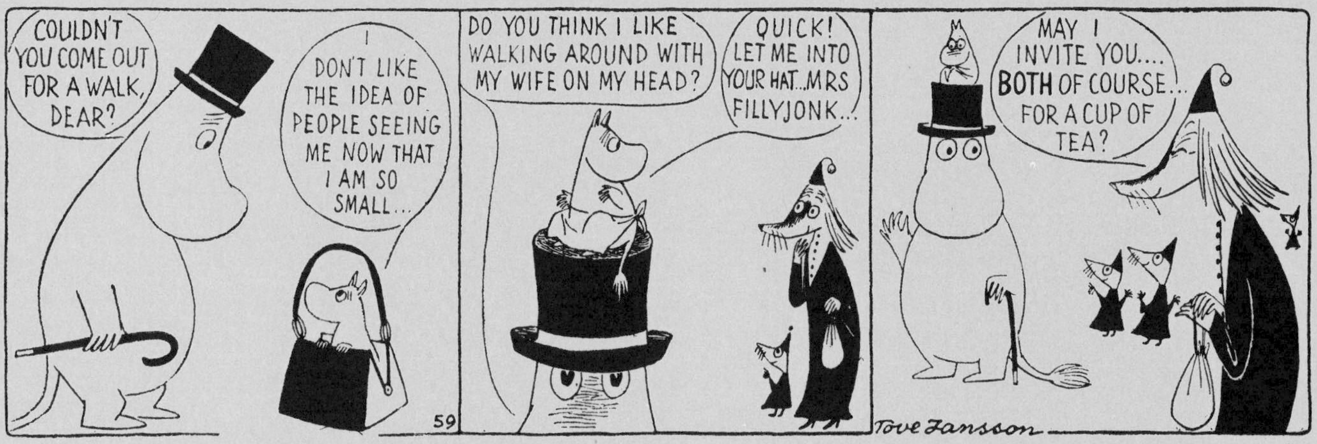
COULDN'T YOU COME OUT FOR A WALK, DEAR?
I DON'T LIKE THE IDEA OF PEOPLE SEEING ME NOW THAT I AM SO SMALL...
59
DO YOU THINK I LIKE WALKING AROUND WITH MY WIFE ON MY HEAD?
QUICK! LET ME INTO YOUR HAT...MRS FILLYJONK...
MAY I INVITE YOU.... **BOTH** OF COURSE... FOR A CUP OF TEA?
Tove Jansson

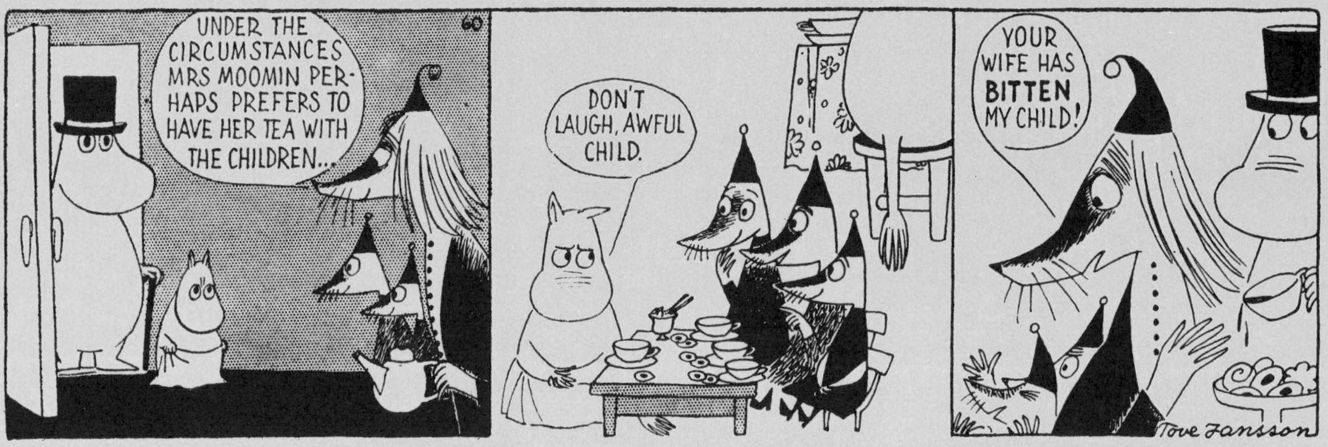
60
UNDER THE CIRCUMSTANCES MRS MOOMIN PER-HAPS PREFERS TO HAVE HER TEA WITH THE CHILDREN...
DON'T LAUGH, AWFUL CHILD.
YOUR WIFE HAS **BITTEN** MY CHILD!
Tove Jansson

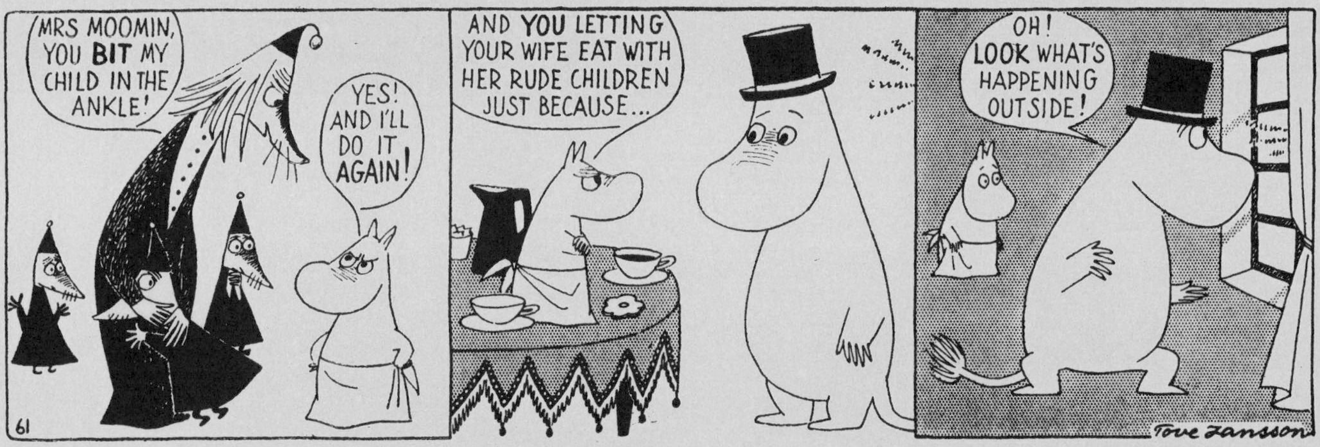
MRS MOOMIN, YOU **BIT** MY CHILD IN THE ANKLE!
YES! AND I'LL DO IT **AGAIN**!
61
AND **YOU** LETTING YOUR WIFE EAT WITH HER RUDE CHILDREN JUST BECAUSE...
OH! **LOOK** WHAT'S HAPPENING OUTSIDE!
Tove Jansson

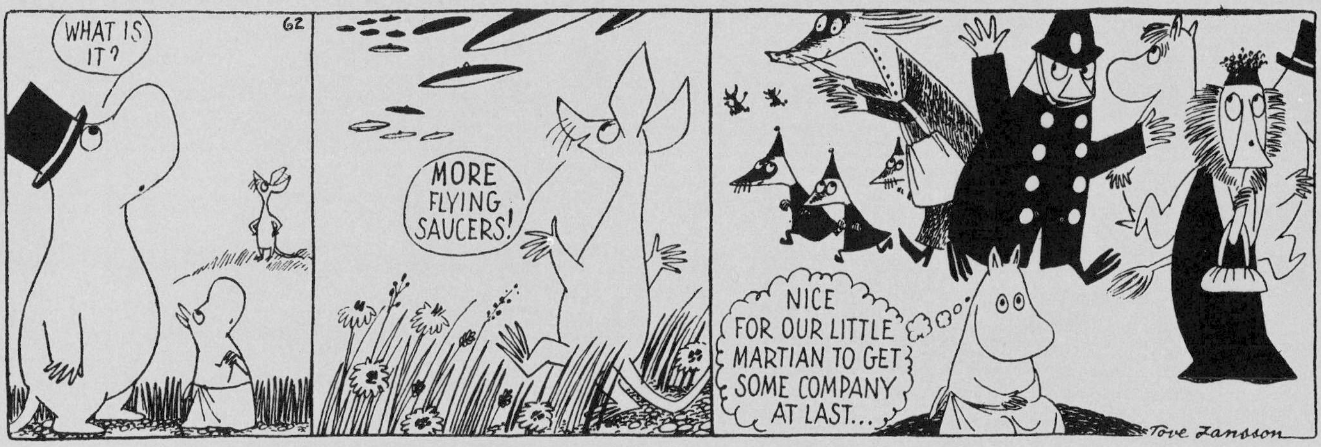
WHAT IS IT?
62
MORE FLYING SAUCERS!
NICE FOR OUR LITTLE MARTIAN TO GET SOME COMPANY AT LAST...
Tove Jansson

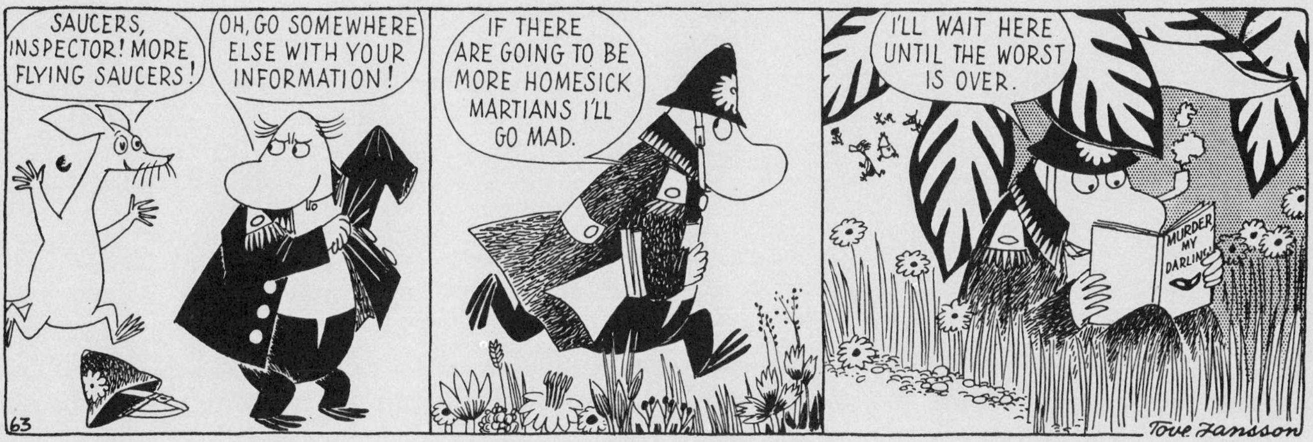
SAUCERS, INSPECTOR! MORE FLYING SAUCERS!
OH, GO SOMEWHERE ELSE WITH YOUR INFORMATION!
IF THERE ARE GOING TO BE MORE HOMESICK MARTIANS I'LL GO MAD.
I'LL WAIT HERE UNTIL THE WORST IS OVER.
MURDER MY DARLING
63
Tove Jansson

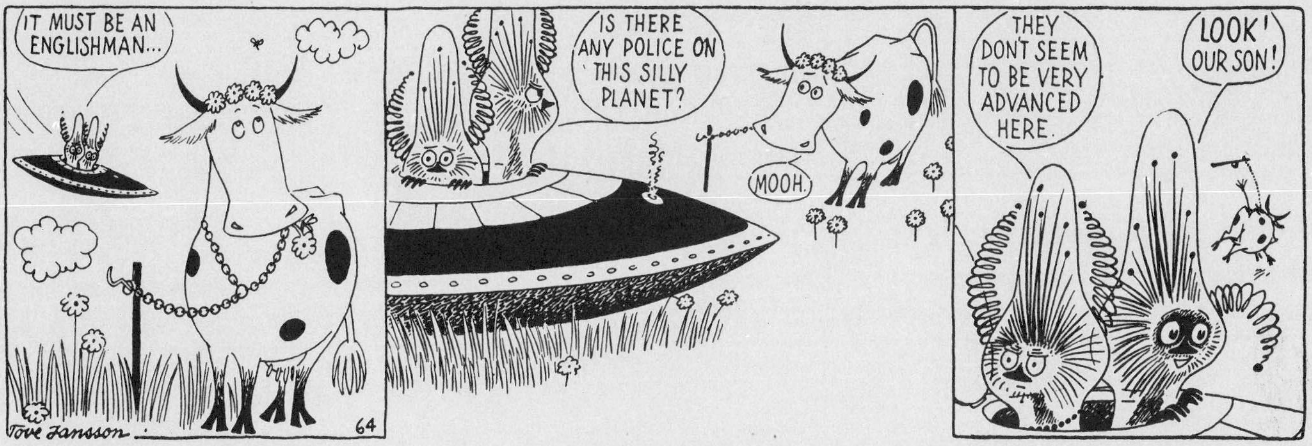
IT MUST BE AN ENGLISHMAN...
Tove Jansson
64
IS THERE ANY POLICE ON THIS SILLY PLANET?
MOOH.
THEY DON'T SEEM TO BE VERY ADVANCED HERE.
LOOK! OUR SON!

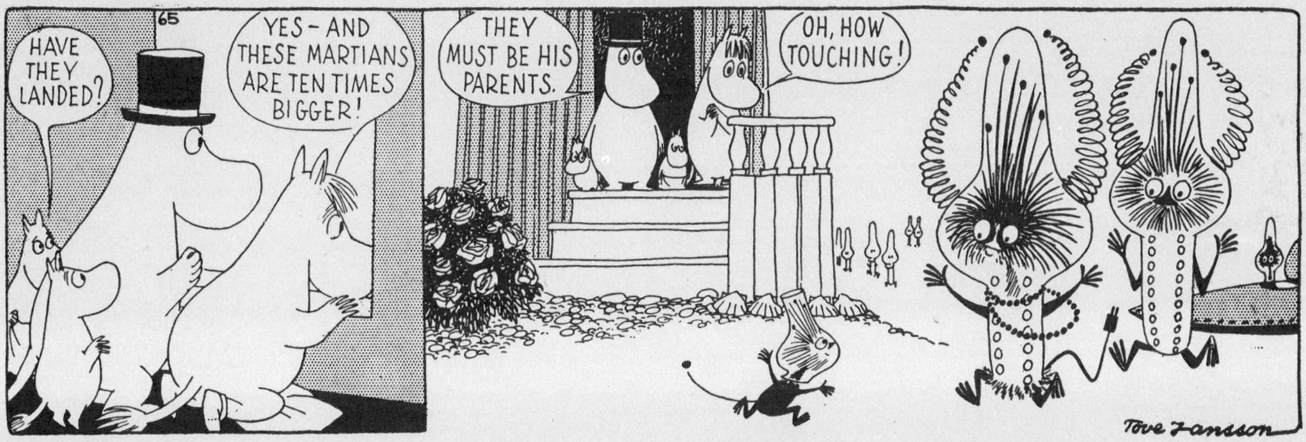
65
HAVE THEY LANDED?
YES - AND THESE MARTIANS ARE TEN TIMES BIGGER!
THEY MUST BE HIS PARENTS.
OH, HOW TOUCHING!
Tove Jansson

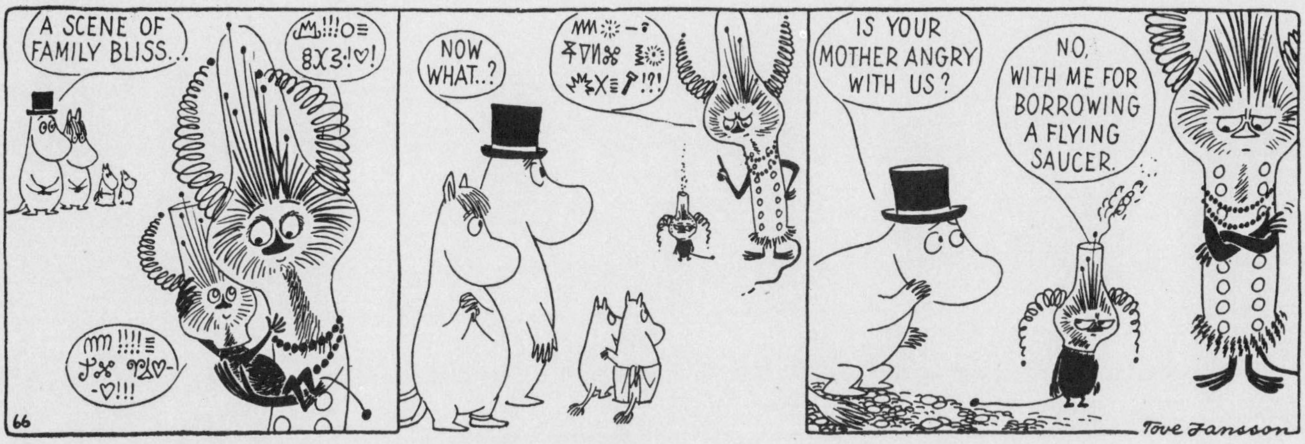
A SCENE OF FAMILY BLISS...
66
NOW WHAT..?
IS YOUR MOTHER ANGRY WITH US?
NO, WITH ME FOR BORROWING A FLYING SAUCER.
Tove Jansson

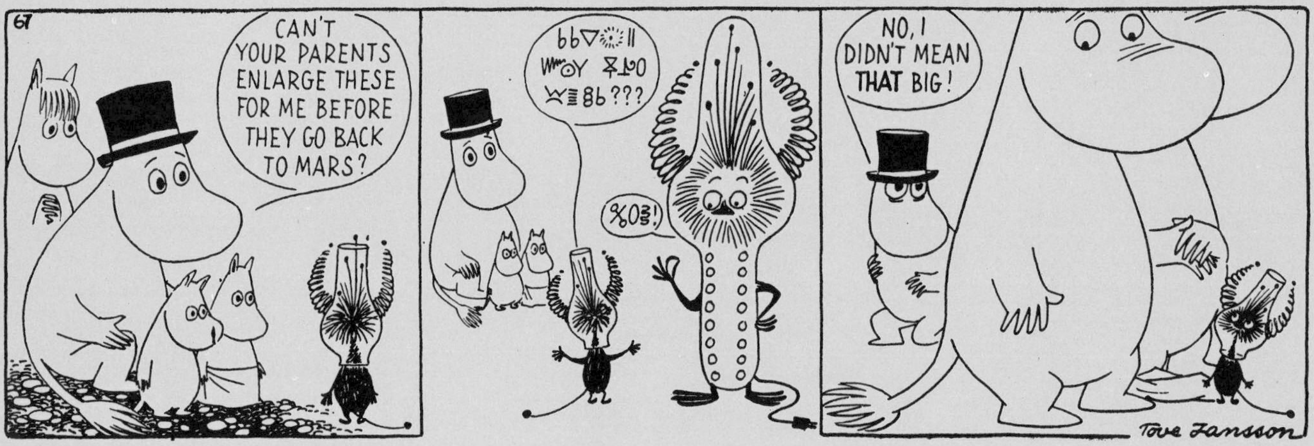
67
CAN'T YOUR PARENTS ENLARGE THESE FOR ME BEFORE THEY GO BACK TO MARS?
NO, I DIDN'T MEAN THAT BIG!
Tove Jansson

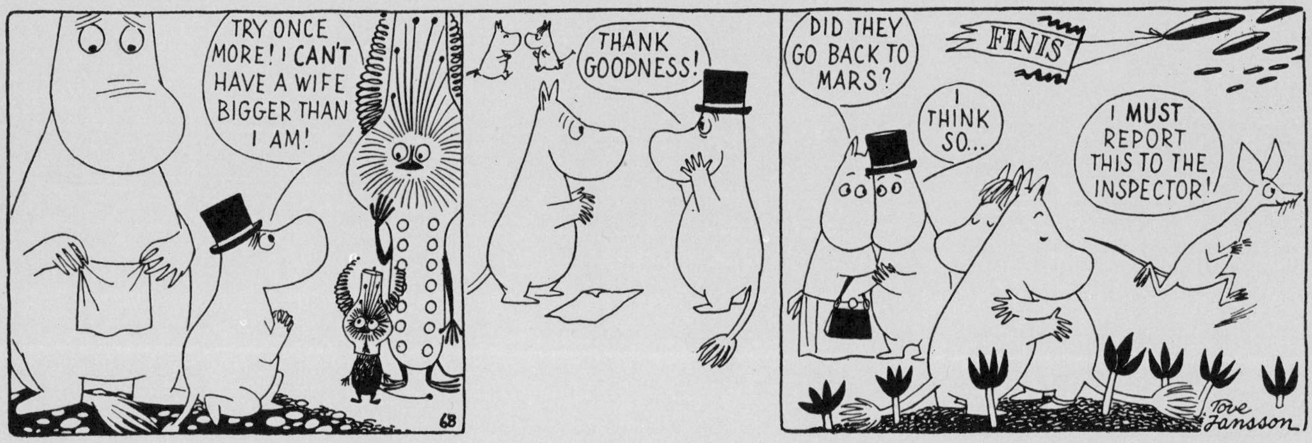
TRY ONCE MORE! I CAN'T HAVE A WIFE BIGGER THAN I AM!
68
THANK GOODNESS!
DID THEY GO BACK TO MARS?
FINIS
I THINK SO...
I MUST REPORT THIS TO THE INSPECTOR!
Tove Jansson

12. Moomin and the Sea

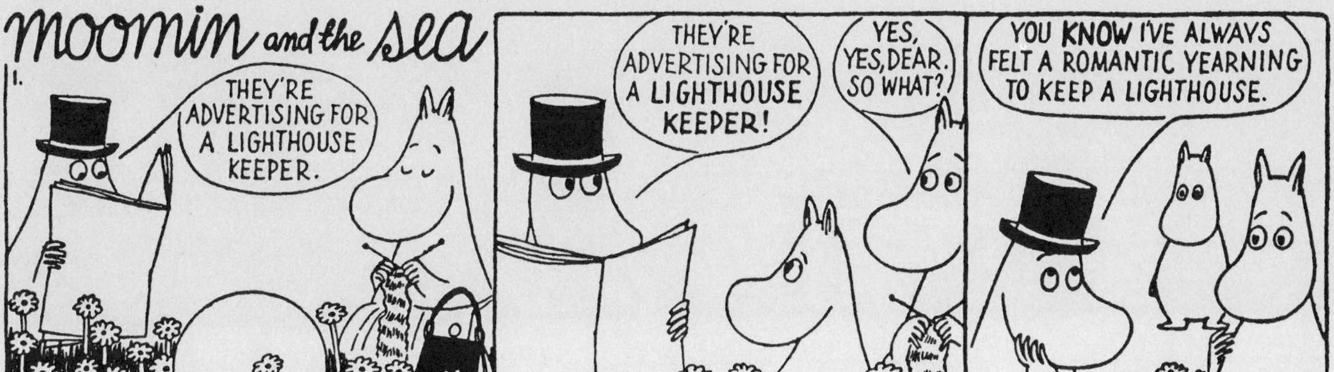
moomin and the sea
1.
THEY'RE ADVERTISING FOR A LIGHTHOUSE KEEPER.
THEY'RE ADVERTISING FOR A LIGHTHOUSE KEEPER!
YES, YES, DEAR. SO WHAT?
Tove Jansson
YOU KNOW I'VE ALWAYS FELT A ROMANTIC YEARNING TO KEEP A LIGHTHOUSE.

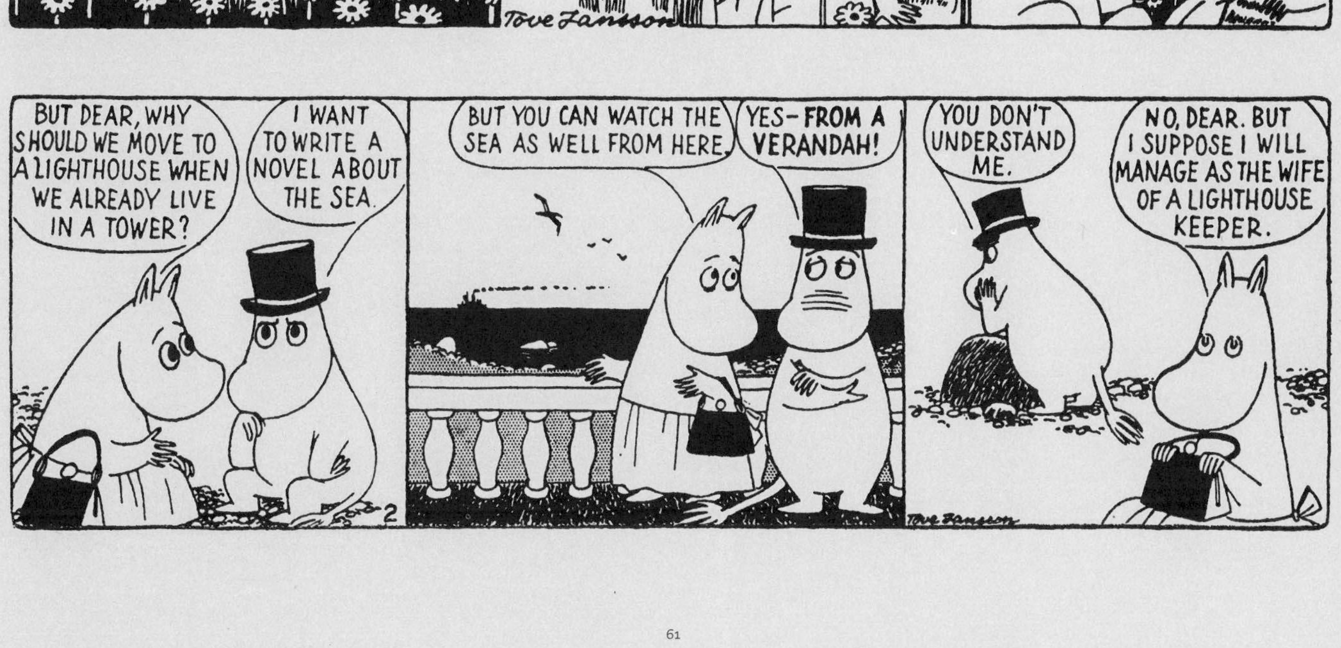
BUT DEAR, WHY SHOULD WE MOVE TO A LIGHTHOUSE WHEN WE ALREADY LIVE IN A TOWER?
I WANT TO WRITE A NOVEL ABOUT THE SEA.
2
BUT YOU CAN WATCH THE SEA AS WELL FROM HERE.
YES- FROM A VERANDAH!
YOU DON'T UNDERSTAND ME.
NO, DEAR. BUT I SUPPOSE I WILL MANAGE AS THE WIFE OF A LIGHTHOUSE KEEPER.
Tove Jansson

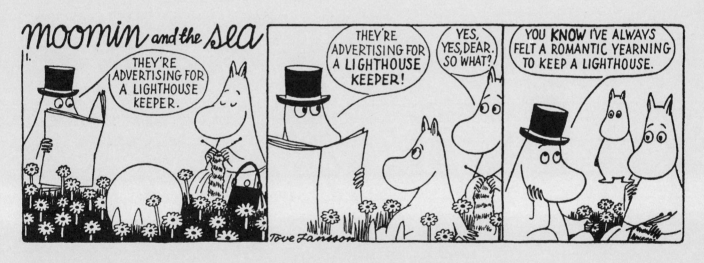

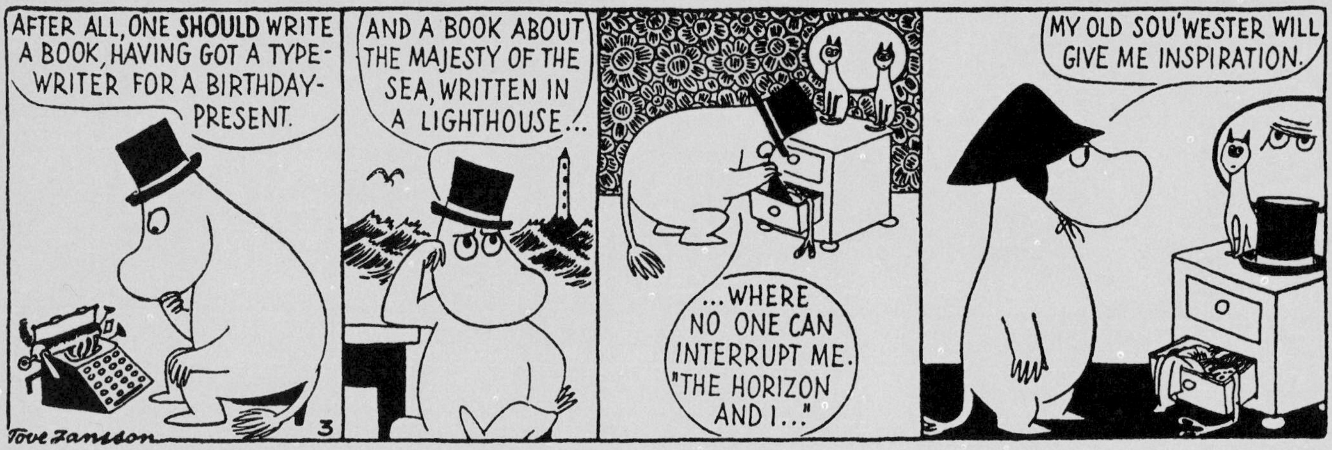
AFTER ALL, ONE SHOULD WRITE A BOOK, HAVING GOT A TYPE-WRITER FOR A BIRTHDAY-PRESENT.
AND A BOOK ABOUT THE MAJESTY OF THE SEA, WRITTEN IN A LIGHTHOUSE...
...WHERE NO ONE CAN INTERRUPT ME. "THE HORIZON AND I..."
MY OLD SOU'WESTER WILL GIVE ME INSPIRATION.
Tove Jansson

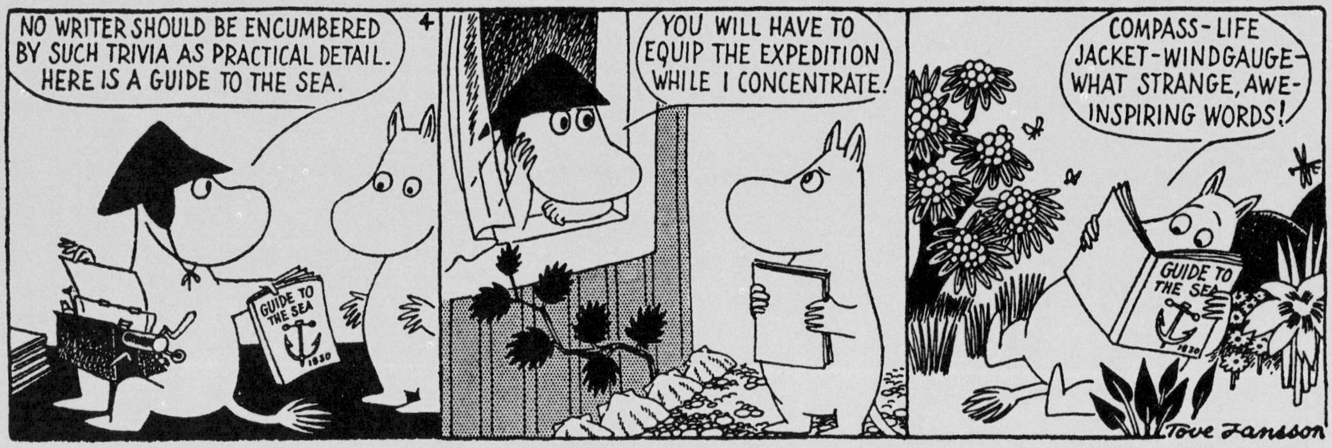
NO WRITER SHOULD BE ENCUMBERED BY SUCH TRIVIA AS PRACTICAL DETAIL. HERE IS A GUIDE TO THE SEA.
GUIDE TO THE SEA
1930
YOU WILL HAVE TO EQUIP THE EXPEDITION WHILE I CONCENTRATE.
COMPASS-LIFE JACKET-WINDGAUGE-WHAT STRANGE, AWE-INSPIRING WORDS!
GUIDE TO THE SEA
Tove Jansson

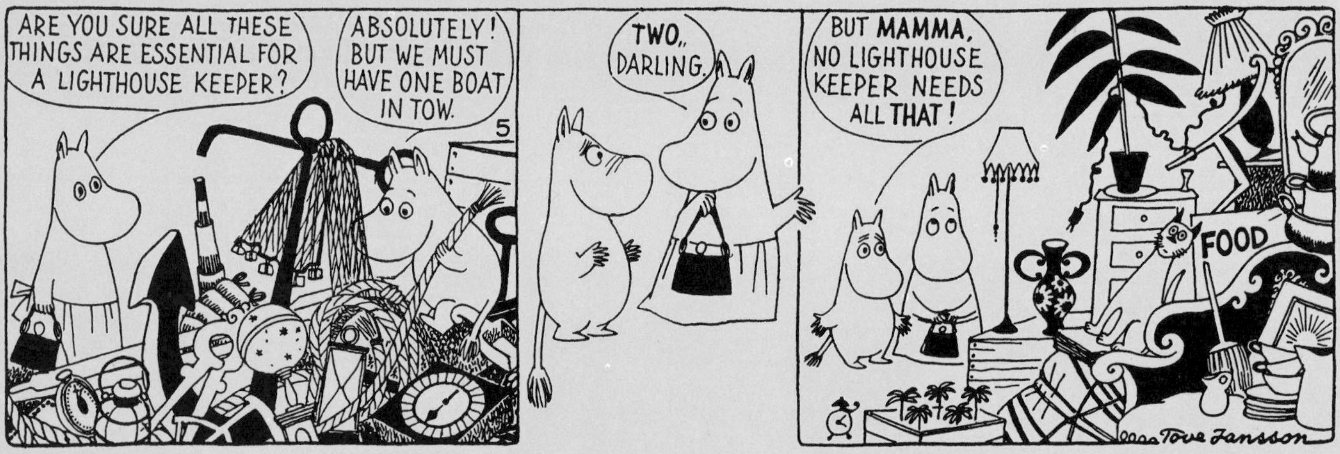
ARE YOU SURE ALL THESE THINGS ARE ESSENTIAL FOR A LIGHTHOUSE KEEPER?
ABSOLUTELY! BUT WE MUST HAVE ONE BOAT IN TOW.
TWO, DARLING.
BUT MAMMA, NO LIGHTHOUSE KEEPER NEEDS ALL THAT!
FOOD
Tove Jansson

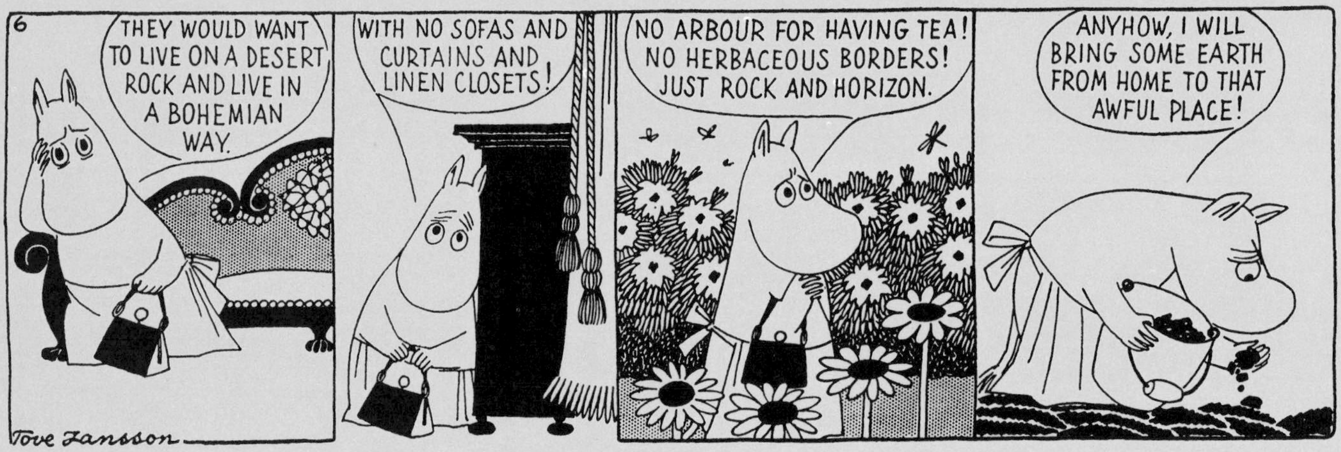
THEY WOULD WANT TO LIVE ON A DESERT ROCK AND LIVE IN A BOHEMIAN WAY.
WITH NO SOFAS AND CURTAINS AND LINEN CLOSETS!
NO ARBOUR FOR HAVING TEA! NO HERBACEOUS BORDERS! JUST ROCK AND HORIZON.
ANYHOW, I WILL BRING SOME EARTH FROM HOME TO THAT AWFUL PLACE!
Tove Jansson

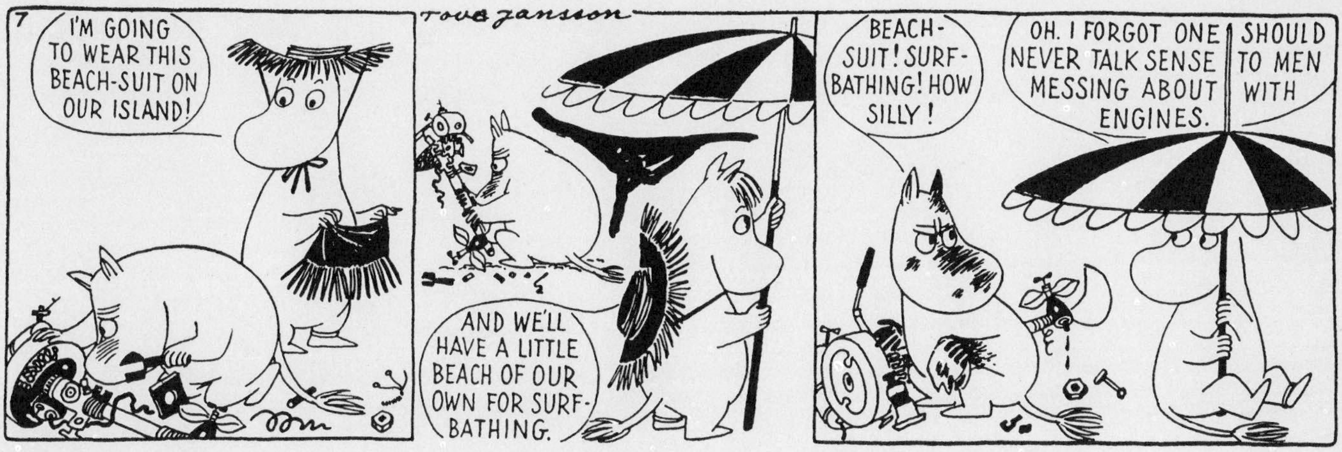
7
I'M GOING TO WEAR THIS BEACH-SUIT ON OUR ISLAND!
Tove Jansson
AND WE'LL HAVE A LITTLE BEACH OF OUR OWN FOR SURF-BATHING.
BEACH-SUIT! SURF-BATHING! HOW SILLY!
OH. I FORGOT ONE SHOULD NEVER TALK SENSE TO MEN MESSING ABOUT WITH ENGINES.

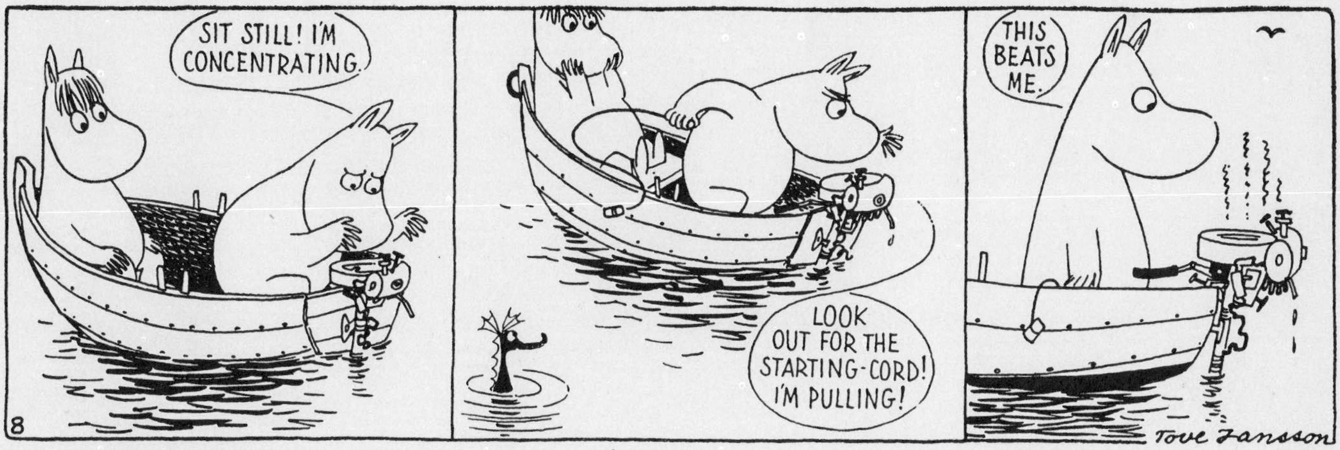
8
SIT STILL! I'M CONCENTRATING.
LOOK OUT FOR THE STARTING-CORD! I'M PULLING!
THIS BEATS ME.
Tove Jansson

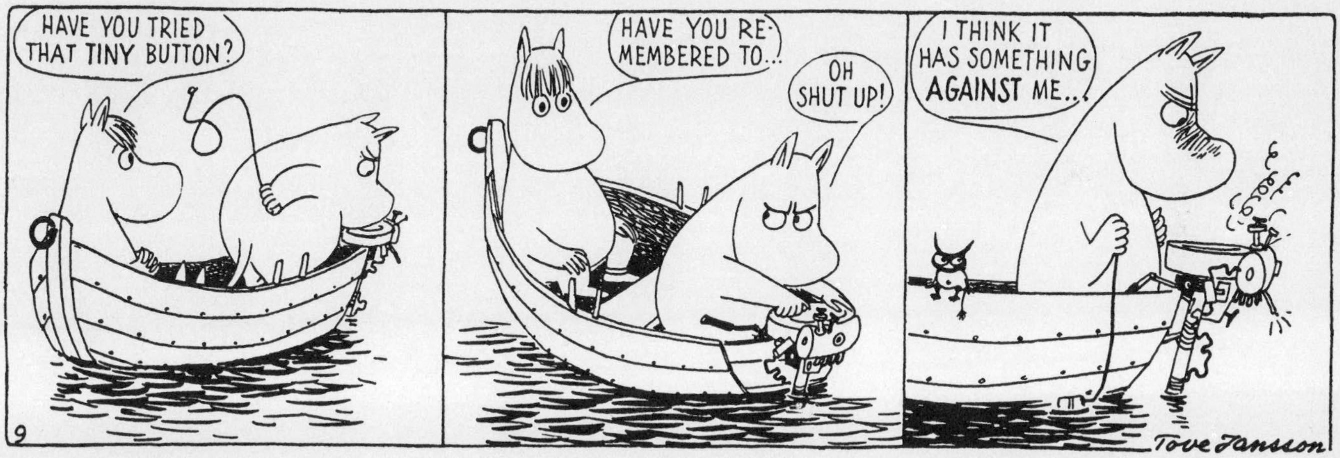
9
HAVE YOU TRIED THAT TINY BUTTON?
HAVE YOU RE-MEMBERED TO...
OH SHUT UP!
I THINK IT HAS SOMETHING AGAINST ME...
Tove Jansson

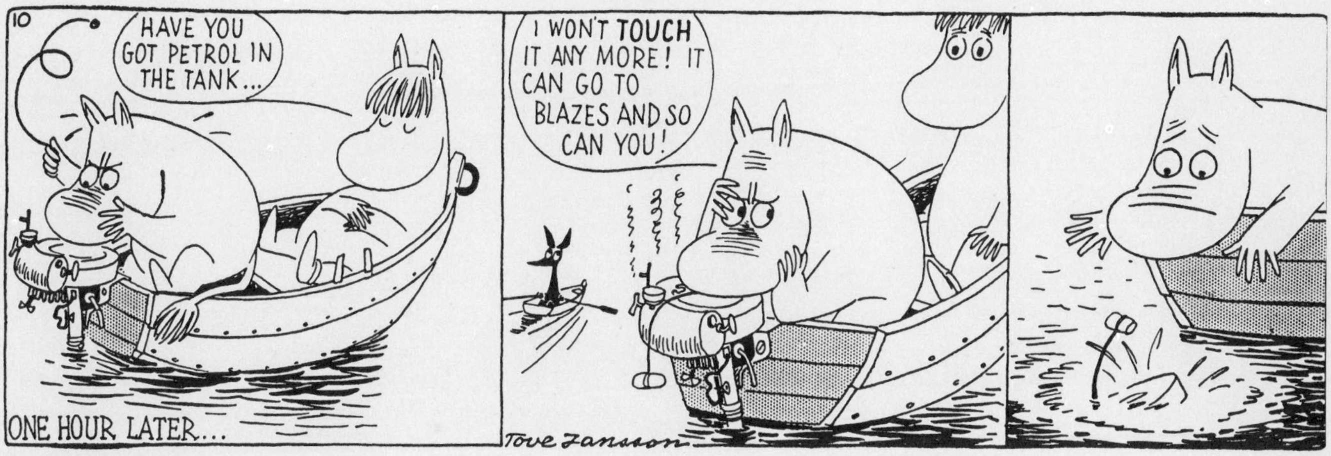
10
HAVE YOU GOT PETROL IN THE TANK...
ONE HOUR LATER...
I WON'T TOUCH IT ANY MORE! IT CAN GO TO BLAZES AND SO CAN YOU!
Tove Jansson

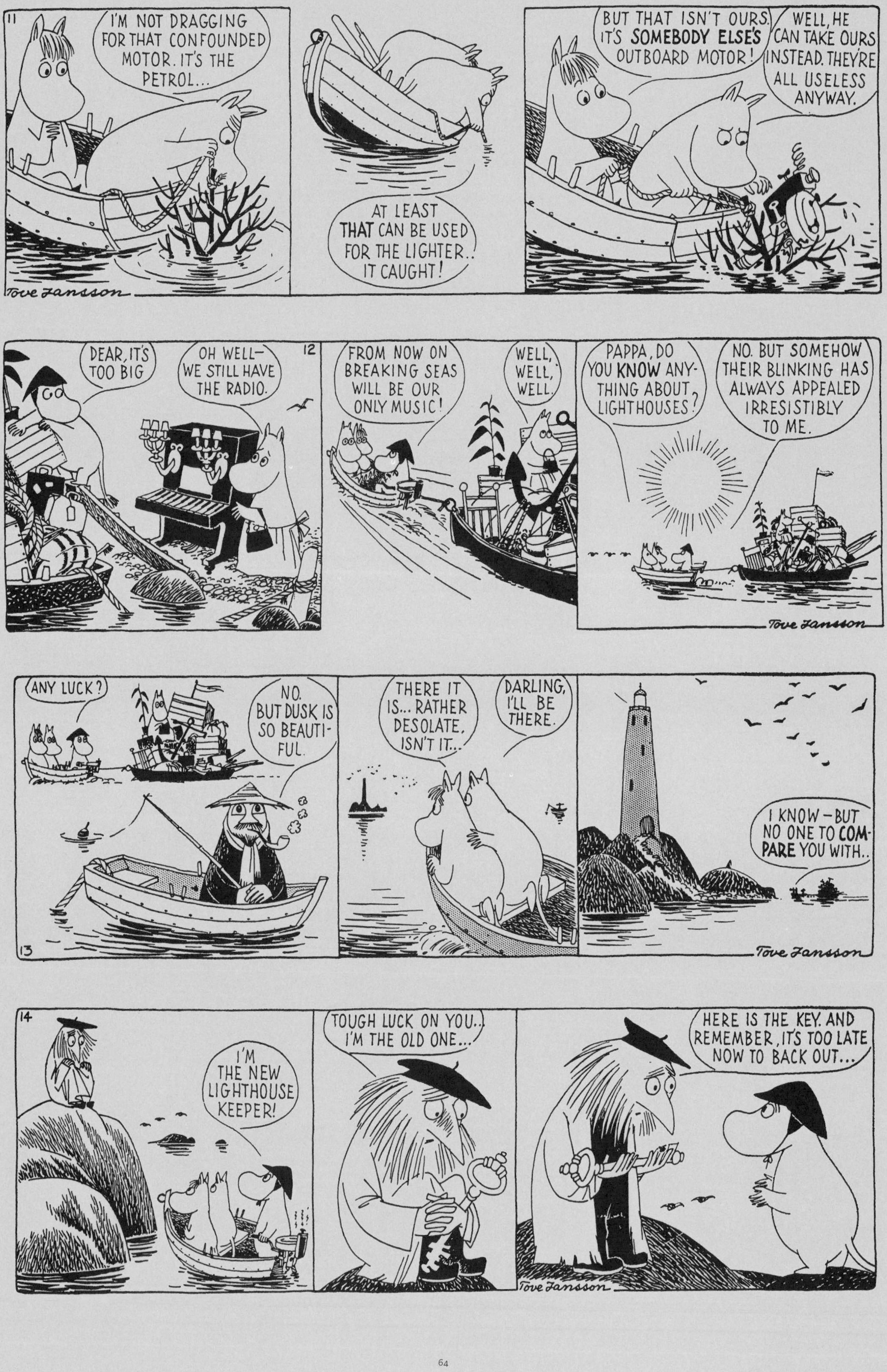
11
I'M NOT DRAGGING FOR THAT CONFOUNDED MOTOR. IT'S THE PETROL...
AT LEAST **THAT** CAN BE USED FOR THE LIGHTER.. IT CAUGHT!
BUT THAT ISN'T OURS. IT'S **SOMEBODY ELSE'S** OUTBOARD MOTOR!
WELL, HE CAN TAKE OURS INSTEAD. THEY'RE ALL USELESS ANYWAY.
Tove Jansson
12
DEAR, IT'S TOO BIG
OH WELL— WE STILL HAVE THE RADIO.
FROM NOW ON BREAKING SEAS WILL BE OUR ONLY MUSIC!
WELL, WELL, WELL.
PAPPA, DO YOU **KNOW** ANYTHING ABOUT LIGHTHOUSES?
NO. BUT SOMEHOW THEIR BLINKING HAS ALWAYS APPEALED IRRESISTIBLY TO ME.
Tove Jansson
13
ANY LUCK?
NO. BUT DUSK IS SO BEAUTIFUL.
THERE IT IS... RATHER DESOLATE, ISN'T IT...
DARLING, I'LL BE THERE.
I KNOW—BUT NO ONE TO **COMPARE** YOU WITH..
Tove Jansson
14
I'M THE NEW LIGHTHOUSE KEEPER!
TOUGH LUCK ON YOU.. I'M THE OLD ONE...
HERE IS THE KEY. AND REMEMBER, IT'S TOO LATE NOW TO BACK OUT...
Tove Jansson

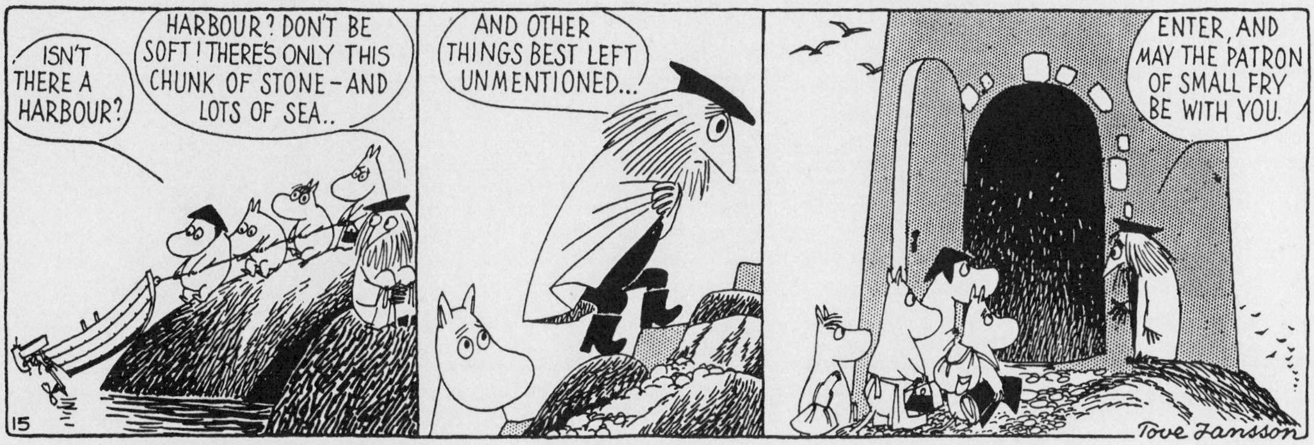
ISN'T THERE A HARBOUR?
HARBOUR? DON'T BE SOFT! THERE'S ONLY THIS CHUNK OF STONE – AND LOTS OF SEA..
AND OTHER THINGS BEST LEFT UNMENTIONED...
ENTER, AND MAY THE PATRON OF SMALL FRY BE WITH YOU.
15
Tove Jansson

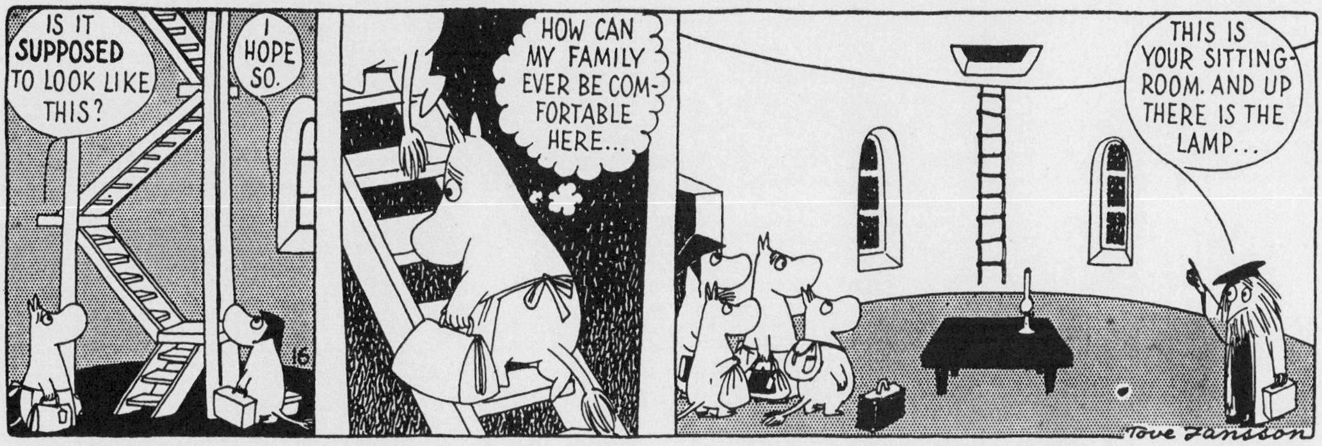
IS IT SUPPOSED TO LOOK LIKE THIS?
I HOPE SO.
16
HOW CAN MY FAMILY EVER BE COM-FORTABLE HERE...
THIS IS YOUR SITTING-ROOM. AND UP THERE IS THE LAMP...
Tove Jansson

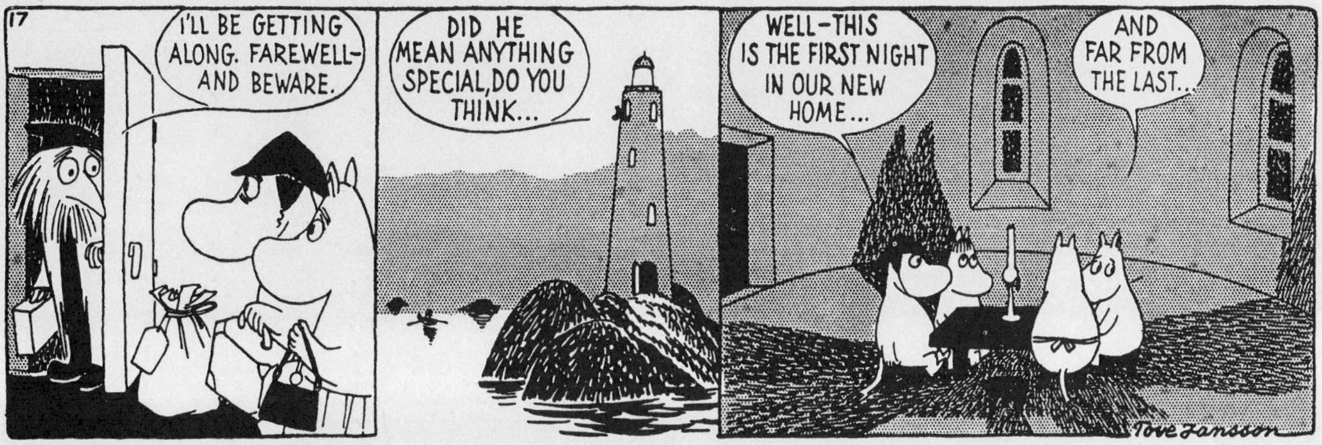
17
I'LL BE GETTING ALONG. FAREWELL – AND BEWARE.
DID HE MEAN ANYTHING SPECIAL, DO YOU THINK...
WELL – THIS IS THE FIRST NIGHT IN OUR NEW HOME...
AND FAR FROM THE LAST...
Tove Jansson

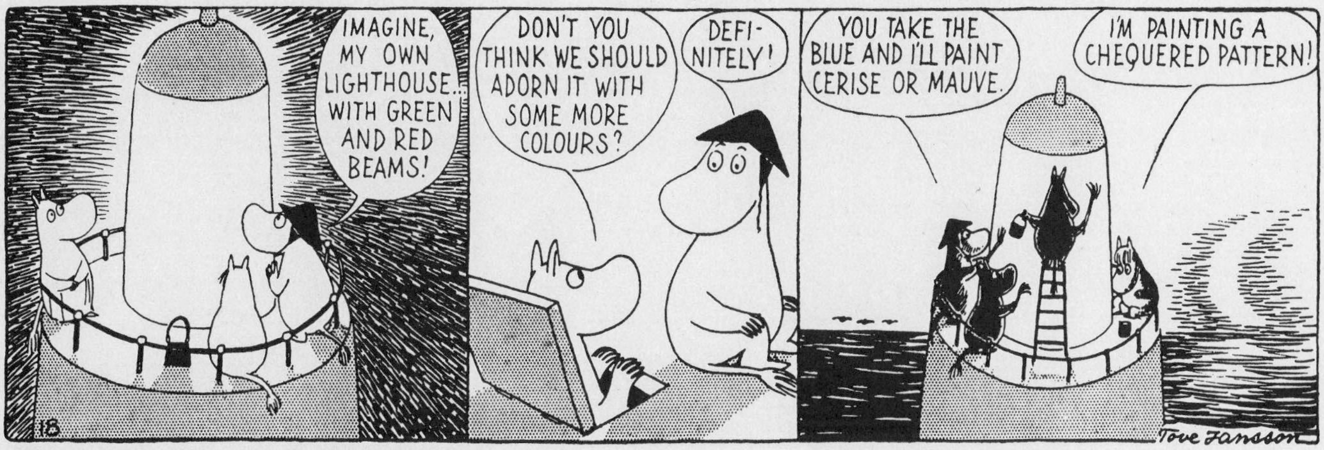
IMAGINE, MY OWN LIGHTHOUSE... WITH GREEN AND RED BEAMS!
18
DON'T YOU THINK WE SHOULD ADORN IT WITH SOME MORE COLOURS?
DEFI-NITELY!
YOU TAKE THE BLUE AND I'LL PAINT CERISE OR MAUVE.
I'M PAINTING A CHEQUERED PATTERN!
Tove Jansson

WHAT A LOT OF STRANGE NOISES THERE ARE IN AN OLD LIGHTHOUSE LIKE THIS....
BUT THOSE WERE STEPS!
DEAR, I'M SURE IT WAS ONLY A RAT.
THOUGH IT DOESN'T IMPROVE MATTERS ANY...
BUT IN THE LIGHT FROM THE MOON SOMETHING CREPT ACROSS THE ROOM.......
HOW ROMANTIC! I'M A REAL LIGHTHOUSE KEEPER!
NEXT MORNING....
HERE, FACING THE MIGHTY SEA, I SHALL GET INSPIRATION FOR MY GREAT SEA-STORY.
DARLING, MOOMIN SAYS THE LIGHTHOUSE IS FULL OF RATS. COULDN'T YOU...
DEAR, I'M CONCENTRATING ON THE PROLOGUE.
A CARGO OF PLANKS ADRIFT! THEY MUST BE SALVAGED!
OH, DON'T BOTHER WE'LL SALVAGE THEM, YOU JUST GO ON WRITING!
CAN'T THEY UNDERSTAND ONE DOESN'T WANT TO BE LEFT IN PEACE ALL THE TIME!
BUT WHAT ARE WE GOING TO DO WITH ALL THE PLANKS?
WE'LL BUILD BEAUTIFUL ROCK-MARKERS!
EVERY ROCK WILL GET A MARK OF IT'S OWN!
IMAGINE, NOW WE HAVE DECORATED THE WHOLE ARCHIPELAGO!

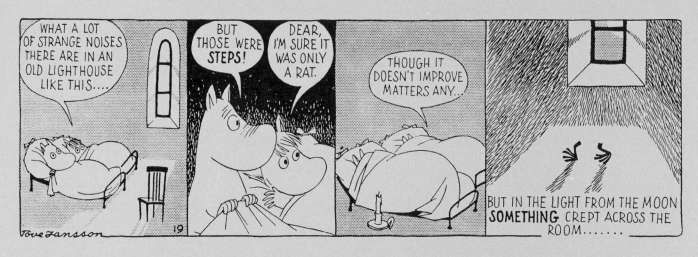

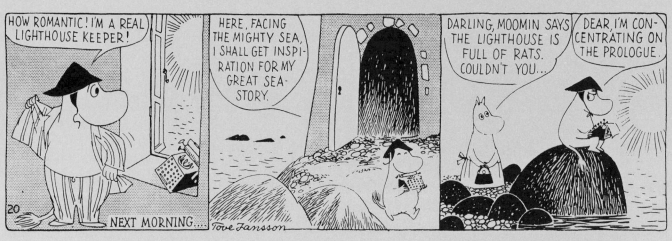

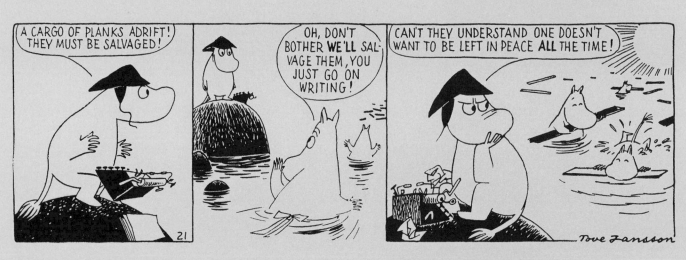

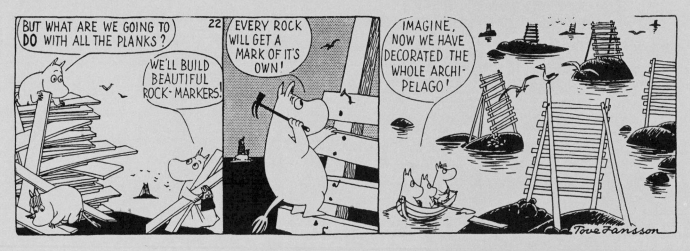

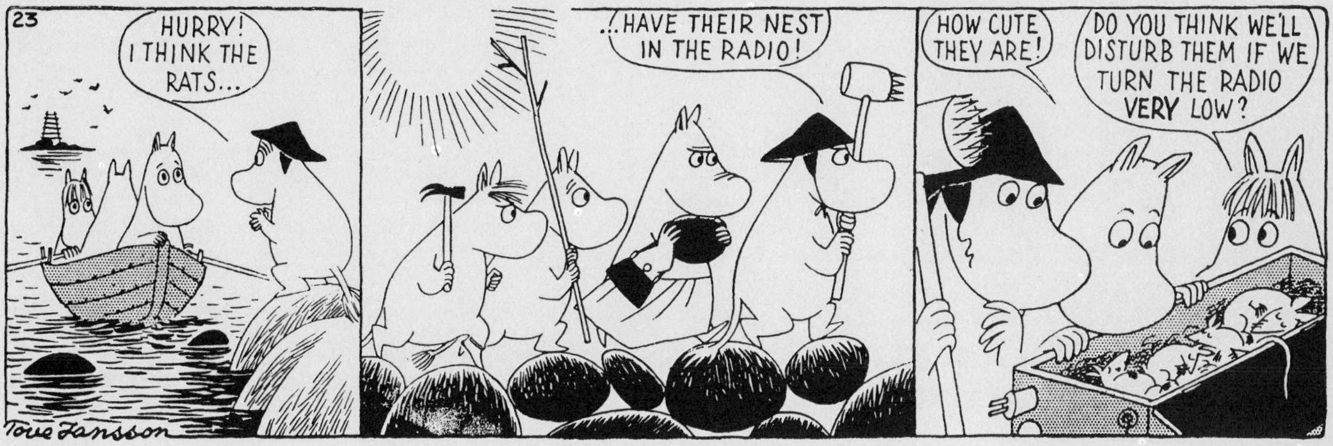
23
HURRY! I THINK THE RATS...
...HAVE THEIR NEST IN THE RADIO!
HOW CUTE THEY ARE!
DO YOU THINK WE'LL DISTURB THEM IF WE TURN THE RADIO VERY LOW?
Tove Jansson

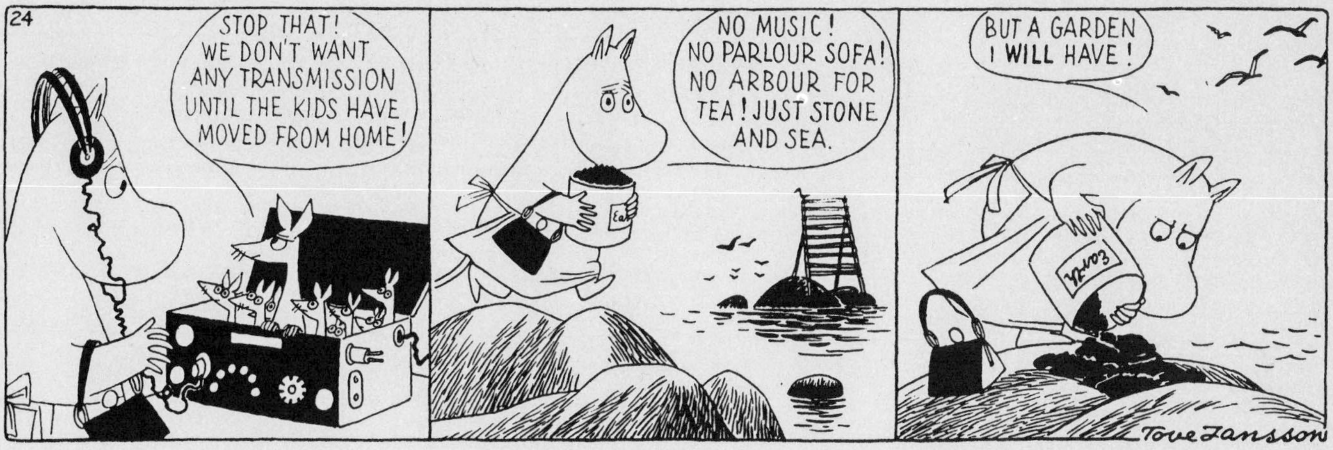
24
STOP THAT! WE DON'T WANT ANY TRANSMISSION UNTIL THE KIDS HAVE MOVED FROM HOME!
NO MUSIC! NO PARLOUR SOFA! NO ARBOUR FOR TEA! JUST STONE AND SEA.
BUT A GARDEN I WILL HAVE!
Tove Jansson

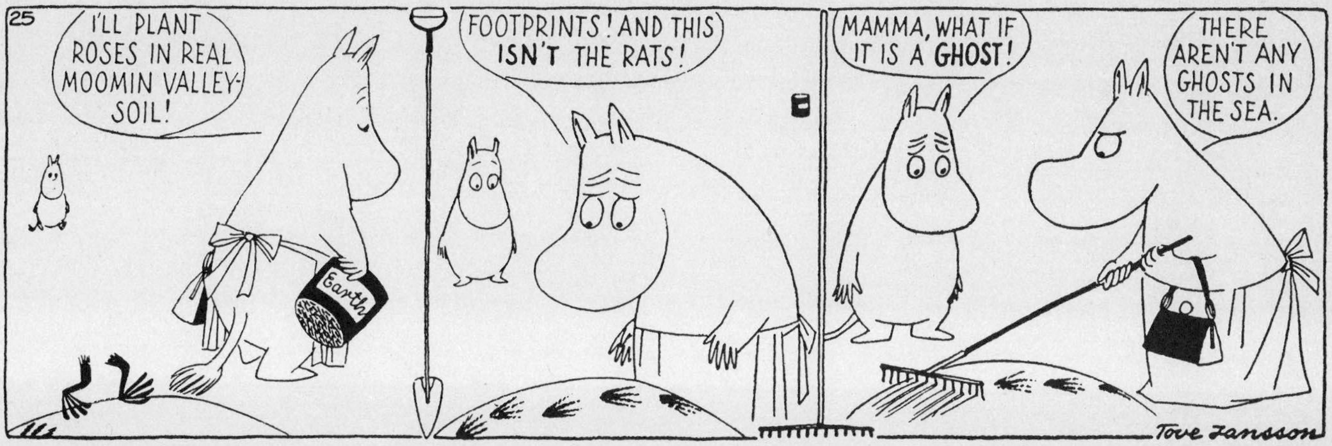
25
I'LL PLANT ROSES IN REAL MOOMIN VALLEY-SOIL!
Earth
FOOTPRINTS! AND THIS ISN'T THE RATS!
MAMMA, WHAT IF IT IS A GHOST!
THERE AREN'T ANY GHOSTS IN THE SEA.
Tove Jansson

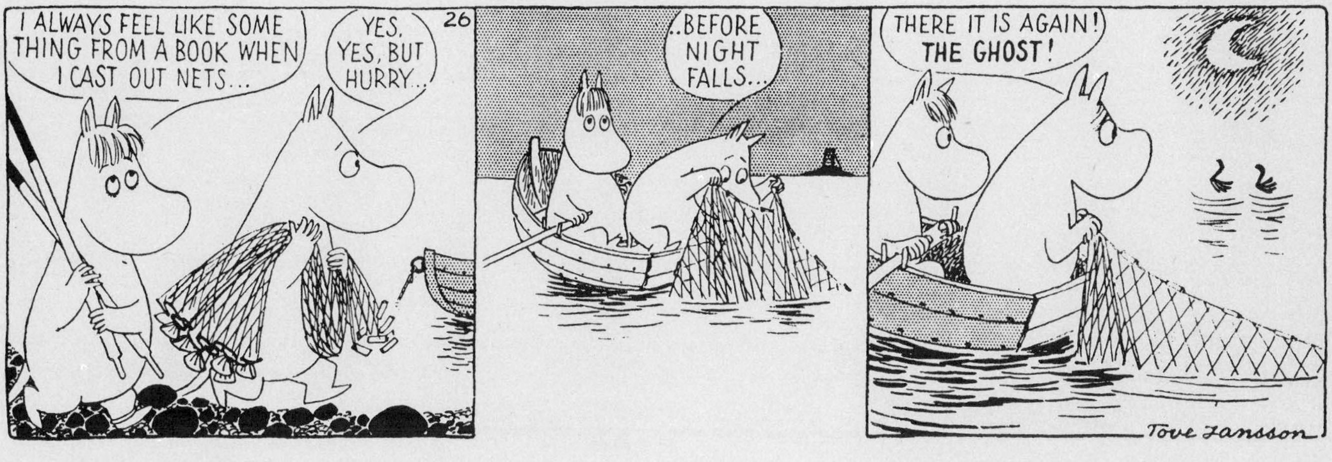
I ALWAYS FEEL LIKE SOME THING FROM A BOOK WHEN I CAST OUT NETS...
YES, YES, BUT HURRY...
26
..BEFORE NIGHT FALLS...
THERE IT IS AGAIN! THE GHOST!
Tove Jansson

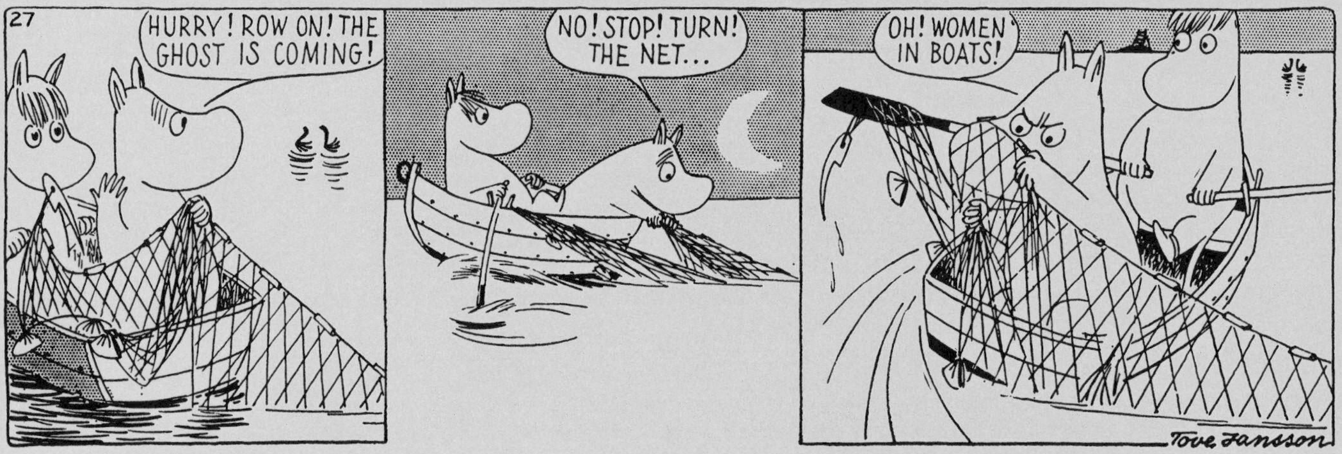
27
HURRY! ROW ON! THE GHOST IS COMING!
NO! STOP! TURN! THE NET...
OH! WOMEN IN BOATS!
Tove Jansson

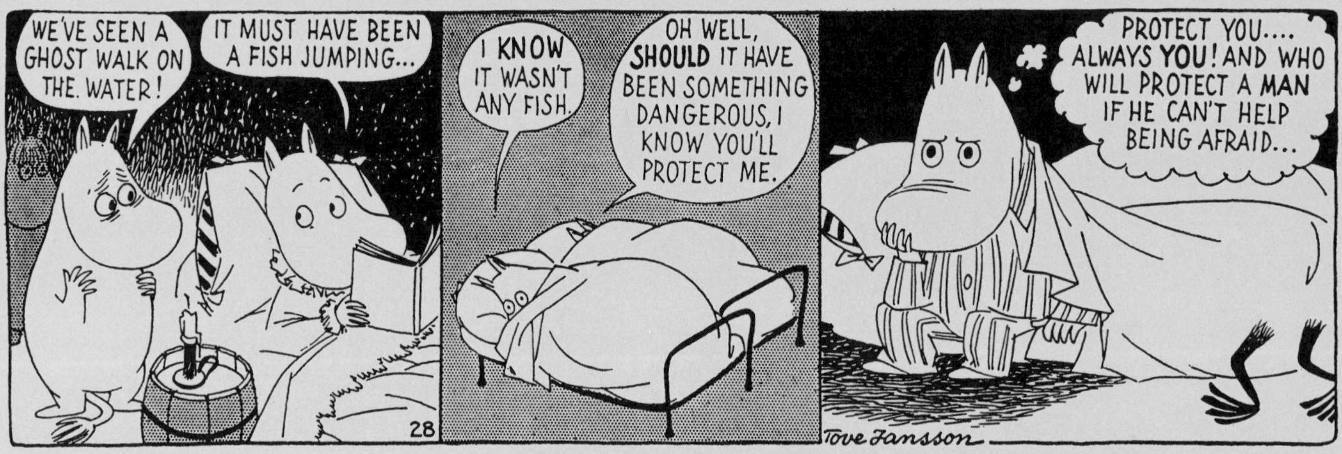
WE'VE SEEN A GHOST WALK ON THE. WATER!
IT MUST HAVE BEEN A FISH JUMPING...
28
I **KNOW** IT WASN'T ANY FISH.
OH WELL, **SHOULD** IT HAVE BEEN SOMETHING DANGEROUS, I KNOW YOU'LL PROTECT ME.
PROTECT YOU.... ALWAYS **YOU**! AND WHO WILL PROTECT A **MAN** IF HE CAN'T HELP BEING AFRAID...
Tove Jansson

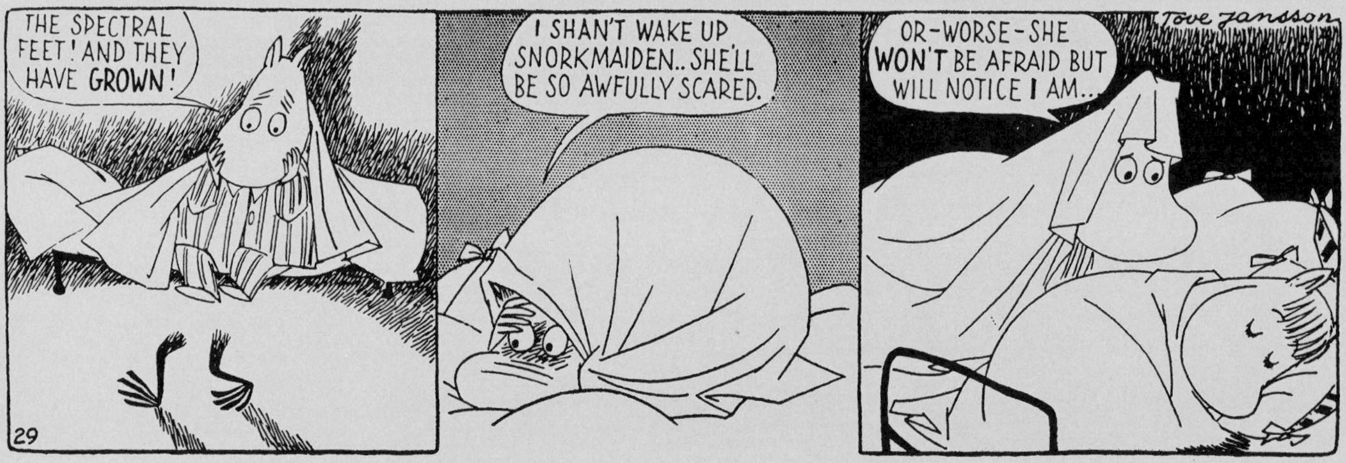
THE SPECTRAL FEET! AND THEY HAVE **GROWN**!
29
I SHAN'T WAKE UP SNORKMAIDEN.. SHE'LL BE SO AWFULLY SCARED.
Tove Jansson
OR-WORSE-SHE **WON'T** BE AFRAID BUT WILL NOTICE **I** AM..

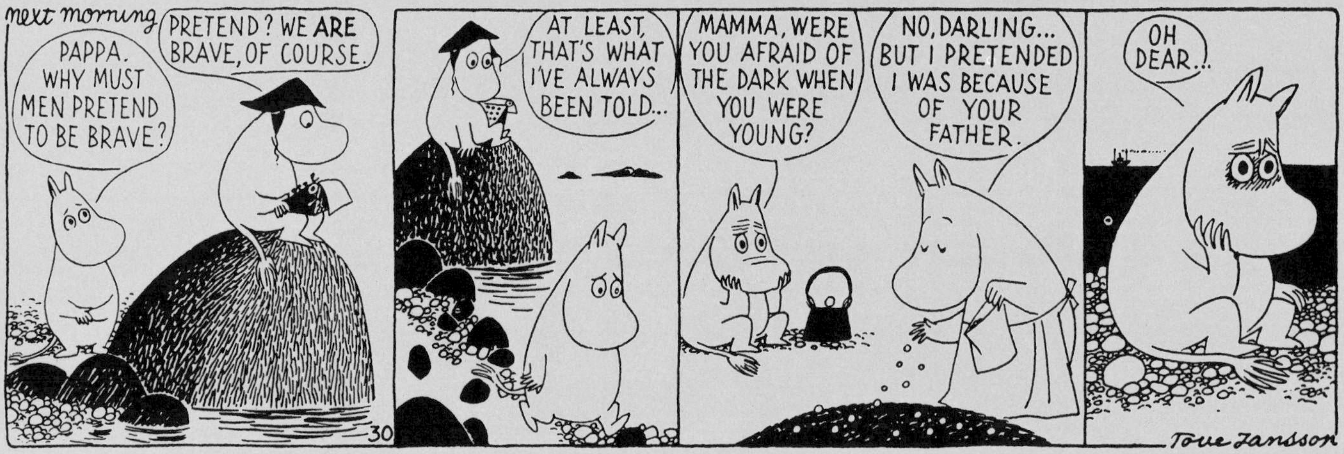
next morning
PAPPA. WHY MUST MEN PRETEND TO BE BRAVE?
PRETEND? WE **ARE** BRAVE, OF COURSE.
30
AT LEAST, THAT'S WHAT I'VE ALWAYS BEEN TOLD...
MAMMA, WERE YOU AFRAID OF THE DARK WHEN YOU WERE YOUNG?
NO, DARLING... BUT I PRETENDED I WAS BECAUSE OF YOUR FATHER.
OH DEAR...
Tove Jansson

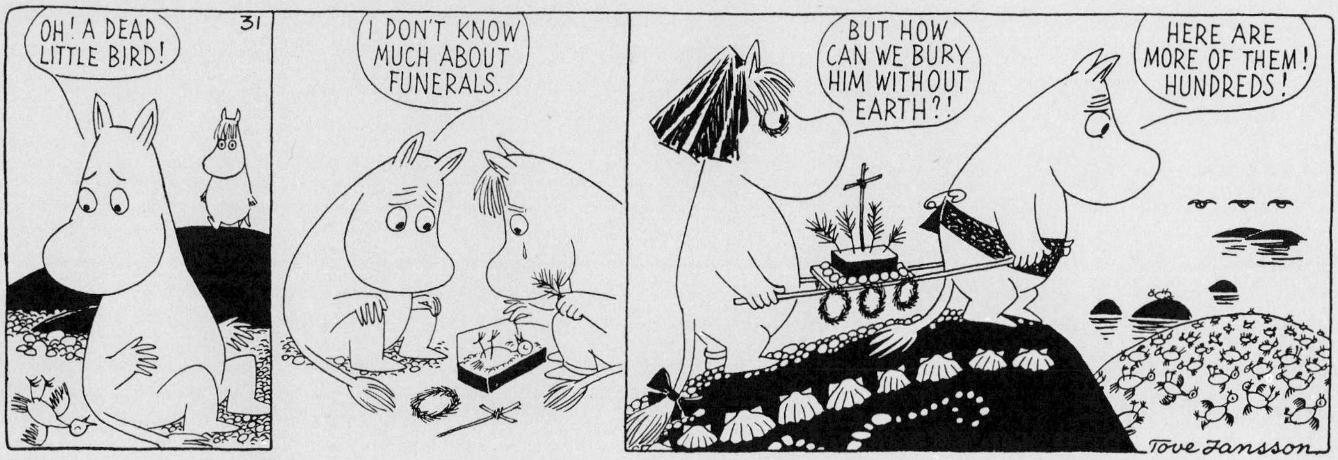
31
OH! A DEAD LITTLE BIRD!
I DON'T KNOW MUCH ABOUT FUNERALS.
BUT HOW CAN WE BURY HIM WITHOUT EARTH?!
HERE ARE MORE OF THEM! HUNDREDS!
Tove Jansson

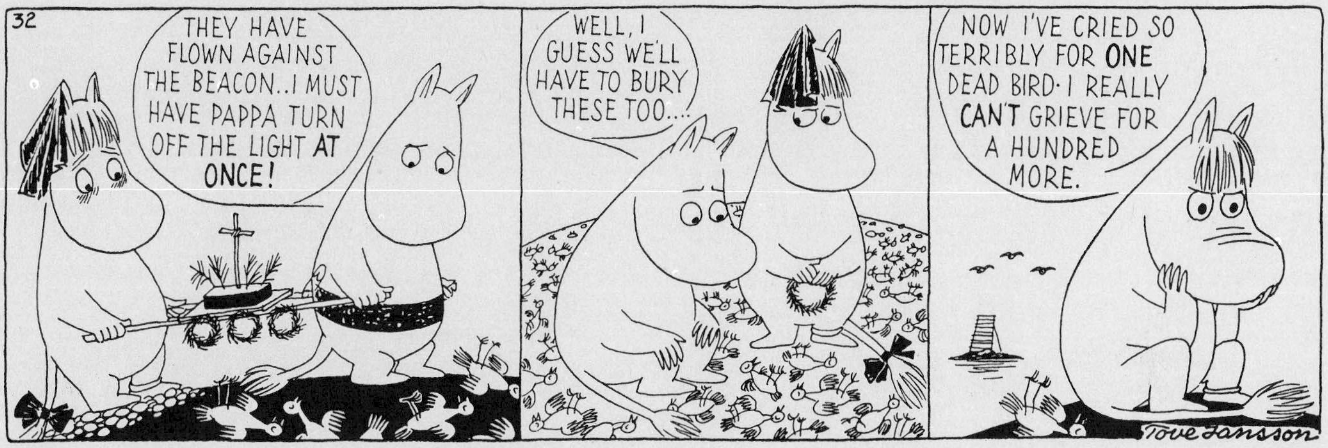
32
THEY HAVE FLOWN AGAINST THE BEACON..I MUST HAVE PAPPA TURN OFF THE LIGHT AT ONCE!
WELL, I GUESS WE'LL HAVE TO BURY THESE TOO....
NOW I'VE CRIED SO TERRIBLY FOR ONE DEAD BIRD· I REALLY CAN'T GRIEVE FOR A HUNDRED MORE.
Tove Jansson

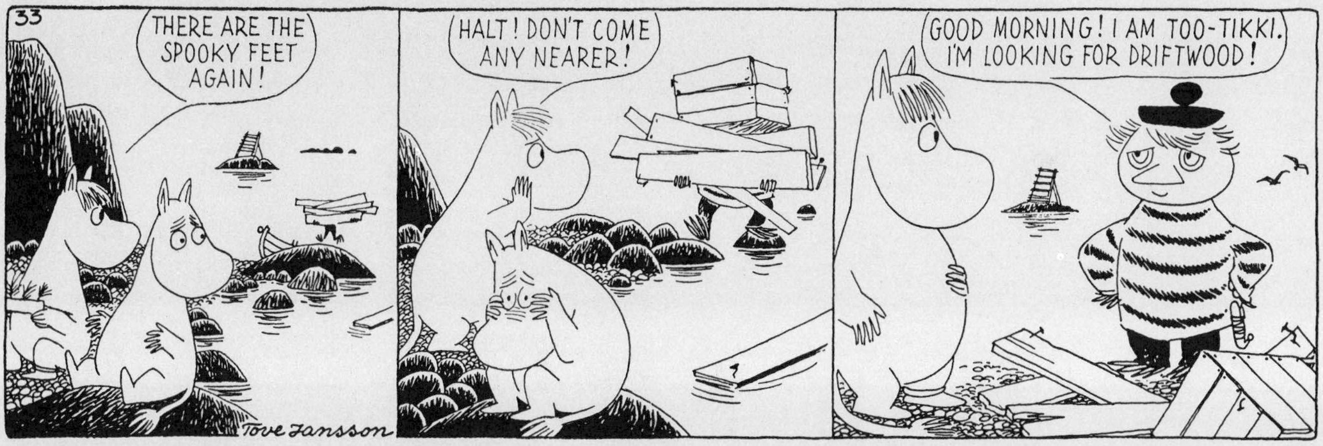
33
THERE ARE THE SPOOKY FEET AGAIN!
Tove Jansson
HALT! DON'T COME ANY NEARER!
GOOD MORNING! I AM TOO-TIKKI. I'M LOOKING FOR DRIFTWOOD!

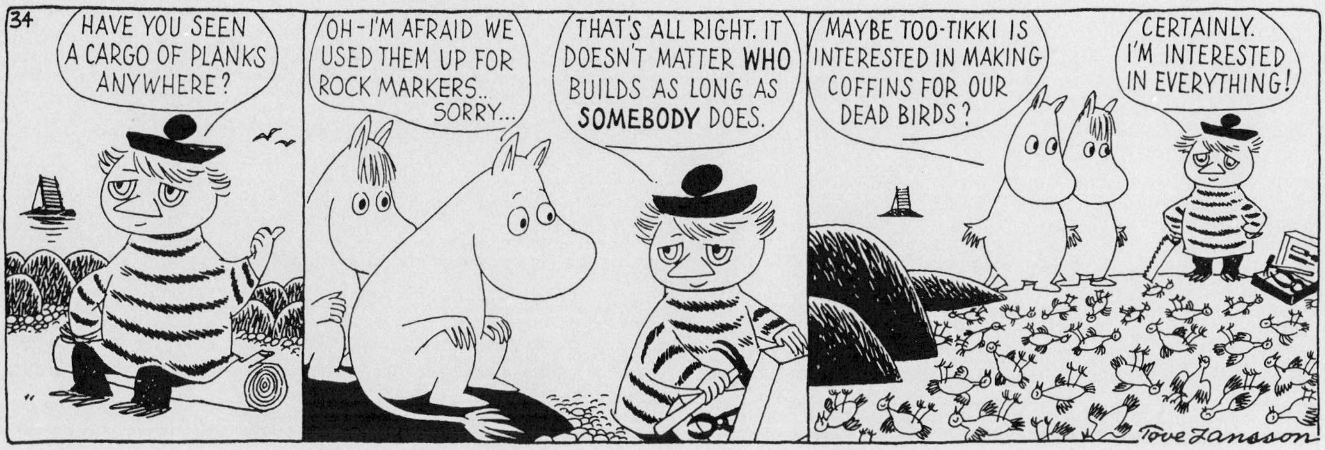
34
HAVE YOU SEEN A CARGO OF PLANKS ANYWHERE?
OH-I'M AFRAID WE USED THEM UP FOR ROCK MARKERS.. SORRY...
THAT'S ALL RIGHT. IT DOESN'T MATTER WHO BUILDS AS LONG AS SOMEBODY DOES.
MAYBE TOO-TIKKI IS INTERESTED IN MAKING COFFINS FOR OUR DEAD BIRDS?
CERTAINLY. I'M INTERESTED IN EVERYTHING!
Tove Jansson

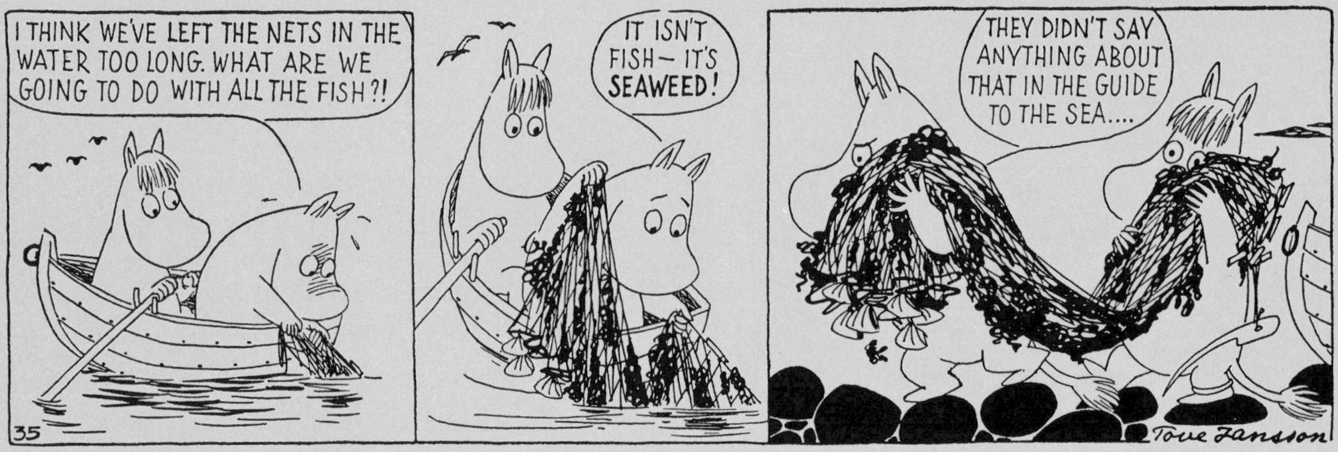
I THINK WE'VE LEFT THE NETS IN THE WATER TOO LONG. WHAT ARE WE GOING TO DO WITH ALL THE FISH ?!
35
IT ISN'T FISH – IT'S SEAWEED!
THEY DIDN'T SAY ANYTHING ABOUT THAT IN THE GUIDE TO THE SEA....
Tove Jansson

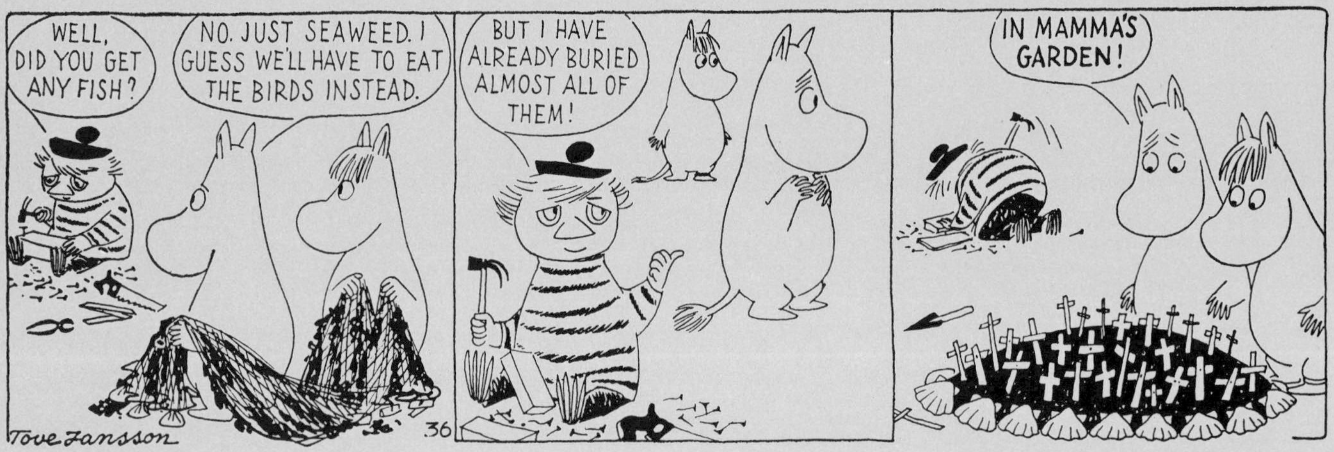
WELL, DID YOU GET ANY FISH?
NO. JUST SEAWEED. I GUESS WE'LL HAVE TO EAT THE BIRDS INSTEAD.
Tove Jansson
BUT I HAVE ALREADY BURIED ALMOST ALL OF THEM!
36
IN MAMMA'S GARDEN!

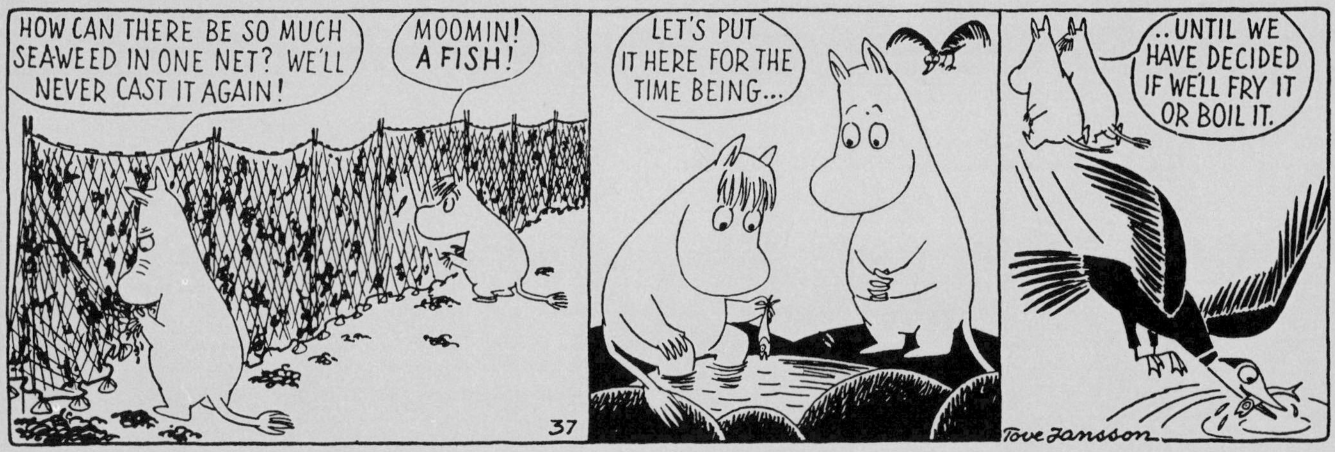
HOW CAN THERE BE SO MUCH SEAWEED IN ONE NET? WE'LL NEVER CAST IT AGAIN!
MOOMIN! A FISH!
37
LET'S PUT IT HERE FOR THE TIME BEING...
..UNTIL WE HAVE DECIDED IF WE'LL FRY IT OR BOIL IT.
Tove Jansson

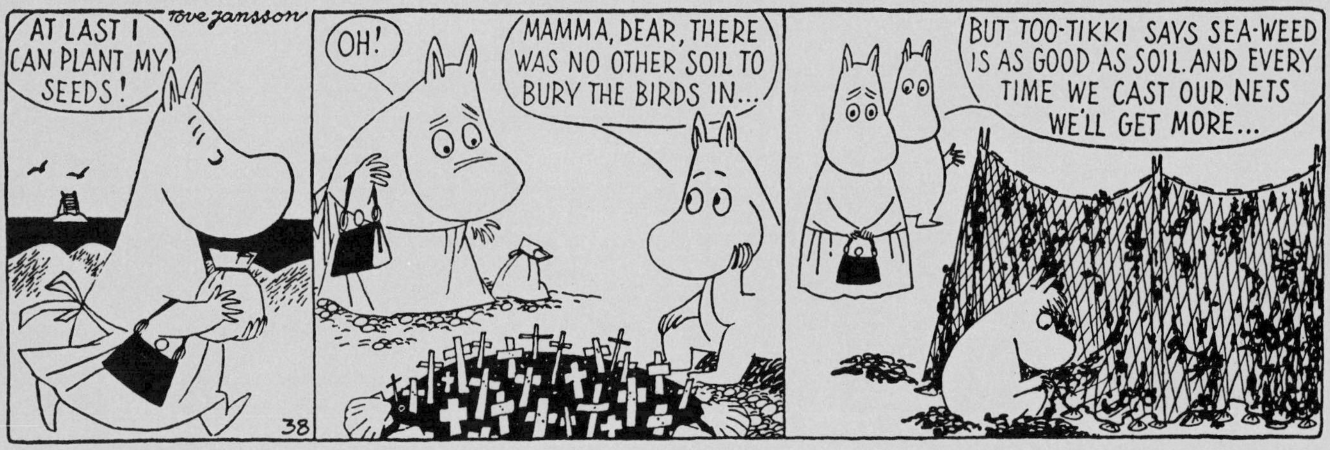
Tove Jansson
AT LAST I CAN PLANT MY SEEDS!
38
OH!
MAMMA, DEAR, THERE WAS NO OTHER SOIL TO BURY THE BIRDS IN...
BUT TOO-TIKKI SAYS SEA-WEED IS AS GOOD AS SOIL. AND EVERY TIME WE CAST OUR NETS WE'LL GET MORE...

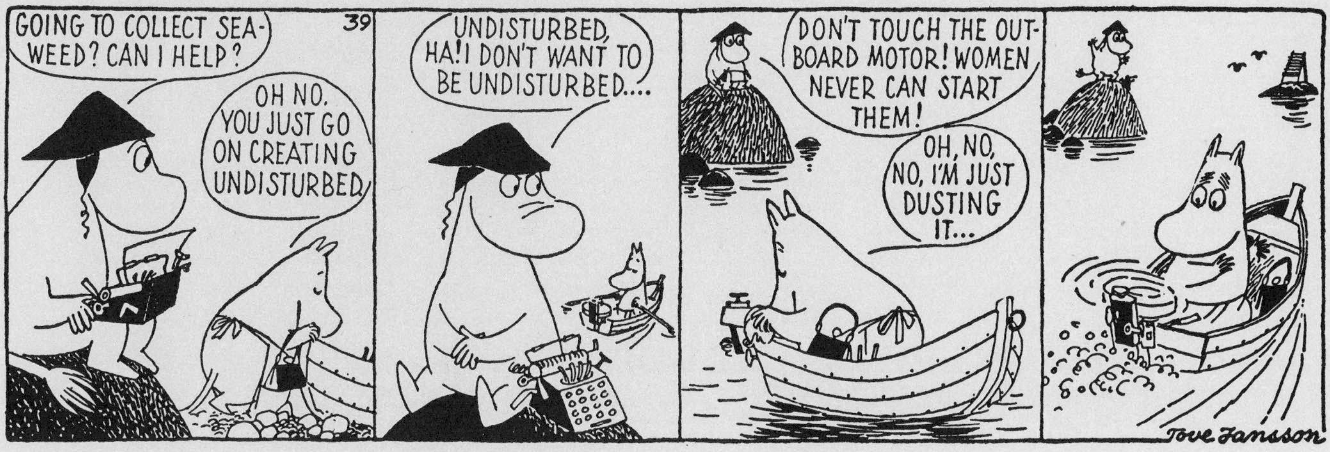
39
GOING TO COLLECT SEA-WEED? CAN I HELP?
OH NO. YOU JUST GO ON CREATING UNDISTURBED.
UNDISTURBED, HA! I DON'T WANT TO BE UNDISTURBED....
DON'T TOUCH THE OUT-BOARD MOTOR! WOMEN NEVER CAN START THEM!
OH, NO, NO, I'M JUST DUSTING IT...
Tove Jansson

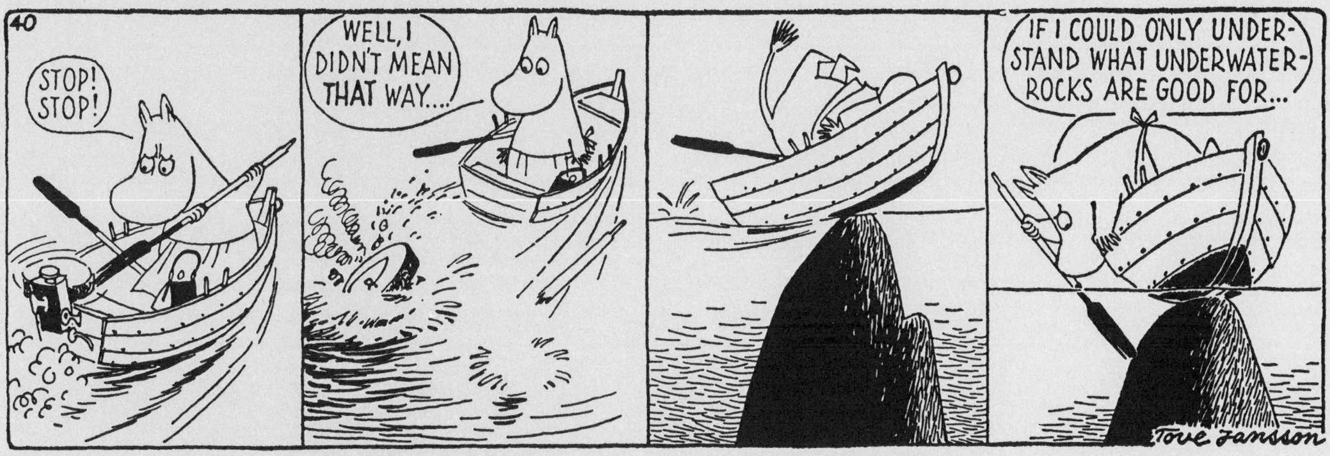
40
STOP! STOP!
WELL, I DIDN'T MEAN THAT WAY....
IF I COULD ONLY UNDER-STAND WHAT UNDERWATER-ROCKS ARE GOOD FOR...
Tove Jansson

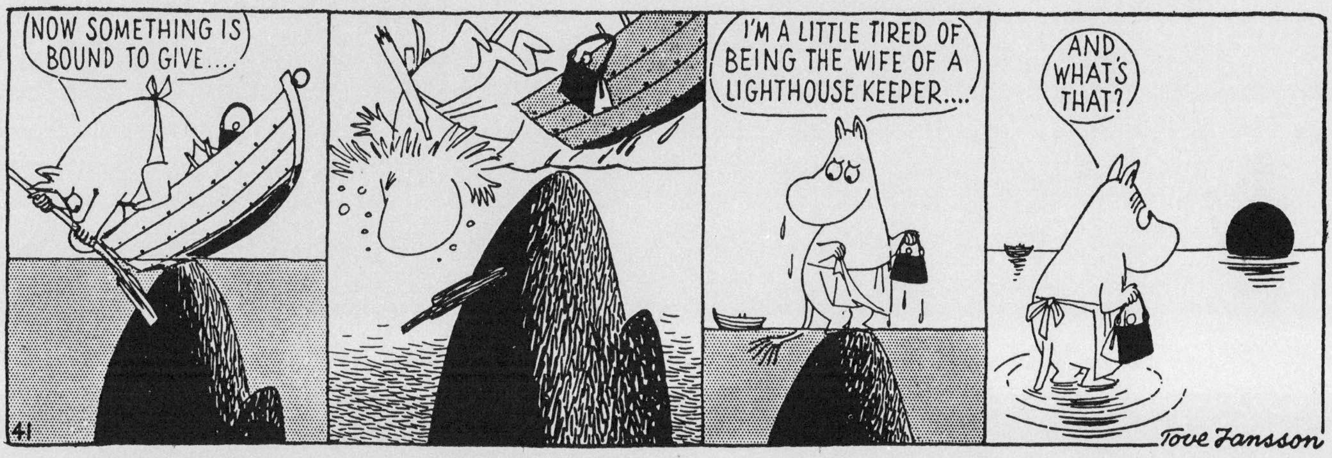
NOW SOMETHING IS BOUND TO GIVE....
41
I'M A LITTLE TIRED OF BEING THE WIFE OF A LIGHTHOUSE KEEPER....
AND WHAT'S THAT?
Tove Jansson

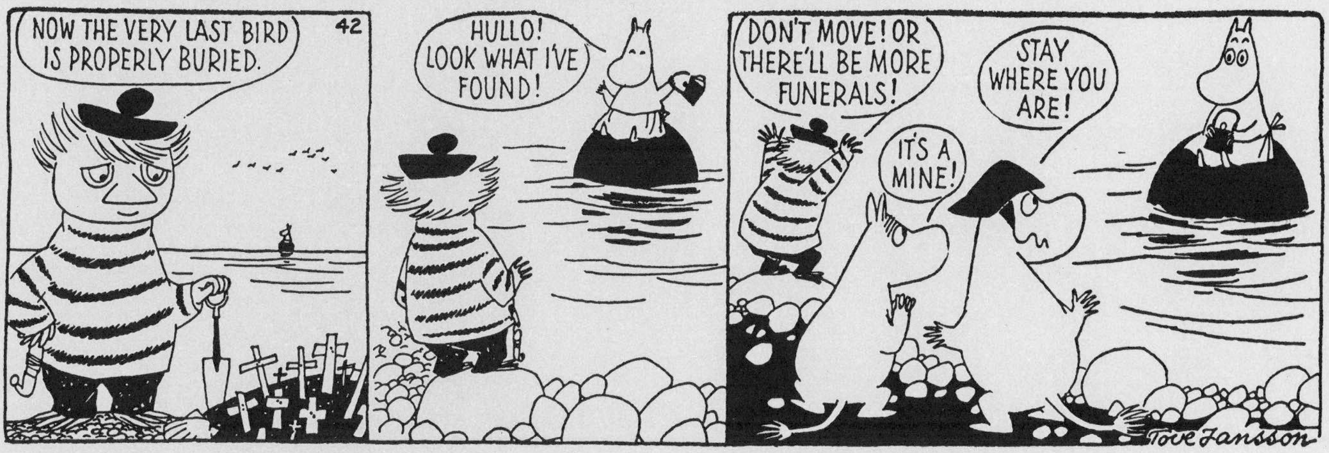
NOW THE VERY LAST BIRD IS PROPERLY BURIED.
42
HULLO! LOOK WHAT I'VE FOUND!
DON'T MOVE! OR THERE'LL BE MORE FUNERALS!
STAY WHERE YOU ARE!
IT'S A MINE!
Tove Jansson

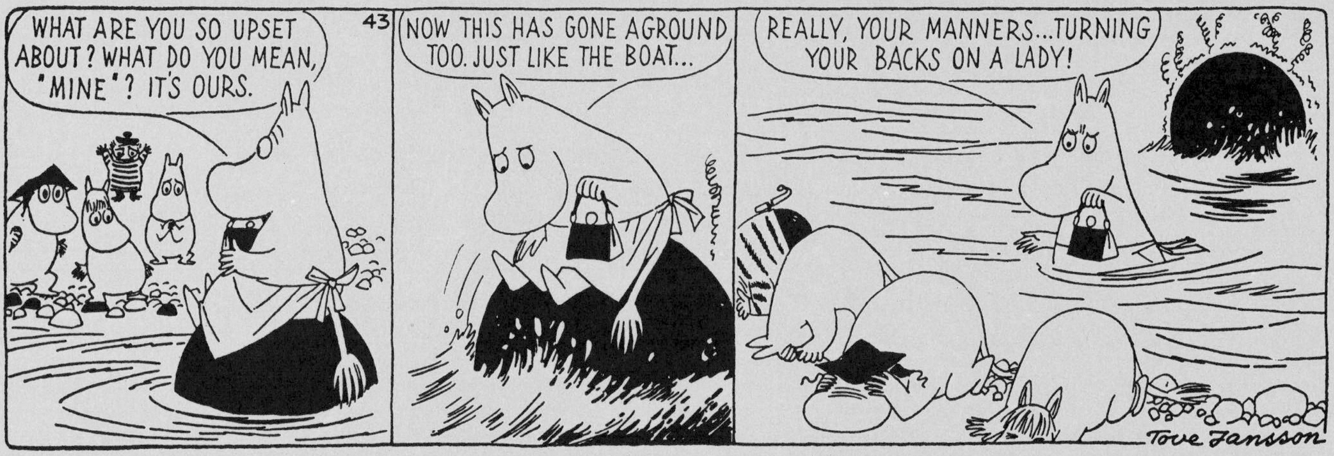
43
WHAT ARE YOU SO UPSET ABOUT? WHAT DO YOU MEAN, "MINE"? IT'S OURS.
NOW THIS HAS GONE AGROUND TOO. JUST LIKE THE BOAT...
REALLY, YOUR MANNERS...TURNING YOUR BACKS ON A LADY!
Tove Jansson

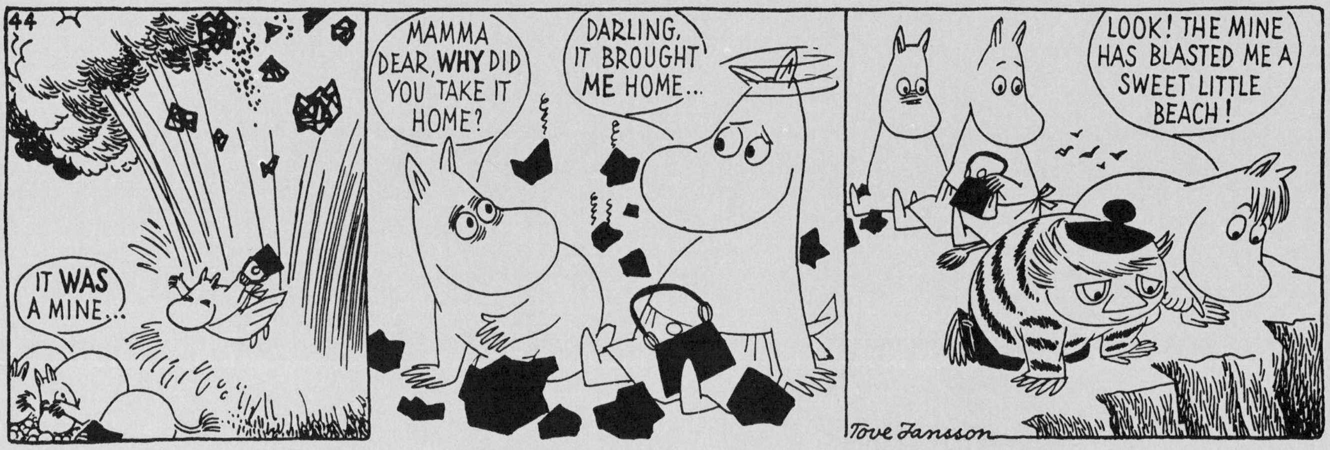
44
IT WAS A MINE...
MAMMA DEAR, WHY DID YOU TAKE IT HOME?
DARLING, IT BROUGHT ME HOME...
LOOK! THE MINE HAS BLASTED ME A SWEET LITTLE BEACH!
Tove Jansson

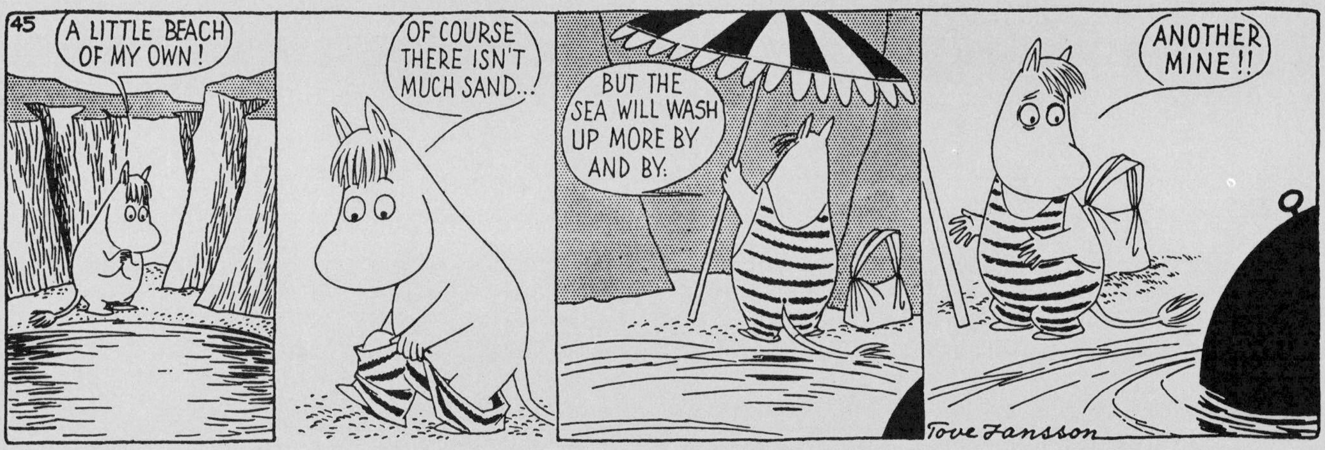
45
A LITTLE BEACH OF MY OWN!
OF COURSE THERE ISN'T MUCH SAND...
BUT THE SEA WILL WASH UP MORE BY AND BY.
ANOTHER MINE!!
Tove Jansson

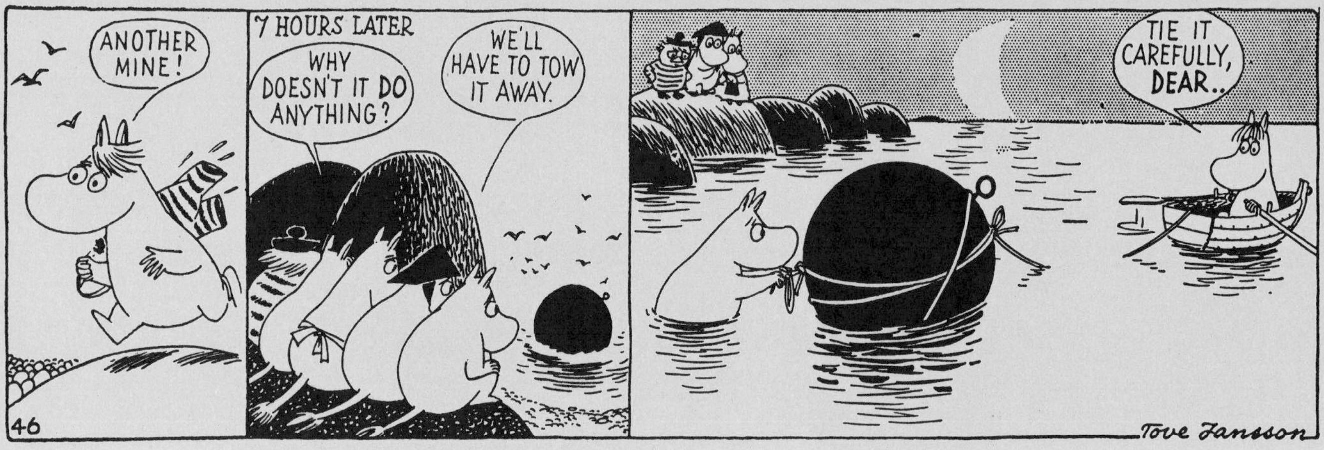
ANOTHER MINE!
46
7 HOURS LATER
WHY DOESN'T IT DO ANYTHING?
WE'LL HAVE TO TOW IT AWAY.
TIE IT CAREFULLY, DEAR..
Tove Jansson

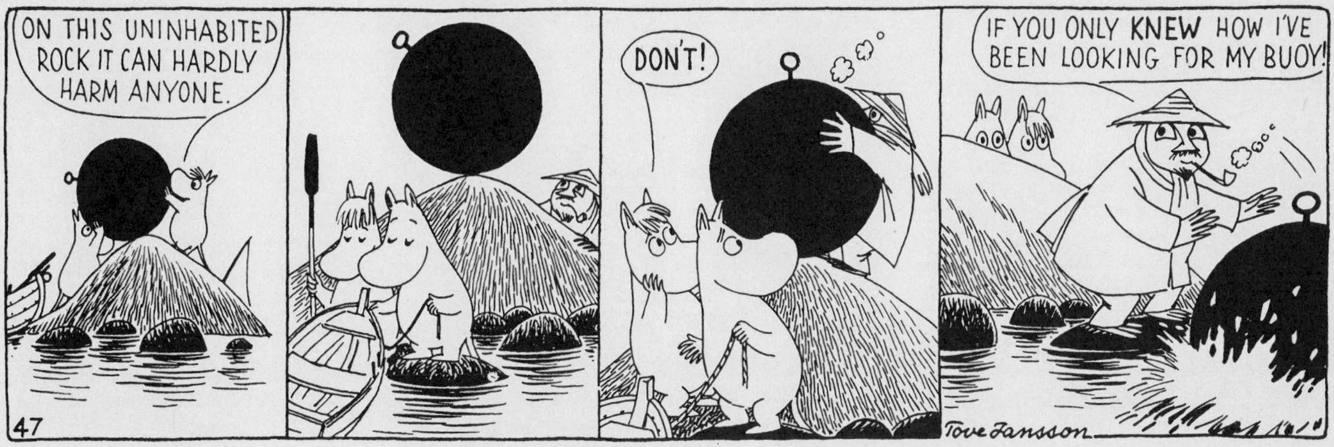
47
ON THIS UNINHABITED ROCK IT CAN HARDLY HARM ANYONE.
DON'T!
IF YOU ONLY KNEW HOW I'VE BEEN LOOKING FOR MY BUOY!
Tove Jansson

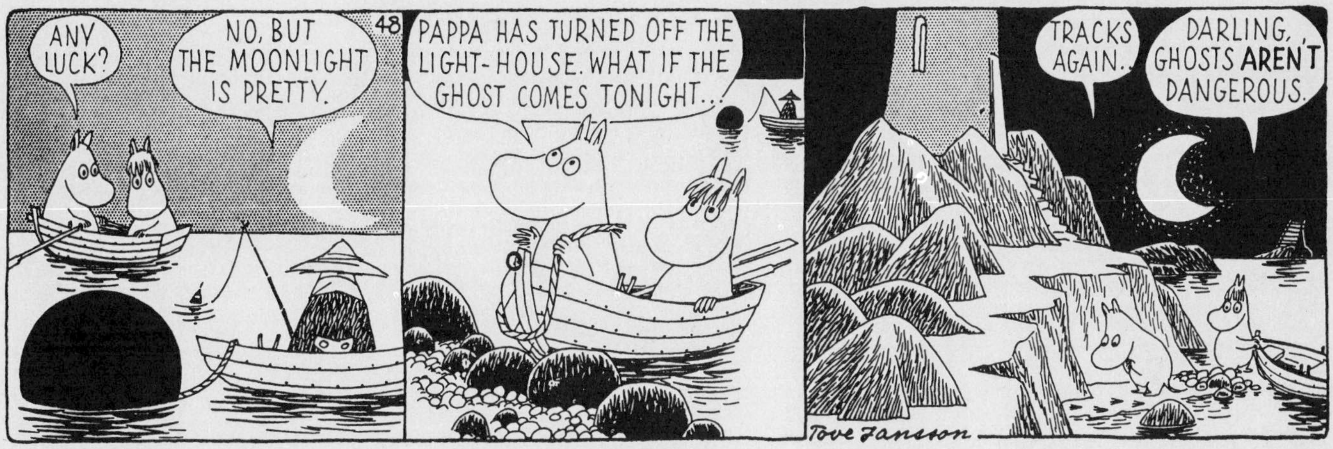
48
ANY LUCK?
NO, BUT THE MOONLIGHT IS PRETTY.
PAPPA HAS TURNED OFF THE LIGHT-HOUSE. WHAT IF THE GHOST COMES TONIGHT...
TRACKS AGAIN...
DARLING, GHOSTS AREN'T DANGEROUS.
Tove Jansson

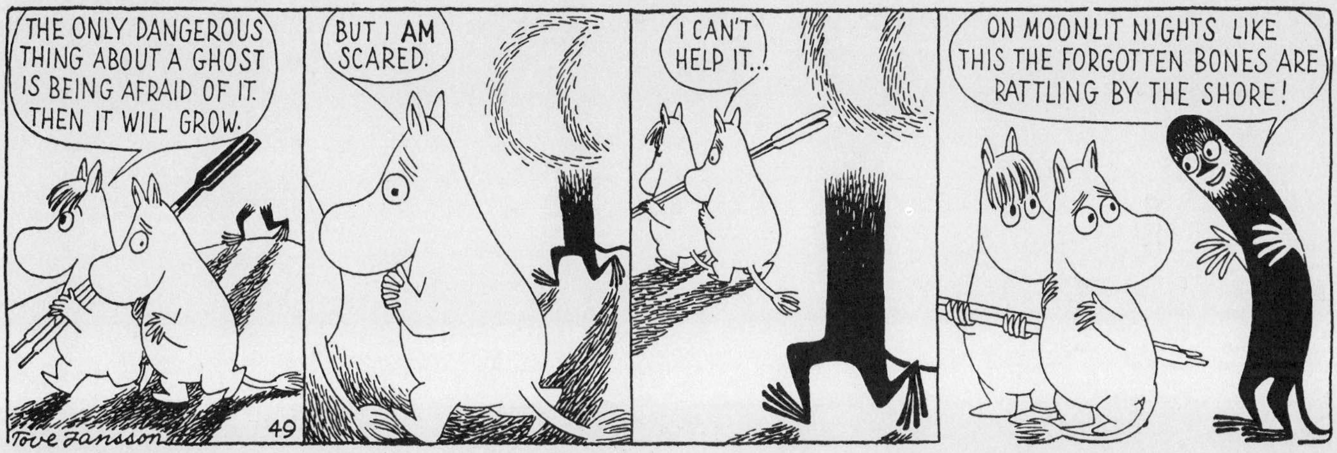
THE ONLY DANGEROUS THING ABOUT A GHOST IS BEING AFRAID OF IT. THEN IT WILL GROW.
Tove Jansson
49
BUT I AM SCARED.
I CAN'T HELP IT...
ON MOONLIT NIGHTS LIKE THIS THE FORGOTTEN BONES ARE RATTLING BY THE SHORE!

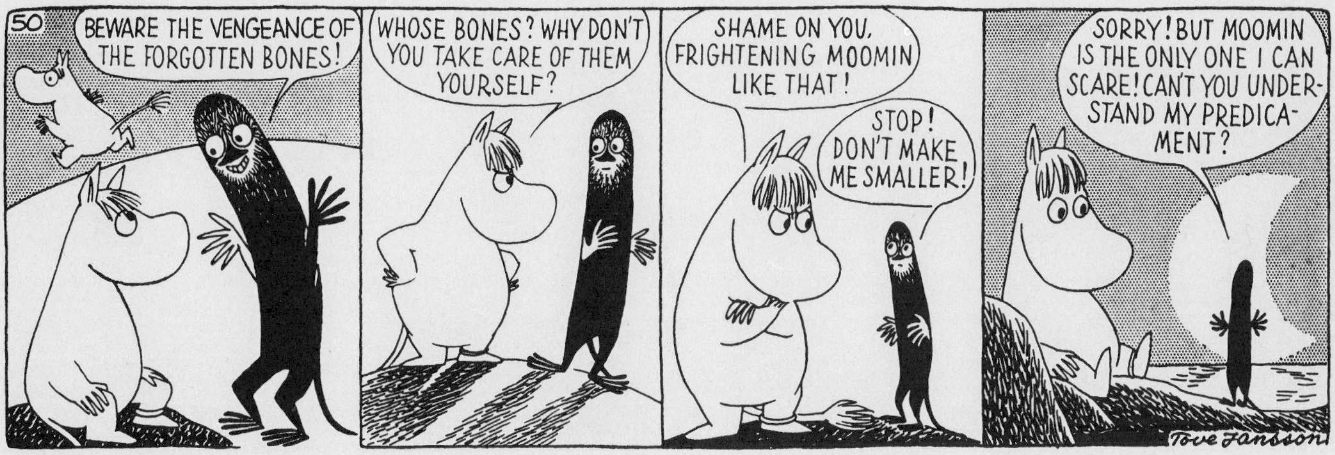
50
BEWARE THE VENGEANCE OF THE FORGOTTEN BONES!
WHOSE BONES? WHY DON'T YOU TAKE CARE OF THEM YOURSELF?
SHAME ON YOU, FRIGHTENING MOOMIN LIKE THAT!
STOP! DON'T MAKE ME SMALLER!
SORRY! BUT MOOMIN IS THE ONLY ONE I CAN SCARE! CAN'T YOU UNDER-STAND MY PREDICA-MENT?
Tove Jansson

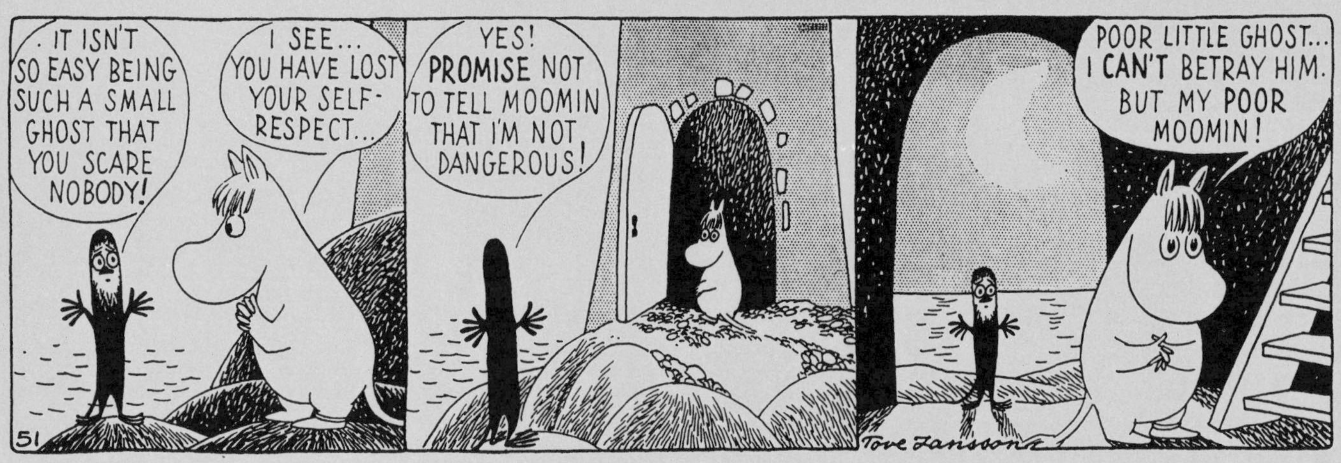
. IT ISN'T SO EASY BEING SUCH A SMALL GHOST THAT YOU SCARE NOBODY!
I SEE... YOU HAVE LOST YOUR SELF-RESPECT...
YES! PROMISE NOT TO TELL MOOMIN THAT I'M NOT DANGEROUS!
POOR LITTLE GHOST... I CAN'T BETRAY HIM. BUT MY POOR MOOMIN!
51
Tove Jansson

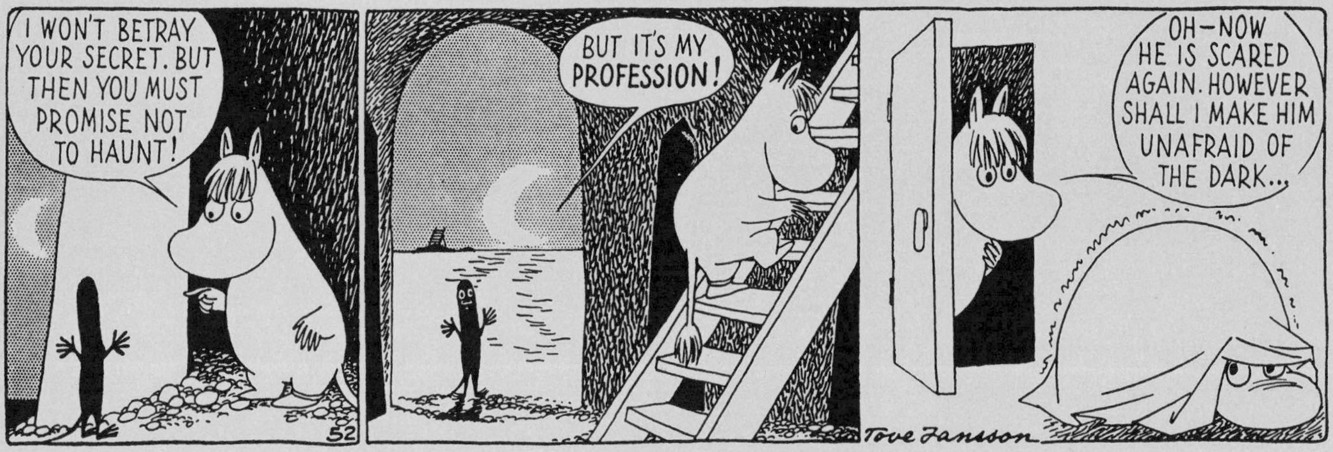
I WON'T BETRAY YOUR SECRET. BUT THEN YOU MUST PROMISE NOT TO HAUNT!
BUT IT'S MY PROFESSION!
OH—NOW HE IS SCARED AGAIN. HOWEVER SHALL I MAKE HIM UNAFRAID OF THE DARK...
52
Tove Jansson

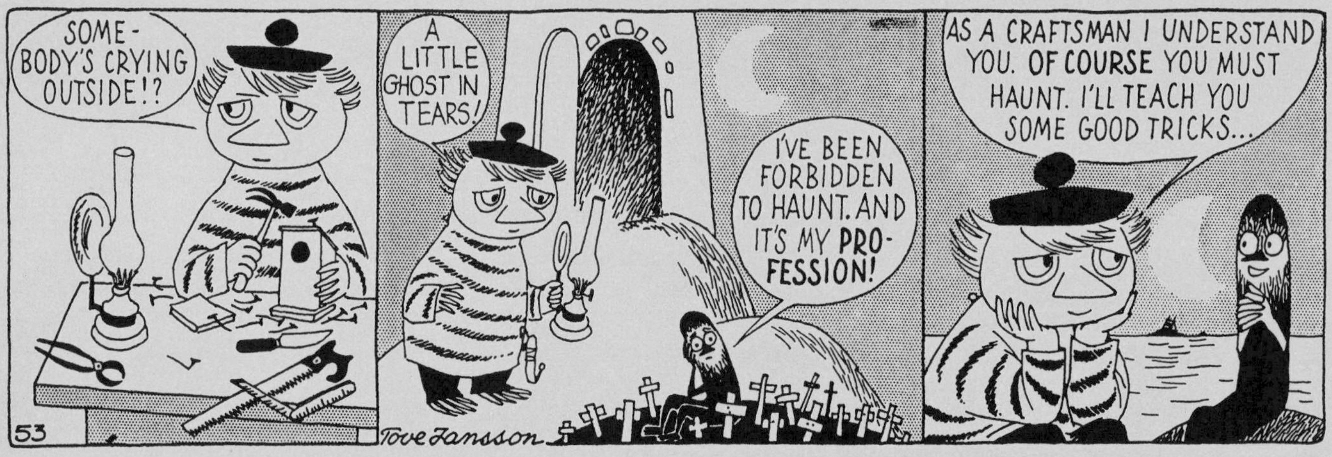
SOME-BODY'S CRYING OUTSIDE!?
A LITTLE GHOST IN TEARS!
I'VE BEEN FORBIDDEN TO HAUNT. AND IT'S MY PRO-FESSION!
AS A CRAFTSMAN I UNDERSTAND YOU. OF COURSE YOU MUST HAUNT. I'LL TEACH YOU SOME GOOD TRICKS...
53
Tove Jansson

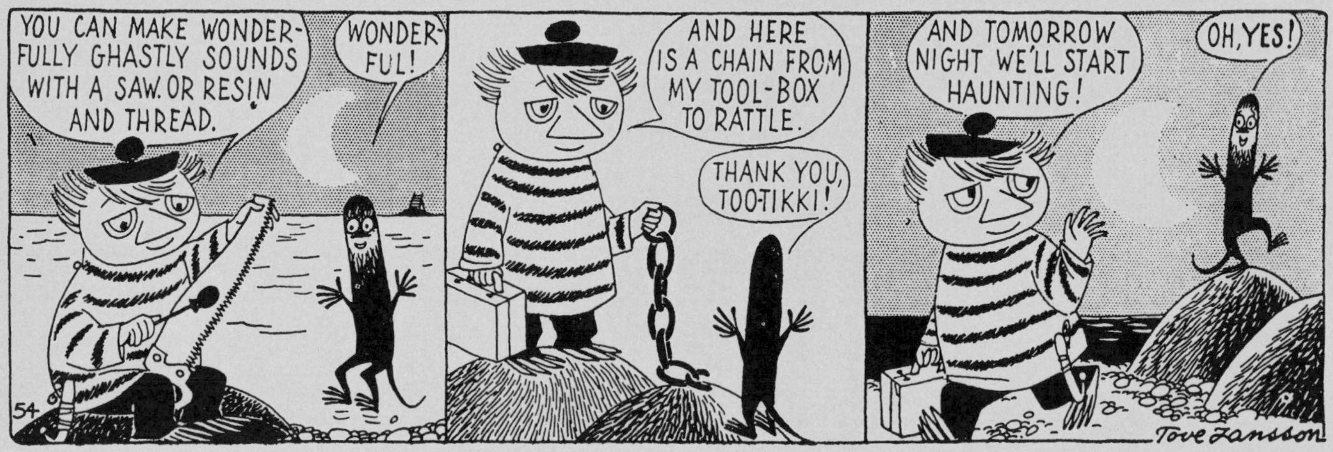
YOU CAN MAKE WONDER-FULLY GHASTLY SOUNDS WITH A SAW. OR RESIN AND THREAD.
WONDER-FUL!
AND HERE IS A CHAIN FROM MY TOOL-BOX TO RATTLE.
THANK YOU, TOO-TIKKI!
AND TOMORROW NIGHT WE'LL START HAUNTING!
OH, YES!
54
Tove Jansson

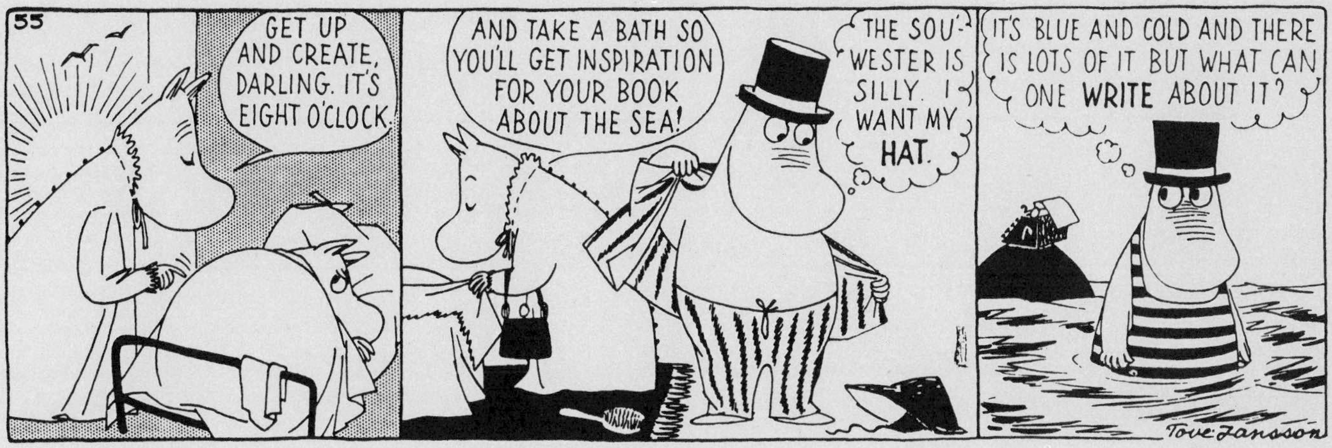
55
GET UP AND CREATE, DARLING. IT'S EIGHT O'CLOCK.
AND TAKE A BATH SO YOU'LL GET INSPIRATION FOR YOUR BOOK ABOUT THE SEA!
THE SOU'-WESTER IS SILLY. I WANT MY **HAT**.
IT'S BLUE AND COLD AND THERE IS LOTS OF IT BUT WHAT CAN ONE **WRITE** ABOUT IT?
Tove Jansson

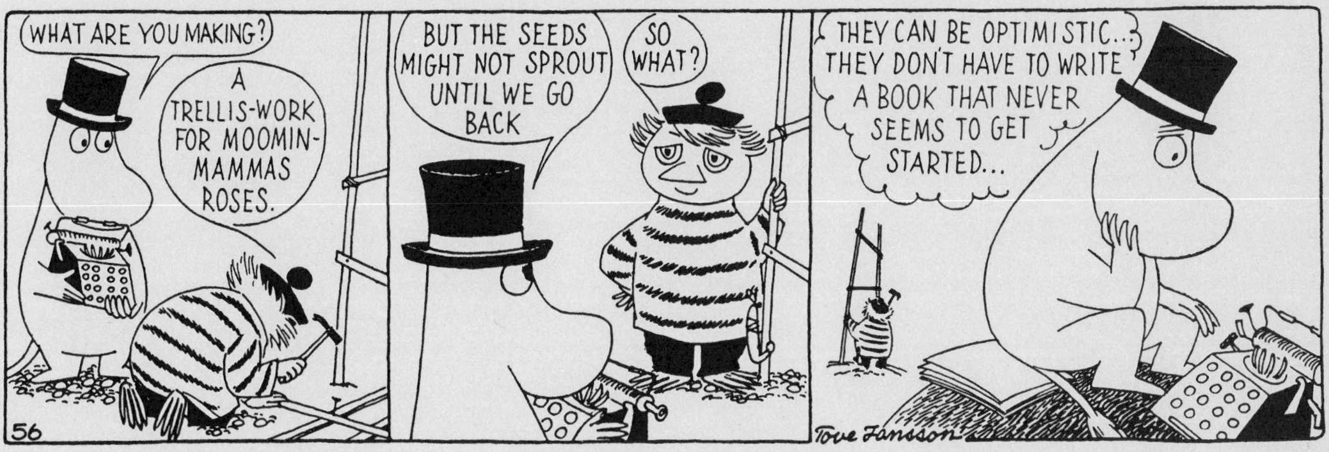
WHAT ARE YOU MAKING?
A TRELLIS-WORK FOR MOOMIN-MAMMAS ROSES.
56
BUT THE SEEDS MIGHT NOT SPROUT UNTIL WE GO BACK
SO WHAT?
THEY CAN BE OPTIMISTIC... THEY DON'T HAVE TO WRITE A BOOK THAT NEVER SEEMS TO GET STARTED...
Tove Jansson

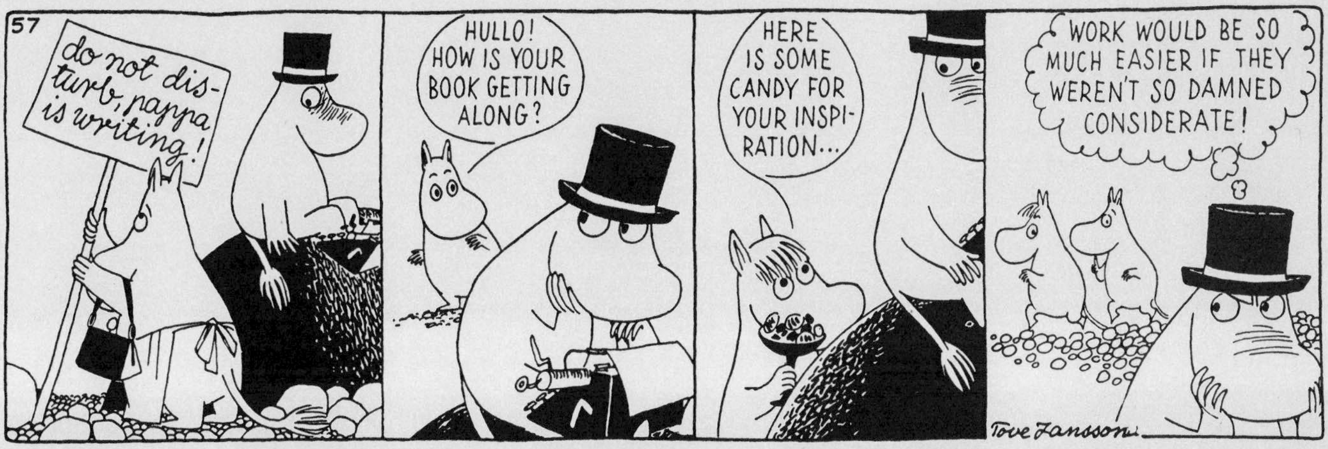
57
do not disturb, pappa is writing!
HULLO! HOW IS YOUR BOOK GETTING ALONG?
HERE IS SOME CANDY FOR YOUR INSPIRATION...
WORK WOULD BE SO MUCH EASIER IF THEY WEREN'T SO DAMNED CONSIDERATE!
Tove Jansson

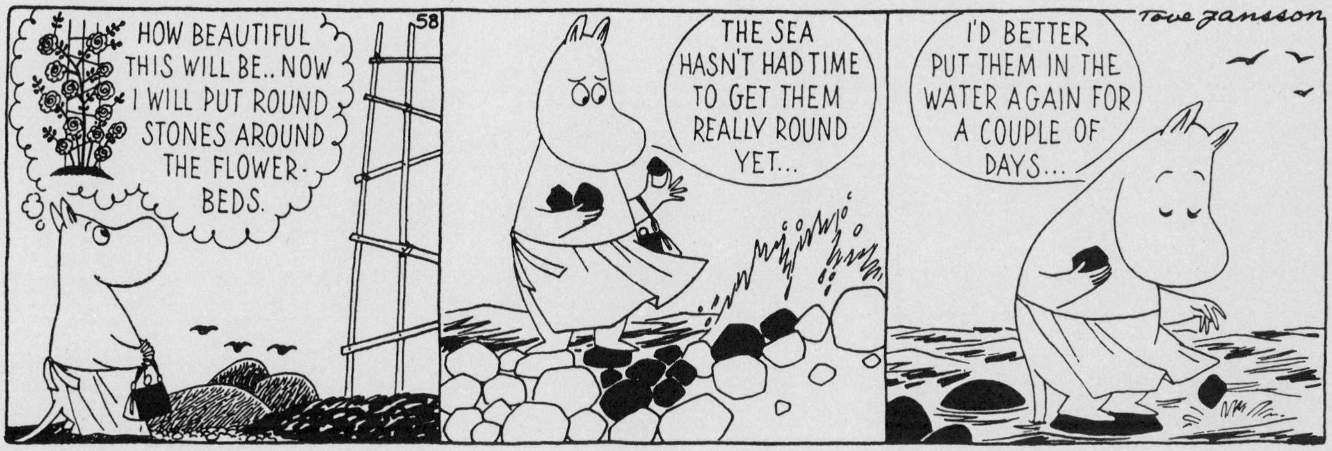
HOW BEAUTIFUL THIS WILL BE.. NOW I WILL PUT ROUND STONES AROUND THE FLOWER-BEDS.
58
THE SEA HASN'T HAD TIME TO GET THEM REALLY ROUND YET...
Tove Jansson
I'D BETTER PUT THEM IN THE WATER AGAIN FOR A COUPLE OF DAYS...

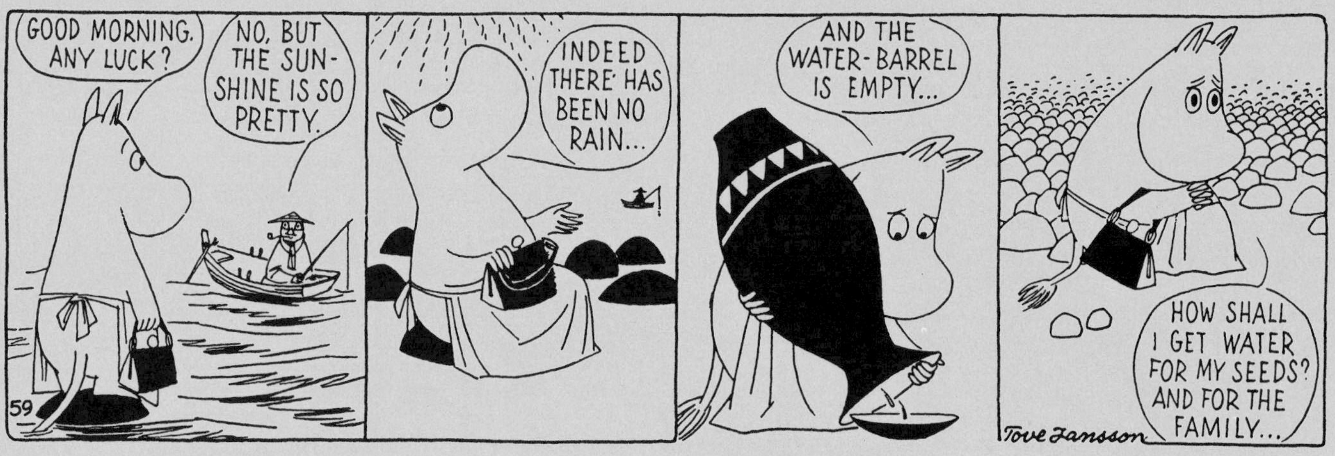
GOOD MORNING. ANY LUCK?
NO, BUT THE SUN-SHINE IS SO PRETTY.
59
INDEED THERE HAS BEEN NO RAIN...
AND THE WATER-BARREL IS EMPTY...
HOW SHALL I GET WATER FOR MY SEEDS? AND FOR THE FAMILY...
Tove Jansson

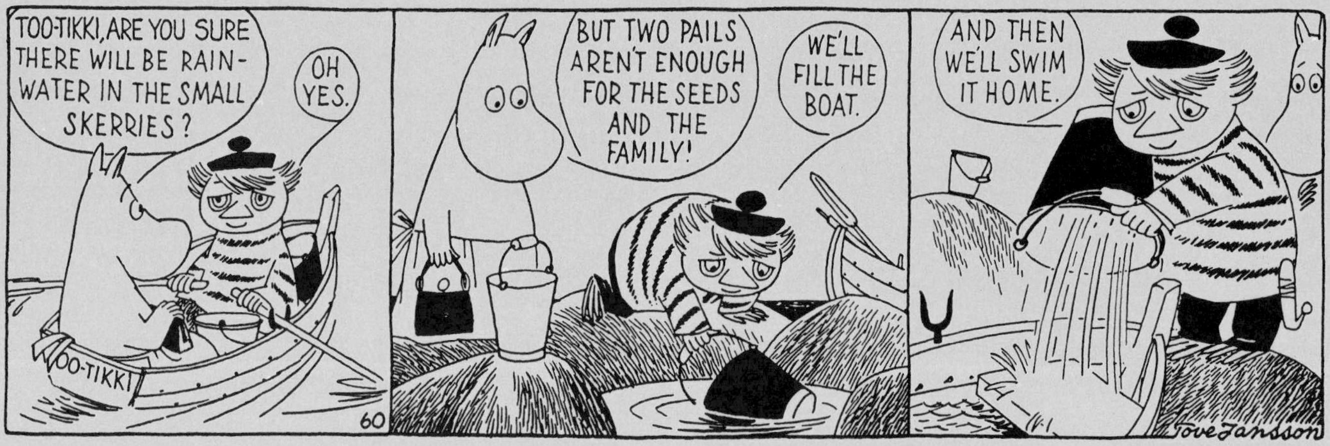
TOO-TIKKI, ARE YOU SURE THERE WILL BE RAIN-WATER IN THE SMALL SKERRIES?
OH YES.
OO-TIKKI
60
BUT TWO PAILS AREN'T ENOUGH FOR THE SEEDS AND THE FAMILY!
WE'LL FILL THE BOAT.
AND THEN WE'LL SWIM IT HOME.
Tove Jansson

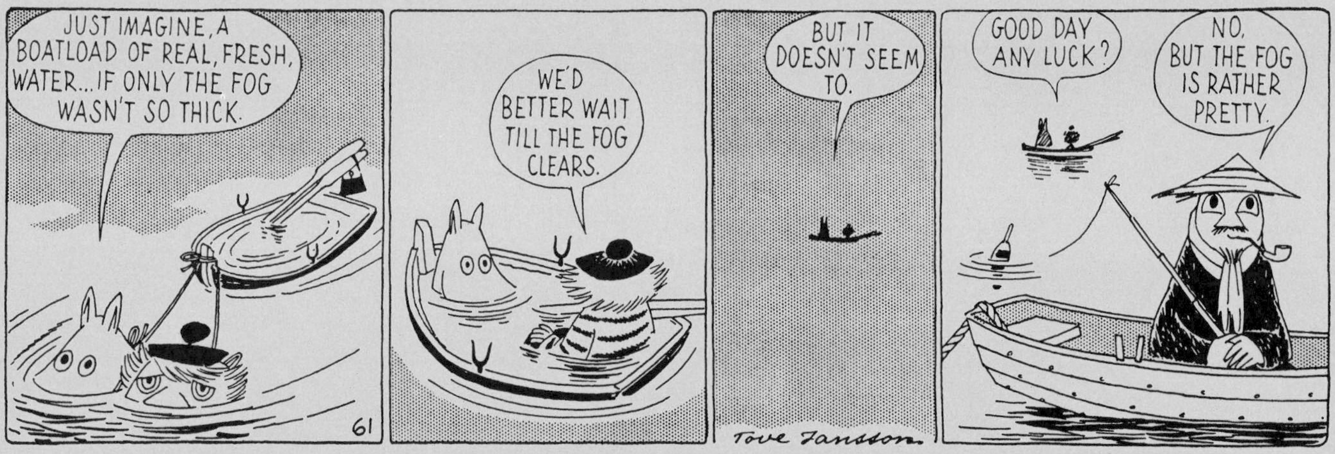
JUST IMAGINE, A BOATLOAD OF REAL, FRESH, WATER... IF ONLY THE FOG WASN'T SO THICK.
61
WE'D BETTER WAIT TILL THE FOG CLEARS.
BUT IT DOESN'T SEEM TO.
Tove Jansson
GOOD DAY ANY LUCK?
NO. BUT THE FOG IS RATHER PRETTY.

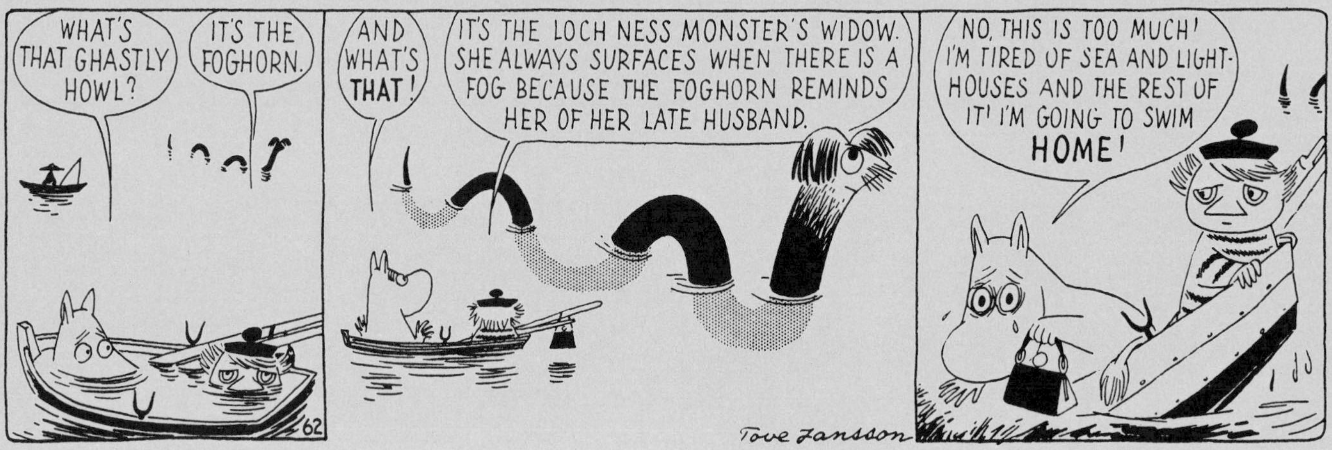
WHAT'S THAT GHASTLY HOWL?
IT'S THE FOGHORN.
62
AND WHAT'S THAT!
IT'S THE LOCH NESS MONSTER'S WIDOW. SHE ALWAYS SURFACES WHEN THERE IS A FOG BECAUSE THE FOGHORN REMINDS HER OF HER LATE HUSBAND.
Tove Jansson
NO, THIS IS TOO MUCH! I'M TIRED OF SEA AND LIGHT-HOUSES AND THE REST OF IT! I'M GOING TO SWIM HOME!

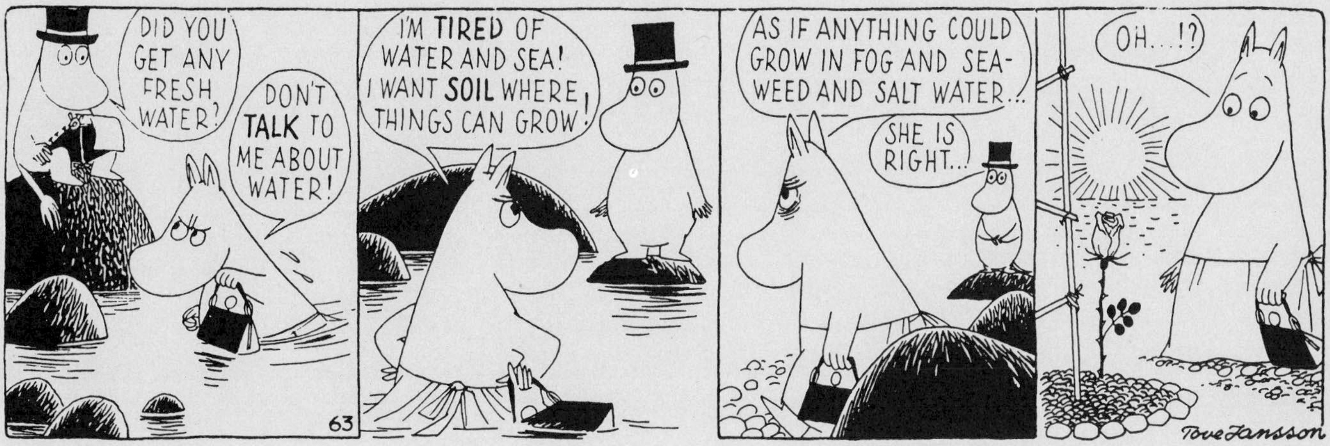
DID YOU GET ANY FRESH WATER?
DON'T **TALK** TO ME ABOUT WATER!
I'M **TIRED** OF WATER AND SEA! I WANT **SOIL** WHERE THINGS CAN GROW!
AS IF ANYTHING COULD GROW IN FOG AND SEA-WEED AND SALT WATER...
SHE IS RIGHT...
OH...!?
63
Tove Jansson

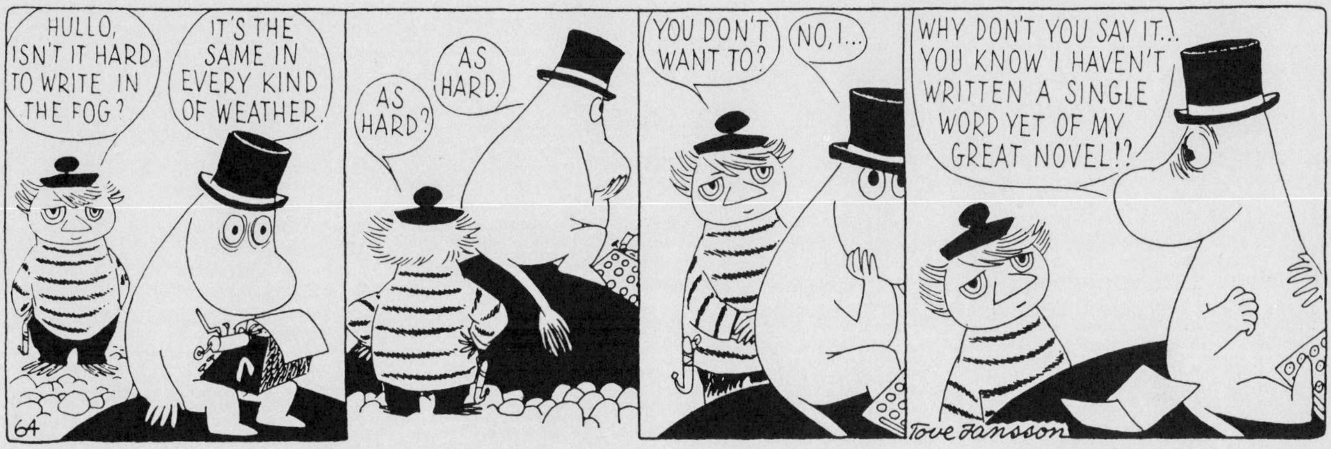
HULLO, ISN'T IT HARD TO WRITE IN THE FOG?
IT'S THE SAME IN EVERY KIND OF WEATHER.
AS HARD?
AS HARD.
YOU DON'T WANT TO?
NO, I...
WHY DON'T YOU SAY IT... YOU KNOW I HAVEN'T WRITTEN A SINGLE WORD YET OF MY GREAT NOVEL!?
64
Tove Jansson

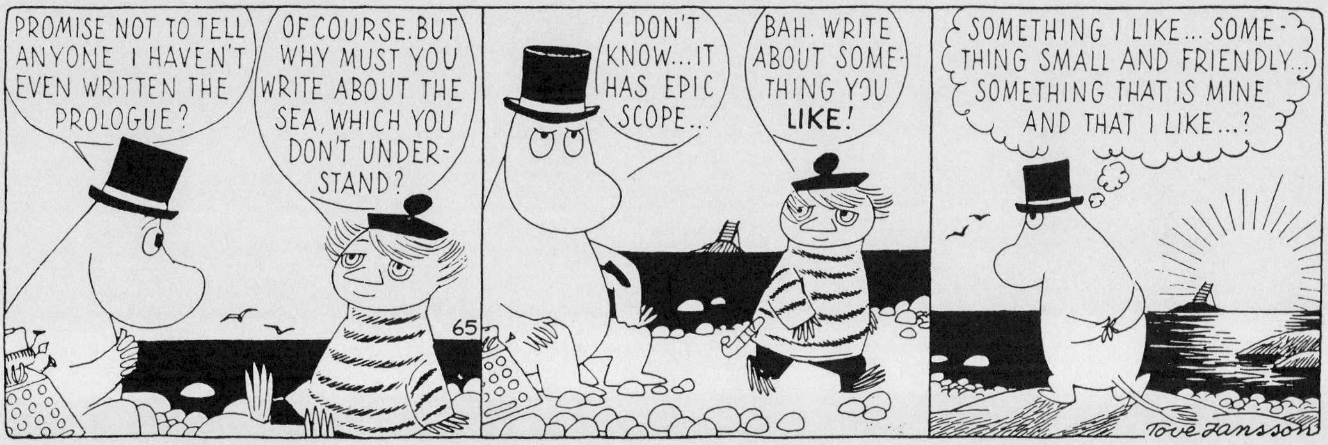
PROMISE NOT TO TELL ANYONE I HAVEN'T EVEN WRITTEN THE PROLOGUE?
OF COURSE. BUT WHY MUST YOU WRITE ABOUT THE SEA, WHICH YOU DON'T UNDER-STAND?
I DON'T KNOW... IT HAS EPIC SCOPE...
BAH. WRITE ABOUT SOME-THING YOU **LIKE**!
SOMETHING I LIKE... SOME-THING SMALL AND FRIENDLY... SOMETHING THAT IS MINE AND THAT I LIKE...?
65
Tove Jansson

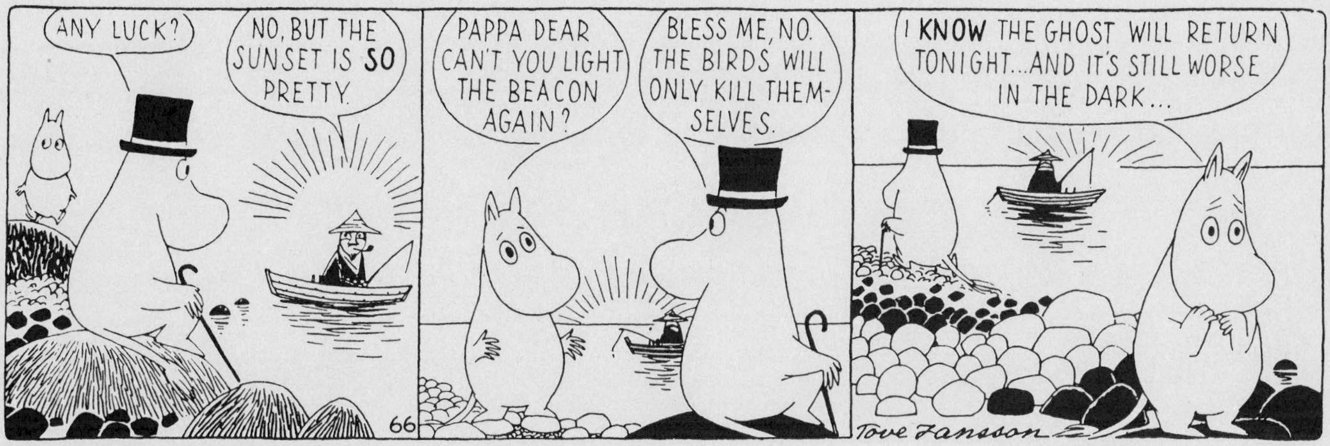
ANY LUCK?
NO, BUT THE SUNSET IS **SO** PRETTY.
PAPPA DEAR CAN'T YOU LIGHT THE BEACON AGAIN?
BLESS ME, NO. THE BIRDS WILL ONLY KILL THEM-SELVES.
I **KNOW** THE GHOST WILL RETURN TONIGHT... AND IT'S STILL WORSE IN THE DARK...
66
Tove Jansson

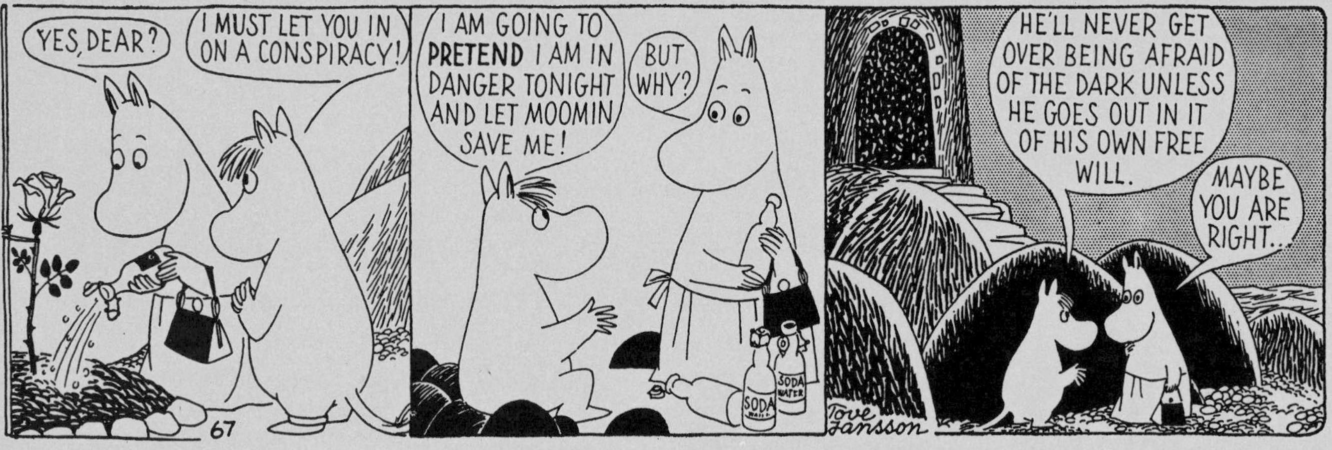
YES, DEAR?
I MUST LET YOU IN ON A CONSPIRACY!
67
I AM GOING TO **PRETEND** I AM IN DANGER TONIGHT AND LET MOOMIN SAVE ME!
BUT WHY?
SODA WATER
HE'LL NEVER GET OVER BEING AFRAID OF THE DARK UNLESS HE GOES OUT IN IT OF HIS OWN FREE WILL.
MAYBE YOU ARE RIGHT...
Tove Jansson

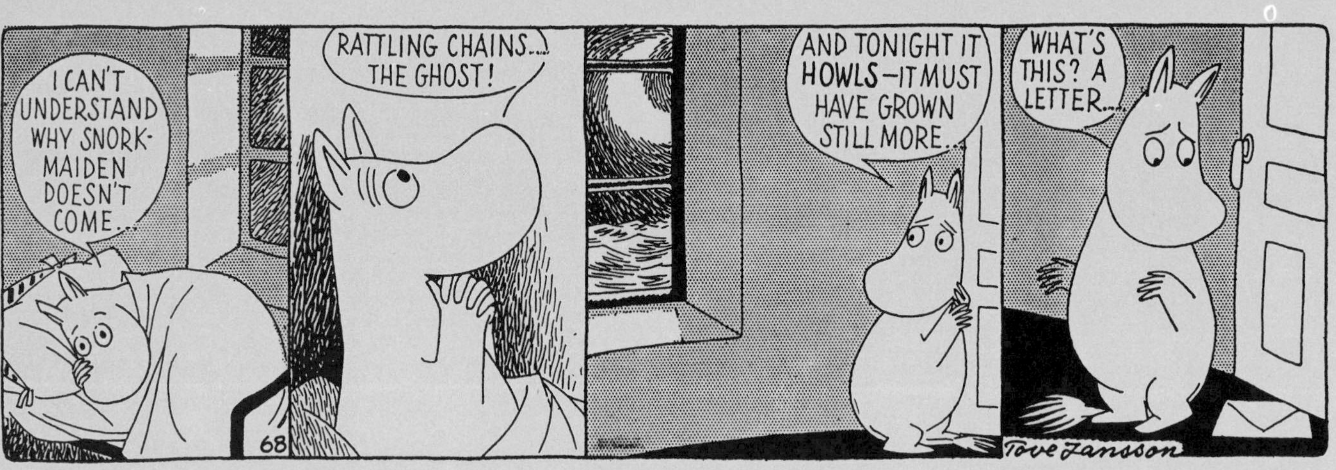
I CAN'T UNDERSTAND WHY SNORK-MAIDEN DOESN'T COME...
68
RATTLING CHAINS... THE GHOST!
AND TONIGHT IT **HOWLS**—IT MUST HAVE GROWN STILL MORE...
WHAT'S THIS? A LETTER...
Tove Jansson

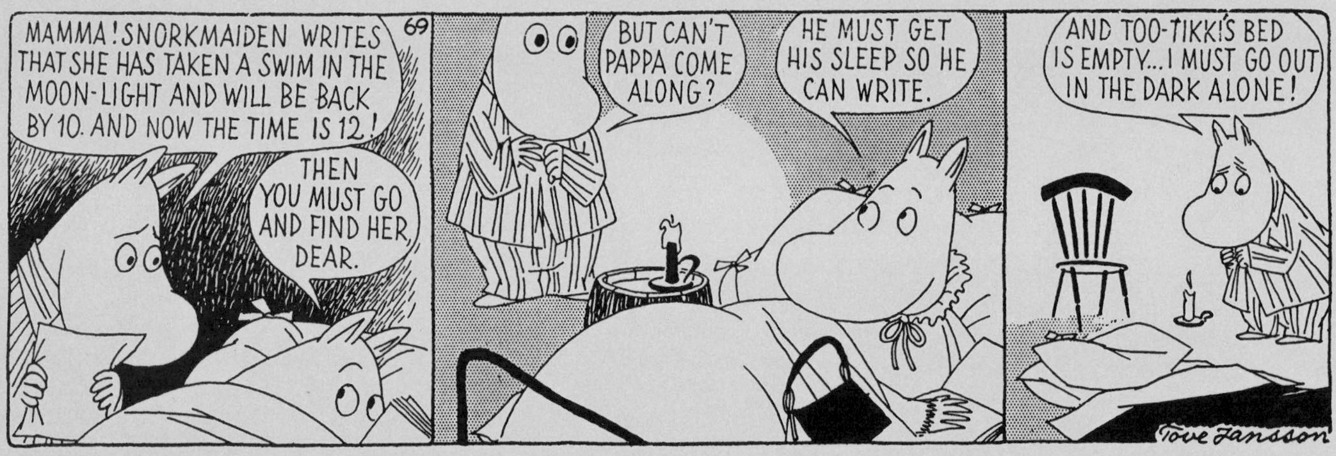
MAMMA! SNORKMAIDEN WRITES THAT SHE HAS TAKEN A SWIM IN THE MOON-LIGHT AND WILL BE BACK BY 10. AND NOW THE TIME IS 12!
69
THEN YOU MUST GO AND FIND HER, DEAR.
BUT CAN'T PAPPA COME ALONG?
HE MUST GET HIS SLEEP SO HE CAN WRITE.
AND TOO-TIKKI'S BED IS EMPTY... I MUST GO OUT IN THE DARK ALONE!
Tove Jansson

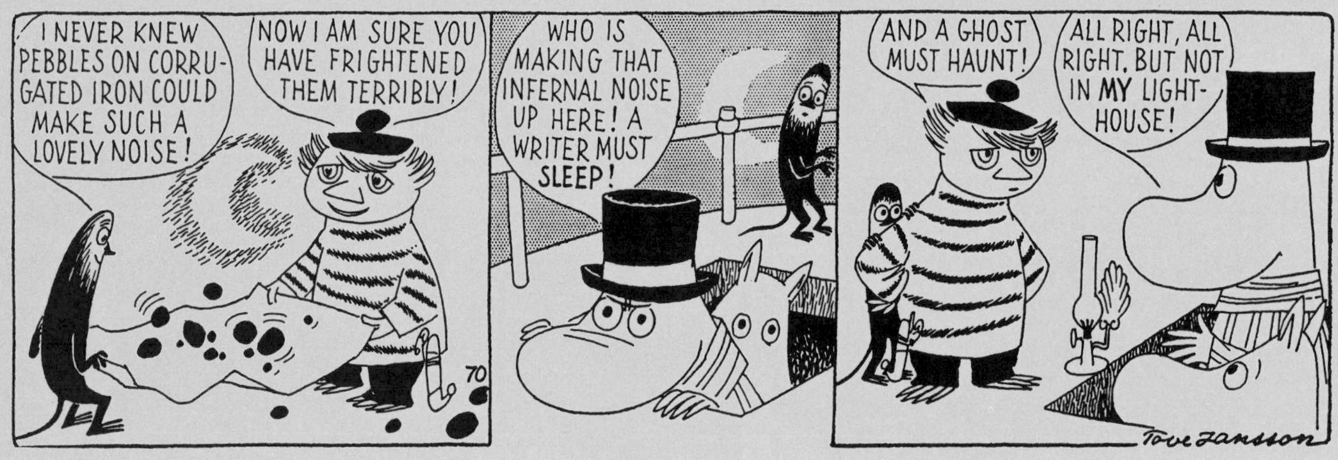
I NEVER KNEW PEBBLES ON CORRU-GATED IRON COULD MAKE SUCH A LOVELY NOISE!
NOW I AM SURE YOU HAVE FRIGHTENED THEM TERRIBLY!
70
WHO IS MAKING THAT INFERNAL NOISE UP HERE! A WRITER MUST **SLEEP**!
AND A GHOST MUST HAUNT!
ALL RIGHT, ALL RIGHT, BUT NOT IN **MY** LIGHT-HOUSE!
Tove Jansson

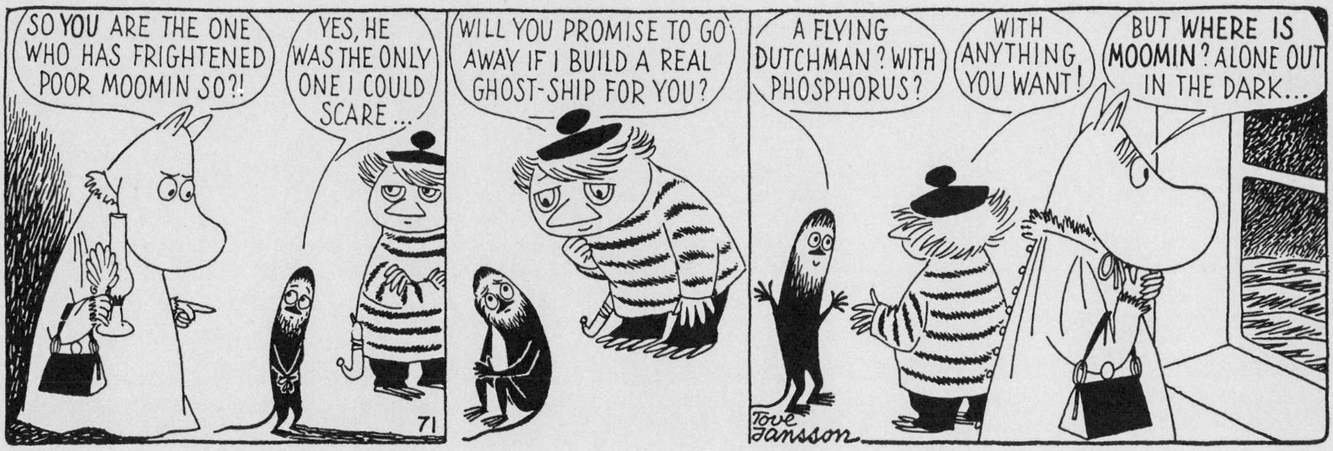
SO YOU ARE THE ONE WHO HAS FRIGHTENED POOR MOOMIN SO?!
YES, HE WAS THE ONLY ONE I COULD SCARE...
71
WILL YOU PROMISE TO GO AWAY IF I BUILD A REAL GHOST-SHIP FOR YOU?
A FLYING DUTCHMAN? WITH PHOSPHORUS?
WITH ANYTHING, YOU WANT!
BUT WHERE IS MOOMIN? ALONE OUT IN THE DARK...
Tove Jansson

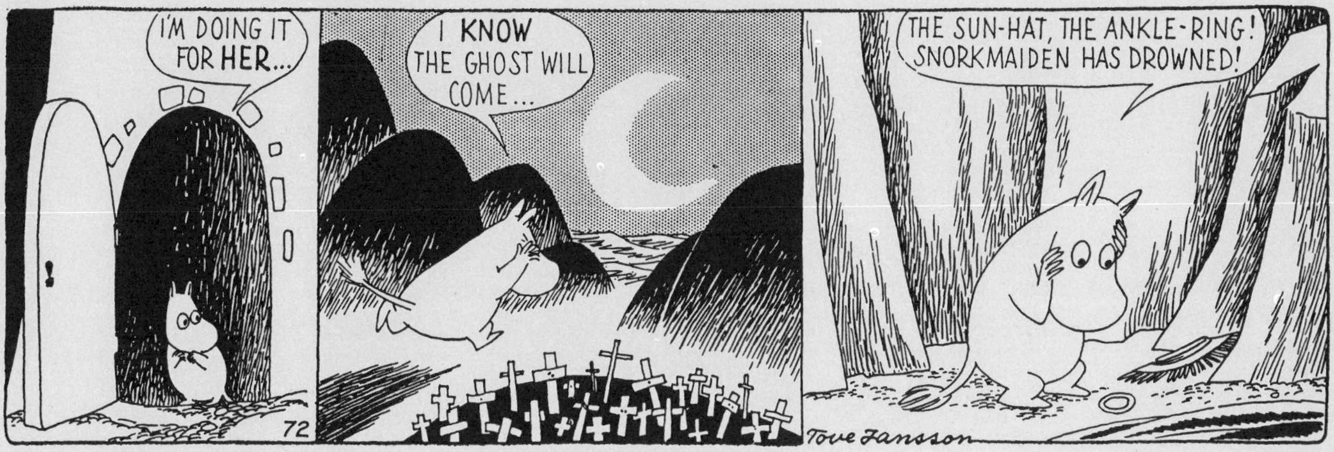
I'M DOING IT FOR HER...
72
I KNOW THE GHOST WILL COME...
THE SUN-HAT, THE ANKLE-RING! SNORKMAIDEN HAS DROWNED!
Tove Jansson

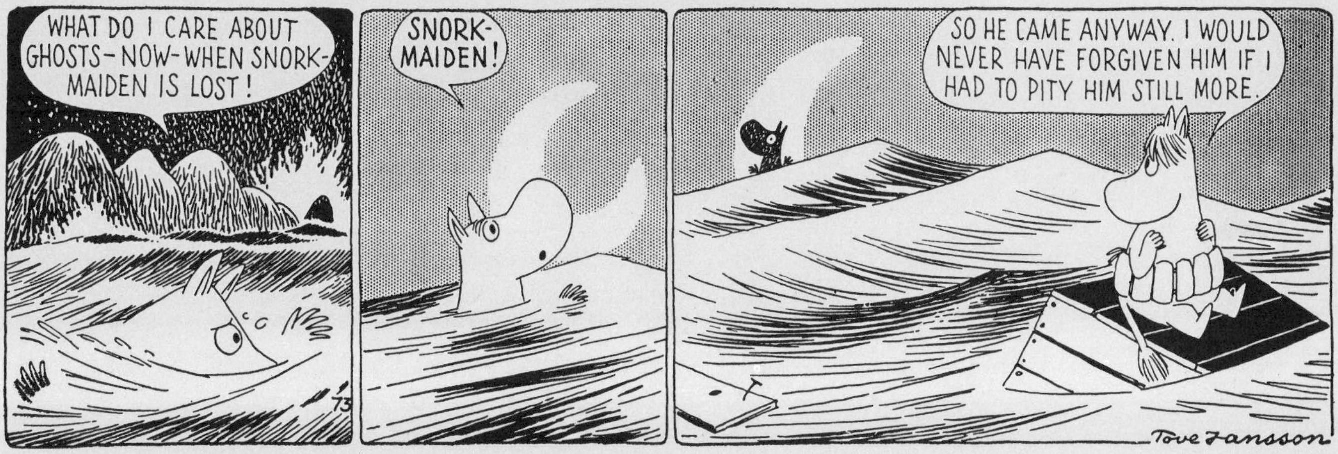
WHAT DO I CARE ABOUT GHOSTS—NOW—WHEN SNORK-MAIDEN IS LOST!
73
SNORK-MAIDEN!
SO HE CAME ANYWAY. I WOULD NEVER HAVE FORGIVEN HIM IF I HAD TO PITY HIM STILL MORE.
Tove Jansson

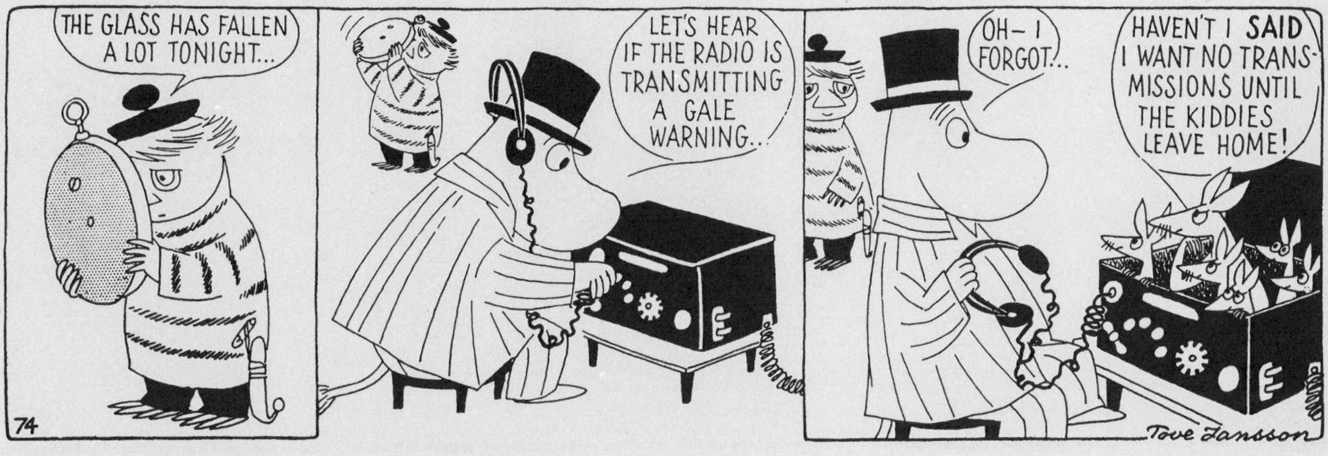
THE GLASS HAS FALLEN A LOT TONIGHT...
74
LET'S HEAR IF THE RADIO IS TRANSMITTING A GALE WARNING...
OH—I FORGOT...
HAVEN'T I SAID I WANT NO TRANS-MISSIONS UNTIL THE KIDDIES LEAVE HOME!
Tove Jansson

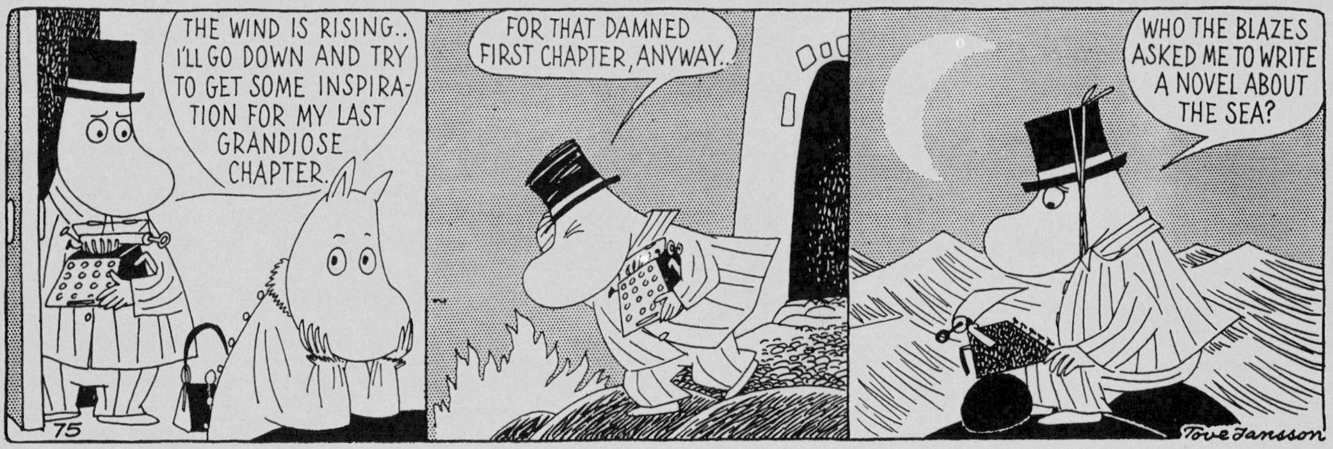
75
THE WIND IS RISING.. I'LL GO DOWN AND TRY TO GET SOME INSPIRATION FOR MY LAST GRANDIOSE CHAPTER.
FOR THAT DAMNED FIRST CHAPTER, ANYWAY...
WHO THE BLAZES ASKED ME TO WRITE A NOVEL ABOUT THE SEA?
Tove Jansson

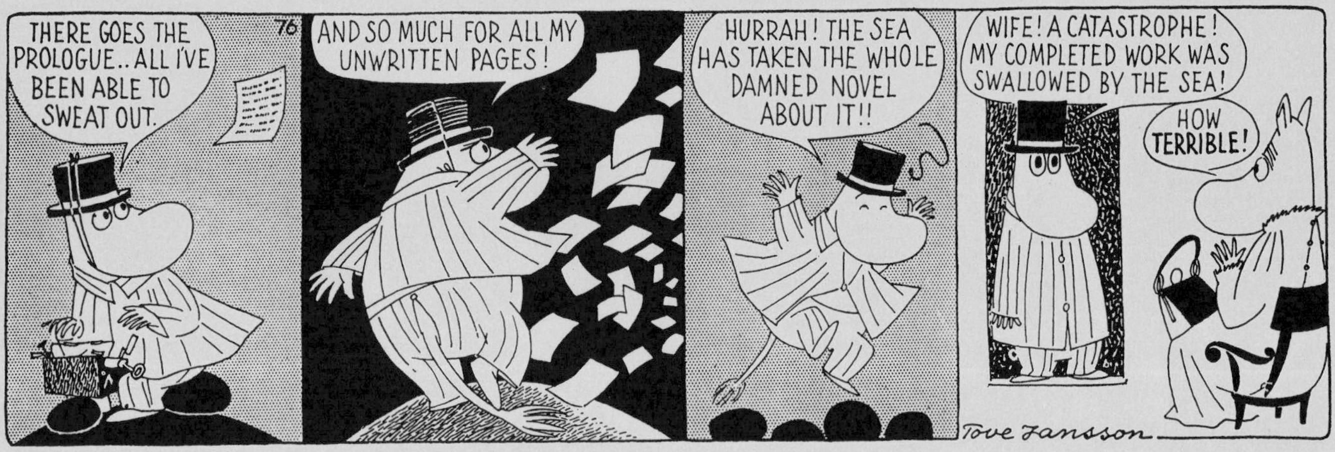
76
THERE GOES THE PROLOGUE.. ALL I'VE BEEN ABLE TO SWEAT OUT.
AND SO MUCH FOR ALL MY UNWRITTEN PAGES!
HURRAH! THE SEA HAS TAKEN THE WHOLE DAMNED NOVEL ABOUT IT!!
WIFE! A CATASTROPHE! MY COMPLETED WORK WAS SWALLOWED BY THE SEA!
HOW TERRIBLE!
Tove Jansson

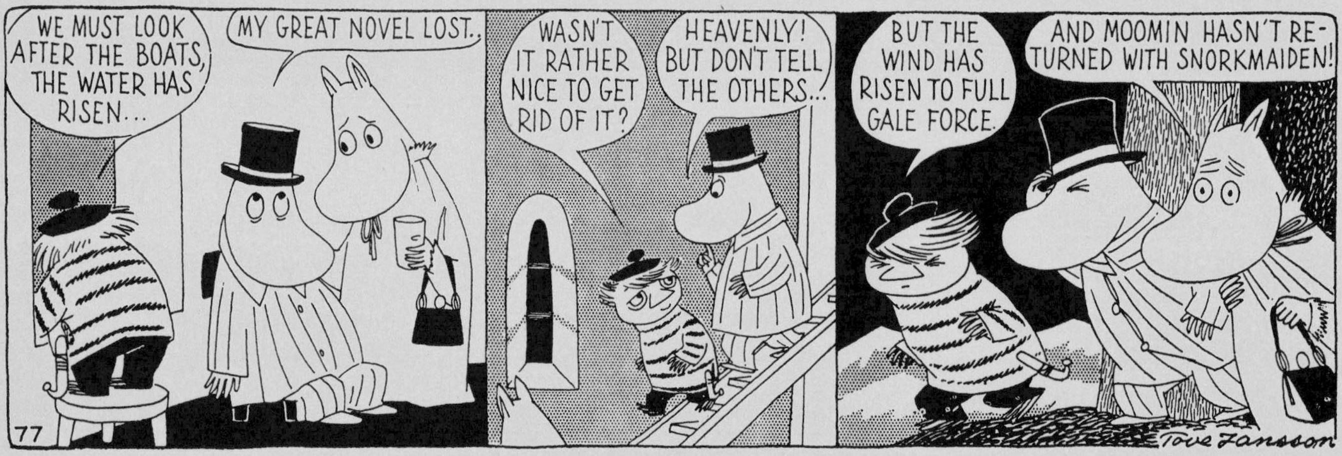
77
WE MUST LOOK AFTER THE BOATS, THE WATER HAS RISEN...
MY GREAT NOVEL LOST..
WASN'T IT RATHER NICE TO GET RID OF IT?
HEAVENLY! BUT DON'T TELL THE OTHERS...
BUT THE WIND HAS RISEN TO FULL GALE FORCE.
AND MOOMIN HASN'T RETURNED WITH SNORKMAIDEN!
Tove Jansson

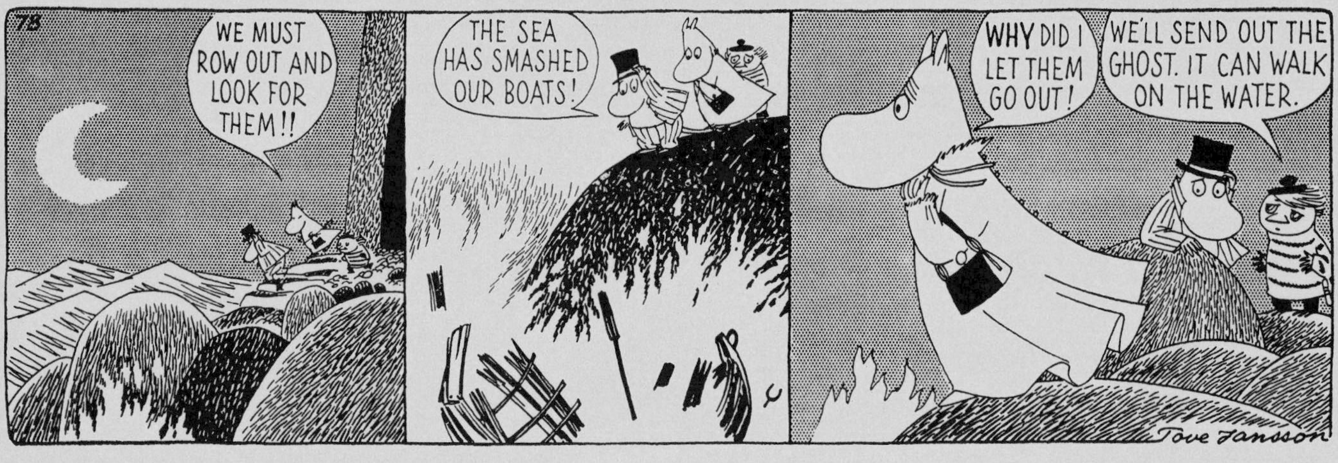
78
WE MUST ROW OUT AND LOOK FOR THEM!!
THE SEA HAS SMASHED OUR BOATS!
WHY DID I LET THEM GO OUT!
WE'LL SEND OUT THE GHOST. IT CAN WALK ON THE WATER.
Tove Jansson

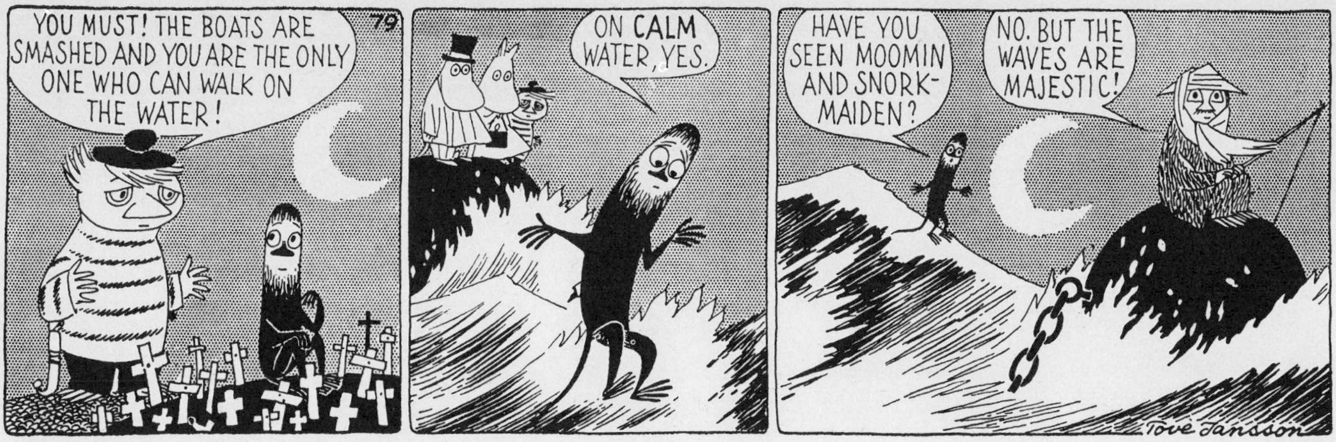
79
YOU MUST! THE BOATS ARE SMASHED AND YOU ARE THE ONLY ONE WHO CAN WALK ON THE WATER!
ON CALM WATER, YES.
HAVE YOU SEEN MOOMIN AND SNORK-MAIDEN?
NO. BUT THE WAVES ARE MAJESTIC!
Tove Jansson

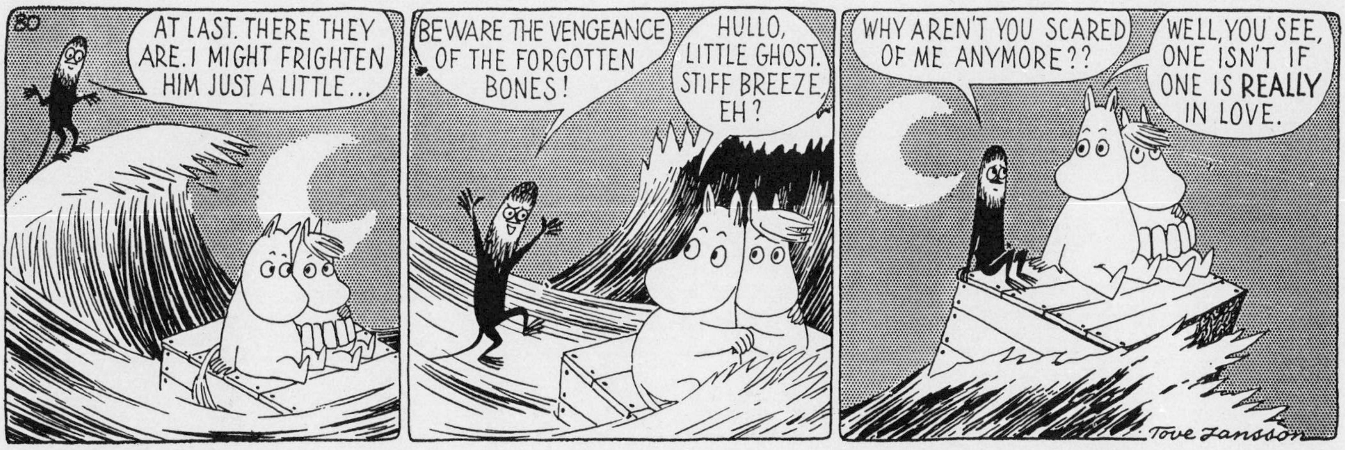
80
AT LAST. THERE THEY ARE. I MIGHT FRIGHTEN HIM JUST A LITTLE...
BEWARE THE VENGEANCE OF THE FORGOTTEN BONES!
HULLO, LITTLE GHOST. STIFF BREEZE EH?
WHY AREN'T YOU SCARED OF ME ANYMORE??
WELL, YOU SEE, ONE ISN'T IF ONE IS REALLY IN LOVE.
Tove Jansson

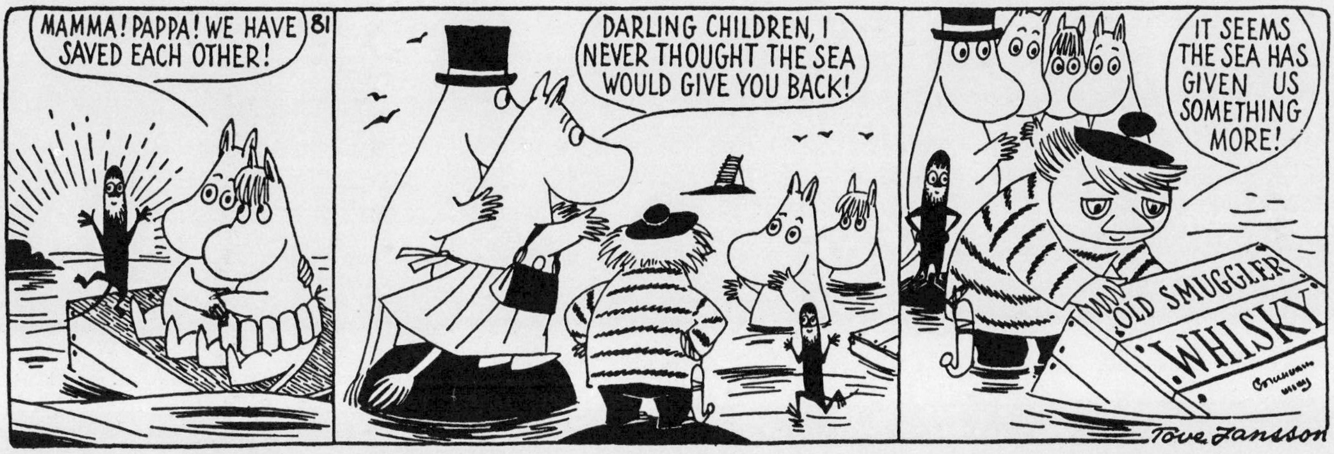
MAMMA! PAPPA! WE HAVE SAVED EACH OTHER!
81
DARLING CHILDREN, I NEVER THOUGHT THE SEA WOULD GIVE YOU BACK!
IT SEEMS THE SEA HAS GIVEN US SOMETHING MORE!
OLD SMUGGLER
WHISKY
Tove Jansson

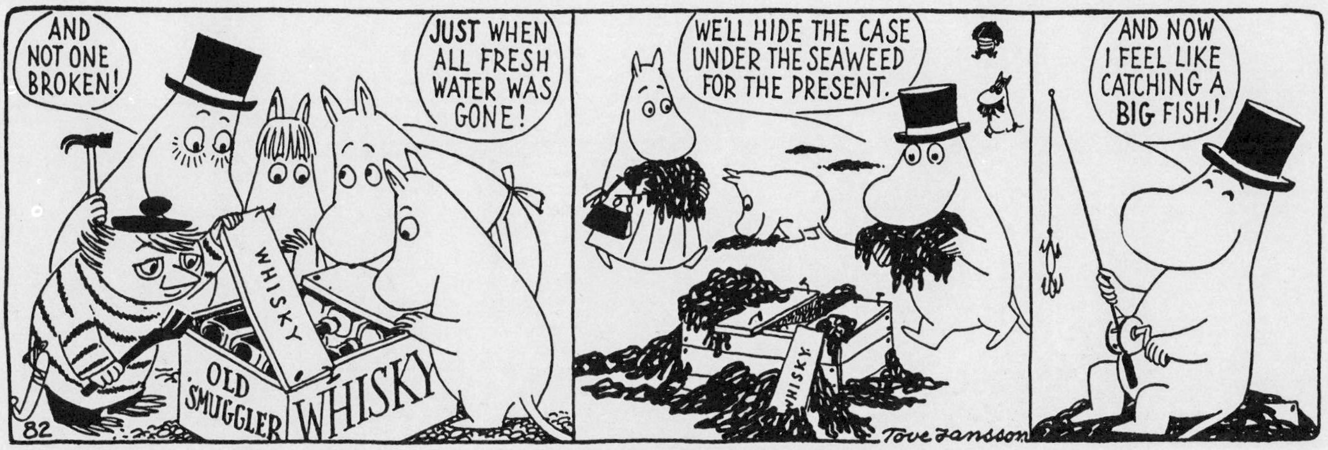
AND NOT ONE BROKEN!
JUST WHEN ALL FRESH WATER WAS GONE!
WHISKY
OLD SMUGGLER
WHISKY
82
WE'LL HIDE THE CASE UNDER THE SEAWEED FOR THE PRESENT.
WHISKY
Tove Jansson
AND NOW I FEEL LIKE CATCHING A BIG FISH!

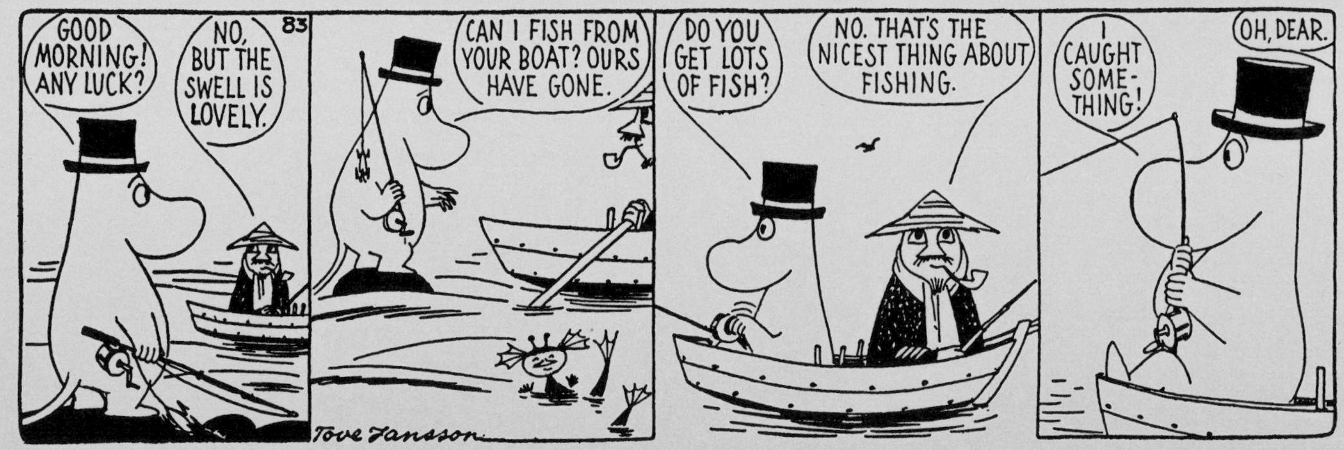
GOOD MORNING! ANY LUCK?
NO, BUT THE SWELL IS LOVELY.
83
CAN I FISH FROM YOUR BOAT? OURS HAVE GONE.
DO YOU GET LOTS OF FISH?
NO. THAT'S THE NICEST THING ABOUT FISHING.
I CAUGHT SOME-THING!
OH, DEAR.
Tove Jansson

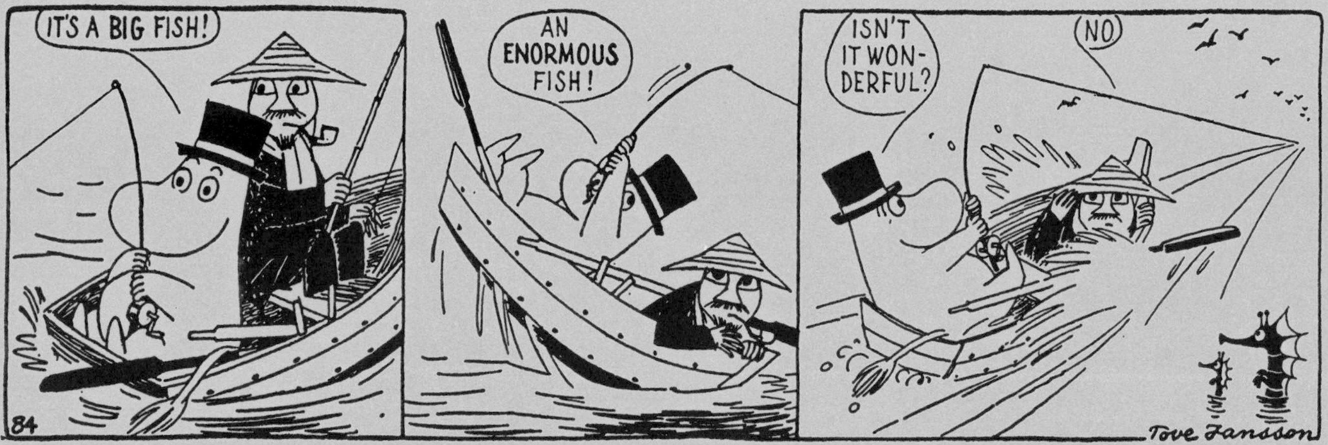
IT'S A BIG FISH!
84
AN ENORMOUS FISH!
ISN'T IT WON-DERFUL?
NO
Tove Jansson

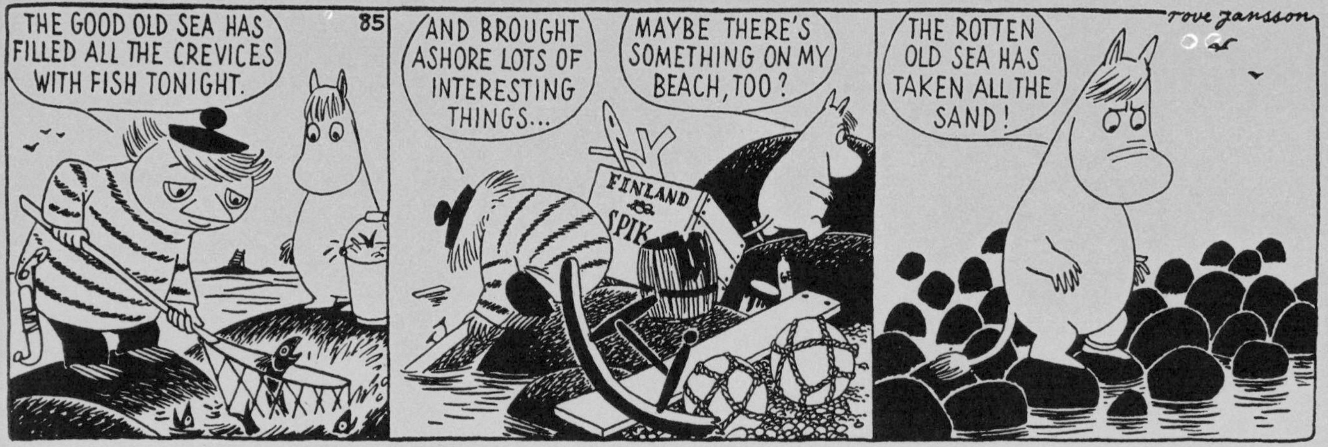
THE GOOD OLD SEA HAS FILLED ALL THE CREVICES WITH FISH TONIGHT.
85
AND BROUGHT ASHORE LOTS OF INTERESTING THINGS...
MAYBE THERE'S SOMETHING ON MY BEACH, TOO?
FINLAND
SPIK
THE ROTTEN OLD SEA HAS TAKEN ALL THE SAND!
Tove Jansson

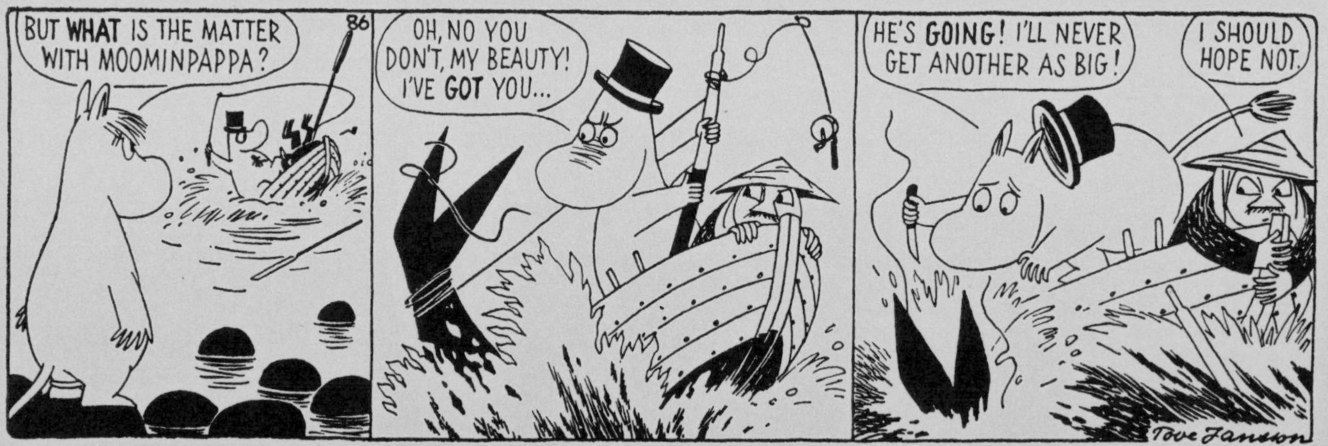
BUT WHAT IS THE MATTER WITH MOOMINPAPPA?
86
OH, NO YOU DON'T, MY BEAUTY! I'VE GOT YOU...
HE'S GOING! I'LL NEVER GET ANOTHER AS BIG!
I SHOULD HOPE NOT.
Tove Jansson

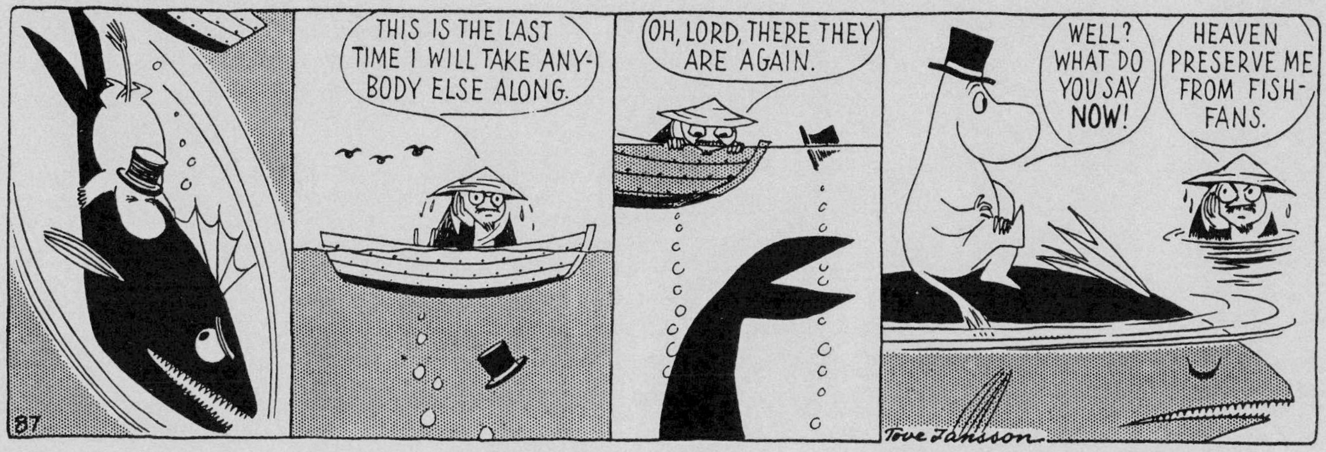
87
THIS IS THE LAST TIME I WILL TAKE ANY-BODY ELSE ALONG.
OH, LORD, THERE THEY ARE AGAIN.
WELL? WHAT DO YOU SAY NOW!
HEAVEN PRESERVE ME FROM FISH-FANS.
Tove Jansson

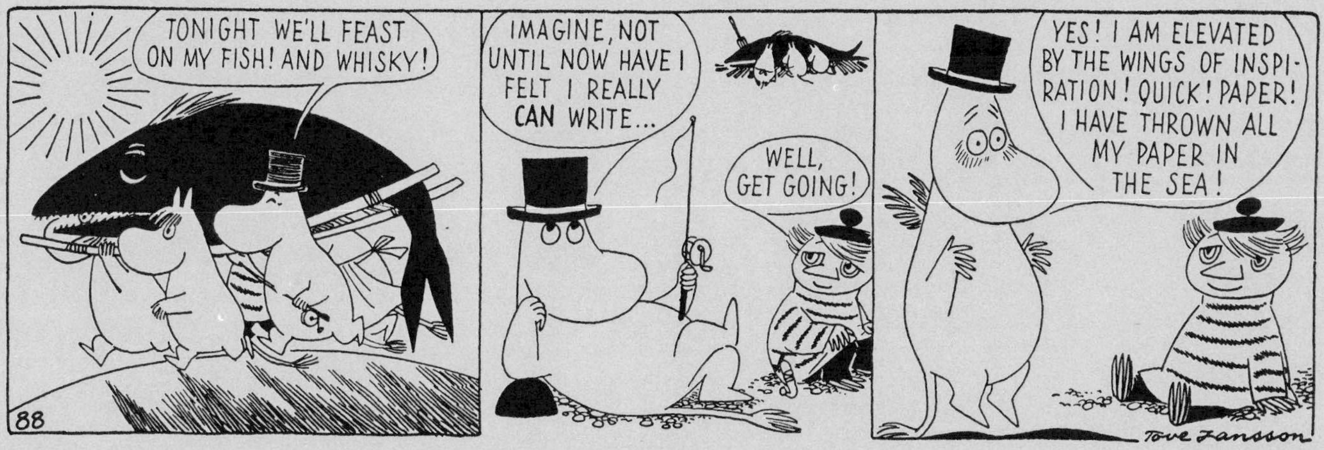
TONIGHT WE'LL FEAST ON MY FISH! AND WHISKY!
88
IMAGINE, NOT UNTIL NOW HAVE I FELT I REALLY CAN WRITE...
WELL, GET GOING!
YES! I AM ELEVATED BY THE WINGS OF INSPI-RATION! QUICK! PAPER! I HAVE THROWN ALL MY PAPER IN THE SEA!
Tove Jansson

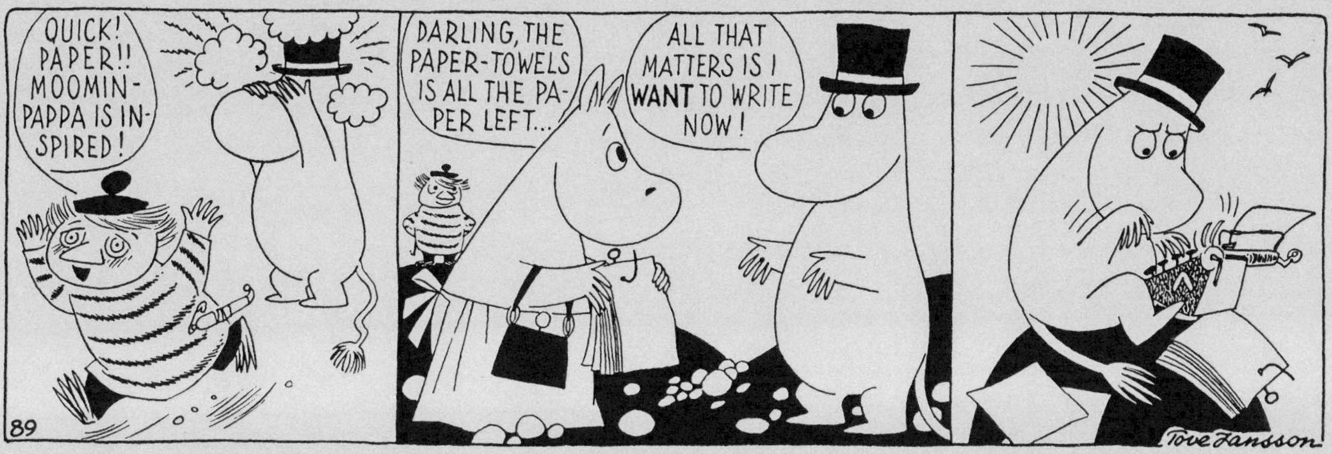
QUICK! PAPER!! MOOMIN-PAPPA IS IN-SPIRED!
89
DARLING, THE PAPER-TOWELS IS ALL THE PA-PER LEFT...
ALL THAT MATTERS IS I WANT TO WRITE NOW!
Tove Jansson

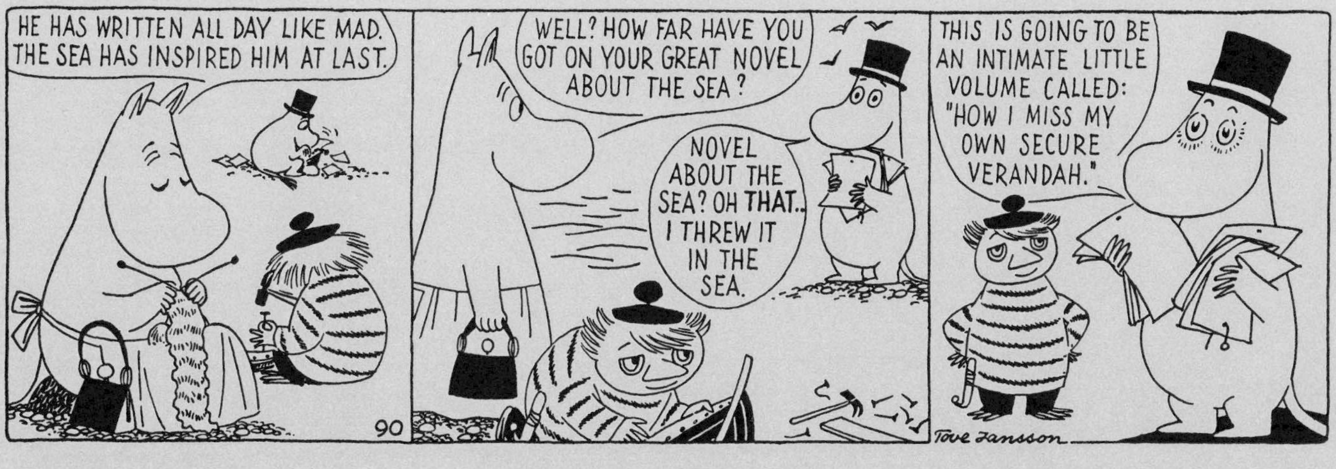
HE HAS WRITTEN ALL DAY LIKE MAD. THE SEA HAS INSPIRED HIM AT LAST.
90
WELL? HOW FAR HAVE YOU GOT ON YOUR GREAT NOVEL ABOUT THE SEA?
NOVEL ABOUT THE SEA? OH THAT.. I THREW IT IN THE SEA.
THIS IS GOING TO BE AN INTIMATE LITTLE VOLUME CALLED: "HOW I MISS MY OWN SECURE VERANDAH."
Tove Jansson

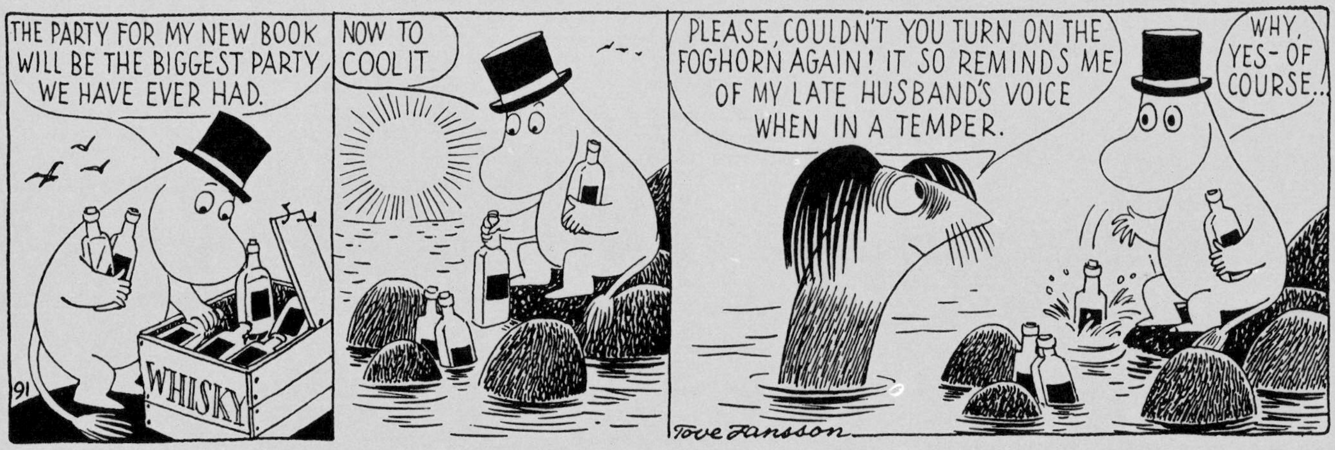
THE PARTY FOR MY NEW BOOK WILL BE THE BIGGEST PARTY WE HAVE EVER HAD.
WHISKY
91
NOW TO COOL IT
PLEASE, COULDN'T YOU TURN ON THE FOGHORN AGAIN! IT SO REMINDS ME OF MY LATE HUSBAND'S VOICE WHEN IN A TEMPER.
WHY, YES- OF COURSE...
Tove Jansson

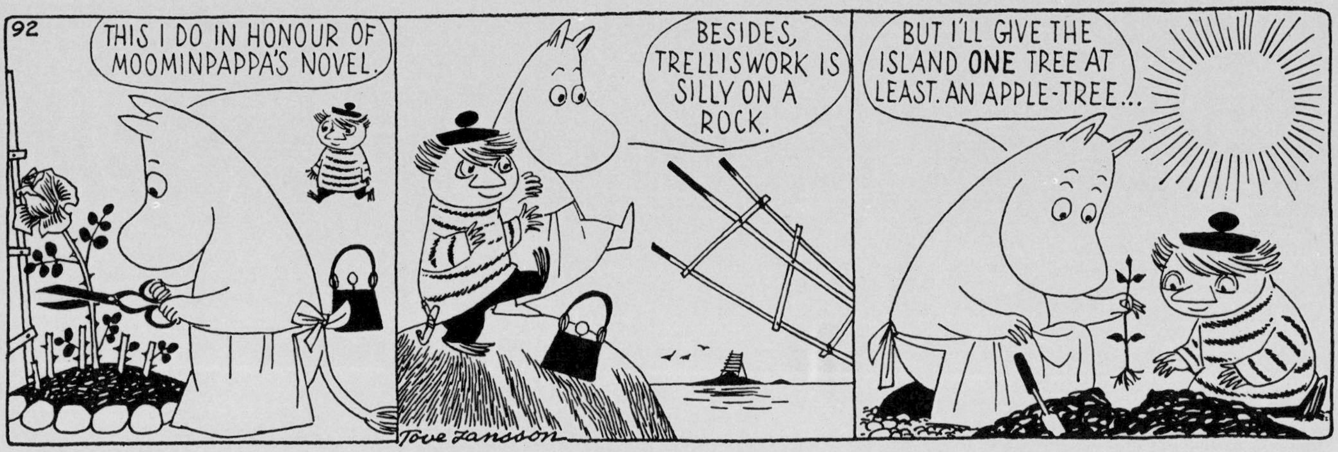
92
THIS I DO IN HONOUR OF MOOMINPAPPA'S NOVEL.
BESIDES, TRELLISWORK IS SILLY ON A ROCK.
Tove Jansson
BUT I'LL GIVE THE ISLAND ONE TREE AT LEAST. AN APPLE-TREE...

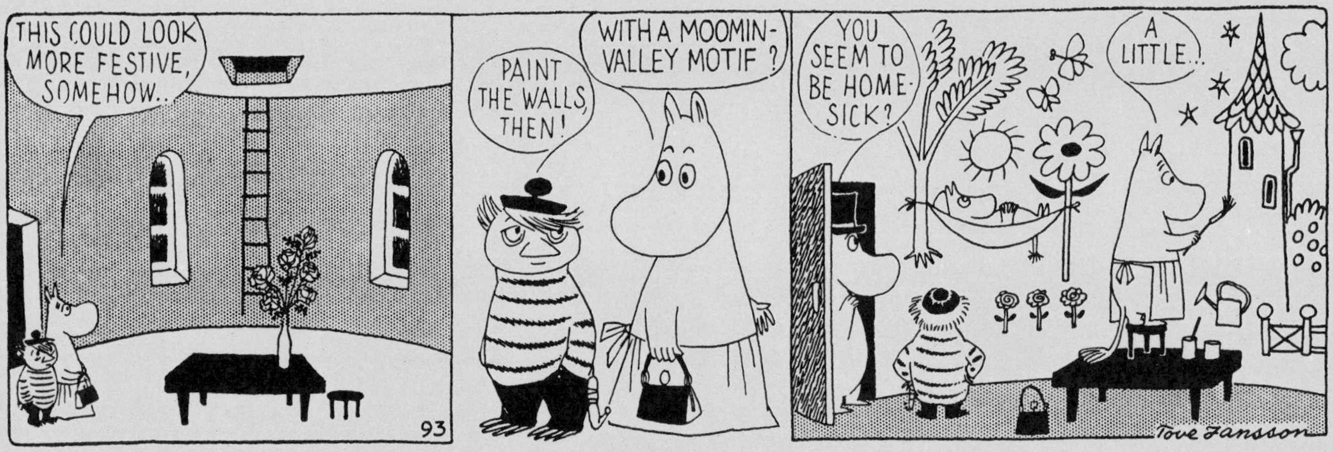
THIS COULD LOOK MORE FESTIVE, SOMEHOW...
93
PAINT THE WALLS, THEN!
WITH A MOOMIN-VALLEY MOTIF?
YOU SEEM TO BE HOME-SICK?
A LITTLE...
Tove Jansson

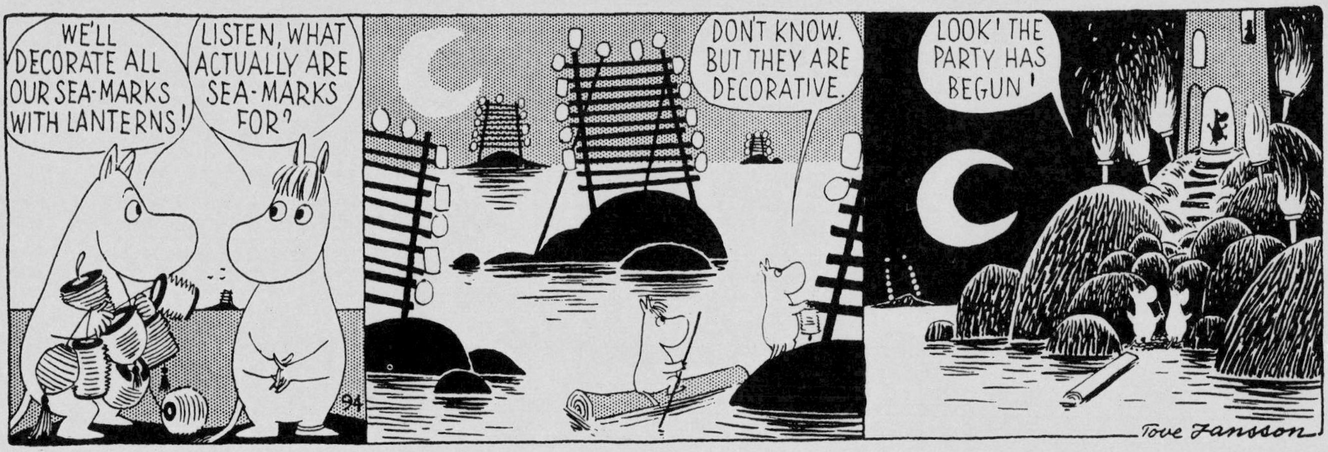
WE'LL DECORATE ALL OUR SEA-MARKS WITH LANTERNS!
LISTEN, WHAT ACTUALLY ARE SEA-MARKS FOR?
94
DON'T KNOW. BUT THEY ARE DECORATIVE.
LOOK! THE PARTY HAS BEGUN!
Tove Jansson

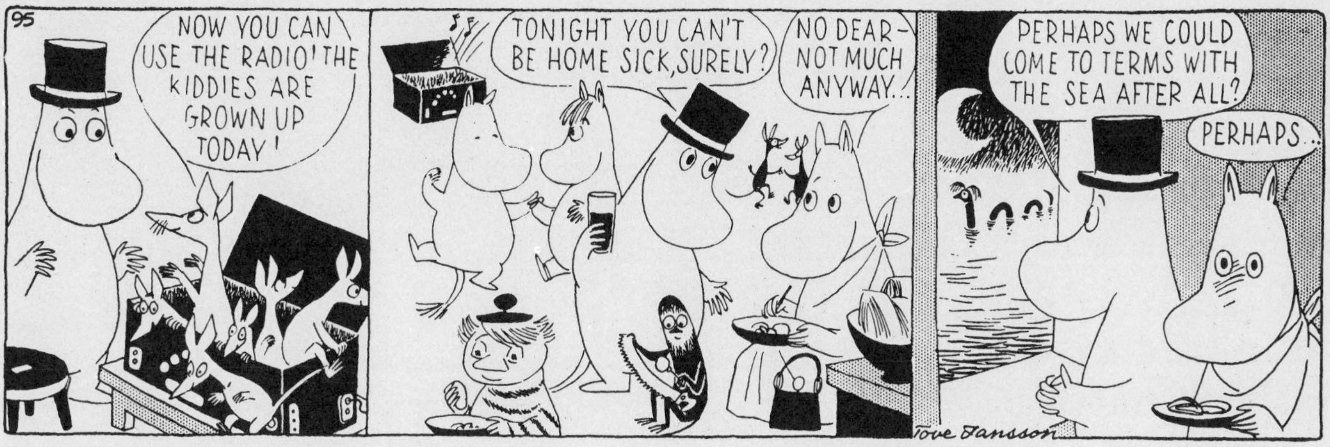
95
NOW YOU CAN USE THE RADIO! THE KIDDIES ARE GROWN UP TODAY!
TONIGHT YOU CAN'T BE HOME SICK, SURELY?
NO DEAR- NOT MUCH ANYWAY...
PERHAPS WE COULD COME TO TERMS WITH THE SEA AFTER ALL?
PERHAPS...
Tove Jansson

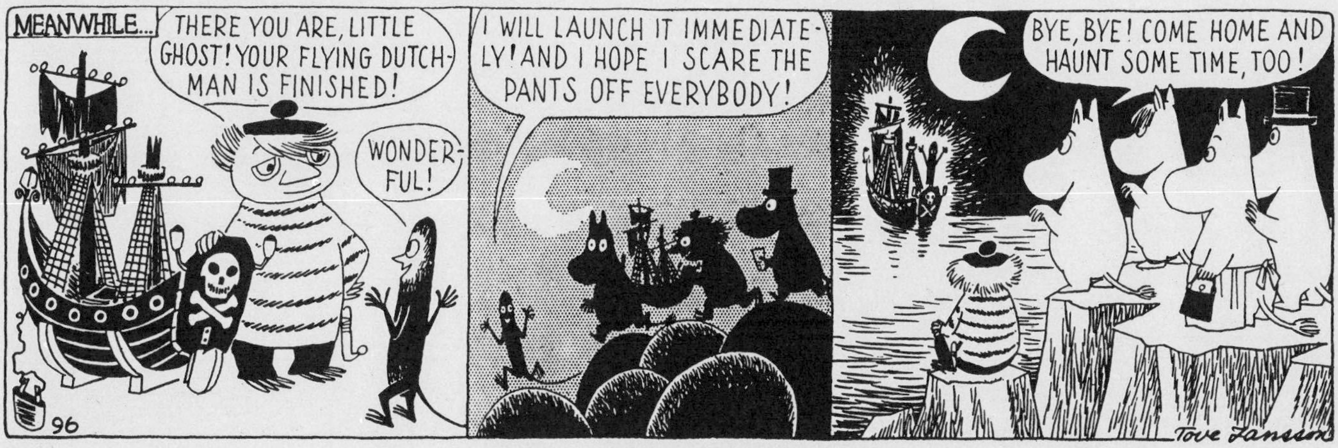
MEANWHILE...
THERE YOU ARE, LITTLE GHOST! YOUR FLYING DUTCH-MAN IS FINISHED!
WONDER-FUL!
96
I WILL LAUNCH IT IMMEDIATE-LY! AND I HOPE I SCARE THE PANTS OFF EVERYBODY!
BYE, BYE! COME HOME AND HAUNT SOME TIME, TOO!
Tove Jansson

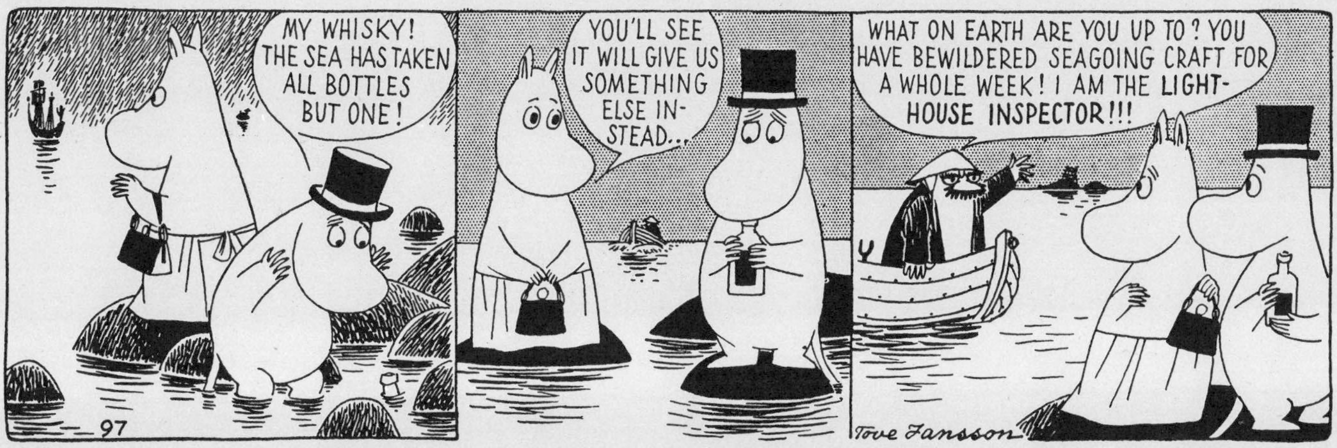
MY WHISKY! THE SEA HAS TAKEN ALL BOTTLES BUT ONE!
97
YOU'LL SEE IT WILL GIVE US SOMETHING ELSE IN-STEAD...
WHAT ON EARTH ARE YOU UP TO? YOU HAVE BEWILDERED SEAGOING CRAFT FOR A WHOLE WEEK! I AM THE LIGHT-HOUSE INSPECTOR!!!
Tove Jansson

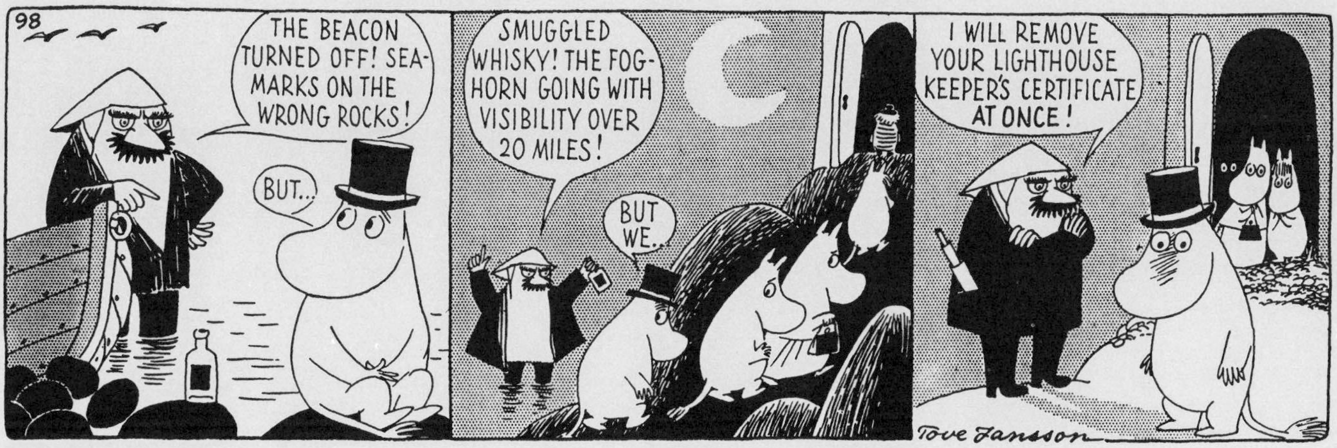
98
THE BEACON TURNED OFF! SEA-MARKS ON THE WRONG ROCKS!
BUT...
SMUGGLED WHISKY! THE FOG-HORN GOING WITH VISIBILITY OVER 20 MILES!
BUT WE...
I WILL REMOVE YOUR LIGHTHOUSE KEEPER'S CERTIFICATE AT ONCE!
Tove Jansson

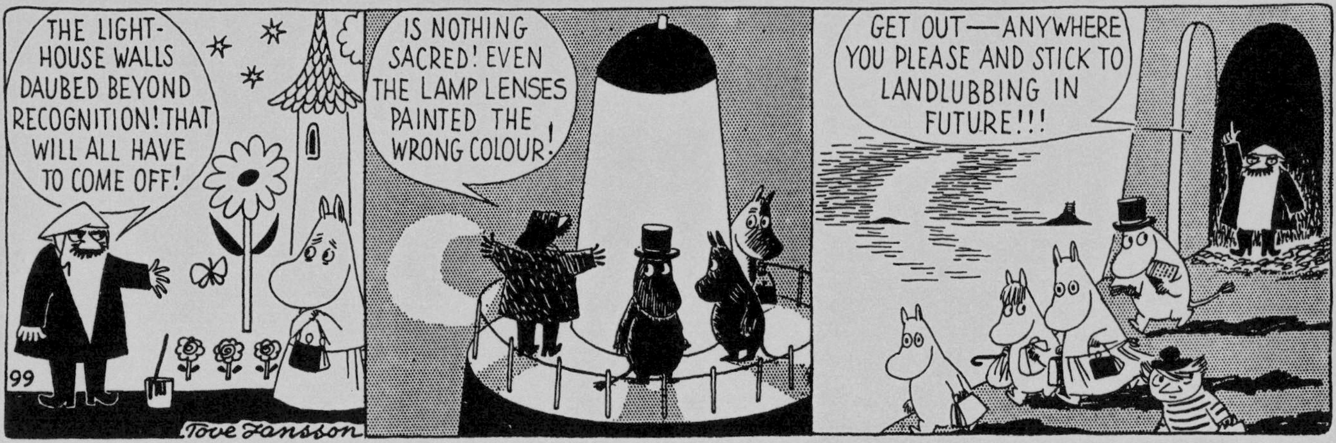
THE LIGHT-HOUSE WALLS DAUBED BEYOND RECOGNITION! THAT WILL ALL HAVE TO COME OFF!
99
Tove Jansson
IS NOTHING SACRED! EVEN THE LAMP LENSES PAINTED THE WRONG COLOUR!
GET OUT—ANYWHERE YOU PLEASE AND STICK TO LANDLUBBING IN FUTURE!!!

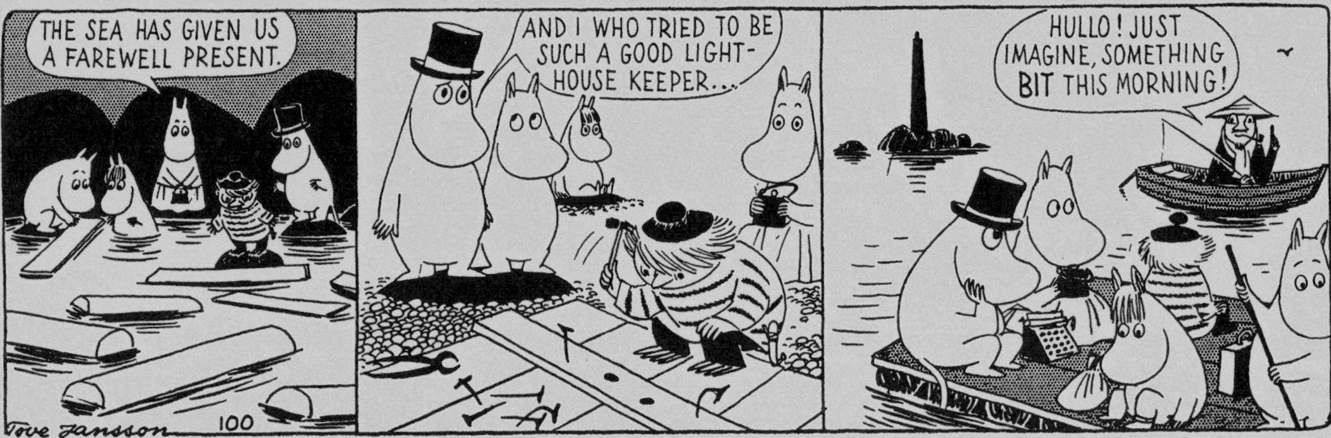
THE SEA HAS GIVEN US A FAREWELL PRESENT.
Tove Jansson
100
AND I WHO TRIED TO BE SUCH A GOOD LIGHT-HOUSE KEEPER...
HULLO! JUST IMAGINE, SOMETHING BIT THIS MORNING!

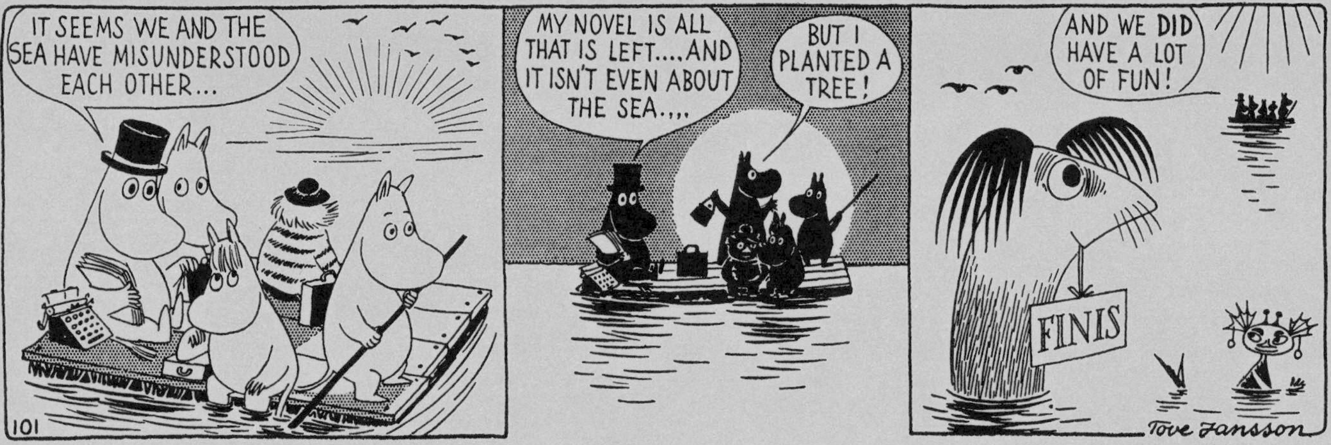
IT SEEMS WE AND THE SEA HAVE MISUNDERSTOOD EACH OTHER...
101
MY NOVEL IS ALL THAT IS LEFT....AND IT ISN'T EVEN ABOUT THE SEA....
BUT I PLANTED A TREE!
AND WE DID HAVE A LOT OF FUN!
FINIS
Tove Jansson

13. Club Life in Moominvalley

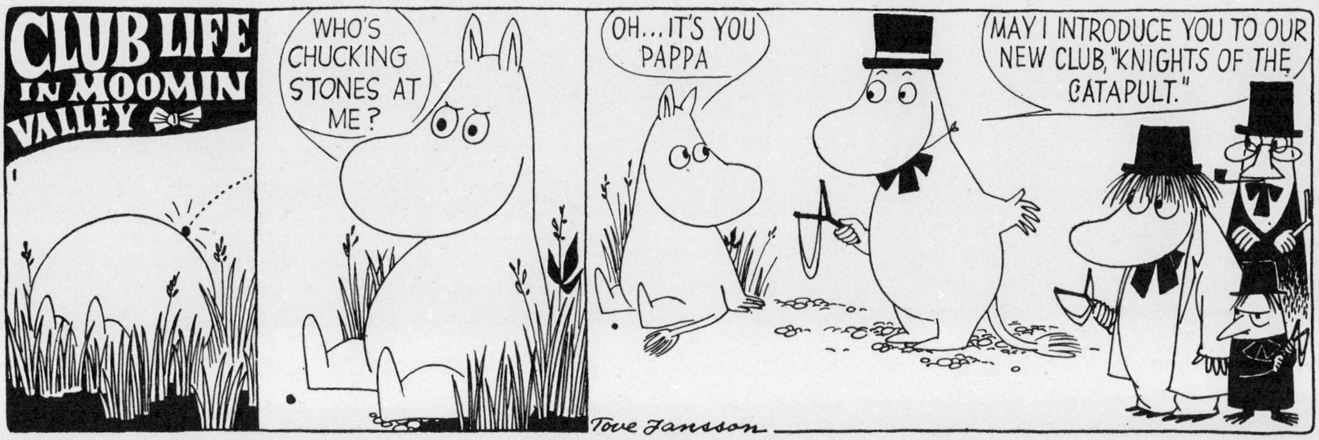
CLUB LIFE IN MOOMIN VALLEY
WHO'S CHUCKING STONES AT ME?
OH... IT'S YOU PAPPA
MAY I INTRODUCE YOU TO OUR NEW CLUB, "KNIGHTS OF THE CATAPULT."
Tove Jansson

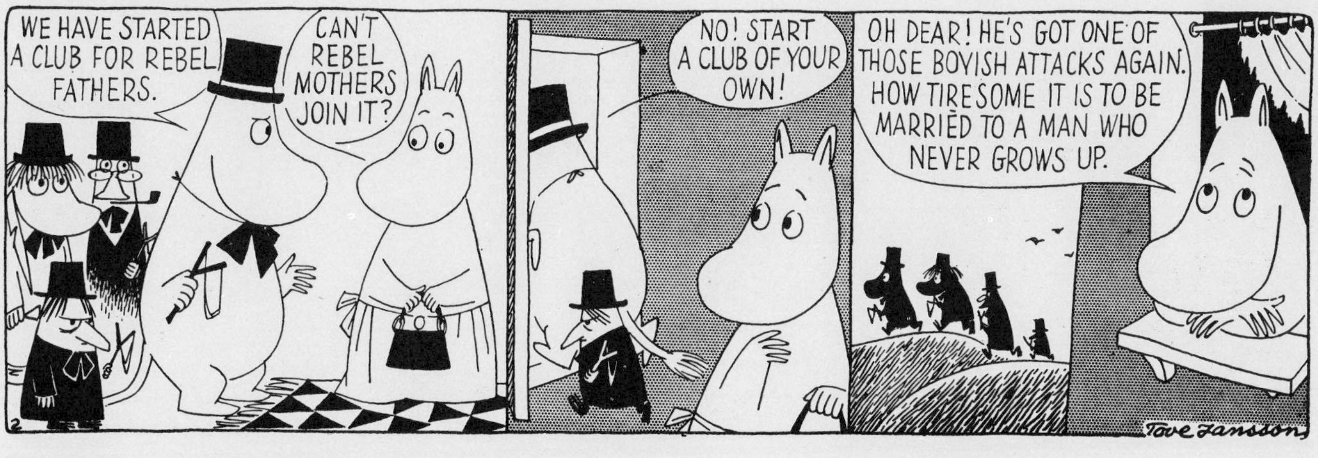
WE HAVE STARTED A CLUB FOR REBEL FATHERS.
CAN'T REBEL MOTHERS JOIN IT?
NO! START A CLUB OF YOUR OWN!
OH DEAR! HE'S GOT ONE OF THOSE BOYISH ATTACKS AGAIN. HOW TIRESOME IT IS TO BE MARRIED TO A MAN WHO NEVER GROWS UP.
Tove Jansson

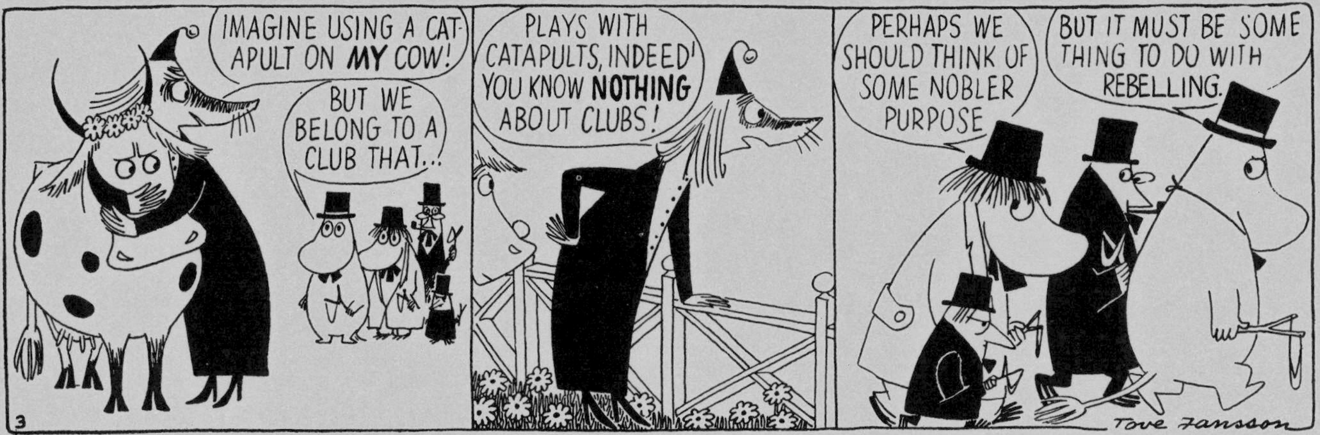
IMAGINE USING A CAT-APULT ON MY COW!
BUT WE BELONG TO A CLUB THAT...
PLAYS WITH CATAPULTS, INDEED! YOU KNOW NOTHING ABOUT CLUBS!
PERHAPS WE SHOULD THINK OF SOME NOBLER PURPOSE
BUT IT MUST BE SOME THING TO DO WITH REBELLING.
Tove Jansson

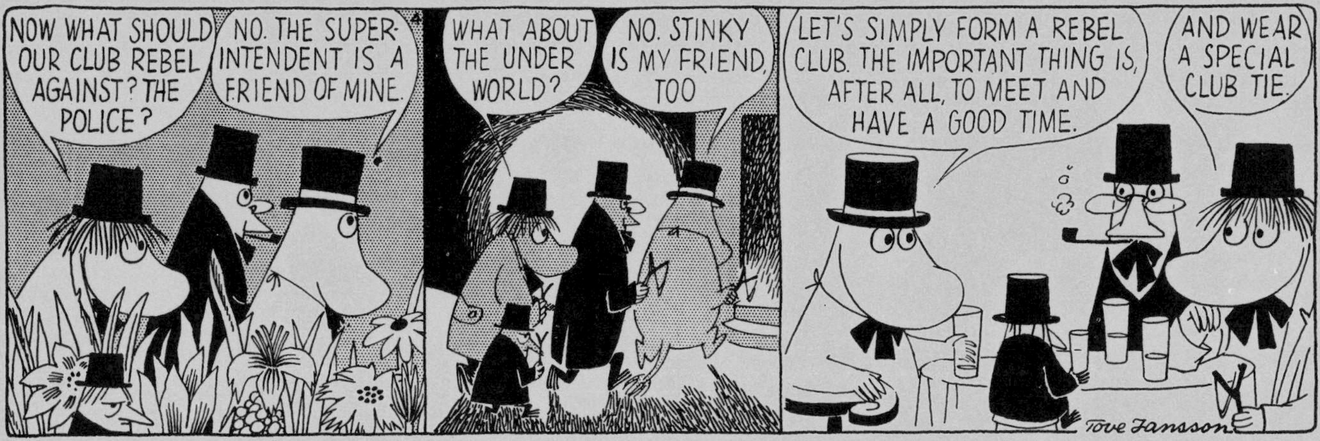
NOW WHAT SHOULD OUR CLUB REBEL AGAINST? THE POLICE?
NO. THE SUPER-INTENDENT IS A FRIEND OF MINE.
WHAT ABOUT THE UNDER WORLD?
NO. STINKY IS MY FRIEND, TOO
LET'S SIMPLY FORM A REBEL CLUB. THE IMPORTANT THING IS, AFTER ALL, TO MEET AND HAVE A GOOD TIME.
AND WEAR A SPECIAL CLUB TIE.
Tove Jansson

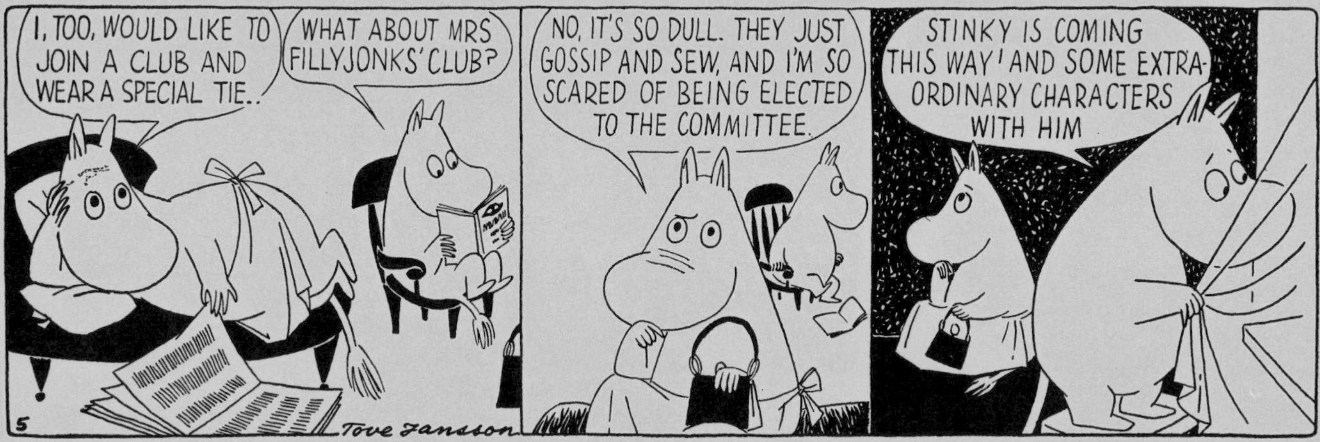
I, TOO, WOULD LIKE TO JOIN A CLUB AND WEAR A SPECIAL TIE..
WHAT ABOUT MRS FILLYJONKS' CLUB?
NO, IT'S SO DULL. THEY JUST GOSSIP AND SEW, AND I'M SO SCARED OF BEING ELECTED TO THE COMMITTEE.
STINKY IS COMING THIS WAY! AND SOME EXTRA-ORDINARY CHARACTERS WITH HIM
Tove Jansson

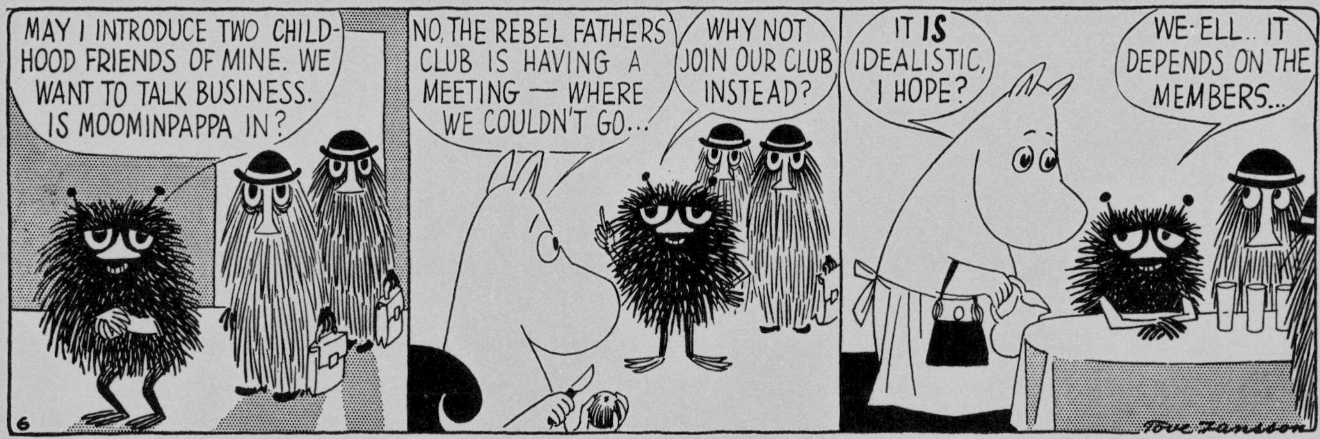
MAY I INTRODUCE TWO CHILD-HOOD FRIENDS OF MINE. WE WANT TO TALK BUSINESS. IS MOOMINPAPPA IN?
NO, THE REBEL FATHERS CLUB IS HAVING A MEETING — WHERE WE COULDN'T GO...
WHY NOT JOIN OUR CLUB INSTEAD?
IT IS IDEALISTIC, I HOPE?
WE-ELL.. IT DEPENDS ON THE MEMBERS...
Tove Jansson

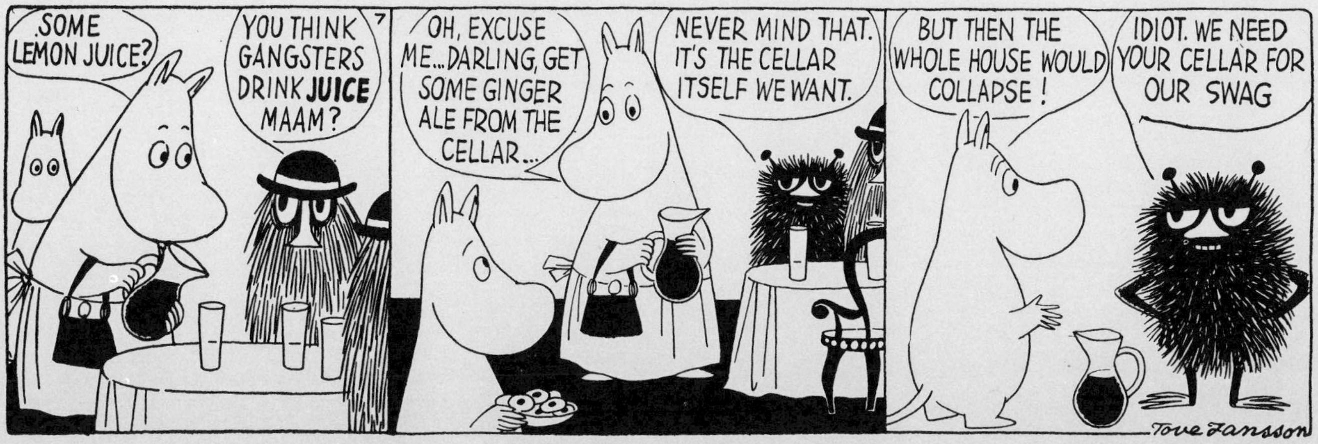
7
SOME LEMON JUICE?
YOU THINK GANGSTERS DRINK **JUICE** MAAM?
OH, EXCUSE ME...DARLING, GET SOME GINGER ALE FROM THE CELLAR...
NEVER MIND THAT. IT'S THE CELLAR ITSELF WE WANT.
BUT THEN THE WHOLE HOUSE WOULD COLLAPSE !
IDIOT. WE NEED YOUR CELLAR FOR OUR SWAG
Tove Jansson

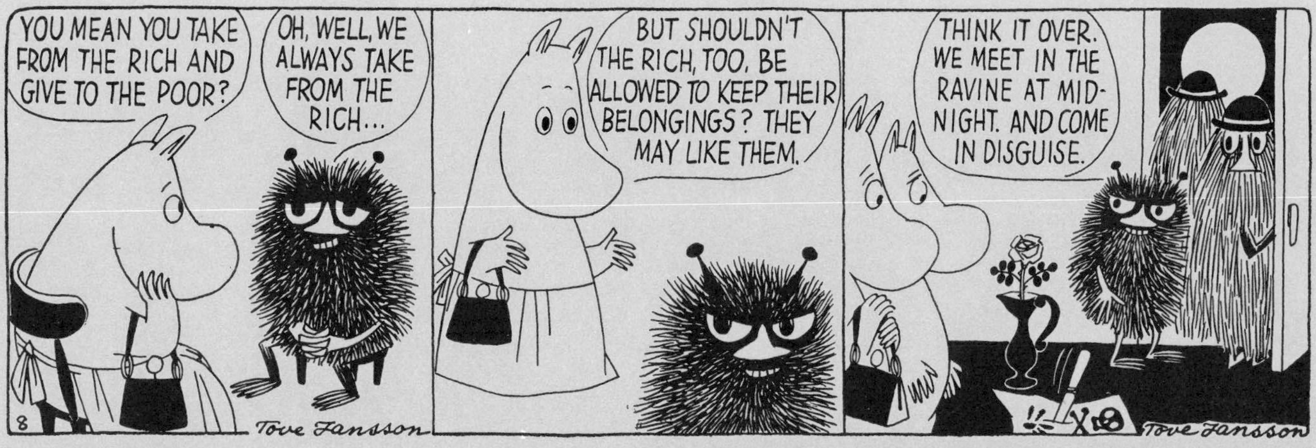
8
YOU MEAN YOU TAKE FROM THE RICH AND GIVE TO THE POOR?
OH, WELL, WE ALWAYS TAKE FROM THE RICH...
Tove Jansson
BUT SHOULDN'T THE RICH, TOO, BE ALLOWED TO KEEP THEIR BELONGINGS? THEY MAY LIKE THEM.
THINK IT OVER. WE MEET IN THE RAVINE AT MIDNIGHT. AND COME IN DISGUISE.
Tove Jansson

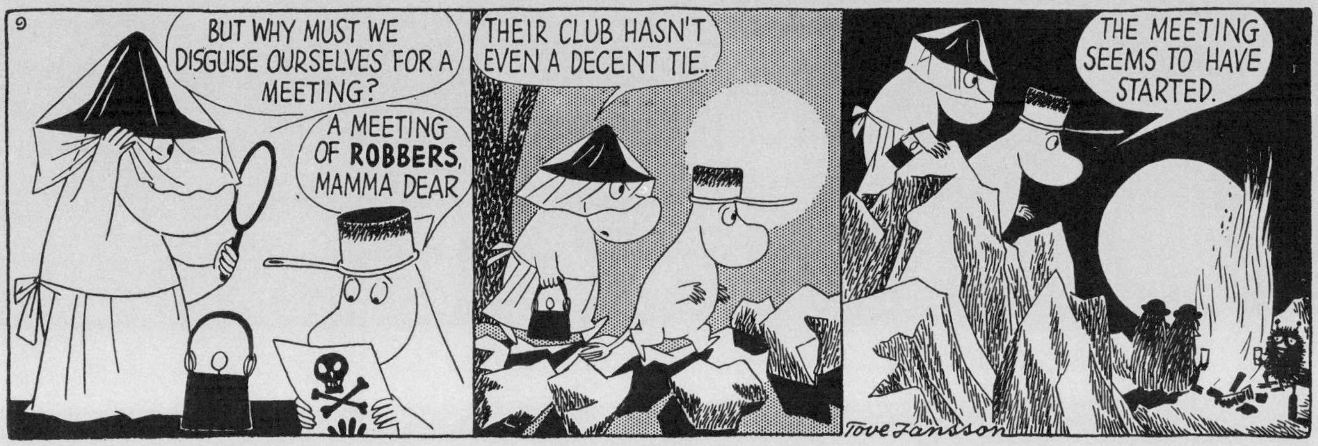
9
BUT WHY MUST WE DISGUISE OURSELVES FOR A MEETING?
A MEETING OF **ROBBERS**, MAMMA DEAR
THEIR CLUB HASN'T EVEN A DECENT TIE...
THE MEETING SEEMS TO HAVE STARTED.
Tove Jansson

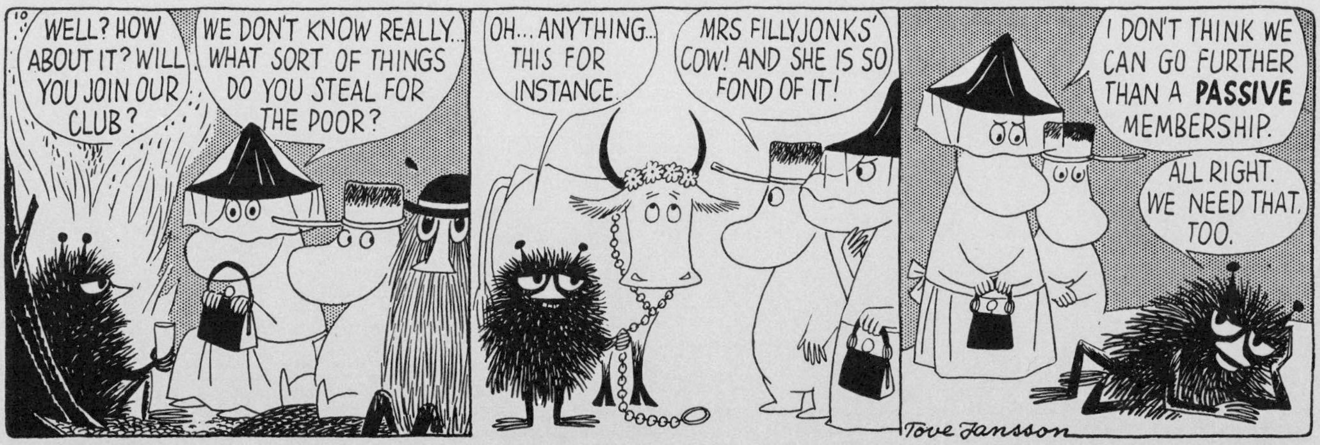
10
WELL? HOW ABOUT IT? WILL YOU JOIN OUR CLUB?
WE DON'T KNOW REALLY... WHAT SORT OF THINGS DO YOU STEAL FOR THE POOR?
OH... ANYTHING... THIS FOR INSTANCE.
MRS FILLYJONKS' COW! AND SHE IS SO FOND OF IT!
I DON'T THINK WE CAN GO FURTHER THAN A **PASSIVE** MEMBERSHIP.
ALL RIGHT. WE NEED THAT, TOO.
Tove Jansson

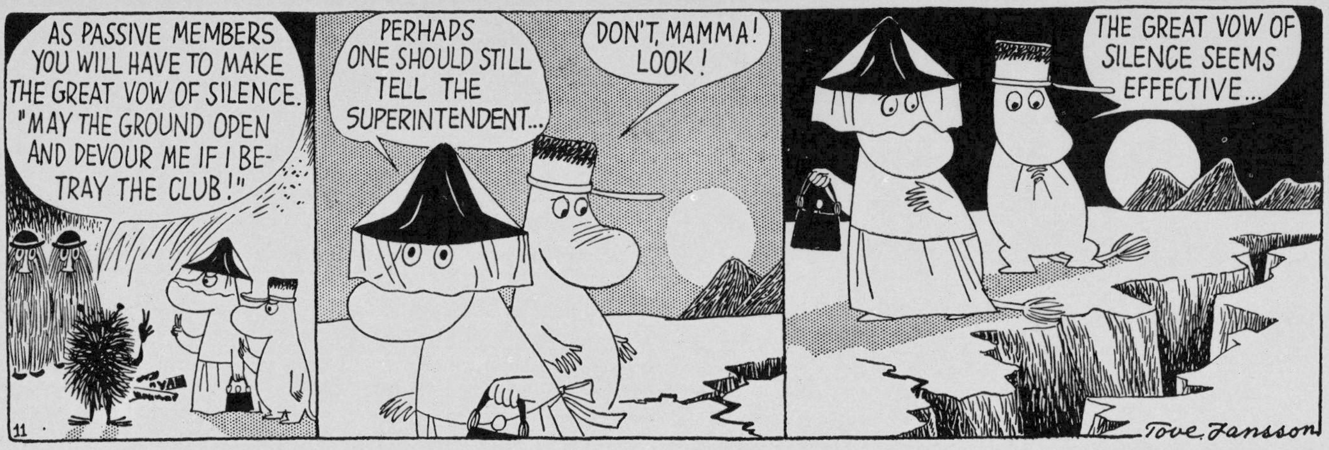
AS PASSIVE MEMBERS YOU WILL HAVE TO MAKE THE GREAT VOW OF SILENCE. "MAY THE GROUND OPEN AND DEVOUR ME IF I BETRAY THE CLUB!"
PERHAPS ONE SHOULD STILL TELL THE SUPERINTENDENT...
DON'T, MAMMA! LOOK!
THE GREAT VOW OF SILENCE SEEMS EFFECTIVE...
Tove Jansson

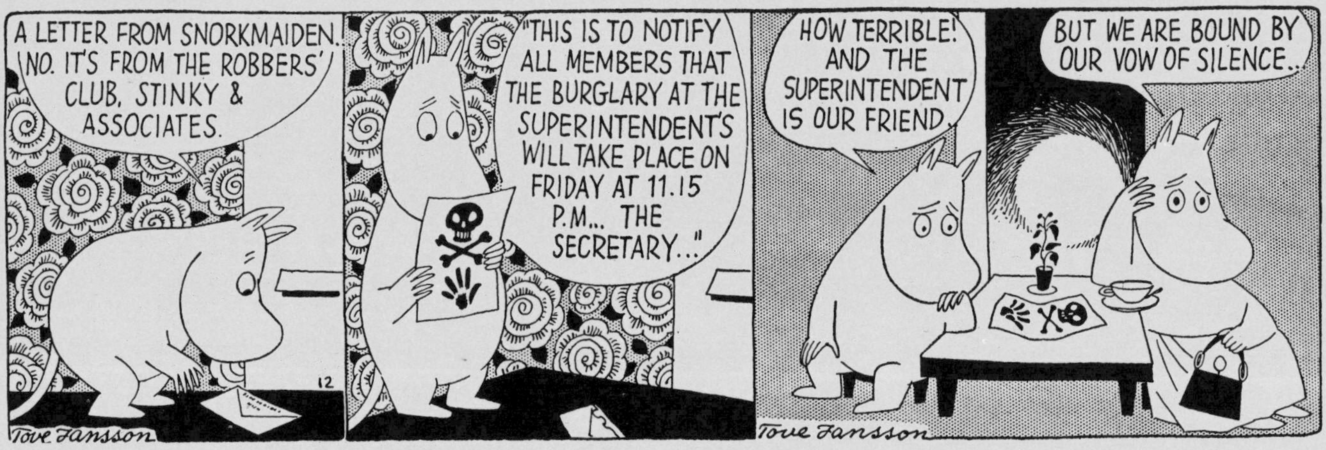
A LETTER FROM SNORKMAIDEN.. NO. IT'S FROM THE ROBBERS' CLUB, STINKY & ASSOCIATES.
"THIS IS TO NOTIFY ALL MEMBERS THAT THE BURGLARY AT THE SUPERINTENDENT'S WILL TAKE PLACE ON FRIDAY AT 11.15 P.M... THE SECRETARY..."
HOW TERRIBLE! AND THE SUPERINTENDENT IS OUR FRIEND.
BUT WE ARE BOUND BY OUR VOW OF SILENCE..
Tove Jansson
Tove Jansson

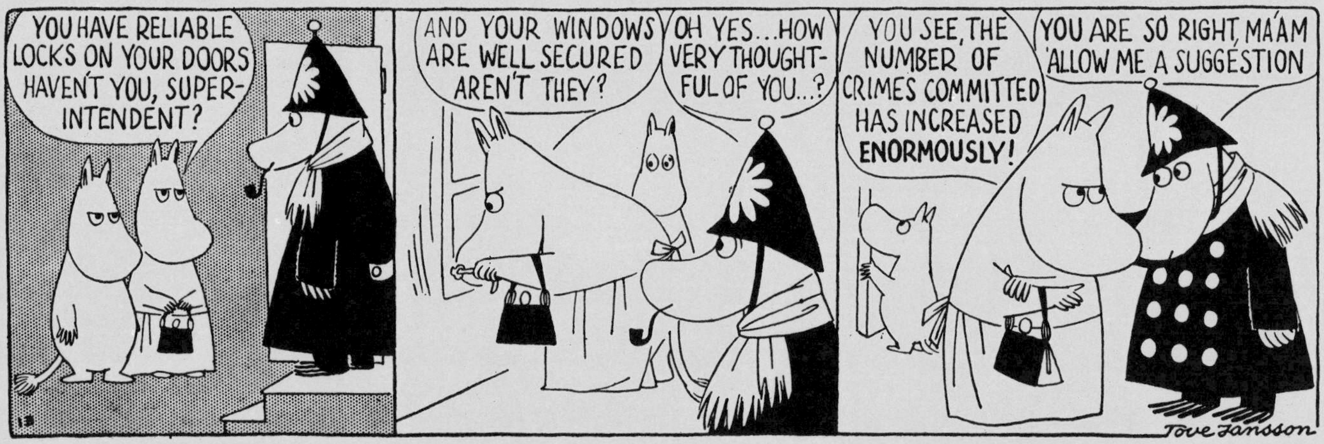
YOU HAVE RELIABLE LOCKS ON YOUR DOORS HAVEN'T YOU, SUPERINTENDENT?
AND YOUR WINDOWS ARE WELL SECURED AREN'T THEY?
OH YES...HOW VERY THOUGHTFUL OF YOU...?
YOU SEE, THE NUMBER OF CRIMES COMMITTED HAS INCREASED ENORMOUSLY!
YOU ARE SO RIGHT, MA'AM 'ALLOW ME A SUGGESTION
Tove Jansson

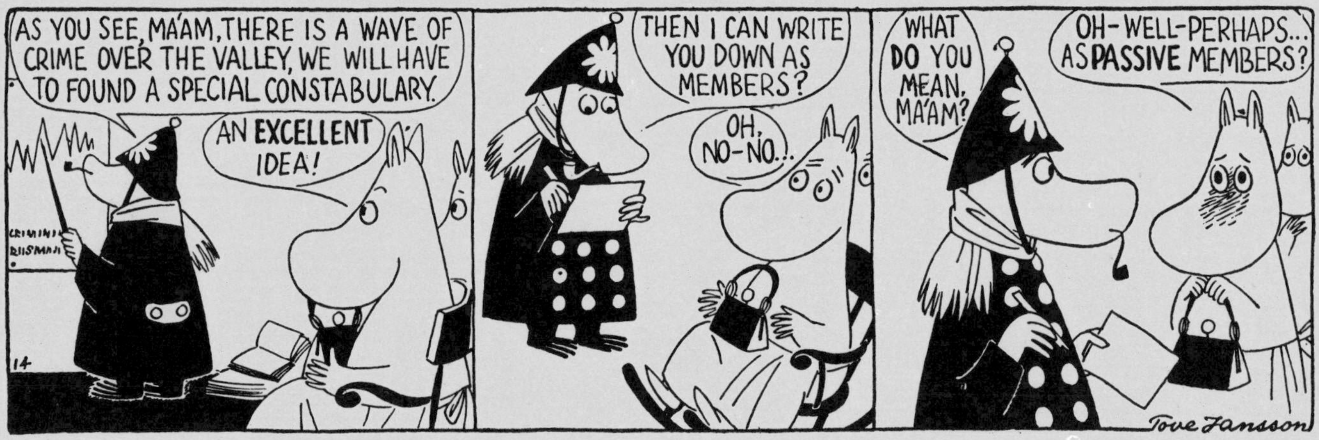
AS YOU SEE, MA'AM, THERE IS A WAVE OF CRIME OVER THE VALLEY, WE WILL HAVE TO FOUND A SPECIAL CONSTABULARY.
AN EXCELLENT IDEA!
THEN I CAN WRITE YOU DOWN AS MEMBERS?
OH, NO-NO..
WHAT DO YOU MEAN, MA'AM?
OH-WELL-PERHAPS... AS PASSIVE MEMBERS?
Tove Jansson

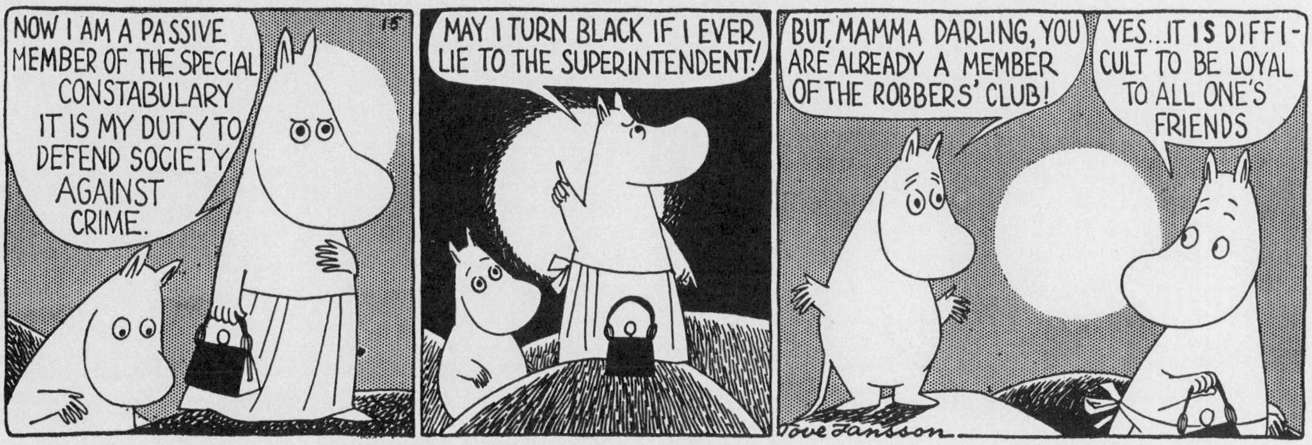
15
NOW I AM A PASSIVE MEMBER OF THE SPECIAL CONSTABULARY IT IS MY DUTY TO DEFEND SOCIETY AGAINST CRIME.
MAY I TURN BLACK IF I EVER LIE TO THE SUPERINTENDENT!
BUT, MAMMA DARLING, YOU ARE ALREADY A MEMBER OF THE ROBBERS' CLUB!
YES...IT IS DIFFICULT TO BE LOYAL TO ALL ONE'S FRIENDS
Tove Jansson

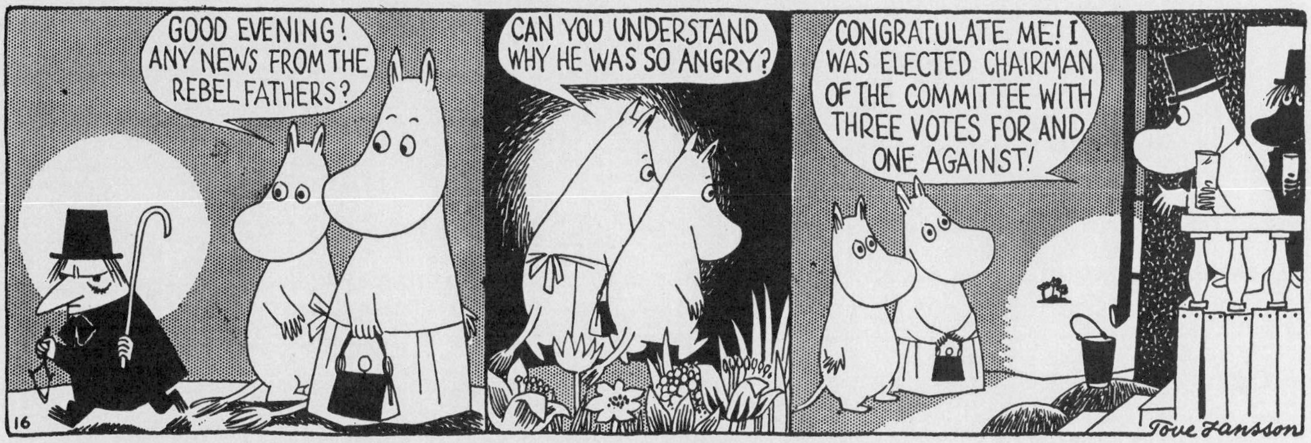
16
GOOD EVENING! ANY NEWS FROM THE REBEL FATHERS?
CAN YOU UNDERSTAND WHY HE WAS SO ANGRY?
CONGRATULATE ME! I WAS ELECTED CHAIRMAN OF THE COMMITTEE WITH THREE VOTES FOR AND ONE AGAINST!
Tove Jansson

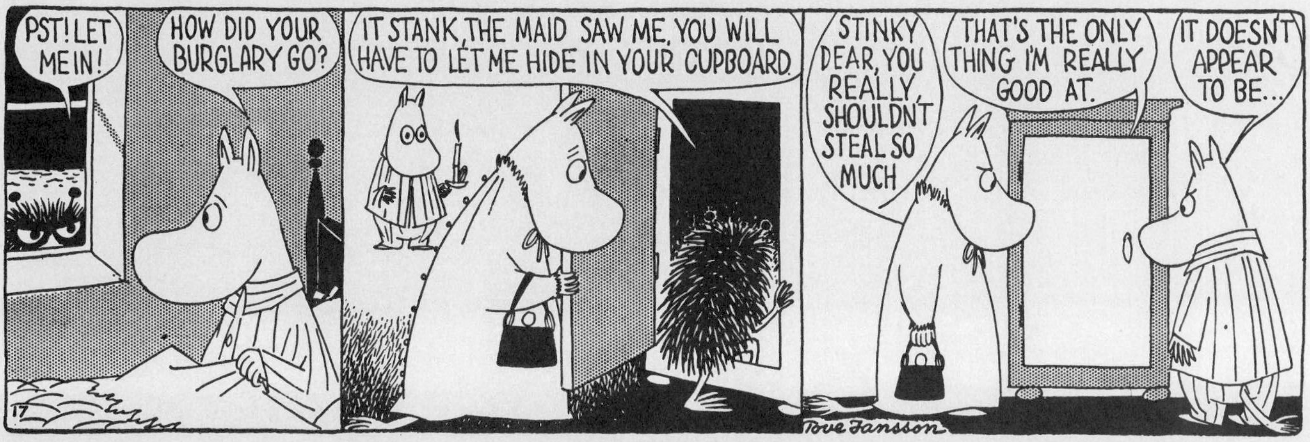
17
PST! LET ME IN!
HOW DID YOUR BURGLARY GO?
IT STANK, THE MAID SAW ME, YOU WILL HAVE TO LET ME HIDE IN YOUR CUPBOARD
STINKY DEAR, YOU REALLY, SHOULDN'T STEAL SO MUCH
THAT'S THE ONLY THING I'M REALLY GOOD AT.
IT DOESN'T APPEAR TO BE...
Tove Jansson

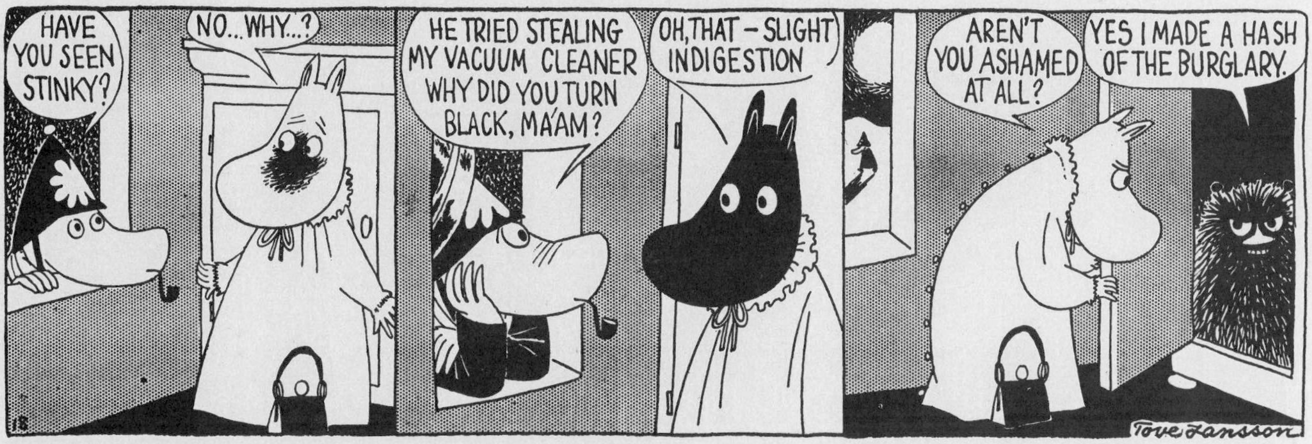
18
HAVE YOU SEEN STINKY?
NO...WHY...?
HE TRIED STEALING MY VACUUM CLEANER WHY DID YOU TURN BLACK, MA'AM?
OH, THAT – SLIGHT INDIGESTION
AREN'T YOU ASHAMED AT ALL?
YES I MADE A HASH OF THE BURGLARY.
Tove Jansson

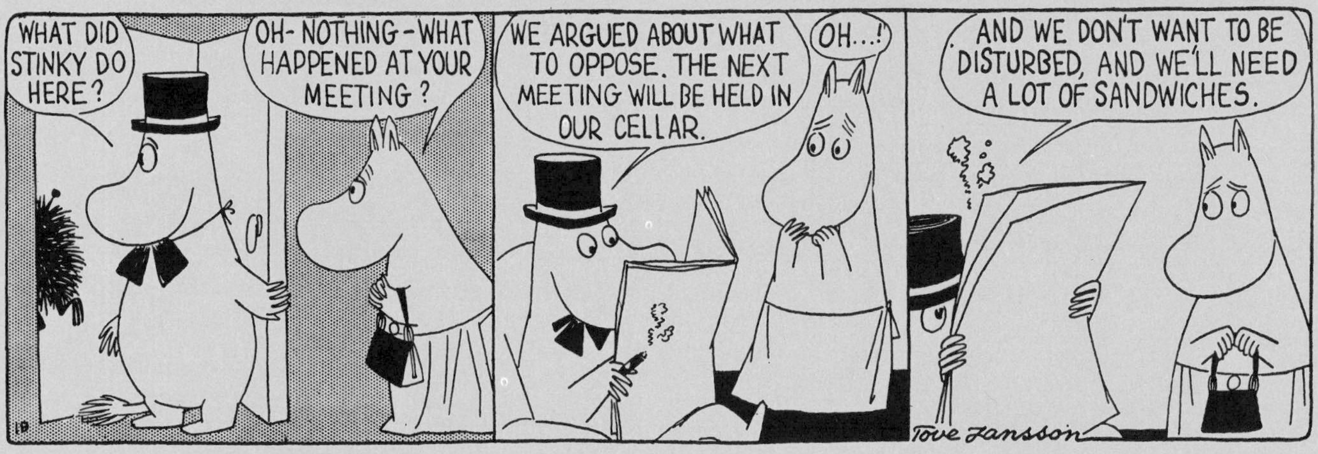

WHAT DID STINKY DO HERE?
OH- NOTHING - WHAT HAPPENED AT YOUR MEETING?
WE ARGUED ABOUT WHAT TO OPPOSE. THE NEXT MEETING WILL BE HELD IN OUR CELLAR.
OH...!
AND WE DON'T WANT TO BE DISTURBED, AND WE'LL NEED A LOT OF SANDWICHES.
Tove Jansson

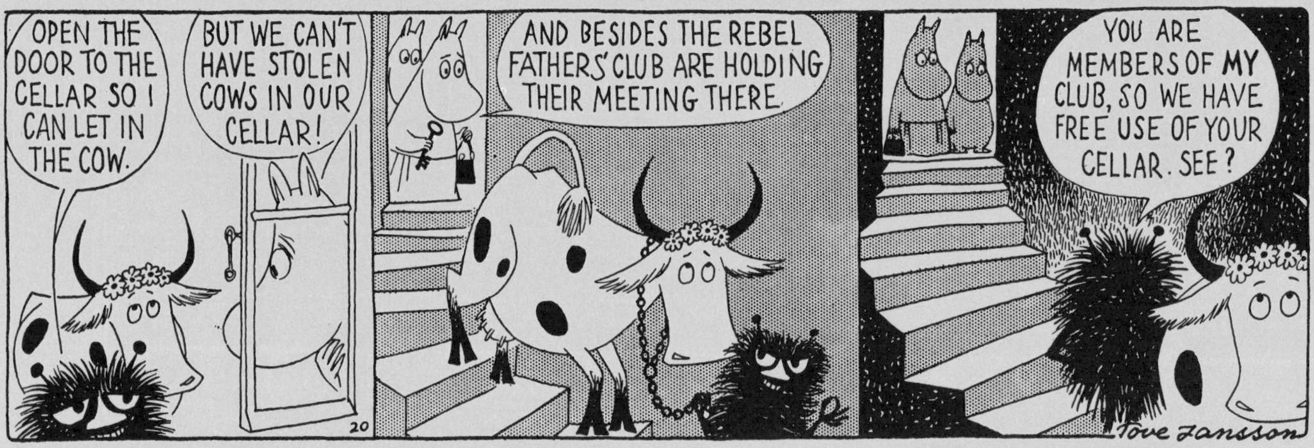

OPEN THE DOOR TO THE CELLAR SO I CAN LET IN THE COW.
BUT WE CAN'T HAVE STOLEN COWS IN OUR CELLAR!
AND BESIDES THE REBEL FATHERS' CLUB ARE HOLDING THEIR MEETING THERE.
YOU ARE MEMBERS OF **MY** CLUB, SO WE HAVE FREE USE OF YOUR CELLAR. SEE?
Tove Jansson

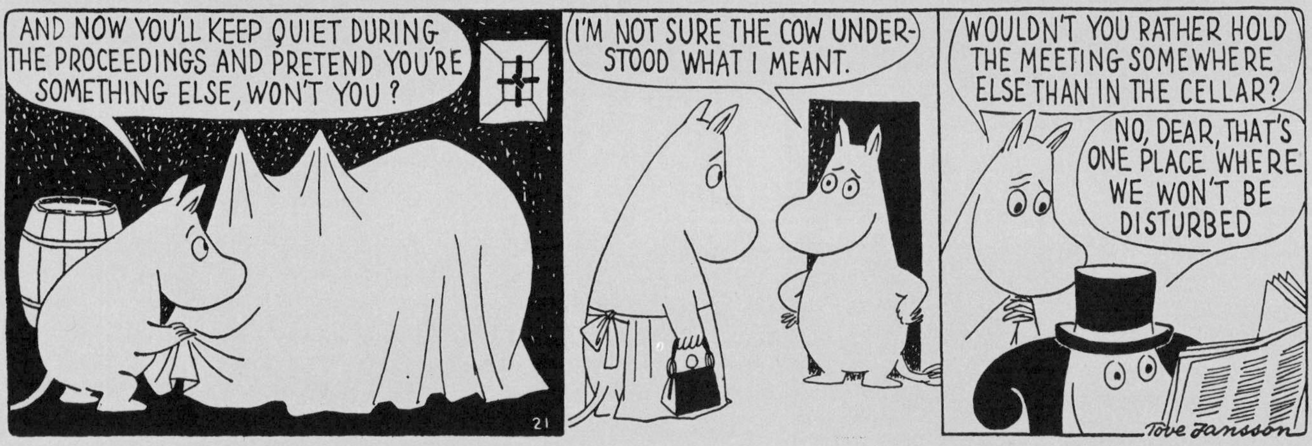

AND NOW YOU'LL KEEP QUIET DURING THE PROCEEDINGS AND PRETEND YOU'RE SOMETHING ELSE, WON'T YOU?
I'M NOT SURE THE COW UNDER-STOOD WHAT I MEANT.
WOULDN'T YOU RATHER HOLD THE MEETING SOMEWHERE ELSE THAN IN THE CELLAR?
NO, DEAR, THAT'S ONE PLACE WHERE WE WON'T BE DISTURBED
Tove Jansson

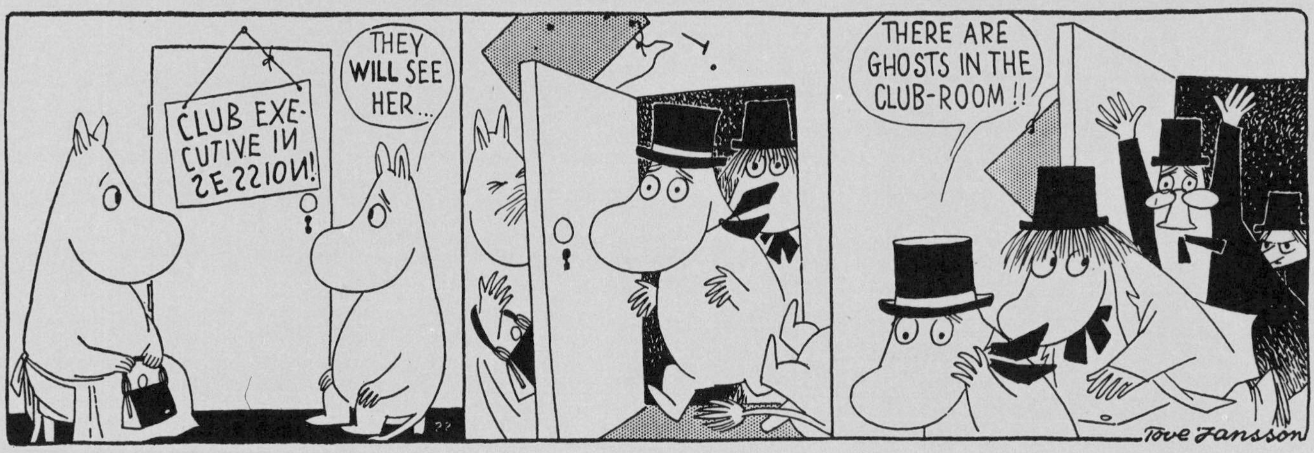

CLUB EXE-CUTIVE IN SESSION!
THEY **WILL** SEE HER...
THERE ARE GHOSTS IN THE CLUB-ROOM!!
Tove Jansson

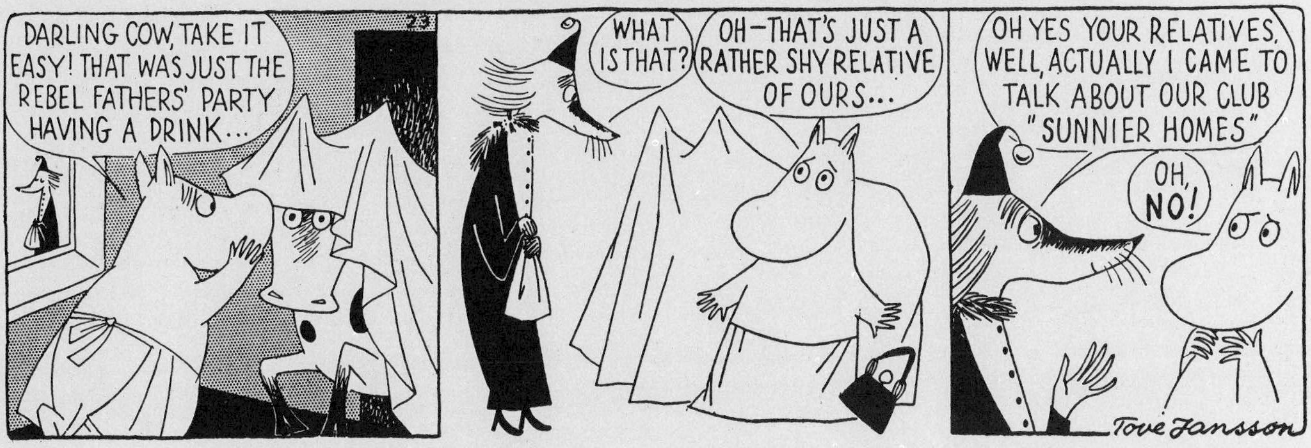
23
DARLING COW, TAKE IT EASY! THAT WAS JUST THE REBEL FATHERS' PARTY HAVING A DRINK...
WHAT IS THAT?
OH—THAT'S JUST A RATHER SHY RELATIVE OF OURS...
OH YES YOUR RELATIVES. WELL, ACTUALLY I CAME TO TALK ABOUT OUR CLUB "SUNNIER HOMES"
OH, NO!
Tove Jansson

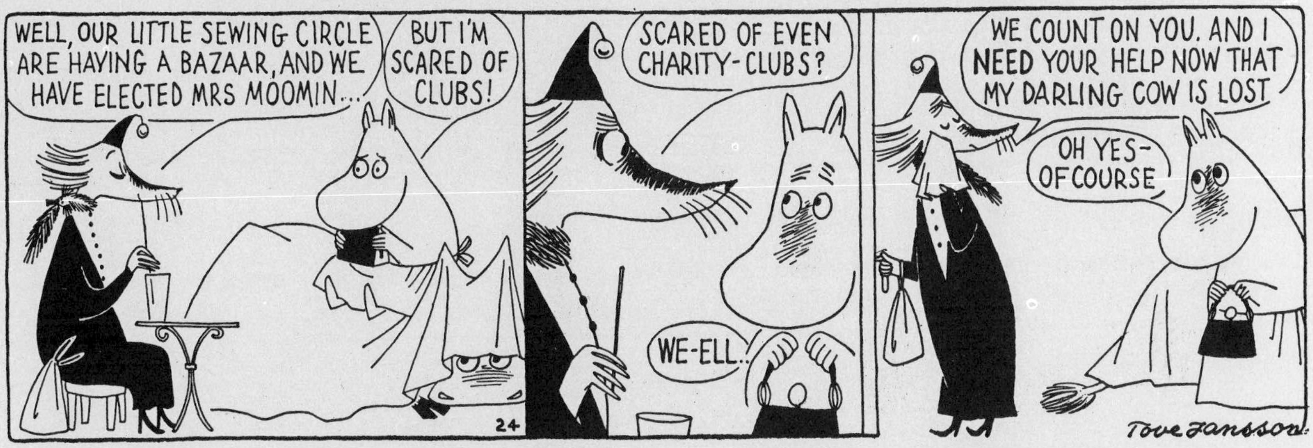
WELL, OUR LITTLE SEWING CIRCLE ARE HAVING A BAZAAR, AND WE HAVE ELECTED MRS MOOMIN...
BUT I'M SCARED OF CLUBS!
24
SCARED OF EVEN CHARITY-CLUBS?
WE-ELL...
WE COUNT ON YOU. AND I NEED YOUR HELP NOW THAT MY DARLING COW IS LOST
OH YES-OF COURSE
Tove Jansson

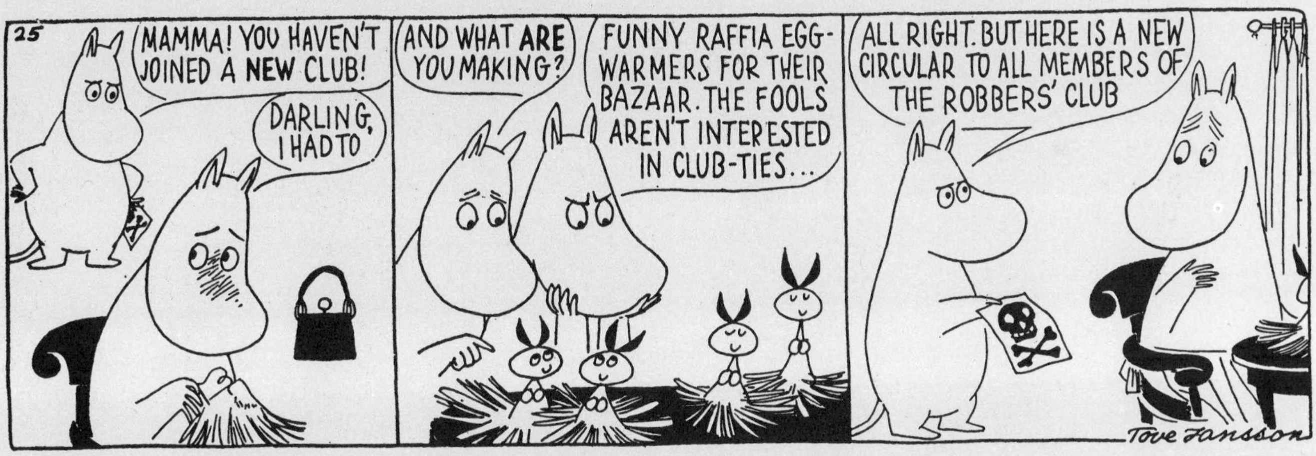
25
MAMMA! YOU HAVEN'T JOINED A NEW CLUB!
DARLING, I HAD TO
AND WHAT ARE YOU MAKING?
FUNNY RAFFIA EGG-WARMERS FOR THEIR BAZAAR. THE FOOLS AREN'T INTERESTED IN CLUB-TIES...
ALL RIGHT. BUT HERE IS A NEW CIRCULAR TO ALL MEMBERS OF THE ROBBERS' CLUB
Tove Jansson

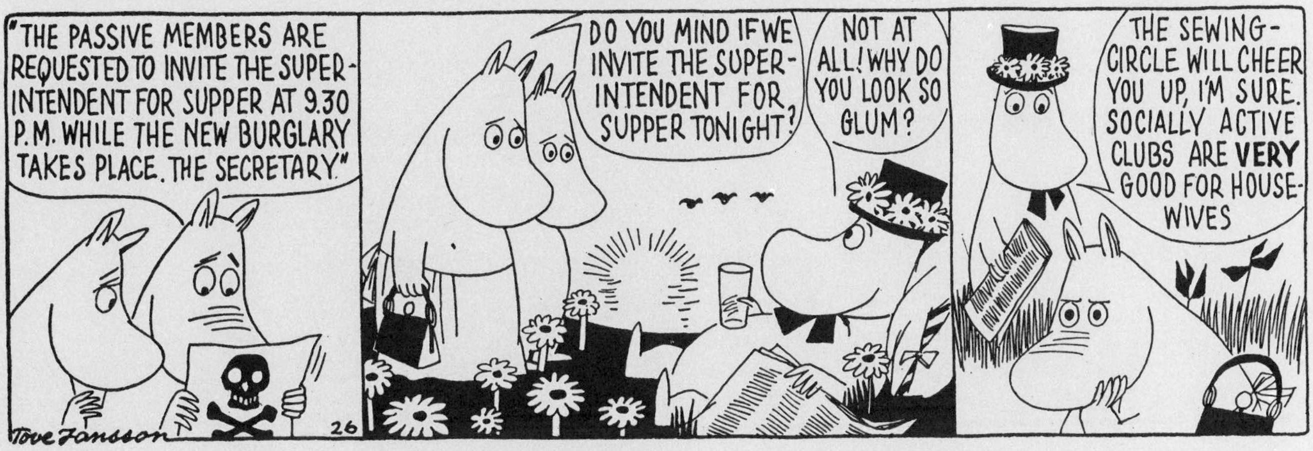
"THE PASSIVE MEMBERS ARE REQUESTED TO INVITE THE SUPER-INTENDENT FOR SUPPER AT 9.30 P.M. WHILE THE NEW BURGLARY TAKES PLACE. THE SECRETARY."
Tove Jansson
26
DO YOU MIND IF WE INVITE THE SUPER-INTENDENT FOR SUPPER TONIGHT?
NOT AT ALL! WHY DO YOU LOOK SO GLUM?
THE SEWING-CIRCLE WILL CHEER YOU UP, I'M SURE. SOCIALLY ACTIVE CLUBS ARE VERY GOOD FOR HOUSE-WIVES

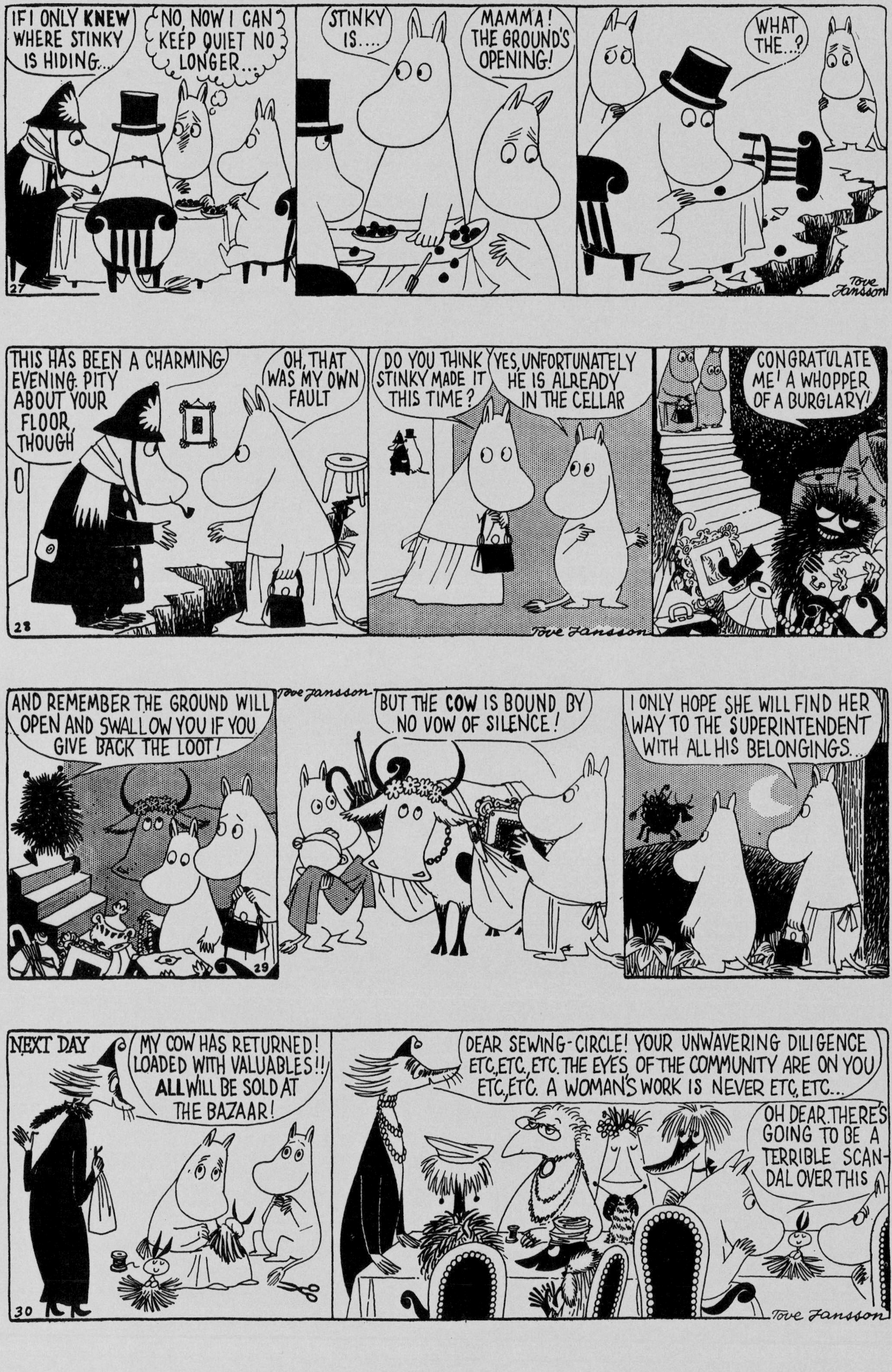
IF I ONLY KNEW WHERE STINKY IS HIDING...
NO, NOW I CAN KEEP QUIET NO LONGER...
STINKY IS....
MAMMA! THE GROUND'S OPENING!
WHAT THE...?
Tove Jansson
27
THIS HAS BEEN A CHARMING EVENING. PITY ABOUT YOUR FLOOR, THOUGH
OH, THAT WAS MY OWN FAULT
DO YOU THINK STINKY MADE IT THIS TIME?
YES, UNFORTUNATELY HE IS ALREADY IN THE CELLAR
CONGRATULATE ME! A WHOPPER OF A BURGLARY!
Tove Jansson
28
AND REMEMBER THE GROUND WILL OPEN AND SWALLOW YOU IF YOU GIVE BACK THE LOOT!
Tove Jansson
BUT THE COW IS BOUND BY NO VOW OF SILENCE!
I ONLY HOPE SHE WILL FIND HER WAY TO THE SUPERINTENDENT WITH ALL HIS BELONGINGS...
29
NEXT DAY
MY COW HAS RETURNED! LOADED WITH VALUABLES!! ALL WILL BE SOLD AT THE BAZAAR!
DEAR SEWING-CIRCLE! YOUR UNWAVERING DILIGENCE ETC, ETC, ETC. THE EYES OF THE COMMUNITY ARE ON YOU ETC, ETC. A WOMAN'S WORK IS NEVER ETC, ETC...
OH DEAR. THERE'S GOING TO BE A TERRIBLE SCANDAL OVER THIS
Tove Jansson
30

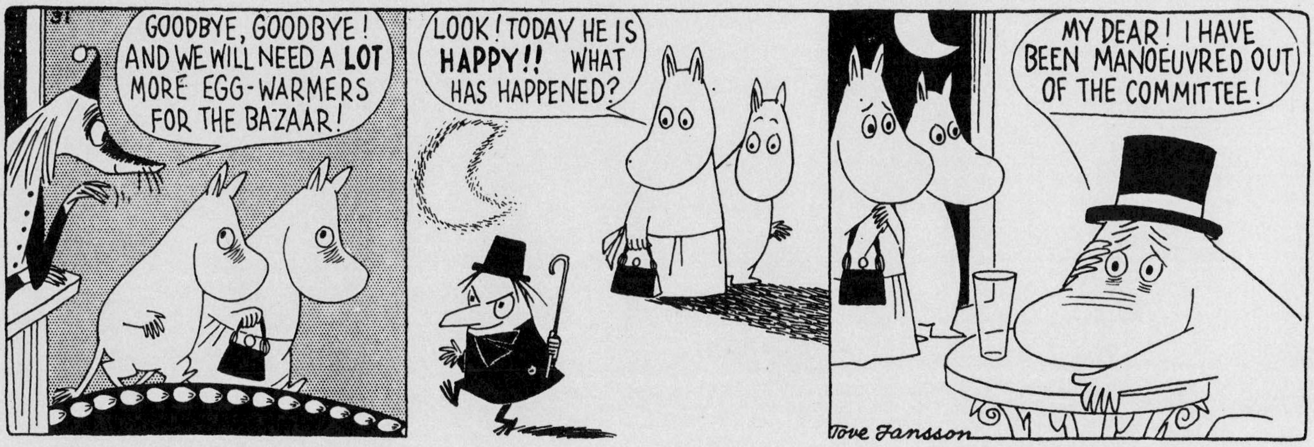
31
GOODBYE, GOODBYE! AND WE WILL NEED A **LOT** MORE EGG-WARMERS FOR THE BAZAAR!
LOOK! TODAY HE IS **HAPPY!!** WHAT HAS HAPPENED?
MY DEAR! I HAVE BEEN MANOEUVRED OUT OF THE COMMITTEE!
Tove Jansson

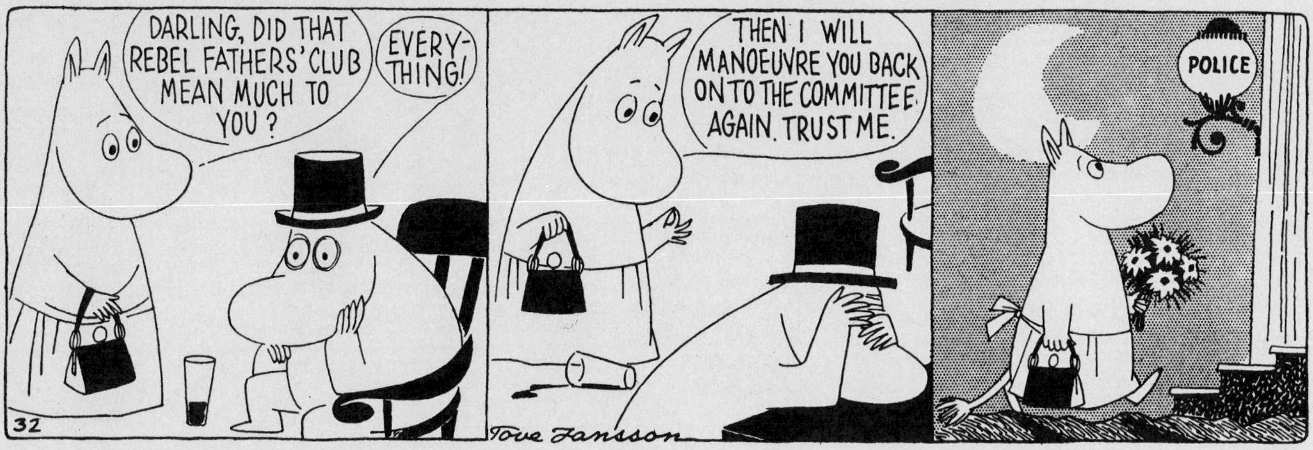
32
DARLING, DID THAT REBEL FATHERS' CLUB MEAN MUCH TO YOU?
EVERYTHING!
THEN I WILL MANOEUVRE YOU BACK ON TO THE COMMITTEE AGAIN. TRUST ME.
Tove Jansson
POLICE

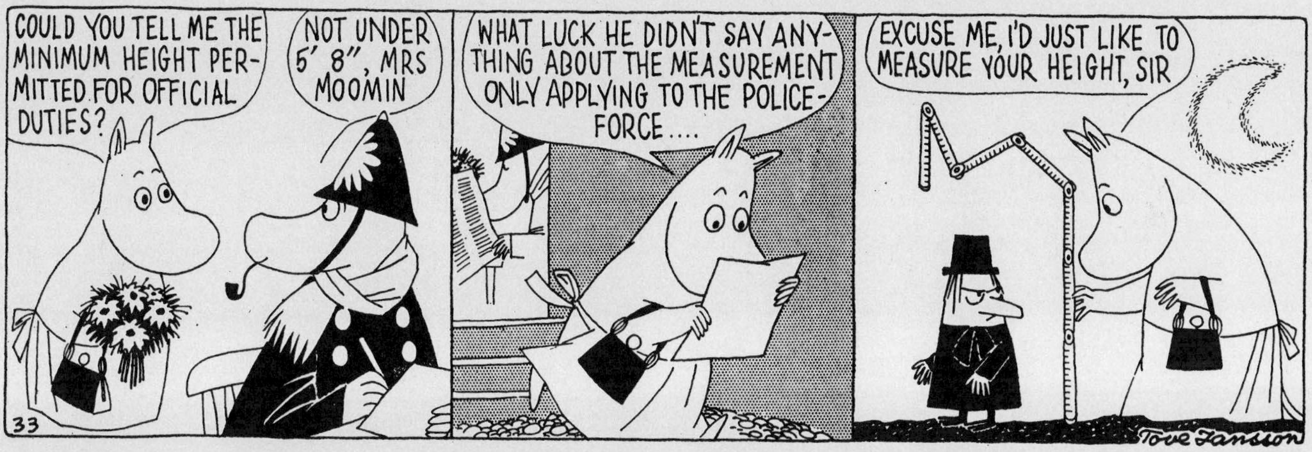
33
COULD YOU TELL ME THE MINIMUM HEIGHT PERMITTED FOR OFFICIAL DUTIES?
NOT UNDER 5' 8", MRS MOOMIN
WHAT LUCK HE DIDN'T SAY ANYTHING ABOUT THE MEASUREMENT ONLY APPLYING TO THE POLICE-FORCE....
EXCUSE ME, I'D JUST LIKE TO MEASURE YOUR HEIGHT, SIR
Tove Jansson

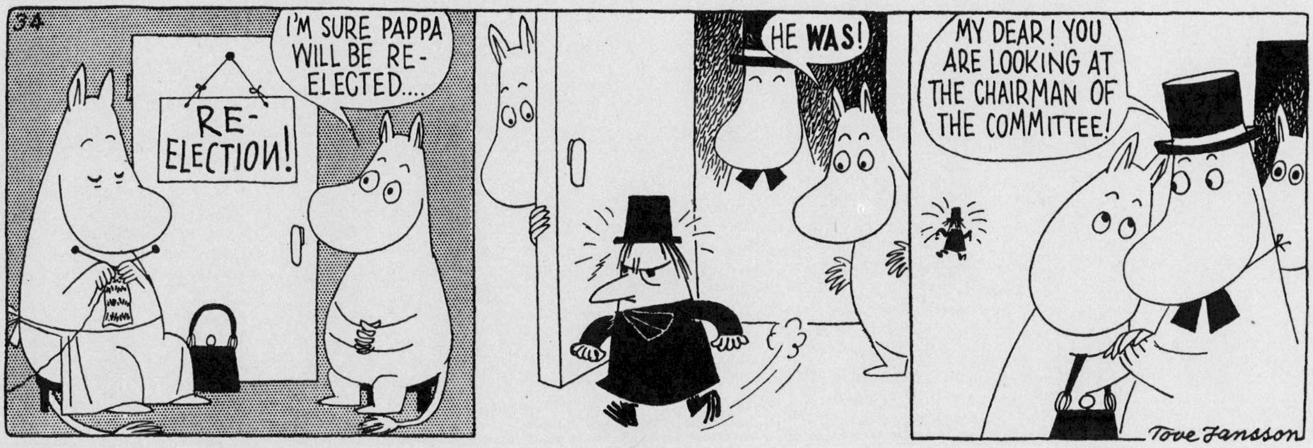
34
RE-ELECTION!
I'M SURE PAPPA WILL BE RE-ELECTED....
HE **WAS**!
MY DEAR! YOU ARE LOOKING AT THE CHAIRMAN OF THE COMMITTEE!
Tove Jansson

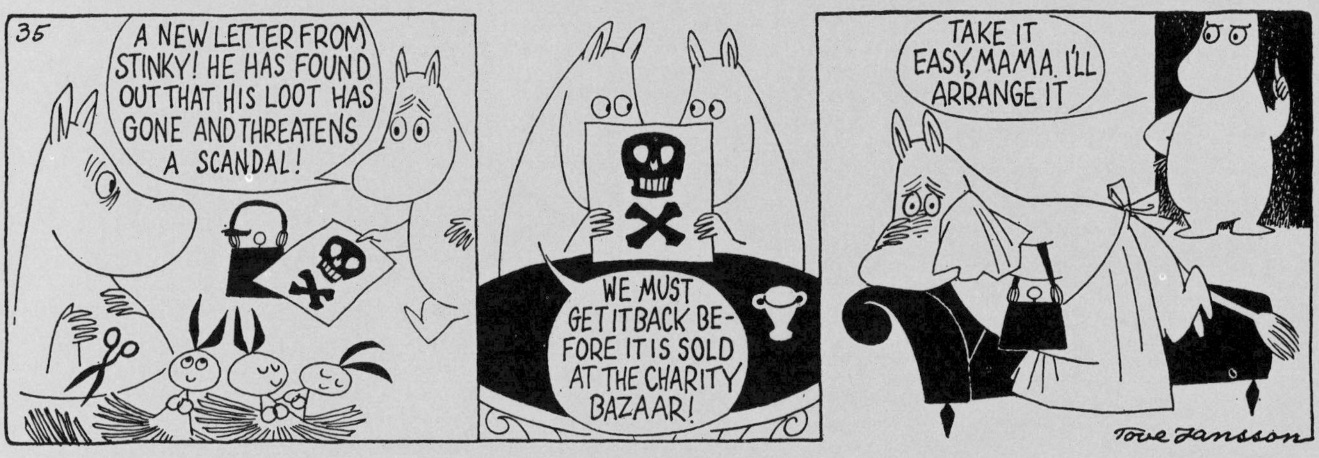
35
A NEW LETTER FROM STINKY! HE HAS FOUND OUT THAT HIS LOOT HAS GONE AND THREATENS A SCANDAL!
WE MUST GET IT BACK BEFORE IT IS SOLD AT THE CHARITY BAZAAR!
TAKE IT EASY, MAMA. I'LL ARRANGE IT
Tove Jansson

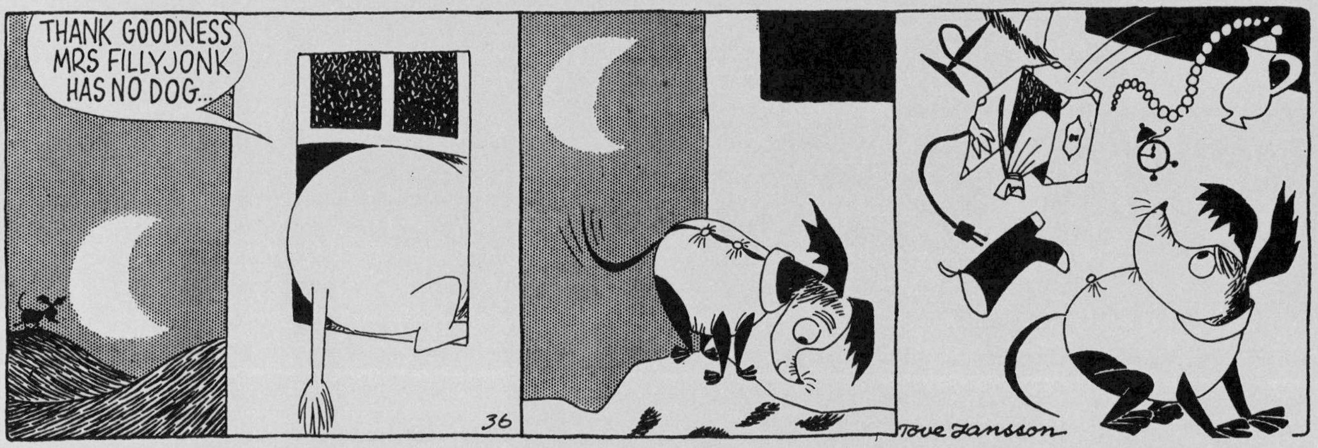
THANK GOODNESS MRS FILLYJONK HAS NO DOG...
36
Tove Jansson

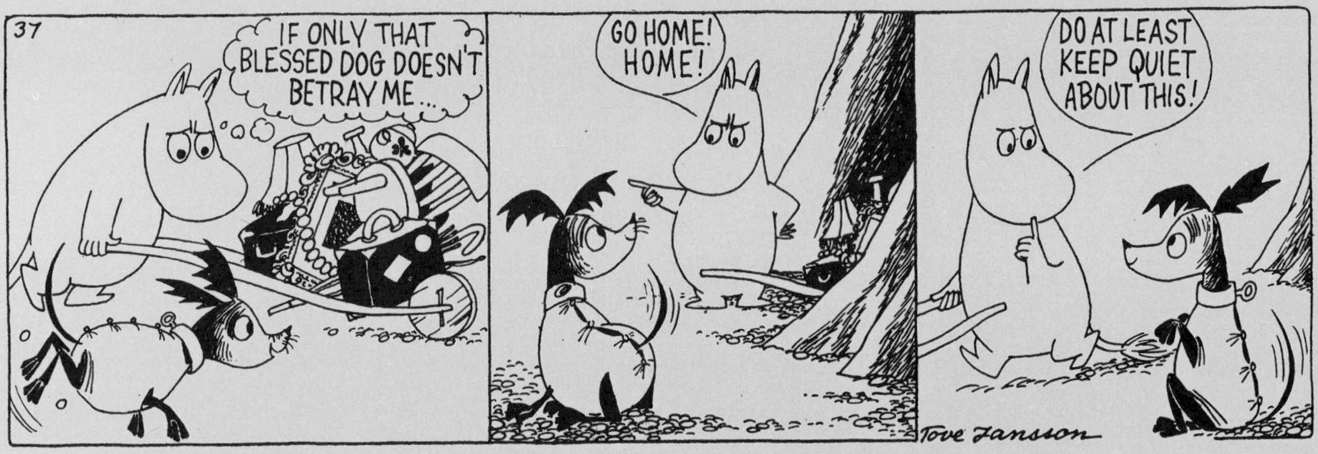
37
IF ONLY THAT BLESSED DOG DOESN'T BETRAY ME...
GO HOME! HOME!
DO AT LEAST KEEP QUIET ABOUT THIS!
Tove Jansson

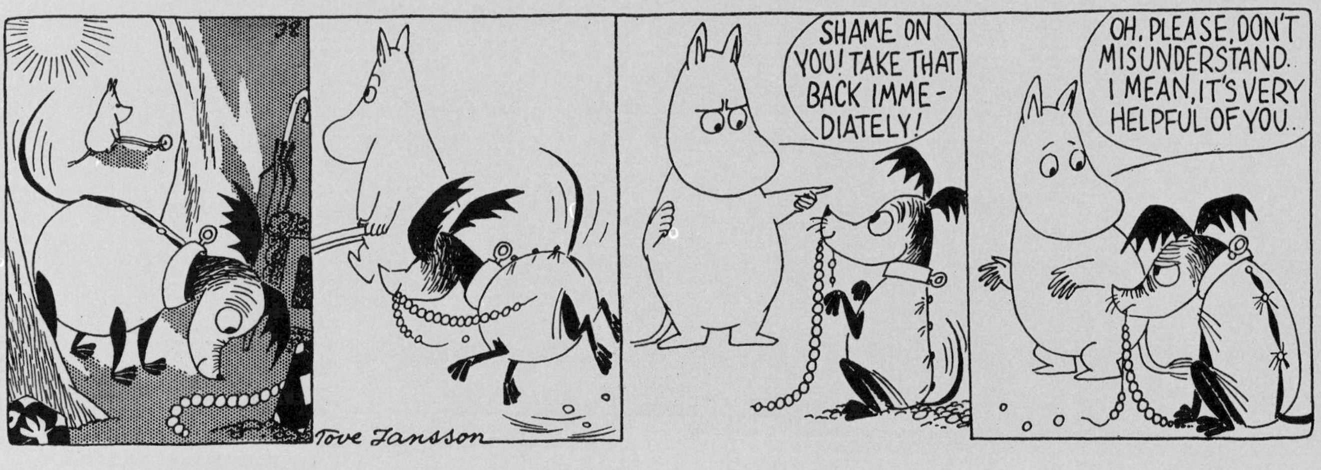
Tove Jansson
SHAME ON YOU! TAKE THAT BACK IMMEDIATELY!
OH, PLEASE, DON'T MISUNDERSTAND. I MEAN, IT'S VERY HELPFUL OF YOU..

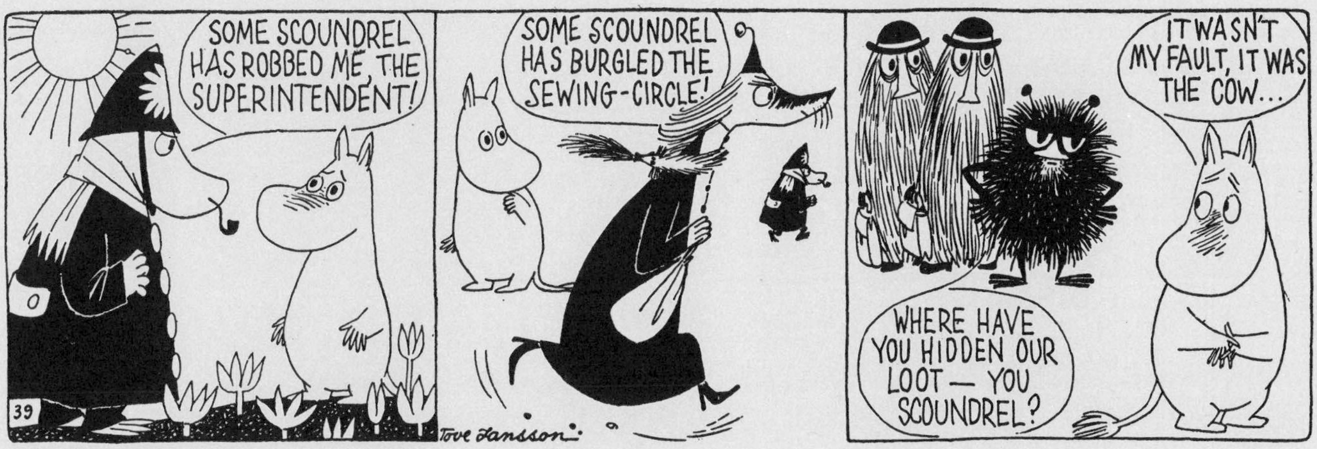
39
SOME SCOUNDREL HAS ROBBED ME, THE SUPERINTENDENT!
SOME SCOUNDREL HAS BURGLED THE SEWING-CIRCLE!
Tove Jansson
IT WASN'T MY FAULT, IT WAS THE COW...
WHERE HAVE YOU HIDDEN OUR LOOT — YOU SCOUNDREL?

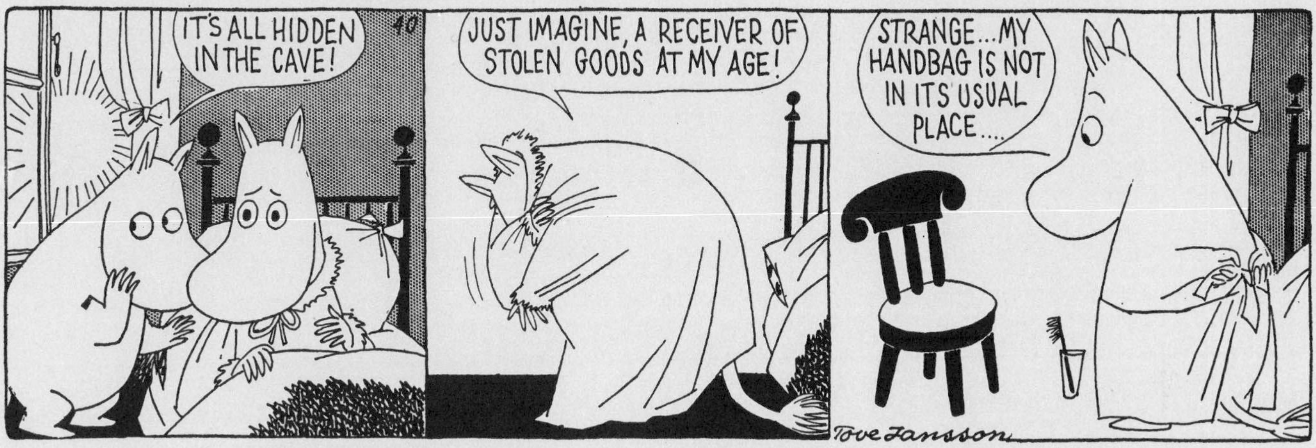
40
IT'S ALL HIDDEN IN THE CAVE!
JUST IMAGINE, A RECEIVER OF STOLEN GOODS AT MY AGE!
STRANGE...MY HANDBAG IS NOT IN ITS USUAL PLACE....
Tove Jansson

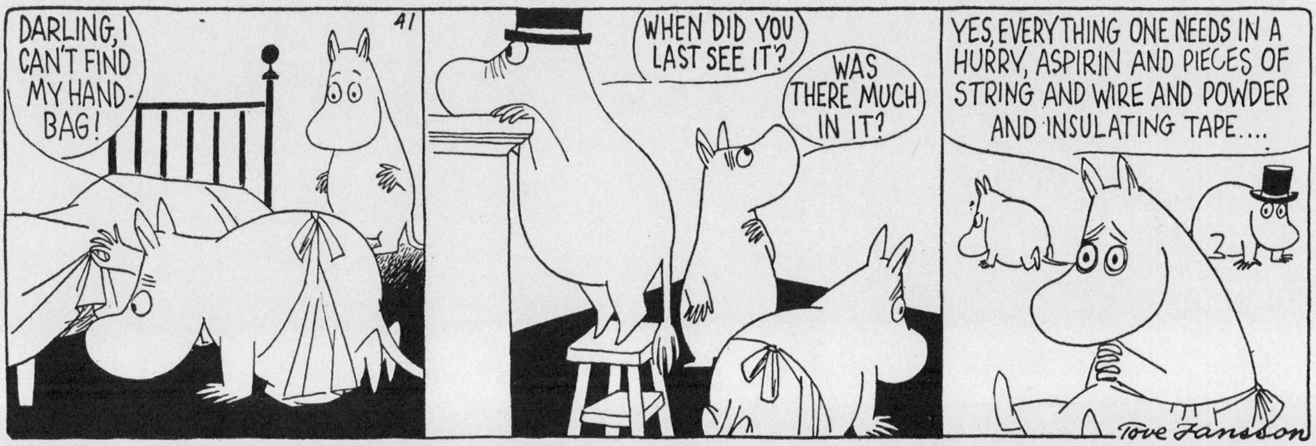
41
DARLING, I CAN'T FIND MY HAND-BAG!
WHEN DID YOU LAST SEE IT?
WAS THERE MUCH IN IT?
YES, EVERYTHING ONE NEEDS IN A HURRY, ASPIRIN AND PIECES OF STRING AND WIRE AND POWDER AND INSULATING TAPE....
Tove Jansson

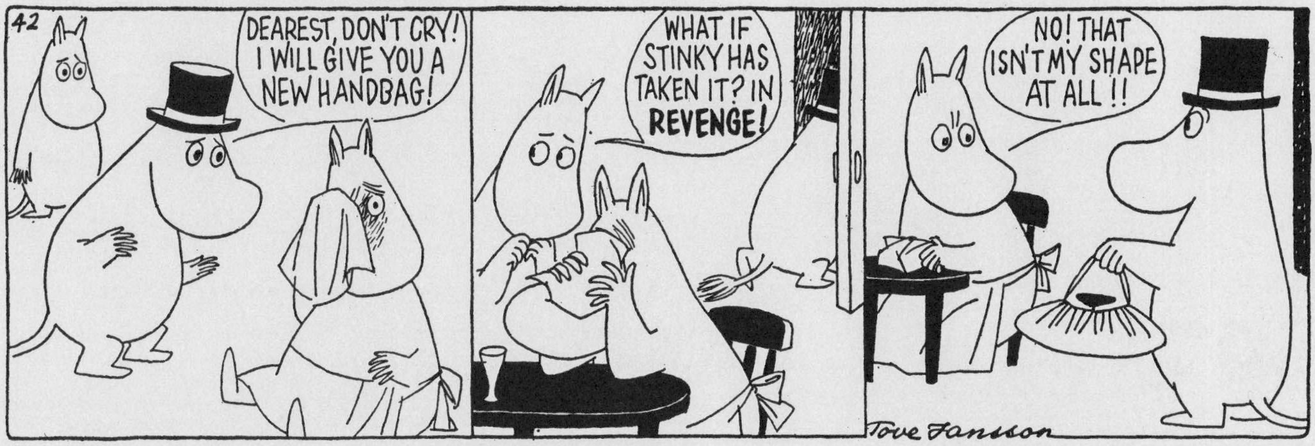
42
DEAREST, DON'T CRY! I WILL GIVE YOU A NEW HANDBAG!
WHAT IF STINKY HAS TAKEN IT? IN REVENGE!
NO! THAT ISN'T MY SHAPE AT ALL!!
Tove Jansson

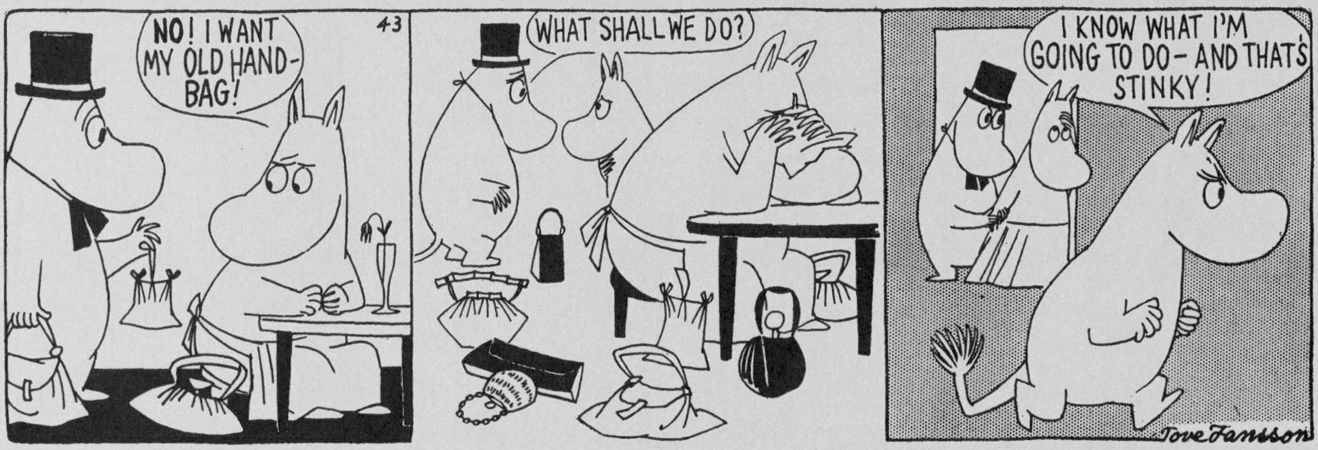
43
NO! I WANT MY OLD HAND-BAG!
WHAT SHALL WE DO?
I KNOW WHAT I'M GOING TO DO – AND THAT'S STINKY!
Tove Jansson

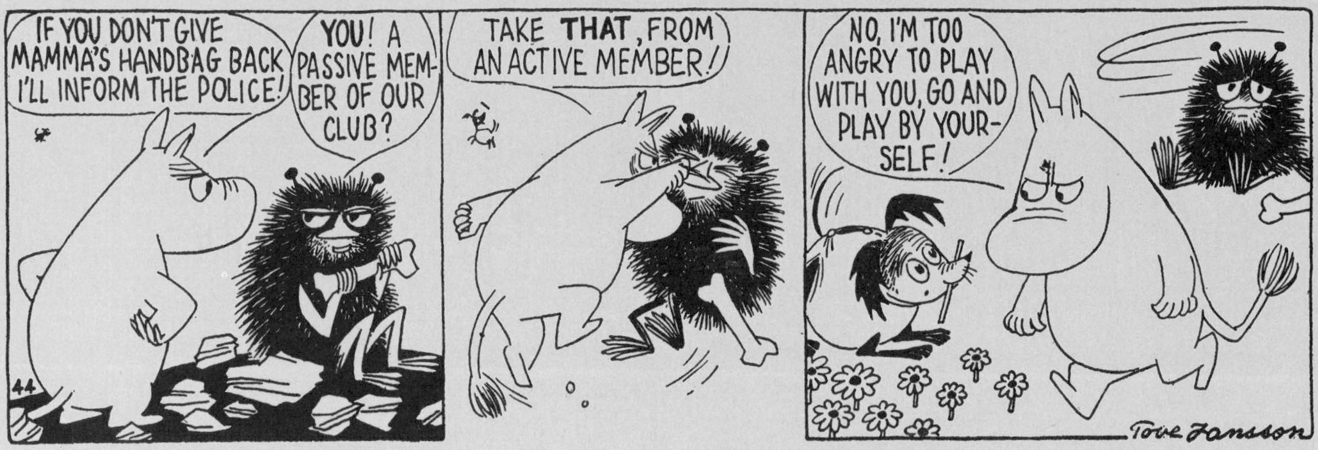
IF YOU DON'T GIVE MAMMA'S HANDBAG BACK I'LL INFORM THE POLICE!
YOU! A PASSIVE MEM-BER OF OUR CLUB?
44
TAKE THAT, FROM AN ACTIVE MEMBER!
NO, I'M TOO ANGRY TO PLAY WITH YOU, GO AND PLAY BY YOUR-SELF!
Tove Jansson

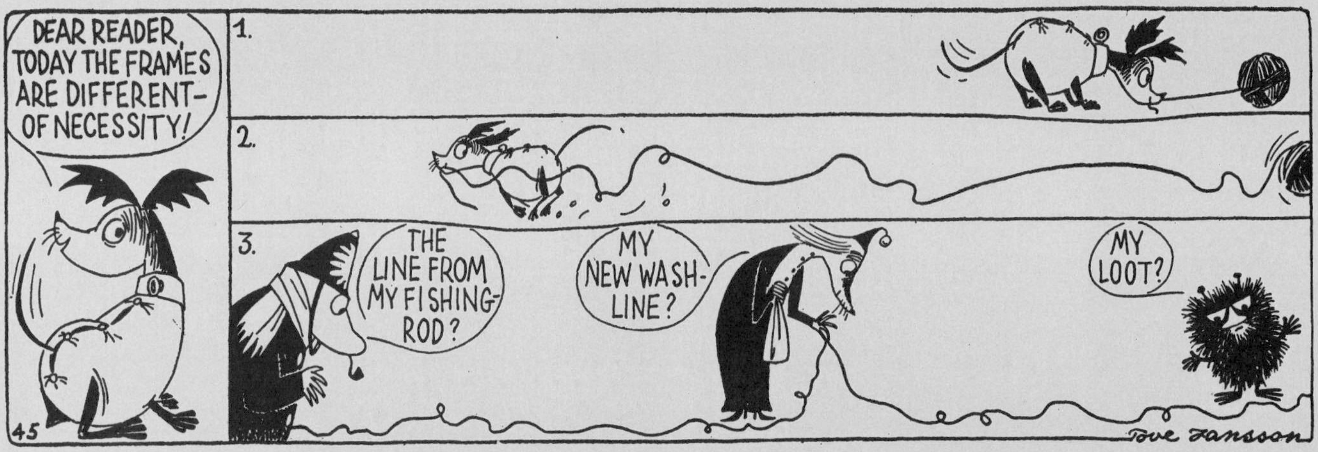
DEAR READER, TODAY THE FRAMES ARE DIFFERENT- OF NECESSITY!
45
1.
2.
3.
THE LINE FROM MY FISHING-ROD?
MY NEW WASH-LINE?
MY LOOT?
Tove Jansson

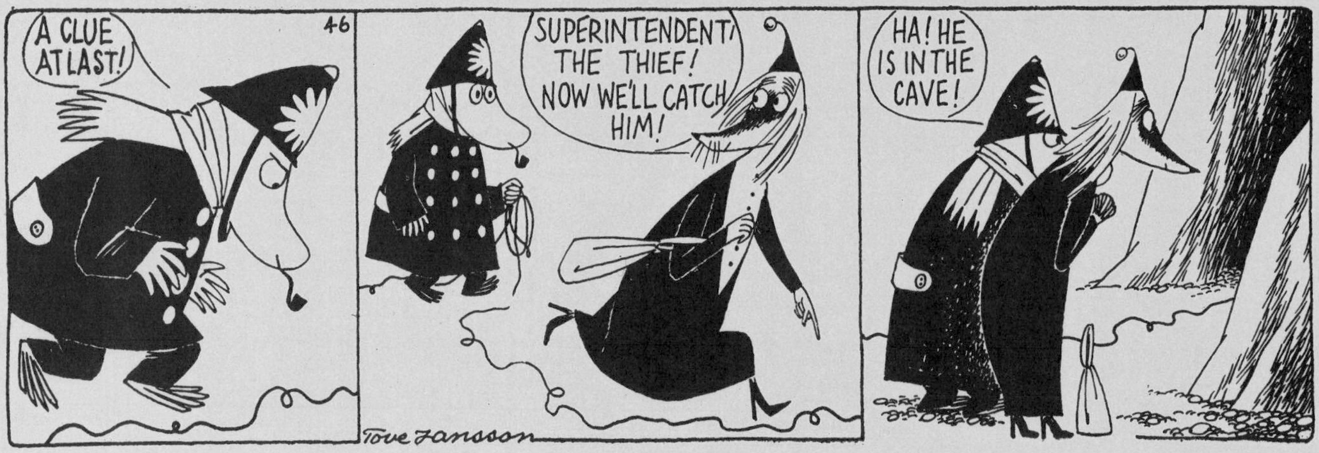
46
A CLUE AT LAST!
SUPERINTENDENT! THE THIEF! NOW WE'LL CATCH HIM!
Tove Jansson
HA! HE IS IN THE CAVE!

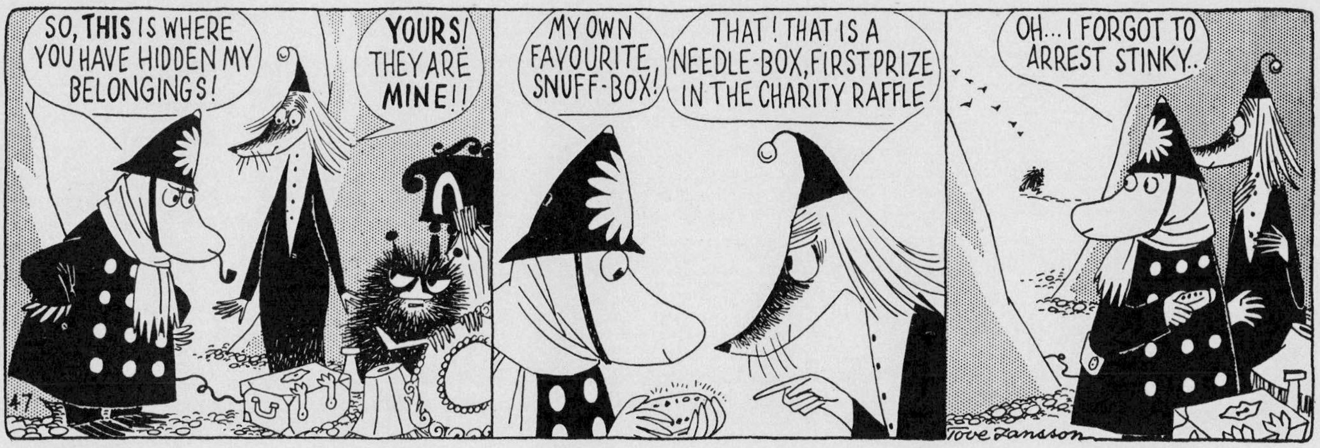
SO, THIS IS WHERE YOU HAVE HIDDEN MY BELONGINGS!
YOURS! THEY ARE MINE!!
MY OWN FAVOURITE SNUFF-BOX!
THAT! THAT IS A NEEDLE-BOX, FIRST PRIZE IN THE CHARITY RAFFLE
OH... I FORGOT TO ARREST STINKY..

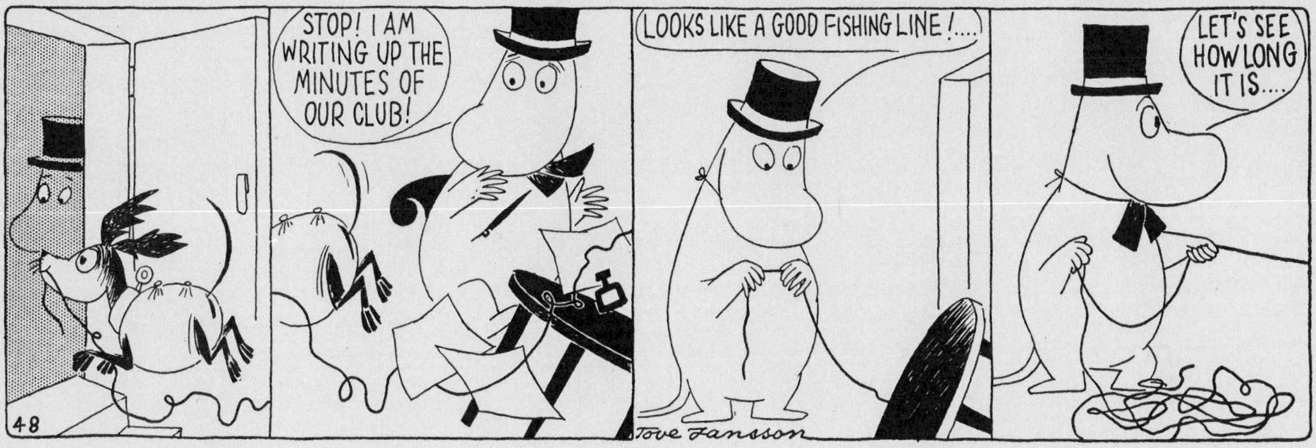
STOP! I AM WRITING UP THE MINUTES OF OUR CLUB!
LOOKS LIKE A GOOD FISHING LINE!....
LET'S SEE HOW LONG IT IS....

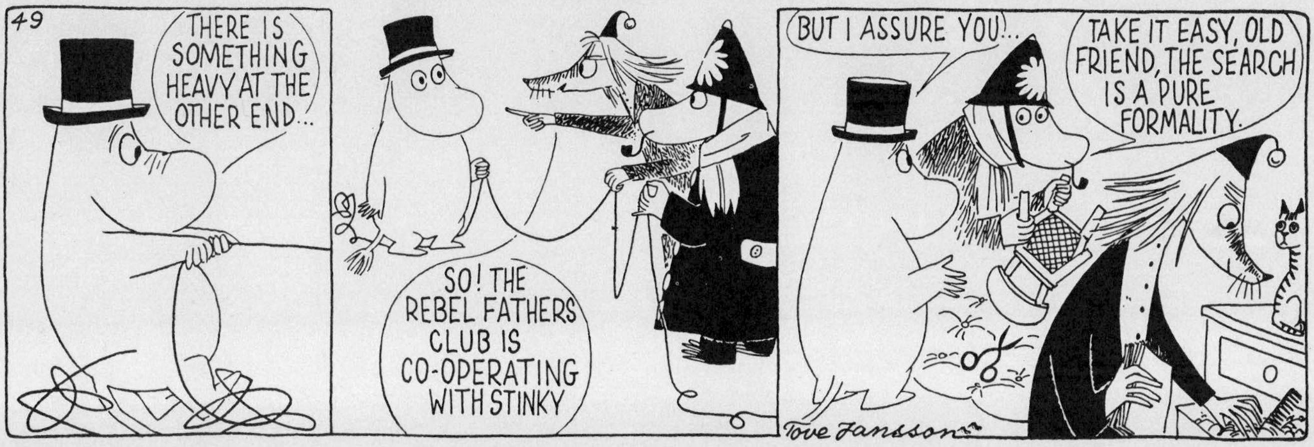
THERE IS SOMETHING HEAVY AT THE OTHER END...
SO! THE REBEL FATHERS CLUB IS CO-OPERATING WITH STINKY
BUT I ASSURE YOU...
TAKE IT EASY, OLD FRIEND, THE SEARCH IS A PURE FORMALITY.

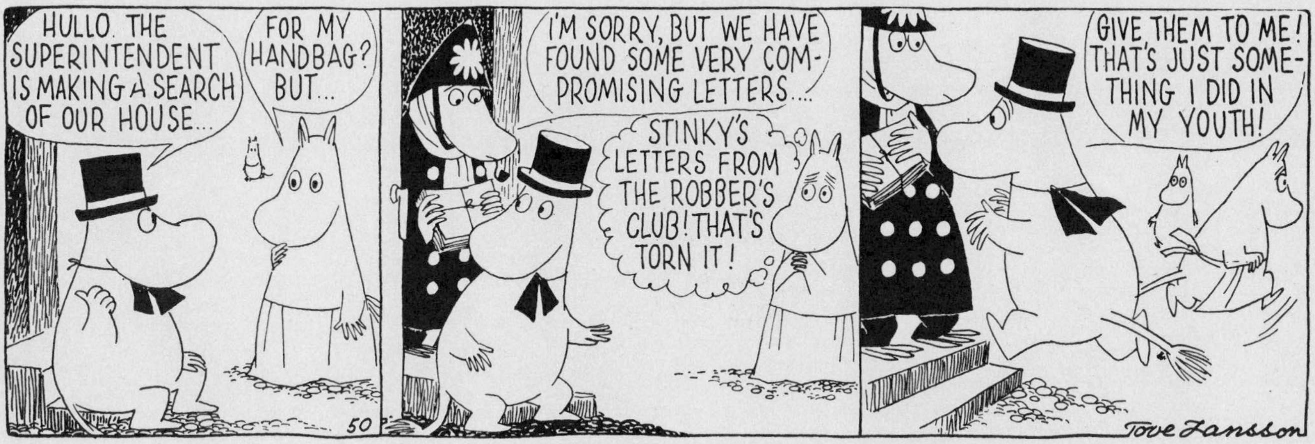
HULLO. THE SUPERINTENDENT IS MAKING A SEARCH OF OUR HOUSE...
FOR MY HANDBAG? BUT...
I'M SORRY, BUT WE HAVE FOUND SOME VERY COM-PROMISING LETTERS....
STINKY'S LETTERS FROM THE ROBBER'S CLUB! THAT'S TORN IT!
GIVE THEM TO ME! THAT'S JUST SOME-THING I DID IN MY YOUTH!

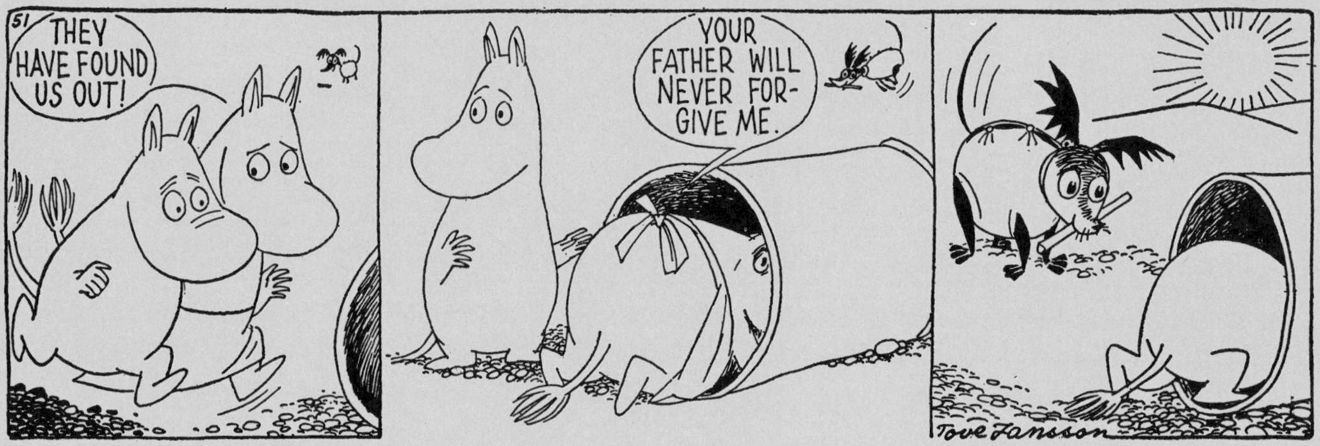
51
THEY HAVE FOUND US OUT!
YOUR FATHER WILL NEVER FORGIVE ME.
Tove Jansson

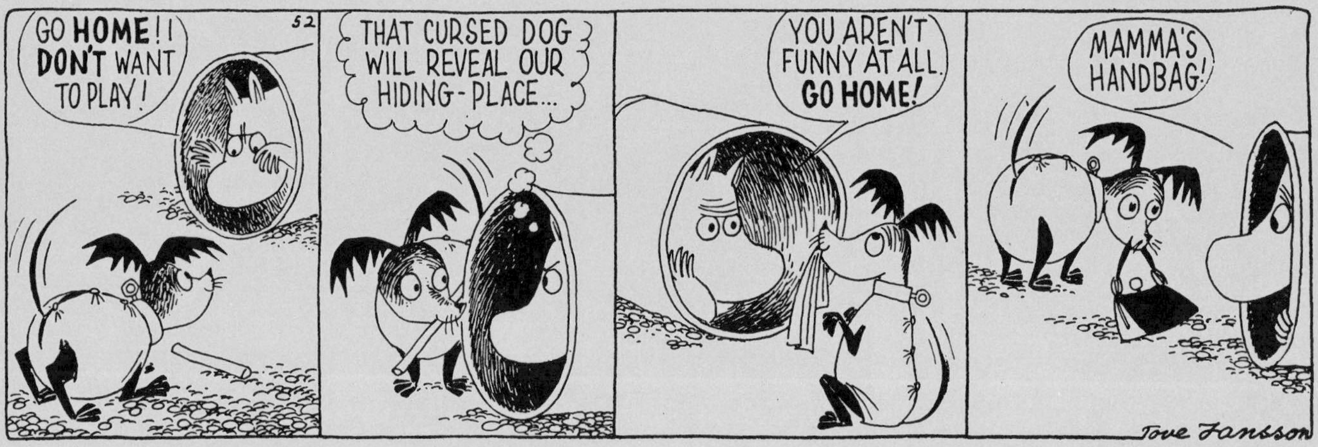
52
GO **HOME**! I **DON'T** WANT TO PLAY!
THAT CURSED DOG WILL REVEAL OUR HIDING-PLACE...
YOU AREN'T FUNNY AT ALL. **GO HOME!**
MAMMA'S HANDBAG!
Tove Jansson

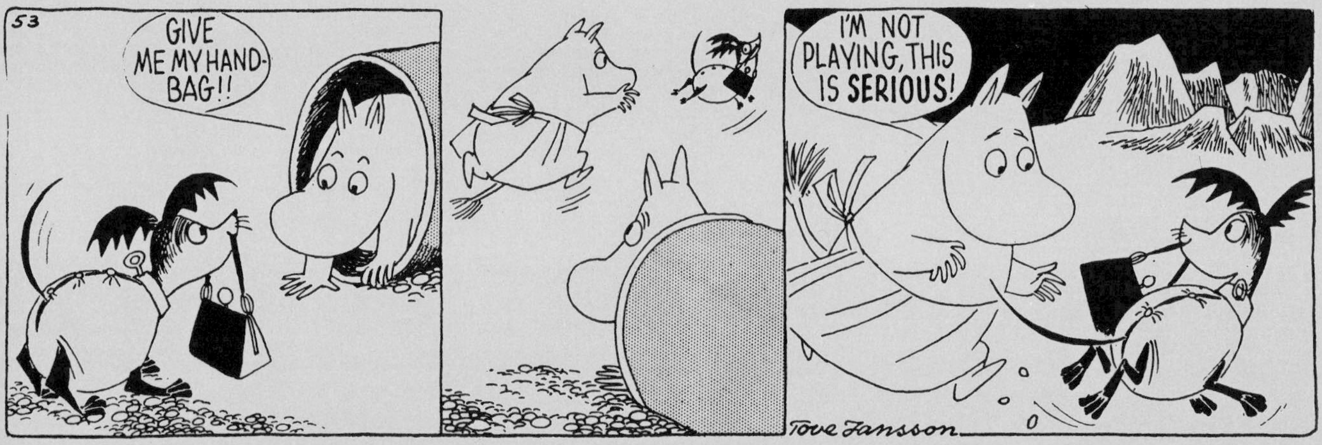
53
GIVE ME MY HANDBAG!!
I'M NOT PLAYING, THIS IS **SERIOUS!**
Tove Jansson

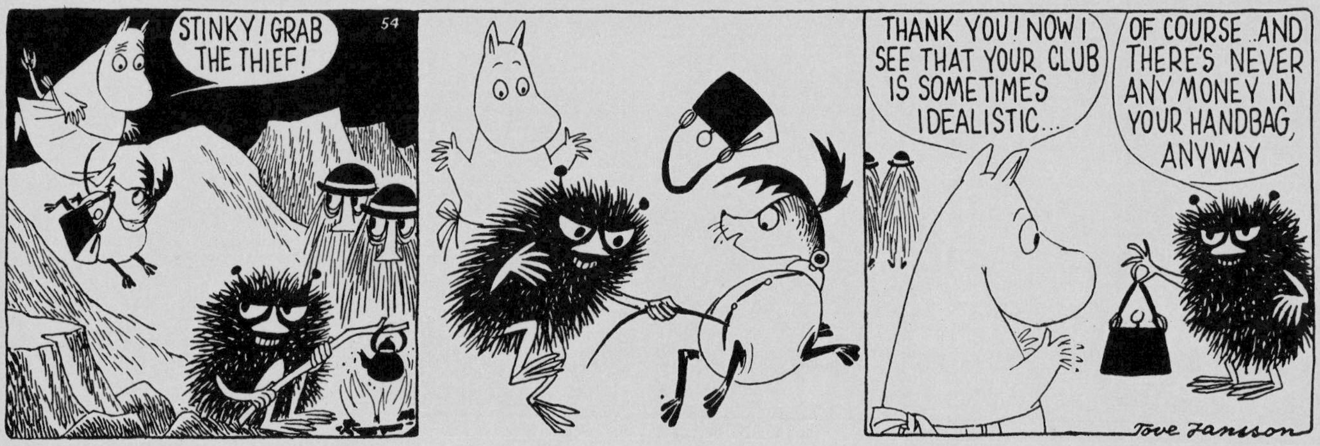
54
STINKY! GRAB THE THIEF!
THANK YOU! NOW I SEE THAT YOUR CLUB IS SOMETIMES IDEALISTIC...
OF COURSE ..AND THERE'S NEVER ANY MONEY IN YOUR HANDBAG, ANYWAY
Tove Jansson

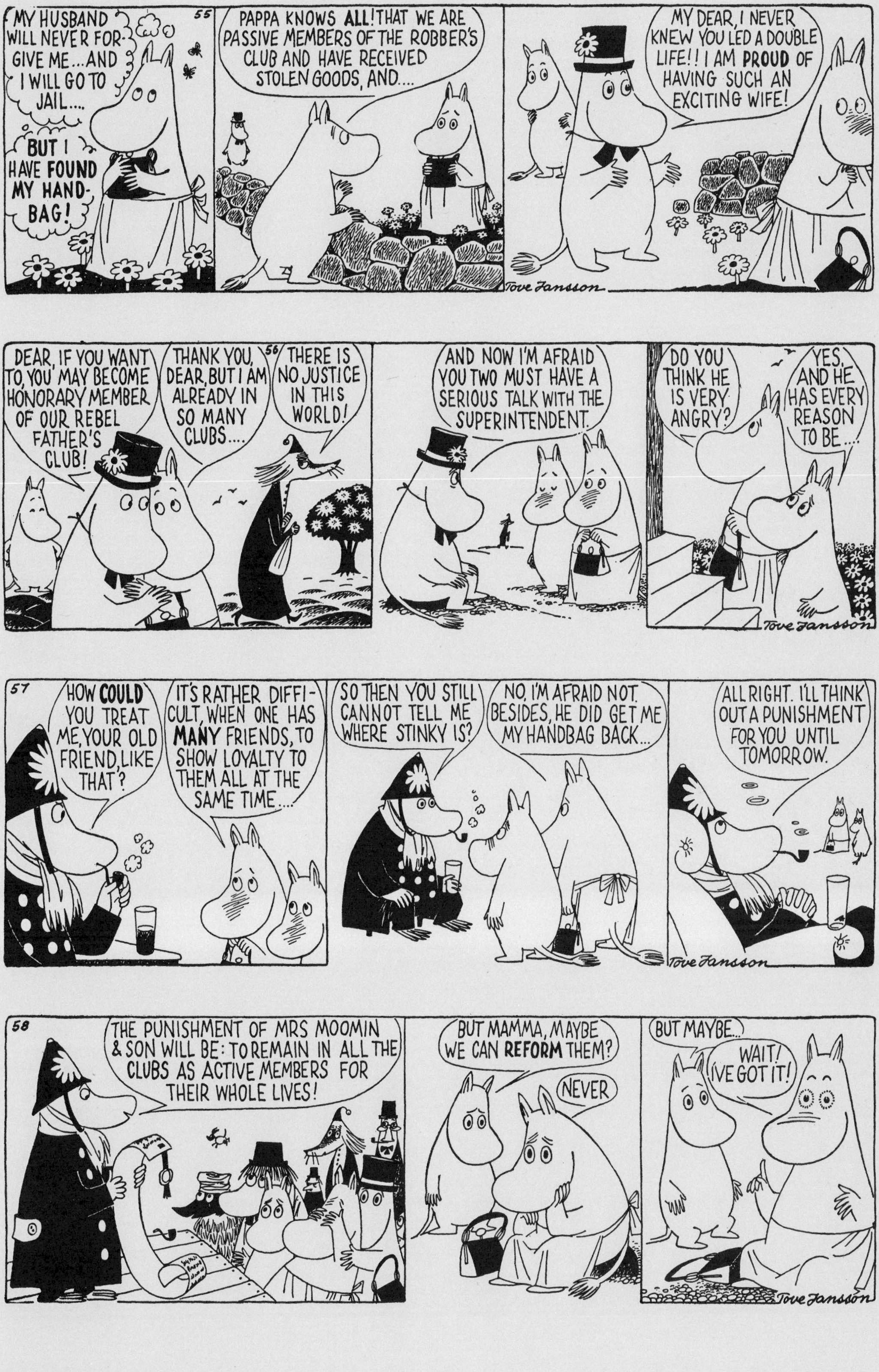
55
MY HUSBAND WILL NEVER FOR-GIVE ME...AND I WILL GO TO JAIL....
BUT I HAVE **FOUND** MY HAND-BAG!
PAPPA KNOWS **ALL**! THAT WE ARE PASSIVE MEMBERS OF THE ROBBER'S CLUB AND HAVE RECEIVED STOLEN GOODS, AND....
MY DEAR, I NEVER KNEW YOU LED A DOUBLE LIFE!! I AM **PROUD** OF HAVING SUCH AN EXCITING WIFE!
Tove Jansson
56
DEAR, IF YOU WANT TO, YOU MAY BECOME HONORARY MEMBER OF OUR REBEL FATHER'S CLUB!
THANK YOU, DEAR, BUT I AM ALREADY IN SO MANY CLUBS....
THERE IS NO JUSTICE IN THIS WORLD!
AND NOW I'M AFRAID YOU TWO MUST HAVE A SERIOUS TALK WITH THE SUPERINTENDENT.
DO YOU THINK HE IS VERY ANGRY?
YES, AND HE HAS EVERY REASON TO BE....
Tove Jansson
57
HOW **COULD** YOU TREAT ME, YOUR OLD FRIEND, LIKE THAT?
IT'S RATHER DIFFI-CULT, WHEN ONE HAS **MANY** FRIENDS, TO SHOW LOYALTY TO THEM ALL AT THE SAME TIME....
SO THEN YOU STILL CANNOT TELL ME WHERE STINKY IS?
NO, I'M AFRAID NOT. BESIDES, HE DID GET ME MY HANDBAG BACK...
ALL RIGHT. I'LL THINK OUT A PUNISHMENT FOR YOU UNTIL TOMORROW.
Tove Jansson
58
THE PUNISHMENT OF MRS MOOMIN & SON WILL BE: TO REMAIN IN ALL THE CLUBS AS ACTIVE MEMBERS FOR THEIR WHOLE LIVES!
BUT MAMMA, MAYBE WE CAN **REFORM** THEM?
NEVER
BUT MAYBE...
WAIT! I'VE GOT IT!
Tove Jansson

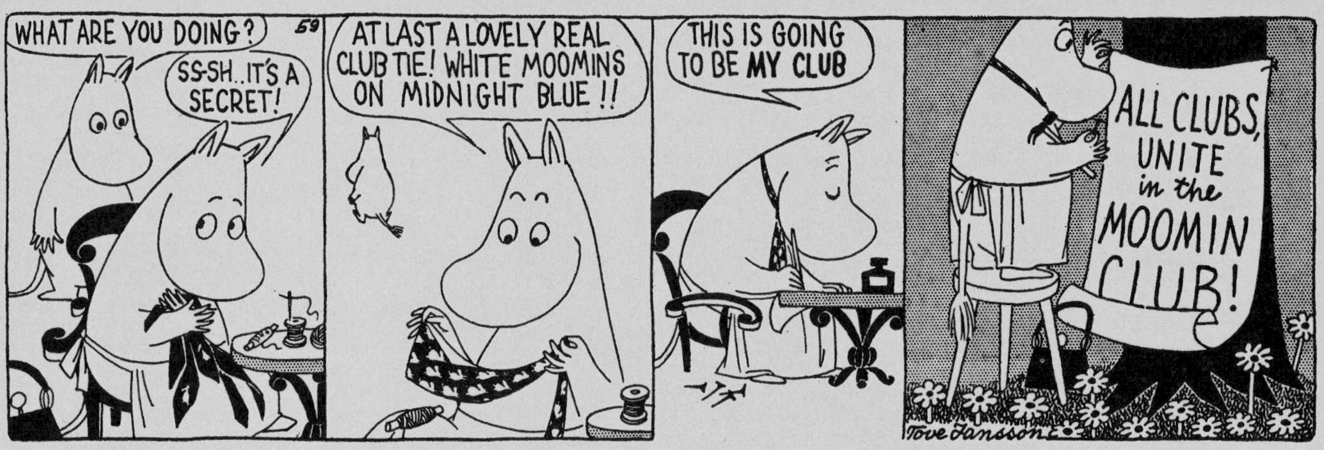
WHAT ARE YOU DOING?
59
SS-SH..IT'S A SECRET!
AT LAST A LOVELY REAL CLUB TIE! WHITE MOOMINS ON MIDNIGHT BLUE!!
THIS IS GOING TO BE **MY CLUB**
ALL CLUBS, UNITE in the MOOMIN CLUB!
Tove Jansson

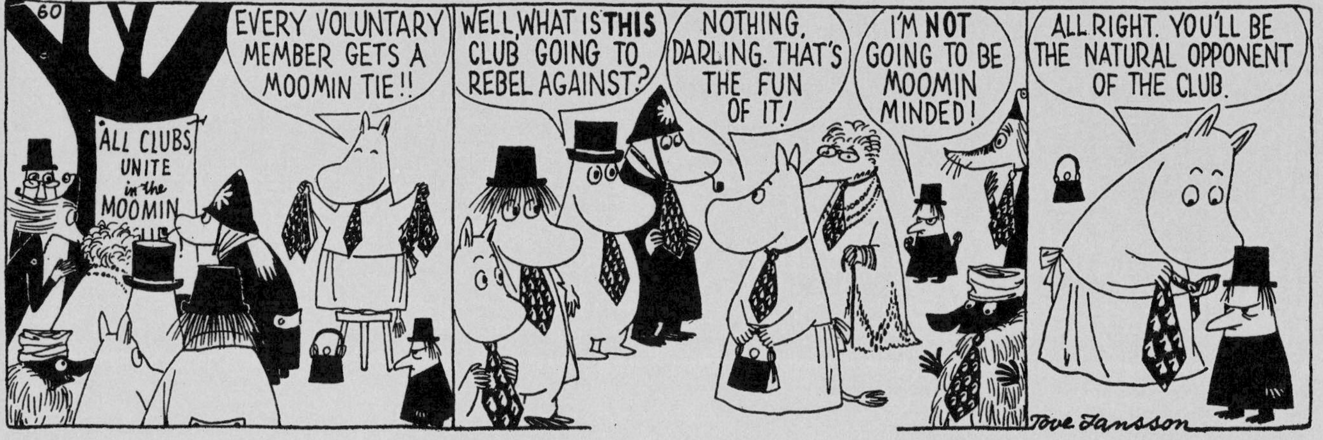
60
ALL CLUBS, UNITE in the MOOMIN
EVERY VOLUNTARY MEMBER GETS A MOOMIN TIE!!
WELL, WHAT IS **THIS** CLUB GOING TO REBEL AGAINST?
NOTHING, DARLING. THAT'S THE FUN OF IT!
I'M **NOT** GOING TO BE MOOMIN MINDED!
ALL RIGHT. YOU'LL BE THE NATURAL OPPONENT OF THE CLUB.
Tove Jansson

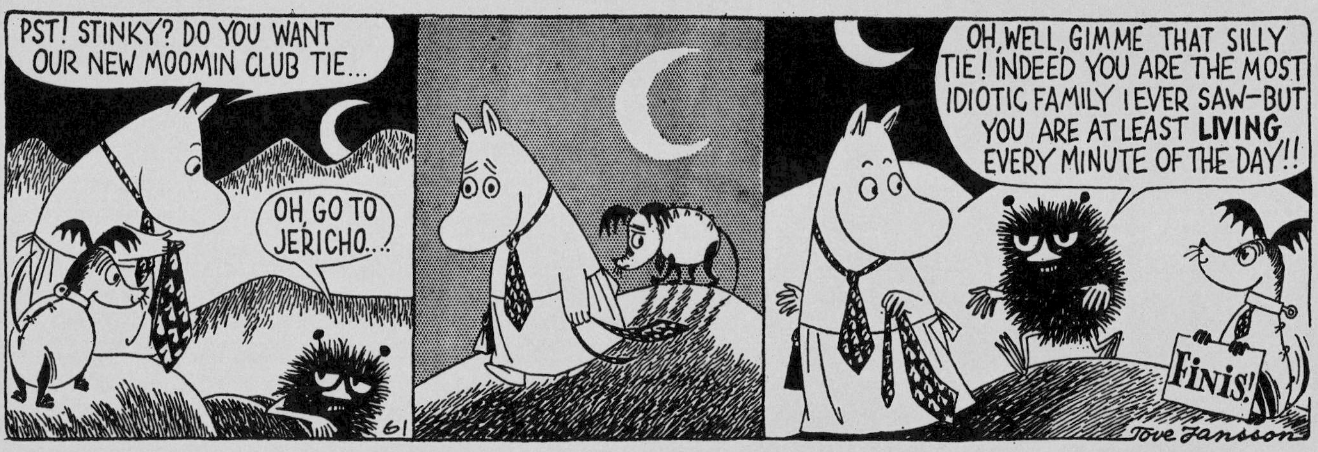
PST! STINKY? DO YOU WANT OUR NEW MOOMIN CLUB TIE...
OH, GO TO JERICHO...
61
OH, WELL, GIMME THAT SILLY TIE! INDEED YOU ARE THE MOST IDIOTIC FAMILY I EVER SAW—BUT YOU ARE AT LEAST **LIVING** EVERY MINUTE OF THE DAY!!
FINIS!
Tove Jansson

Tove Jansson: To Live in Peace, Plant Potatoes, and Dream

Throughout her memoir *Sculptor's Daughter*, artist and author Tove Jansson describes a childhood environment much like that inhabited by the captivating characters in her Moomin comics—a magically ramshackle house filled with affectionate family, numerous friends, and a varied array of voracious guests—all set in the midst of a richly verdant seaside valley. After her birth in Helsinki in August of 1914, her family spent their summers along the shore, first at her grandparents' sprawling home on the archipelago of Stockholm, and later at her family's cottage near Porvoo on the Pellinge Islands of Finland. Her tender memories of these days are perhaps the most compelling motif within all of her works. Whether collecting pearly shells to line the flower beds, dragging errant treasures from the waves, or rubbing precious stream pebbles with margarine to make them glimmer, it was the ephemeral pleasures of nature and the company of loved ones that provided Jansson with her earliest inspiration.

Liberal and artistic parents also helped to kindle young Jansson's innate talents, and foster her often remarked upon tolerance for the idiosyncratic. As the eldest daughter of a sculptor, Viktor Jansson, and a graphic artist/illustrator, Signe Hammarsten-Jansson, Tove was immersed in a creative and often raucously eccentric household. A pet monkey named Poppolino, who was reputedly fond of wearing argyle sweaters, and a nanny who read Plato were only two of the less than conventional members of this extended Jansson "family," and it was most likely these peculiar but beloved figures who became the models for the dreamers, philosophers, and dilettantes who populate her fictional world. In the Valley of the Moomins, whether it be Moominmamma's soothing, homespun wisdom or Sniff's egocentric desire for wealth and fame, everyone's unique perspective is accorded equal consideration. These whimsically drawn creatures are comically human, and Jansson's emotionally rich but often fiscally impoverished bohemianism is probably reflected in the Moomin's sensual frivolity. Tiny bikinis, shimmery chandeliers, whiskey, jewels, and roses are evidence of the importance of relishing the moment, a maxim Jansson was said to have followed most of her life.

The smell of wet plaster and sight of a father sculpting away at his modeling clay, as well as the diligence of a mother who read every book she illustrated so that she would have the proper feel, and thus look, of a character, were Jansson's formative images of her parents' devotion to their art, and it was only natural that she followed their lead. At the age of fifteen, she published her first drawings in the politically progressive *Garm* magazine, and soon after left for the Konstfack art academy in Stockholm. At nineteen, she continued her studies at the Helsinki Art Society's drawing school at the Finnish National Gallery, while concurrently traveling around the continent and exhibiting both abroad and in Finland. In 1938 Jansson took yet further lessons in Paris at both the Ecole d'Adrien Holy and Ecole des Beaux Arts, and by the end of the decade, she was recognized as one of Finland's most gifted young artists. The vanity and vacuity of the modern art world are certainly mirrored in the first volume of *Moomin*, and Jansson lampoons her own romantic nature. When Sniff instructs poor Moomintroll to create art that is "baffling" and "bewildering," as surely that will earn them riches, his happy go lucky, tubby-tummied friend answers that he wants only to "live in peace, plant potatoes and dream!" Tove Jansson knew all too well that a velvet beret doesn't make one an artist, and soon returned home to Finland for good.

It was in the pages of *Garm* in 1940 that Jansson first introduced Moomintroll as a sort of signature figure within her illustrations. In 1945, his charming family was introduced in her first children's book, *Småtrollen och den Stora Översvämningen* (*The Little Trolls and the Great Flood*), although it was the third in the series, *Trollkarlens Hatt* (*The Magician's Hat*, or as titled in English, *Finn Family Moomintroll*) that captured the widest readership and affirmed her lifelong reputation as an adored children's author. In the early 1950s, the Associated Press in England contacted Jansson about turning her beloved trolls' escapades into a comic strip for adults. Having already drawn a successful comic exploit titled *Mumintrollet och jordens undergång* (*Moomintrolls and the End of the World*) for *Ny Tid*, a Finland-Swedish newspaper, Jansson took them up on their proposal. In 1953 the *London Evening News* began running *Moomin* on a daily basis, and it was soon published in over 40 papers around the world. Jansson drew the strip for five years, until she realized that the grueling schedule of a daily and being creative on demand did not suit her meandering attitude towards life. As one of her fictional alter-egos, Mymble, instructs those who worry and fret: "Lie on the bridge and watch the water flowing past. Or run, or wade through the swamp in your red boots. Or roll yourself up and listen to the rain falling on the roof. It's very easy to enjoy yourself."

In addition to the ten children's novels, which have been translated into 34 languages, three whimsical picture books, and the comics collected in these volumes, Jansson was passionately prolific in her other artistic pursuits, writing a number of poetic, often bittersweet, novels for adults, as well as painting vividly engaging murals for such public institutions as the Aurora Children's Hospital in Helsinki. Her devotion to a life of creativity and imagination did not go unrewarded, and she received a number of significant prizes for her work: among these are the Nils Holgersson plaquette in 1953, the esteemed Hans Christian Andersen medal in 1966, the Swedish Academy prize in 1972, the Pro Finlandia medal in 1976, and on multiple occasions, the Finnish State prize for literature. Six years before her death in 2001, the eighty year old Jansson was awarded the honorary title of professor at the Åbo Akademi University in 1995, a fitting tribute for a vital woman who taught the world some of life's most fundamental lessons: float on clouds, wear red boots, and always, always, live in peace.

—Alisia Grace Chase, PhD

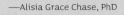